Blood And Whiskey

ROYAL BASTARDS MC: HELENA, MT
BOOK ONE

JENA DOYLE

DIRTY WORDS PUBLISHING LLC

Cover Art: Syn Ink Books LLC

Developmental Edit: Rebecca Hartwell at Hartbound Editing

Line Edit: Misha Robinson at Verity Ink Editorial

Proofreading: Kimberly Hunt at Revision Division

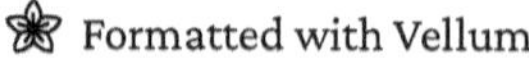 Formatted with Vellum

For the others...
I see you. I am you. I love you.
Cheers.

Royal Bastards MC
Series Sixth Run

Kristine Dugger : Crazy Psycho

KL Ramsey : Lost in Yonkers

Barbara Nolan: Loving Smoke

Crimson Syn: Tormented by Regret

Elizabeth N. Harris: Warden

Liberty Parker : Butcher's Destruction

Morgan Jane Mitchell : Hard Knox

B.B. Blaque: Royal Family

Darlene Tallman : Kraken's Release

H.J. Marshall: Roughstock

Claire Shaw : Tyres

Kathleen Kelly : Highway

J. Lynn Lombard : Jaded Red

India R. Adams : Praying for Fire

Nikki Landis : Grim's Justice

Dani René : REV

Verlene Landon : Snagged by Hook

Kris Anne Dean : Scorched Souls

ROYAL BASTARDS MC SERIES SIXTH RUN

J.L. Leslie : Worth it All

Jena Doyle: Blood and Whiskey

K.D. Latronico: Wherever I May Roam

Sapphire Knight : Toxic Biker

Nicole James : Taking What's Ours

Rae B. Lake: Sins and Paradise

Kristine Allen: Blade

Roux Cantrell: Hell Bent

Daphne Loveling : Deadly North

M Merin : Big Timber

Amy Davies:Seized by Solo

J.A. CollardAuthor : In Too Deep

Elle Boon : Royally Embraced

Murphy Wallace : Misery and Ecstasy

Theta James: Demon in the Shadows

Chelle C. Craze & Eli Abbott

Royal Bastards MC Facebook Group - https://www.facebook.com/groups/royalbas
tardsmc/

Website- https://www.royalbastardsmc.com/

Royal Bastards Code

PROTECT: The club and your brothers come before anything else, and must be protected at all costs. **CLUB** is **FAMILY**.

RESPECT: Earn it & Give it. Respect club law. Respect the patch. Respect your brothers. Disrespect a member and there will be hell to pay.

HONOR: Being patched in is an honor, not a right. Your colors are sacred, not to be left alone, and **NEVER** let them touch the ground.

OL' LADIES: Never disrespect a member's or brother's Ol'Lady. **PERIOD.**

CHURCH is **MANDATORY.**

LOYALTY: Takes precedence over all, including well-being.

HONESTY: Never **LIE, CHEAT,** or **STEAL** from another member or the club.

TERRITORY: You are to respect your brother's property and follow their Chapter's club rules.

TRUST: Years to earn it...seconds to lose it.

NEVER RIDE OFF: Brothers do not abandon their family.

I stared at my father's corpse and tried to will the tears to come. The toughest man I'd ever known had finally succumbed to the cancer attacking his body. His once strong and steady countenance had been eaten away until he was skin and bones, and at the end, he could barely hold his head up.

"It hardly looks like him," my sister, Maeve, said as she grabbed my hand, intertwining her fingers with mine.

I nodded, admitting to myself that he hadn't been himself for the last six months. I'd always thought of my father as tough and agile. I'd seen him break even the wildest stallions, the most feral mares. The majority of the Vanderbilt reputation in Helena had been because of him, because he refused to bend or break to anyone. Being a Vanderbilt meant more than a name and a fortune. It meant being the meanest, roughest cattle ranchers in Montana, and now that he was gone, I didn't know how we'd hold on to that reputation.

"Can you believe the paparazzi came?" Avalon, Maeve's identical twin, asked, standing on the other side of me while she peered over her shoulder. I followed her line of sight to the cameras at the back of the crowd. "Can't even leave us to grieve in peace."

"Has Guin seen them yet?" I asked, glancing around the rest of the cathedral, hoping to spot my eldest sister, but I only found the rest of my siblings. Of the seven of us, I was the second youngest, but I was probably the closest to my father, which was to say none of us were very close to him at all. He'd once told me I reminded him the most of our mother, who had passed away shortly after giving birth to my youngest brother. She, too, had a wild spirit. Guin had inherited the rougher side of our father's disposition. She'd been known to cut grown men down to size and make them weep in the boardroom.

"God, I hope not," Avalon said, rolling her eyes. "We don't need a fight in the pews."

"Come on," I said, nodding to the rest of the family in the first row. "Let's go sit down before she does anything dramatic."

Avalon smirked and Maeve giggled, but when I found Guin's stare, she didn't give the media a passing glance, seemingly too focused on the casket up front.

"They're ready to start," Percy said. Even though Guin was the oldest child, he was the oldest son, and since Father had passed away, he stood to inherit control of the family business. Liam was after him, then Maeve, Avalon, me, and Galahad. Guin already held the CEO spot at Vanderbilt Energy and had been the primary shareholder in both the ranch and energy companies for the last five years. But no one had expected Father to die so suddenly, so no one knew quite what to do now that he was gone.

Maeve, Avalon, and I refocused our attention to the front as the priests started the ceremony.

"Dearly beloved," said Father Derry, "we are gathered here today to honor our cherished friend, Uther."

As he continued, I blinked back the burn in my eyes and tried not to think about what we must look like from an outsider's perspective. My strawberry blond hair had been styled perfectly on the back of my head, and I hadn't cried yet, so my deep emerald eyes were still crystal clear. But inside, I was falling apart. Guin, too, shared these characteristics, but her gaze had turned harsh and angry when she'd gone to work for Father and learned how to play dirty like him. My other siblings shared my mother's characteristics—dark curly hair, penetrating bright blue eyes, deep olive skin. This did not save them from turning bloodthirsty. Save for Galahad and me, Father had put them in positions of nepotistic power at Vanderbilt Holdings as soon as they'd graduated. I didn't know why I'd been spared, but I could guess. And now I'd never have the opportunity to know for sure.

"It has been many years since we gathered to mourn the passing of his adoring wife, Priscilla. They are together now in their rest." The mention of my mother brought my attention back to the present. I'd like to believe she'd loved my father before her death, but like Percy and his wife, their marriage had been arranged for financial reasons. I couldn't imagine what that must be like. I would walk through hot coals before I'd marry a man nearly twenty years older than me, much less be made to pop out heirs like my uterus was a candy machine.

Two long hours and several eulogies later, the funeral ended. My brothers and two of my father's closest friends stood to carry his casket out of the cathedral and into the hearse, where his body would be driven back to our mansion and buried in the family graveyard. Most of the attendees would follow in order to attend the wake.

"Get it together," Guin said, nodding toward the door as she faced us. "Don't let them see you sweat."

Sniffling and holding my head high, I held hands with Maeve and Avalon as we walked down the aisle behind the procession, Guin and Galahad trailing us. We ignored the flashing camera lights and sudden inhales from the gawking paparazzi. They'd never left our family alone, not once in my entire life.

What a screwed-up life we lived. Sure, we were the richest family in Montana, perhaps the country. My Vanderbilt ancestors had lived on our land for over a hundred and fifty years, and in that time, they'd built the biggest ranch this side of the Missouri. What we didn't make in cattle and horses, we earned from the turbine farm and the natural gas company that Guin ran.

Sometimes, my father used to joke that we had more money than he knew what to do with. I'd like to think he wasn't as wicked as my brother and sister, but they must have learned it from somewhere. I remembered him as the man who taught me how to ride my first horse, who brought me on camping trips with the ranch hands, who ensured I went to the best boarding schools in the world. My father was a hard man, no denying that. For every good memory I had of him, there were at least four more that probably required therapy. But I loved him, and watching him rot away to skin and bones had devastated me. At least his pain was over now. He could rest in peace.

I blinked into the sunshine when I stepped outside, the bright blinding light searing my retinas after so long under the soft glow of the cathedral. I'd made it two steps before faltering as the sound of thunder echoed up the street, a herd of motorcycles heading in our direction.

"Oh great, what's this now?" Maeve whispered, tightening her fingers around mine.

Everyone stopped, anticipation buzzing in the tension between us as we waited to see if it was the Bloody Scorpions or the Royal Bastards. Neither would be welcomed at my father's funeral, but at least we didn't have any bad blood with the Scorpions.

They weren't good people, not by any stretch of the imagination, but their property didn't border ours. We'd never had any reason to fight with them. The Royal Bastards, on the other hand, owned the land to the north, and as much as my father had tried to buy it out from under them, they wouldn't budge. Lord only knew what they did with it. They certainly didn't raise enough cattle or horses to make a profit. There was something off about them. Rumors had spread through Helena that they were monsters possessed by demons, that they changed into massive flesh-eating beasts on the full moon.

I scoffed thinking about it. I'd never believed in any of that, even if my father had always said they were responsible for my mother's death. The way he'd told the tale, she had gotten lost on their territory one night. They'd found her and tore her to pieces like animals, leaving nothing behind but a bloody patch in the snow. We didn't even get to bury a body. Father had taken his revenge, he'd said. I shivered to think of what that had entailed. I was too young to remember much about my mother, and I blamed the Bastards for that every day.

The sounds of rumbling engines grew closer, and the leader turned the corner at the end of the street, his pack of bikers behind him nearly fifty strong.

"It's the Bastards," Avalon murmured, her voice dripping with either curiosity or fear. For her, those might have been the same.

"Shit," Guin hissed. "What are they doing here?"

The swarm drew closer, slowing down as they crossed in front of the cathedral. All heads turned to face us and my knees locked into place. The ruthless outlaw motorcycle club had been known to shoot people on sight, and I held my breath, waiting to see if they'd rain bullets down on us. Instead, they glared as they passed, the silence in their stares seemingly enough of a threat.

It said they knew Uther Vanderbilt had been the only thing standing in their way. None of his children would be capable of holding them off from taking what they considered theirs. The war between our families may have been in a stalemate, but it wouldn't be for much longer.

I wasn't the only one that recognized this for what it was. Guin pushed past me and the twins, staring down these imbeciles that had the audacity to crash my father's funeral. The world slowed as I made eye contact with the second one in line, his dark gaze peering directly at me, as if he had pointed me out specifically.

Chills raced down my spine, my fingers curling into a fist seemingly on their own, the air turning to ice in my lungs despite the deceptively warm winter day.

It was like fate was trying to tell me something in that one moment of vulnerability, like everything that had ever happened to me had been leading up to this moment, and only now would the rest of my life truly begin.

I turned off the television, wincing at the forecast for a blizzard starting early tomorrow morning. I didn't mind the snow, but six feet seemed excessive, especially for this side of Montana. In the sudden silence, voices echoed from the hallway outside of my room.

"You saw the way they looked at us," said Percy.

"It was a threat, no doubt about it," Liam said. "But this is drastic, even for you."

"It's time she was married," Percy cut in. "It's time you all were."

"Have you learned nothing from your own arrangement?" Liam hissed.

"It's the way Vanderbilts have always done it," Percy replied. "And now that I'm in charge of the mess Father left behind—"

Liam's cold snicker stopped my eldest brother's rant, sending an equally chilly frost through my blood. "You're so self-righteous, I bet you suck your own dick every morning."

"Fuck off, Liam." Percy tsked.

"You're only in charge because the shareholders wouldn't accept Guin as Father's replacement."

"And you think the ranch hands would?" Percy said, stabbing the proverbial knife deeper into Liam's heart. "Any idea how to run an eighteen-million-dollar ranch with no day workers?"

"They'll come back," Liam said. "They always do."

"No, they won't," Percy whined. "They saw that demonstration the Bastards put on a week ago. They don't want any part of it, and none of them will take orders from me."

"I wonder why," Liam said with a sardonic snort. "You never once worked the ranch with them."

"Why would I?" Percy said. "That's what we pay them for."

"Mother would be rolling over in her grave if she knew she raised a son so greedy that he would do this to one of his sisters."

I straightened, smoothing my hands down the dress I'd purchased from Prada's spring line. If nothing else, I'd look flawless for whatever awaited me in the hallway. I opened my bedroom door and raised my eyebrows at my brothers.

"What are you two scheming about?"

Liam shook his head and pinched the bridge of his nose, but Percy flashed his innocent smile, the one that said he'd done something terrible but was hoping he'd get away with it.

"Dear sister," he said, straightening the sleeves of his suit jacket. "It's good to see you."

I narrowed my eyes, sensing a trap. I'd known him my entire life and not once had he ever come to fetch me from my bedroom with such feigned propriety. "You, too. What can I do for you?"

"I've got a surprise," Percy said. "We have visitors, and I require your assistance."

Liam snorted and rolled his eyes. "You might as well be honest with the girl."

"Honest?" I cleared my throat to hide my nervousness.

Percy inhaled deeply and took a step inside my room, Liam following closely behind him. "Our family has been at odds with the Royal Bastards Motorcycle Club for as long as any of us can remember," Percy said. "The feud goes back decades. They killed our mother."

Okay, I still didn't see what this had to do with me.

"You may have noticed the ranch has been quiet since Father passed away. Most of the workers have abandoned us," Percy continued, straightening and lacing his fingers behind his back, the very essence of upper class training. "This has forced me to take...*drastic* measures to keep our family safe."

Liam sipped at his tumbler of whiskey, and that was my first clue that whatever Percy was about to say would anger me. Liam didn't drink this early, and he certainly didn't have the same dependency that Father or Guin did. Whatever this was wouldn't be good.

"The only group the Bastards hate more than the Vanderbilts are the Bloody Scorpions," Percy continued. "Those two have a national rivalry and a long history of tearing each other apart."

I gulped as alarm skidded over my skin, prickling my hair, revolting in my gut.

"The Scorpions have agreed to lend us some men to help us with the rest of the harvest and provide protection from whatever the Bastards are up to. In fact, they've laid out reasonable terms." Percy tilted his chin higher, staring down his nose while he rubbed at his mouth with a finger, apparently considering his next words carefully.

"And what is it they want in return?" My voice had turned husky with trepidation, the words coming out in more of a growl than an innocent question.

"A big pile of cash, of course," Percy said.

"Of course," I agreed. *Typical.*

"And certain...assurances that our alliance will continue after the winter thaws." Percy cleared his throat as Liam shifted uncomfortably next to me.

"What assurances?" I asked, tightening my fingers into fists to keep my hands from shaking.

Percy paused, pursing his lips while his penetrating blue gaze drifted between me and our brother.

"They require a marriage to their president," Liam said, taking another long sip.

Silence fell between us as tension built, my fury reaching a new tipping point. It had been a week since we'd buried Father, nearly two since he passed, and I missed him more in that moment than I had in the days since. He'd been a force to be reckoned with, a Goliath among a whole town of little Davids, Percy being the smallest. He'd yearned for our father's approval, ached to be like the great man himself. But no matter what he did, he never would, and it wasn't because he was greedy like Liam said. No, it was because he was a coward.

"This must be a joke," I said, crossing my arms. "You can't possibly think to marry one of our siblings off to the president of an outlaw gang."

"They're not outlaws." Percy balked and let out an exhausted laugh, as if my suggestion was ludicrous. "There are no pending charges against Marx O'Kelley. I had my man check."

"Why can't we get the local police to protect us?" I said. "Or the wildlife commission? There must be a better—"

"This is the way Vanderbilts handle business," Percy snapped. "I was married when Lillian was three years younger than you."

It hit me then, and I felt like an idiot for not realizing it sooner. None of my other siblings had been ambushed by these two this early. None of them had been sequestered alone with the two eldest men in our family. No, it was me. The useless one. The one that was easier to sell off because I didn't have a position with the company and I'd spent my time after college riding my horse and trying to please my father.

I'd never been good enough to work at Vanderbilt Holdings. I'd never been good enough to earn Father's approval. Now, my only use was being traded in some antiquated business deal. And these morons had waited until Guin left for Utah before confronting me about it. My eldest sister wouldn't have stood for this. She'd always done whatever she could to protect the younger ones, the proverbial mother bear after our own had died. Now, I yearned for that defense, knowing I had to do it myself.

"You want *me* to marry this man?" I asked, my fury escalating into full-blown panic. My pulse sped up, my muscles trembling as I told myself this was just a dream.

I'll wake up any second. I will.

"Sol," Percy said. "This alliance with the Scorpions will assuage the forces seeking to bring us down. Do you think I like selling my siblings out? Do you think I enjoy making deals with the lowest form of human this world has to offer?"

"I think you would kiss their shit-covered boots if it meant you didn't have to do any dirty work on your own." My entire body quaked, but I tensed my muscles to hide it from him. I couldn't show any sign of weakness or he'd tear out my throat.

Liam snickered while Percy gasped and raised his eyebrows.

"Marrying Lillian was not something I wished, either," he said, taking a step closer so he towered over me. "When Father bought her for me, she was penniless and living on scraps."

"Do you listen to yourself when you talk?" I raised my chin to stare him in the eyes, nearly six foot in my stilettos. He might still have had two inches on me, but I was the one who had inherited our mother's senses. Despite being eight years younger than Percy, I could knock him down to size with a few choice words and a sneer. "You had to marry Lillian because you were caught going to that perverted island owned by that disgusting friend of yours. Statutory rape is still a felony, especially if the victim has been bribed into it."

"Isolde," Percy tried to cut in.

"If you didn't marry Lillian, Father would have had to disown you." I was on a roll now, dragging out the dustiest of Percy's skeletons just so he'd feel some sense of shame. "And that's not to mention the man you nearly killed in high school."

"That's enough," Percy barked, clapping in front of my face, startling me into silence. "You will do this, or I will cut off your trust."

"You can't," I said, confidence starting to waver.

"Despite the disturbing *allegations* against me, the shareholders have voted me in charge of our holdings, including the ranch, the energy company, and Vanderbilt investments." Percy squared his jaw and narrowed his eyes. "You may have what pittance Father put in his will for you once it's divided between us, but how long do you suppose that will last?" He scoffed and gestured to my Louboutin shoes, my Prada dress, and the thousands of dollars of jewelry I'd purchased in the matter of months. "Look at you."

"Percy," Liam cut in, giving our brother a stare that asked him to be more gentle.

"You're ungrateful for everything I've done for you, everything *he's* done for you." Percy rolled his eyes, and my resolve only grew more infuriated.

"Don't you dare bring our father into this," I snarled. I had to restrain myself from stomping my foot like a toddler. "If he were still alive, he would have found a way to keep the ranchers. He wouldn't have sold me off to a motorcycle club like a prized sow."

Percy let out a pitying sigh. "You barely knew him, Sol. He thought of us no better than his horses. For some of us, he had more of an investment in the filthy beasts."

I supposed he meant that as a slight to me because he believed Galahad and I had the most distant relationship with our father. He had been fifty when I was born, fifty-five when Galahad came along, and most of my older siblings were off at boarding school or college for the better part of my childhood. My father loved me. He was hard on me, hard on all of us, but I felt his love and protection every day.

Perhaps Percy envied that about me. Perhaps he was resentful that I'd been given the time and luxury of an older father with more patience. But that wasn't my fault, and I didn't deserve for him to take it out on me.

I blinked back tears as my reality closed in around me, trying to remember what Guin had always said.

"Look out for yourself first. No one in this world can take anything from you unless you let them."

I wouldn't let this happen. I would find some way out of this, some way to fight him. I'd call Guin. We could fight this together. I just needed to buy myself some time to get in touch with her.

I canted my head up and matched my brother's stern glare with one of my own. "And what's in it for me?"

He straightened and furrowed his brows. "What?"

"If I go along with this, if I agree to this ridiculous match and protect the family, and that is a big if...what will you do for me?"

Clearly, he hadn't seen this coming. He pursed his lips and shoved his hands in his pockets. "What do you want?"

I knew right where to hit him, how to make it hurt. "You will take your controlling share of Vanderbilt Holdings, and you will transfer it to someone else. Guin or Liam or both for all I care. Just as long as it's not you."

Both brothers froze at that, and I could almost hear Percy's heart pounding. If I'd been older, if I'd had more experience with the company, if I'd been smart enough, I could have asked for control myself. As it was, I thought of the next best thing.

"No," Percy said. "I couldn't do that even if I wanted to. The shareholders—"

"I don't care about the shareholders. You're a smart man; you'll figure it out. Or you can marry the Scorpion yourself." When he didn't immediately agree, just rolled the idea around in his privileged brain, I decided to press my luck. "I could make this easy for you, Percy, or I could make it *really* difficult. What do you suppose the *Helena Gazette* would make of this, or the *New York Sun*?"

"You'd blow up more than me if you did that," Percy said. "I sense an empty threat."

"You'll have to drag me down the aisle kicking and screaming," I said. "The press chewed us up at Father's funeral. What would they make of a spineless Vanderbilt that sells off his sister at the first hint of trouble?"

The roar of motorcycles echoed down the driveway, vibrating deep in my chest as my anger and resentment grew into a scalding, raging fire.

"They're here," Percy said, turning to Liam.

"Who?" I balked and raised my eyebrows, belatedly realizing the answer to my own question. It wouldn't have been the Bastards, and other than that pack of mangy beasts, there was only one other motorcycle group in Helena.

The Bloody Scorpions.

"You expect me to just go along with this?" I said. "You're delusional."

"If you come willingly," Percy said, "I'll consider your terms. I'll take it to the board as soon as you're married. Don't make a fuss and don't embarrass yourself in front of them. This is our only shot at protecting the Vanderbilt name."

As soon as you're married.

I knew what that meant. I'd get no such considerations from him. He viewed me as a possession, something he could trade or barter for services rendered. But I saw right through him, and he might think he bit harder but he hadn't seen me bare my teeth yet.

"Come along, little sister," Percy said, nodding toward the hallway. "Time to meet the in-laws." I glared at him, switching my ire to Liam as he gave me a sympathetic stare.

Deciding I would play along *for now,* I smoothed my hands down the front of my dress, pulled my best Guin attitude up around me, and followed them out.

My heels clacked on the marble stairs as I descended the staircase, and I nearly stumbled when I saw the group of outlaws standing in the foyer of my father's house. The one closest to me had a scar that went over his eye and down the side of his cheek. Another wore big rings on his fingers and had tattoos that said, "Fuck or Fite." I grimaced at the misspelled word, wondering if there was a hidden meaning or if he'd just been a victim of a bad artist.

All of them wore leather vests with patches proclaiming them as members of the Bloody Scorpions, the enormous sigil stitched onto the back almost as intimidating as it was comical. Most importantly, they looked at least ten years older than me. They radiated danger and violence, the stench of it hanging in the air as powerfully as any perfume or deodorizing spray. It made me gag, and every instinct I had told me to run or attack.

Just get through today. I'll figure it out after this.

I took a deep breath, ignoring the way they stared as I walked past them into the same parlor where I'd once run into my father's lap and gleefully told him about my day.

"Ahh," Percy said, waltzing into the room with his arms out wide. "Marx, thank you for meeting us on such short notice."

"Well, when the Vanderbilts say they have the deal of the century, I'm willing to hear them out," said the man seated on the couch opposite the fireplace, currently propping his filthy boots on a coffee table that had once belonged to my sixth great-grandmother.

"Would you care for a drink?" Percy turned to the bar cart in the opposite corner, but Marx raised a tumbler.

"Already indulged myself." He took a sip and smacked his lips together with an obnoxious pop. "This is some high-quality shit. But I expected as much from the looks of things."

Making himself quite at home. I almost sneered.

Liam pat me on the shoulder before walking to the fireplace and leaning a hand on the mantel, turning to face me.

"I trust you remember Liam." Percy gestured to our brother before nodding in my direction. "And Isolde."

Marx stood and looked at me. At six feet tall with a pale complexion and dark, sinister eyes, his slimy grin stretched ear to ear, showcasing a front tooth that had been encased in gold. His salt-and-pepper hair suggested he was closer to my father's age than my own, and I wondered again what twisted nightmare had brought me here. Like the others, he stank of pure demonic chaos; I could almost see the evil pouring out of him. Percy lifted his whiskey tumbler to me and bit on the end of a cigar.

"Well, well, well," Marx said, stalking closer. Covered in grime and tattoos, he didn't bother trying to hide his perusal of my body, raking his penetrating gaze down to my heels and back up again. "Aren't you a sight for sore eyes?"

I gulped, swallowing against a dry throat, holding my head higher.

"Isolde, I'd like you to meet Marx." Percy glared at me, as if telepathically reminding me to be on my best behavior. "Marx, my youngest sister. Per your request."

His request? This vile, stinking cockroach.

"Boy, you sure do know how to breed 'em, huh?" Marx clapped and glanced at Percy, his grin widening.

"In the terms of our arrangement, you'll marry Isolde and receive a sizable dowry. After that—"

"Yes, yes," Marx cut in, tilting his head back while he stared down at me. "You need ranchers to get you through the winter."

"And protection from the Bastards," Percy added. "With no ranchers and my father gone, we're out in the open."

"You know, my sire used to say that a man who can't protect his family himself ain't no real man at all." Marx raised his eyebrows and turned back to Percy with a smirk, perhaps hoping my brother would respond. He didn't. He only tensed and took another drink of whiskey. I winced at his use of the word "sire" but didn't think more of it.

When Marx returned his attention to me, he raised a hand to brush hair back behind my ear. "How about you, sweet thing? How do you feel about this arrangement?"

I gulped and straightened to keep from visibly revolting at the touch. His hands smelled like excrement and he probably hadn't brushed his teeth in twenty years, the sharp points of his canine teeth looking longer now that I was close to him. He had a certain evilness to his aura, something pale and soulless. It made me sick. I couldn't stand the thought of having to be intimate with him, much less pretend this was anything more than a business arrangement.

"I'll do anything to protect my family." I squared my jaw and held his gaze, unable to smother the burning inferno in my blood.

He met my stare with an intense one of his own, his aging brown eyes telling the tale of how he'd lived up until now.

"See, now this one"—Marx waved his finger at me and turned to my brothers—"you shoulda put her in charge. There's fire in her soul. She woulda made a hell of a biker."

"Well, there's still time yet," I said. "We've got a while until our marriage."

"You think so?" Marx balked and shook his head. "No, my sweet little piece of ass. We're gonna be married as soon as the snow melts."

No. NO.

My heart hammered and dropped to the ground as I focused on Percy and Liam, begging for them to deny him.

"I won't do the deal until I've got my end of the bargain." Marx tsked and took a step around me, circling me like he would a farm animal. He slid his gaze over my body, as disgusting as raw garbage, like the worst kind of assault despite the fact he'd barely touched me. "You've got a few more days to say your goodbyes before I come to collect my...*delectable* reward."

I hated my brother. I held his stare with a wrath in my own, hoping to insinuate how much I despised him with that one expression. I'd never considered myself a violent person, but the blackest parts of my soul reared up as Marx stepped behind me. I would find a way to bring my brother to ruin. He was a terrible person who had been given the lap of luxury for far too long. He'd done despicable things and gotten away with them, only to continue to wreak havoc on the people closest to him.

My father should have shipped him off to military school as soon as he could instead of coddling him.

Well, no longer. Even if this arrangement with the Scorpions didn't fall through, I'd use whatever influence I had to stab my brother between the ribs and pierce his heart. Perhaps I could even swipe his legs out from under him.

"God, you have a tight little ass, huh?" He spanked me hard on the right butt cheek, and I gasped, clenching my eyes shut at the objectification. No one in my entire life had ever touched me so harshly, much less in front of my family. Sure, I'd had lovers who liked it rougher than that, but this was the Vanderbilt parlor. My siblings were five feet away. Members of his MC had witnessed the whole thing, and snickers echoed from the foyer. I did my best not to sob.

Marx leaned in to my ear, pressing his lips against my hair so he could whisper, "I bet you fuck like a mare in heat, don't you? You want to be ridden hard and put away wet? Hmm?"

"Bite your tongue, Scorpion." I sneered, snapping my head to face him. "Or I'll have it removed."

"Ohh, I like that fight in you," he said. "Keep that up after we're married and we'll be happy, indeed."

That, I found even more revolting. If I were going to destroy this, destroy *them*, I'd have to be more discreet. I couldn't upset the heavily armed bikers when they were here in full force. In no universe would that end well.

Marx chuckled and finished his circle around me, turning to my brothers and holding his arms out. "Gentlemen, you have my most hearty approval. I'll marry the little bitch and you'll have your deal."

My stomach soured, churning my breakfast back up my esophagus, and my knees threatened to give out on me.

"Fantastic," Percy said, nodding to the paperwork on the table in front of him. "Isolde, that's all." He waved me away like I was a fly that had annoyed him for too long, like I had no say in my own future.

I glanced at Liam, who grimaced before looking away. Despite how much he might have stood up for me once upon a time, I now hated him as much as I hated Percy.

Silently promising both of them my vengeance, I turned on my heels and headed out of the parlor, straight for the liquor cabinet.

This was quite possibly the worst day of my life, including the death of my beloved father, and I couldn't face another moment of it sober.

"Uther Vanderbilt is dead," Kodiak said from his spot at the head of the table. As the alpha shifter and president of the Helena chapter of the Royal Bastards MC, he sat at the helm of our business and pack dealings. "Rumor has it, his entire ranch staff has abandoned the family after our little show."

The rest of the motorcycle club whooped and clapped around us. Even I had to admit, giving those privileged fuckers a scare felt good. They'd been trying to buy up the Bastard territory for decades, going so far as to lease the area surrounding us in a desperate attempt to squeeze us out. It hadn't worked, and as long as we had the support from the rest of the RBMC globally, they wouldn't be able to.

"I talked to Jameson earlier this morning," Kodiak continued, glancing at me to his right. As president of the National Chapter, Jameson oversaw all of our holdings. We wouldn't have been able to put our next phase of plans into motion without his consent. Since he was on board, we were moving ahead. "Vanderbilt stocks are in a free fall. They're at their most vulnerable. Now is the time for a coordinated attack."

"What did you have in mind?" Lycan said. Our road captain knew these Montana mountains better than anyone. If we were going to put an ambush in place, he'd be the best person to coordinate it.

Kodiak straightened his shoulders and ran his hands over his bald scalp, glancing down at the map in front of us. "They won't be able to maintain this land with no one to work it. We've got the funds to secure our southern border." He pointed to a spot just below the edge of our territory, right where Vanderbilt land butted up against Royal Bastard territory and ran parallel to the area controlled by the Bloody Scorpions. "We can steal it out from under them and cut a new deal with the banks."

If there were anyone the Bastards hated more than the Vanderbilts, it was the fucking Scorpions. Not every chapter of the RBMC was like us, and not every chapter of the Scorpions was like them. There was a reason we'd taken up residence in Big Sky country. The rest of the world didn't know our kind existed, and we liked to keep it that way.

Every full moon, we escaped to the heart of our property to give over to the gift that had been handed down to us through the generations. Tons of legends and stories had been written about werewolves, but none had ever really hit the mark. Yes, we had to turn when the moon grew to its fullest. No, we couldn't help it. But we weren't slaves to our baser natures; we didn't lose our sense of identity when it happened. It was more like we coexisted with our feral selves. And humans couldn't be *turned* into a shifter. One was born a shifter, or they weren't. End of story.

The RBMC Helena chapter was one of the only shifter safe havens left in the US, especially since our existence had to remain a secret from the rest of the world. It was forbidden to tell anyone that wasn't afflicted themselves, and if Kodiak found out someone had, he'd be well within his rights to kill that shifter immediately.

The Scorpions, on the other hand, were bloodsucking leeches. Unlike the myths about vampires, they rode in the daylight and they weren't afraid of crucifixes. But the stories did get one thing straight —we wolves lived to tear their hearts out with our teeth.

Just thinking about it made my canines tingle.

The Scorpions cared about nothing except blood, money, and power. They treated their women like shit, keeping an outdated (and disgusting) approach to motorcycle clubs—old ladies were meant to be used and abused until they were turned, and that was to say nothing of the way they treated their hang-arounds. Might as well say blood bags or vamp junkies. Those poor souls lived to feed the Scorpion vampires and prayed to be made into one. Most died before they ever were.

It was just another reason why we made it our personal mission to protect Helena from those motherfuckers. If they got into town, they'd turn this place into a blood-soaked wasteland, just like they did to Silverton and Crystal Acres.

"And what about the eastern border?" Our sergeant at arms, Moose, pulled on a cigarette and glanced down at the plans with dark. skeptical eyes. "If we're busy fucking around down south, won't that leave us open to the side?"

"I'm hoping the mountain range will keep us protected," Ruby said. Kodiak's sister was almost as dominant as he was, and for that reason, she held a primary spot on his council. As enforcers, she and Serpent kept everyone in the pack in line. Ranked just below the alpha, me, and Moose, no one would fuck with her, not if they wanted to keep their head attached to their bodies.

"Won't that renew the war?" Moose asked.

"If it does, we're ready for that, too," Serpent joked, giving the sarge a playful wink. He barely cracked a smile for anything, but whatever made him grin had to be horrendous and downright deadly. There was a reason the stoic enforcer had been nicknamed after a venomous snake. I'd seen him do things to people with poisons that haunted my nightmares, even despite his claws and teeth.

"We've been loading up on arms," Ruby added. "Not to mention the tricks Serp has up his sleeve."

Lycan leaned his head back and howled, causing the others to join in. I shifted in my seat, watching my oldest friends in the world as they processed this new plan. It *could* work, even if it was risky. When he was alive, Uther Vanderbilt had the whole of the Montana government in his pocket. He blamed the Bastards for killing his wife (which we didn't do), and as retribution, he'd sent assassins in during a full moon, killing off damn near half our numbers.

After the previous alpha died, Uther had cut a tentative truce with Kodiak, predicated on the fact the Vanderbilts wouldn't do any further business with the Scorpions. They stayed out of our way, and we stayed out of theirs. Now that the patriarch was dead, his slimy idiot of a son had stepped in to take his place.

I knew enough about Percival Vanderbilt to know his father's cool head for business had skipped right over him. Liam and Guinevere were a different story, but that wasn't who the shareholders had given the power to, and now all of us braced for the fallout, even if that meant bloodshed.

"The drive-by at the funeral was enough to shake them," our tail gunner, Larentia, added. She had eyes like a hawk and better aim than anyone else on the council. "Let's see what they do next."

"I agree," I said. "Nothing is going to happen over the winter, not while everyone is bracing for a storm."

"Speaking of which," Kodiak said, shifting gears. "We need three volunteers to head up to the Fiver Cabin. The guys up there now are switching out rotation."

A collective groan came from the entire MC and the room went silent. The RBMC owned three thousand acres outside of Helena that we'd maintained for decades. We raised cattle, bred horses, and culled sheep—enough to launder the funds we got from other activities. Being located in the dead center of the country made us a prime stopping spot for anyone that wanted to run guns or drugs, and being this close to Canada gave us an advantage for international trade. Just because we turned furry one night out of the month didn't mean we weren't an MC in every other sense. Millions of dollars passed through our hands every year, but with that came the hard work of keeping the ranch held together.

The Fiver Cabin sat at the top of our property, at the highest altitude. We occasionally moved the cattle and horses through there, but this year, we were letting the sheep have the barn. Three men could run it, though four or five was better. It was never unoccupied when we housed animals at the Fiver, and the four Bastards that were there now had been there since the last moon. Now that the weather stations were predicting a blizzard to dump six feet of snow in the next two days, whoever volunteered to go next would be stuck up there for the foreseeable future.

It was a hard fucking job, but if it didn't get done, it could demolish a big chunk of our income. Not to mention the fact we preferred to shift together. Wolves were pack animals after all, and my inner beast protested the thought of being separated from Kodiak and the others for the upcoming moon. But I was the second for a reason. The strongest members of the pack protected the rest from the worst parts of this life.

"I'll go," I said.

"You always go," Kodiak added, clapping my shoulder and smiling. If there were anyone in this world I would consider my best friend, it would be this grizzly motherfucker in front of me. We'd been born into the pack together and raised by the shifters that came before us. He'd had the scent of an alpha ever since he was a pup, and the only other shifter our age who came close was me. We'd been best friends ever since.

"I'm the veep," I said. "It's my job to do the shitty jobs no one else wants to do."

That made everyone chuckle.

"Sign me up," Lycan said, shooting me a wink and a smile.

I snorted and rolled my eyes. "Great. Stuck in that tiny house with your ass for the next few weeks. Make sure your emergency contact is up to date."

Lycan had been given his road name because he got around like a bitch in heat. Men, women, enbies, it didn't fucking matter. He liked what he liked, and no one else in the MC gave a shit where he stuck his dick. He loved to party, and three weeks stuck with him in the cabin meant we'd play as hard as we worked. He and Larentia were twins, and where he'd gotten the more jovial side of the family gene, she'd gotten the angrier and meaner side. But that was what they said about wolves—the males had one brain cell to share between them while the females did all the work.

"That means I'm in, too," Poe said. The quiet brother had been our secondary tail gunner since he joined a few years ago. Tall, dark, and mysterious, he rarely talked about his past. But he and Lycan had formed a bond immediately, and now, they'd barely be separated from each other. I'd say it reminded me of my own friendship with Kodiak, but we were strictly platonic, and those two liked to share whoever passed through their beds...sometimes even each other. If I didn't know any better, I'd think the two of them had been mated, but they didn't wear each other's scents, so if it was going to happen, it hadn't happened yet.

"Thank you," Kodiak said. "One last thing. I need someone to head out west and meet up with Saddle from the Washington chapter for an exchange." A few other brothers raised their hands, and once the business was settled, Kodiak announced the end of church. "Try to be back by the full moon, yeah?"

The council of Kodiak's most trusted advisers howled in response, the thrill of the upcoming shift humming in the tension surrounding us. It was only ten days until then, and the closer the moon got to its full brightness, the more our beasts rode the surface. Even this far out, my wolf raked its claws against its cage inside my mind, desperate for the chance to run free.

"All right, you Bastards," Kodiak said, bringing me back to the present. "It's one of the last nights we'll be here together, so have fun. Don't get into too much trouble."

"Yeah," Ruby cut in. "Don't make me have to bang your heads together after I get wrecked. It'll be worse for you if you do."

I watched my found-siblings file out of the meeting room to the front area where the old ladies, MC princesses, and hang-arounds waited to party with the rest of us. When Kodiak didn't immediately go with them, I raised my eyebrows at my best friend.

"Something on your mind, brother?" he asked.

"How you doing?" I drummed my fingers on the wooden table bearing the Bastards crest, the symbol of our combined strength across this country and the rest of the world. All of the Helena chapter was connected to Kodiak through the pack bond, a preternatural tether that hummed just below the surface of my skin. Through it, I could sense the all of them, but since he was alpha and I was his second, not to mention his best friend, I noticed Kodiak more keenly than the others.

Today he felt like shit.

Kodiak smiled, crinkling the umber skin near his eyes. At six five and two hundred and fifty pounds, he'd gotten his nickname because he was the biggest and baddest motherfucker in Helena. In his wolf form, he was nearly as big as a Kodiak bear, and ten times stronger. He'd fought the old alpha for the top spot, and though it nearly killed him, the pack followed him because of that strength. He was a juggernaut: once he got going, nothing could stand in his way. The only person in the pack that could take him on and last more than a few minutes was me.

"Living the dream," he said, but I smelled the sickly scent of anxiety pouring off him.

"Don't lie to me," I said. "I know you better than that."

He ran his hands over his forehead and sighed. "Don't ever have daughters."

I barked out a laugh. He'd had two kids right out of high school with his girlfriend, Kendra, who later passed away in a tragic car accident we believed had been caused by the Scorpions. He'd been raising them on his own since then. The eldest had just turned eighteen and the youngest would turn sixteen at the end of the month. I could only imagine the chaos in that house, even with Ruby stepping in to help. It would be a few years until they each went through their transition, and the closer that got, the more they'd act out.

"Ginny wants to go to college in Hawaii, and Henny's dating three boys at the same time."

That made me chuckle harder because it reminded me of him at their age. "Do the three boys know about each other?"

Kodiak shook his head and sighed. "Man, *I* don't even want to know."

I patted his shoulder and gave it a reaffirming squeeze. "You're a good wolf, Kodiak, and an even better father."

"Yeah, yeah," he said, and it was only when he let his guard down like this that I saw the weariness in his eyes, the bags that hung under them, and the stress that pulled at his wrinkles.

"Your girls love you, and I'd kill anyone who said you didn't do the best you could. They know that. It's all they need." I tried to smile against the twinge in my heart that reminded me their mother was gone, that my own parents were gone, that we'd lost so many people in this war against those fucking bloodsucking demons.

"Thank you for always being there for them," he said. "I'll never be able to repay you for that."

"Please," I said, giving him a playful shove. "You wouldn't have been able to keep me away." I loved those girls like my own daughters, like the nieces I'd never have being an only child.

"Alpha," came the voice from the doorway. "I'd like to give an update, if I could."

Kodiak and I glanced over to Morwyn, the pack healer. She had a special connection with Kodiak, one that existed outside the normal hierarchy. She could draw on the entire power of the pack if she needed to heal our family, and she was the only one that could order him around. When it came to an emergency, Kodiak deferred to her.

"Sure, Morwyn." Kodiak nodded toward the front of the club-house. "Go get some pussy, Ry. It's gonna be a long couple of weeks in that cabin with Lycan and Poe."

"Fuck, don't remind me." I pushed to my feet and gave Kodiak's shoulder one last clap before stalking out to the main area where the revelry had already started. Lycan and Poe sat at the back with Serpent and Moose, hang-arounds in their laps, beers in their hands. A few of the MC princesses stood over by the bar, pouring a round of tequila shots for Lycan's sister. They held the glasses up and shouted a cheers to the Royal Bastards and the pack's continued health before shooting them back.

If it had been any other night and if I'd had nothing else going on in the morning, I would have stayed to see what kind of trouble I'd get into. One of the hang-arounds had been eyeing me all day, and I ached to slip my dick into someone warm and wet, especially since I didn't know how long it would be until I could do it again.

But the Fiver Cabin needed a ton of work to keep running, and I'd have to get up early as hell tomorrow to make sure we got there before the snow blocked the roads. Once that happened, there'd be no getting back down until the weather cleared. That could be anywhere from a week to a couple of months. Luckily for me, I liked Lycan and Poe enough to tolerate them for that long, and they liked each other enough to leave me alone.

The snow had already started in the higher elevations by the time I got to the three-bedroom log cabin up in the mountains. Lycan and Poe would probably show up sometime in the late morning, but I wanted to get here to check everything out beforehand.

The brothers that had been here before us kindly left a fresh stack of firewood on the porch, and I stomped my boots on the mat before opening the door to go inside. A few secondhand couches sat in the living room to my left and a small dining room table occupied the empty space in the kitchenette to the right with four chairs around it. At least the last round of Bastards washed all the dishes before they left, so I didn't have to pick up after them before unpacking my shit. I walked up the wooden stairs to the second floor landing, immediately heading to the primary bedroom on the left.

It wasn't huge, only large enough for a queen-size bed and a dresser, but the other rooms only had twin- or full-size mattresses, and at six four, I needed something bigger than that.

I dropped my bag on the floor before checking that the rest of the rooms had been stripped and vacated the way mine had. Not that Lycan or Poe would give a shit, but I appreciated the consideration from our brothers.

Once satisfied that the house was in working order for the few weeks we might be trapped here, I went out back and trudged down the hill to the barn. The livestock guard dogs, Judge and Pete, howled at my approach, both born and bred to keep predators away from our flock.

"Hey ya, boys," I said, stepping inside. Judge bounded up to me, his massive paws nearly the size of my own feet. He nudged his head into my hand, expecting a few pats before he went back to his rounds. Pete was only a year old, basically a puppy compared to Judge, who had lived up here for almost five years. Both were mutts, but with the mastiff blood in them, they had grown to be over a hundred pounds each. They loved their herd, and they kept predators away better than even me or Kodiak. The dogs smelled the wolf in me, and my animal side considered them honorary members of the pack.

After making sure the sheep were accounted for, I went to check on the mule, Larry. He honked his greeting, making me laugh and give him a few scratches behind the ears.

"You ready for the blizzard, huh?" I teased.

He flapped his tail and nodded, pulling his ears back when I got him in the right spot.

We kept five horses up here for the brothers to ride when they stayed, so I made my way to the next stall and checked on each one of them, pausing when I got to Nemesis. She was a huge quarter horse at almost sixteen hands, and she didn't like anyone except me.

Perhaps she, too, could scent the wolf in us and had decided I was the most trustworthy out of the rest.

"There she is," I said when she whinnied and came closer, nodding her giant nose into my palm. "I know, I know. I've been away so long. I won't do it again."

She harrumphed and gave me more of her annoyed cries, reading me the riot act for having sent the other brothers up here instead. Whenever they tried to get close to her, she bit or kicked them to push them away. Kodiak had wanted to get rid of her, and if it weren't for my insistence, he would have.

"You've just got spirit is all. Isn't it?" I rubbed her nose and smiled when she blinked affectionately, nudging me again. "I promise we'll go for a ride before the snow hits."

I checked on the other horses, decided to get Poe out here to clean their pens once he arrived, and headed to the smaller shed where we kept the pallets of hay. Once satisfied that the Fiver Cabin would keep us fed and warm for the next few weeks, I went back to get Nemesis, making sure to give her a good rubdown before putting on her saddle.

Then, I walked her out of the barn and climbed onto her back, grabbing the reins.

"We'll just do a quick sweep, okay?" I gave her a good pat on the neck before nudging her to go.

She set off like she hadn't been run properly in months. Laughing, I held on and encouraged her. I knew that was a lie. The guys would let her out in the pasture even if they couldn't ride her themselves, but with me on top, Nemesis was indomitable. She opened up those legs and let me have it, whipping through the woods, panting in the cooling air. There was no greater feeling on earth than flying across the earth on horseback—except for maybe doing the same thing in my wolf form or on a bike.

I'd grown up on the Bastards' ranch, and even if it wasn't as big as the Vanderbilts', I'd been around horses my whole life. I wasn't much of a people person, and I found that I enjoyed Nemesis's company more than most humans, maybe more than most of my pack. Between her and me, there was only ever the truth—the feel of the air in our hair, the beat of her heart against mine, the cacophony of the world around us.

Out here in the wild, the rest of the world could have fallen away. With the mountains stretching around us and the enormous trees insulating this tiny cocoon of peace, the war with the Scorpions didn't exist. The Vanderbilts were a million miles away, and time itself faded into nothingness.

We slowed when I got to the lake, and I paused to take in the beauty of the Montana skyline surrounding me. The storm clouds were rolling in, and everything had been cast in a shade of gunmetal and steel, but even that added to the decadence of the ever expansive vastness. The smell of snow permeated the thick, freezing air, accented by the ice and fallen leaves. I wasn't a religious person, and I didn't know if God existed, but when presented with natural splendor like this, it was difficult to argue that there wasn't some divinity in the very earth itself.

Nemesis stopped to rest before carrying me down to the far edge of our property, right where it butted up to state park territory. A break in the fence caught my eye, and I hopped off my horse to get closer and check it out. The wire had been cut straight down the middle, almost like it had been done purposely. I sniffed the air and frowned when neither I nor my wolf picked up anything nefarious.

I'd have to come back out here to repair it before we let any of the animals down this way. I stood up and glanced around, looking for signs that a wolf or mountain lion had gotten in. When I found nothing, I did my best to lay the wire over the hole before mounting Nemesis and circling the rest of the perimeter.

I didn't find any more signs of damage, so I headed back to the house, sensing through the bonds Lycan and Poe had arrived. Despite the cold, they'd ridden their bikes up, leaving my truck as the only reliable way to get around in the snow.

"It's about damn time," Lycan said, howling a laugh when I

walked my horse into the barn. "We were wondering if you'd gotten lost."

I smirked while I placed Nemesis in her stall and took off her saddle, hanging it on the rack just outside her pen. "I spend more time up here than anyone else."

"That's not a good thing," Lycan said, narrowing his bright blue gaze on me. "You need human interaction. The lone wolf dies. You need a pack. You're too young to become the monster in the woods."

He was only a few inches shorter than me, but his natural build made him wider and stockier through the chest. He had wavy blond hair that he kept chin length, and combined with his alabaster skin, high cheekbones, and big, wide smile, I understood why people loved him. I'd never been into guys myself, but objectively, he was beautiful.

"Says the worst monster in the woods," Poe added, circling around the corner with a bale of hay.

Poe was a few years younger than Lycan and me, having come to the Bastards just after his transition, which he'd gone through alone, not knowing what he was. I'd only heard of that a few times in my life, and I winced to think about the kind of hell that must have been on him. He was from Baltimore, and he could be a broody mother-fucker when he wanted to. He liked to read and write poetry in his spare time, something that didn't fit his biker persona until you learned that the shit was darker than the stuff created by his name-sake. Some of the imagery he imagined would live rent-free in my nightmares for the rest of my life.

Where Lycan was tall, blond, and stocky, Poe was all lithe muscle and long limbs. He had short brown hair that he kept swept to the side and big brown eyes that seemed innocent despite the violence I knew he was capable of, and his olive skin spoke of some Mediter-ranean heritage.

"I'm not a *recluse* monster," Lycan said, giving Poe a playful wink while he swiped his tongue over an extended canine. "Just the kind that likes to stalk his victims before he eats them alive."

Poe grinned, and his cheeks turned a bright shade of rosy pink.

"Get the stalls cleaned up," I cut in. "Then we'll head down to the lake. There's a tear in the fence, and we'll need to patch it up before the snow starts."

"Ten four," Lycan said, nodding as I walked back toward the main house.

I took another gulp of whiskey and inhaled against the raging vengeance burning in my blood, steering my SUV up the winding mountain road. Hot furious tears stung my eyes, dripping down my cheeks and blurring my vision, but I wiped them away with my sleeve and kept driving. I hated that I cried when I got angry. It made me look weak when I wanted to appear anything but.

"It'll be okay, Sol," Avalon said over the speaker of my SUV.

"Maybe he's rich," Maeve added. Only eighteen months older than me, the three of us had always been close—though they were understandably closer to each other than either was to me.

"I doubt he'd be marrying a Vanderbilt for the dowry if that was the case," Ava argued.

"I'm just saying," Mae said. "Perhaps the situation is not as dire as it appears."

"Being rich doesn't change our stupid brother selling her off to those barbarians." Ava let out a sardonic huff. "It's a shame Guin already left. If she were here, she'd have his nuts as a necklace. Have you tried calling her?"

"She wouldn't have been able to stop him," I said, taking another long gulp of whiskey. "Not even Liam could change his mind. He blindsided both of us with this arrangement." I grabbed my phone to check for a call back from our eldest sister. I'd been trying for hours, only for it to go to voicemail. "You two need to be careful. He mentioned it was time for all of us to marry, so I suspect you'll be next."

"Over my dead body!" Ava said. I could just imagine her shaking her head and turning beet red.

"I think the Scorpions would even take you like that." I sneered, indignation dripping from each syllable. Like the Bastards, there was something *off* about the Scorpions. Their pale, transparent skin and lifeless eyes could have been taken right out of a horror movie.

"Maybe he'll be good in bed," Mae added. "I'd give up riches and good looks for a big co—"

"Mae!" Ava gasped, clearly affronted. "Don't be gross."

"There's nothing gross about cocks, I assure you," Mae replied with a giggle so much like her twin's. I tried not to grimace thinking about a possible future where I'd have to sleep with the man. I'd heard rumors, of course. The Scorpions treated their women nearly as bad as the Bastards did, but I hoped being a Vanderbilt would change that.

My ass still stung where Marx had gripped me like an object, like the very horse he'd called me. I hated his touch. How would I ever sleep with him? How would I have children with him? Certainly, he would expect that.

I wiped my eyes and sniffed as another bout of irate tears rolled down my cheeks. Tomorrow, I'd find a way out. Tomorrow, I wouldn't let my sorrow have me. But tonight, I needed an outlet, if only for a few hours, if only to get it out of the way so I could think more clearly. Emotional Sol was not a pragmatic Sol, and I'd only be able to come up with a solution if I were more levelheaded...and sober.

"Thank you both for listening," I said. "To be honest, if this had to happen to someone, I'm glad it's me and not one of you."

"I'm sorry it has to be any of us," Ava said.

"It doesn't make any sense," Mae added. "Come home, Sol. Don't face this by yourself."

"No, I need some time," I said. "I'll be back by the morning. I just...I just want to be alone...to gather my thoughts."

"And you'll be able to do that with the fifth of Father's favorite I hear you chugging?" Ava sounded judgmental, but I wouldn't let that deter me. Sure, driving around the back country with a little bit of a buzz probably wasn't the brightest idea I'd ever had, but if any situation called for it, surely being potentially betrothed to one of the worst monsters on the planet was reason enough.

"Is that criticism?" Mae asked.

"Hardly," Ava said. "I'm just worried about the ole gal."

"I love you both," I said. "Please cover for me and don't fret. I'll see you soon."

Before they could argue, I hung up and dialed my eldest sister again.

"Guin, it's me," I said when I got her voicemail. "Please call me back. Our brother—" I hiccuped and swallowed another furious sob. "Our brother has lost his mind. I need your help fighting this... fighting him."

I hung up the phone and squinted, attempting to see through the whiteout of the storm. The blizzard was well underway now, and I chastised myself for leaving. But I couldn't stand to be in that house any longer. Big fluffy snowflakes fell on the windshield faster than the wipers could clear them, and I drank down a big gulp of liquor, wincing as the sting in my throat matched that in my heart.

"I can't believe Percy thought he could command me like this." I shook my head and huffed out a sigh of extreme annoyance, bemoaning the life I could have had if my father hadn't died. Perhaps I would have found someone I loved, someone I truly cared about.

The riling bile in my throat made me grimace as visions of that deplorable beast holding me down and taking what he wanted filled my vivid imagination. His disgusting breath would assault my face, and I nearly vomited remembering it.

Oh, God. Please help me. Please give a sign. Show me how to get out of this.

God and I had never been on the best of terms, especially after She took my mother from me at such a young age. But in that moment, I prayed for absolution. I prayed for some miracle to come sweep me away. I prayed for divine intervention.

The snow fell harder, creating a sheet of white so thick I could barely see. I'd made quite the mess for myself, and if I turned around now, I might be able to make it home before it got too bad. But I was up in the mountains, and making my way down might prove to be more treacherous than climbing up.

I'm such an idiot. A stupid, stupid girl. Just like my brother said.

I took another long pull from the bottle before putting the lid on and chucking it into the passenger seat. The world spun, and I squinted, trying to keep up. I hadn't eaten in hours, and the whiskey took advantage of that, going straight to my brain. Perhaps I'd die out here. Perhaps I'd go sailing off a cliff into a ravine.

What would my dear brother do then? How would he secure his alliance with the Scorpions? I chuckled at my own gallows humor, imagining the look on Percy's face when he got the news of my untimely demise.

No.

I couldn't do that. He'd just thrust it on Maeve or Avalon. Lord knew he couldn't make Guin do anything, and I wondered how I could secure such a position for myself. How had Guin made herself so powerful in our family? She'd been close with our father, sure, but his death seemed not to have changed her life at all. Was it because she was older than me, near the same age as Percy? Or did he have some ulterior motive for her, one that had yet to be revealed?

I could kill him. I could take one of Father's hunting knives and cut his heart out.

I laughed harder, sobbing through my hysterics as I coasted through the unplowed snow. Killing my own brother would certainly land me in Hell, if such a thing existed. Was it worse than selling a sibling out to the highest bidder? Who could say?

The higher up I climbed, the worse the driving conditions got. I'd lost track of where I was an hour ago. I'd grown up in these mountains. I'd been riding my horse through them since I was a girl, but everything became suddenly unfamiliar.

Had I been so caught up in my drama that I'd gotten confused in my own backyard? I eased off the gas, slowing down so I could glance around me. But the flakes fell too heavy for me to make anything out. The world had been blanketed in a thick sheet of frost, and after the sun went down, it all looked the same.

Pursing my lips, I stepped on the gas again, fiddling with the GPS so I could navigate my way out of this mess.

Just as I looked back up, something tiny and orange darted across the road, and I slammed on the brakes, trying to avoid it. The back tires hit a patch of ice, and the end of the vehicle fishtailed around. I struggled to hold on to the steering wheel, jabbing my foot into the brake pedal. Nothing I did gave me control again, and I spun, the seat belt tightening into my chest.

With a loud crunch, the SUV came to a stop and the airbags deployed. My head bounced off the hard cushion, my hands flying backward from the impact. For one peaceful moment, I thought I'd died. The world had gone blissfully quiet, and I thanked God for hearing me, for putting me out of my misery. I wanted it to be true. I wanted Her to have taken me.

The crinkling of soft snowflakes on the windows brought me back to reality, the bitter taste of airbag dust in the back of my throat choking me.

"What the fuck?" I groaned as agony shot down my head and into my torso. I blinked and leaned against the seat, grimacing as the taste of whiskey burned up my esophagus. The windshield had been cracked in the accident, but I could tell that I'd gone off the side of the road and pummeled into a big thick tree.

On the hood, a mere two feet in front of me, sat a medium-size burnt orange fox. Its bright amber gaze met mine, a smirk on its lips, its dainty paws poised in front of it as it thwapped its thick, fluffy tail on the crunched metal.

I'd never been so close to a wild animal, and if the shattered glass wasn't in the way, I could have reached out to touch it. I got the sense that it would let me, that it *wanted* me to. Instead, I panted while we stared at each other.

Was this the being that had darted out in front of me? Was this the creature that had caused my accident to begin with? I'd seen a flash of orange fur just before I'd crashed.

It raised its ears and tilted its head to the side, seemingly curious about me and scolding me at the same time. For what, I didn't know. Perhaps driving drunk in a blizzard. Perhaps acquiescing to my brother's hair-brained schemes in the first place.

"What else am I supposed to do?" I whispered. "I don't know how to fight him."

The fox seemed unamused, simply tapping its tail faster before giving me a slow, indignant blink.

"I'm not Guin," I said as another sob forced its way out of my throat. "I'm not my father." I unclicked my seat belt and hung my head in my hands, wiping away the wetness on my cheeks as grief swelled up in my chest. When my fingers came away bloody, I tilted the rearview mirror at myself, realizing I had a cut on my forehead that had leaked down the side of my face. A bruise had already started to form on my cheek, and if I hadn't been so wasted, I'd probably be crying over how badly I ached from the crash. Instead, I cleared my eyes and glanced back at the fox, who tilted its chin up, giving me a much sterner look.

Be strong, it seemed to say. *You are strong. You are special.*

"I don't think I can be," I murmured, my voice dry and cracked. "I don't know how."

Clearly done with me, it gave one last disparaging stare before hopping off the hood and disappearing into the winter storm. I had only a moment to wonder if I'd actually seen the creature before blinding headlights sent a spear straight through my eyes and out the back of my head, making me slam my eyelids shut and hold up a hand to block them out.

I didn't know who this was, and I scrambled to find my purse on the passenger seat. I always carried pepper spray with me, but the damn thing had flown to the floor in the chaos. I leaned as far as I could go to grab it, digging through the tossed-up mess before gripping the circular device just as footsteps crunched through the snow toward me.

"Are you okay?" came a deep voice outside my window as the beam of a flashlight bounced around in the snow. "Hello?"

Finally, a face came into view, but I could only see his outline as I grabbed the door handle and pushed the barrier open. He was tall with a dark beard and a black cowboy hat on his head.

"Hi," I said, stumbling out of the driver's seat. My foot slipped on the snow and the stranger grabbed my shoulders to hold me up, looking at me with a concerned obsidian gaze. It was the middle of the night and the snow fell hard and fast, but the moon reflected off his mahogany eyes in a way that made them shimmer. I stared at him, transfixed by the beauty and depth of color, and all of my fear suddenly melted away. My anger, my grief, my perceived helplessness...it all vanished. I ran my red-soaked fingers over his face, his soft skin like velvet under my touch. "Are you an angel?"

He narrowed his gaze and furrowed his brows, nodding back toward his truck. "My place isn't too far from here. We'll get you warm and figure out how to get you home."

If I hadn't been so intoxicated, a thousand alarms would have gone off at the thought of getting into a stranger's truck and letting him take me wherever he wanted. But those sirens never came, and as I clutched the pepper spray, I let him lead me back to his Chevy. After securing me in the passenger seat, he went back for my purse and other belongings, making sure to lock the door before closing it behind him and trudging to the truck.

S he smelled like sunshine on a cloudy day, like female and pheromones and strawberries, even despite the blood and whiskey. My wolf sat up at attention, barking and yipping at things it had no business entertaining.

When I heard the crash from the safety of the cabin, I never thought I'd find Isolde fucking Vanderbilt in the driver's seat, covered in crimson and drunk off her ass. What the hell was she doing on Bastard territory? Did she even know she'd stumbled over the property lines?

She clutched her coat tighter around her body and leaned her head against the window, smearing sweat and ruby liquid over the glass. I couldn't care less about that. No, I worried about what would happen when her family heard she was this far away from home and had been picked up by the vice president of their worst enemy.

"Do you know where you are?" I asked as I carefully maneuvered my truck back to the Fiver.

She winced and shook her head, shivering so hard her teeth chattered. "Montana."

I turned the heat up higher, hoping it burned through what must be adrenaline withdrawal. She could still stand, so nothing was broken. But I figured she might have a concussion.

"I mean, do you know where you are in Montana? Do you know what territory you're on?"

She trembled harder. "Vanderbilt."

I shook my head. "Darling, you stumbled onto Bastard property fifteen miles back."

Isolde grimaced. "I'm sorry."

"You don't have to be sorry," I said. "But if you didn't notice, they're calling for six feet of snow. Do you know who you are?"

"Of course," she snarled, giving me a side-eye. "Do *you* know who I am?"

"Everyone in the world knows who you are," I said, ignoring the bite in her tone. "I'm Orion, but everyone calls me Ry."

"Yeah, you're the Bastard that taunted us at my father's funeral."

Technically, the whole pack had shown up to celebrate that piece of shit's demise, but I wasn't about to argue semantics. "Why the fuck are you out this far so late?"

She didn't answer, just curled deeper into herself and peered out the window while I pulled into the driveway of the cabin. The front door burst open as I climbed out of the vehicle, Lycan and Poe emerging with their rifles, prepared to fight off whatever got out with me.

"You okay, Ry?" Lycan said, holding up the Winchester as the passenger side door opened. "Who is it?"

"Put the gun down," I said. "She's not a threat." At least not all banged up like this. I circled around to the girl, helping her trudge through the snow to the front porch. Lycan and Poe backed up, staring at her while she limped inside.

"This is Lycan and Poe," I said. "They won't hurt you. No one will, not while you're here." She glanced at them as their features fell in recognition. I shook my head when Lycan opened his mouth, indicating he needed to keep his thoughts to himself for the time being. "The bathroom is through this way." I pointed toward the back of the cabin. "Clean yourself up and then we'll figure out what to do."

"Thank you," she murmured, clutching her purse and coat as she headed through the space and closed the door behind her.

"That is Isolde Vanderbilt," Poe hissed, his dark eyes wild with both accusation and incredulity.

"Yeah, no shit," I said, trying to keep my voice low. "She wrecked her SUV on Buffalo Landing. I couldn't just leave her there."

"Leave her?" Poe ran his hands back through his hair and gave a sardonic laugh that rose the hackles on the back of my neck. "You should have kept fucking driving like you'd never seen her. We can't keep her here."

"We're not monsters. I'm not leaving a girl trapped in her car in a blizzard." I raised my eyebrows, glancing between my brothers. "Is that what you woulda done, Lycan?"

"I don't know, Ry." My blond brother pursed his lips, running a big, heavy palm over his face and back through his hair. "You get a whiff of her?"

"Yeah, I just spent the last ten minutes in a car with her," I said, straightening with suspicion at his tone. "Leave her alone."

Lycan pulled his lips into a wolfish grin, his eyes flashing ice blue like his inner beast wandered too close to the surface. Only nine days out from the moon, all of our feral sides ran hot. "You staking a claim?"

"She's a Vanderbilt," I growled, ignoring the race in my heart at the thought of either of these fuckers putting a hand on her. I didn't know why, but my animal counterpart and I already felt protective over her, probably because we'd pulled her out of the wreckage.

"She does *not* smell like a Vanderbilt," Lycan added, sticking his nose in the air and sucking in through his mouth like he could still taste her. "What is that?"

"If I didn't know any better," Poe added, "I'd say she was close to her—"

"Knock it off," I snarled, unwilling to consider that possibility.

"Don't touch her. Don't fuck with her. Don't hurt her. Got it?" Lycan held up his hands, clearly conceding my point, and Poe narrowed his eyes on me, evidently seeing far too much. "I'll call Kodiak to let him know. We'll figure out what to do from there."

The alpha would hand my ass to me, even if it was over the phone. But she'd come on *our* territory. She'd crashed on *our* road. My conscience wouldn't let her freeze to death out there, regardless of her last name or what her family had done to mine.

"This isn't good, brother," Lycan said, shaking his head. "Alpha isn't going to like this."

"Let me deal with Kodiak." I cleared my throat and put my hands on my hips. "Poe, you have medical training, yeah?"

He pulled his lips into a thin line and winced. "Some, yeah."

"When she gets out of the shower, check the cut on her head. It looks nasty." I reached into my back pocket for my phone, deciding to call Kodiak despite the late hour. He'd want to know as soon as possible after something like this. Perhaps he could even figure out a way to get her out of here before it became an issue.

"Yeah, okay," Poe said, nodding.

"I don't like this," Lycan said, widening his eyes to show he meant business.

"Me neither," I said.

"If we can't get her down the mountain tonight, she's stuck here with us," Lycan added, glancing at Poe, who scowled and walked back to the gun case so he could return his rifle.

"I know that," I said, my sneer hinting at the frustration racing through my blood. The full moon was in just over a week, and if she was still here, that could spell trouble for everyone involved. I lifted the phone to my ear and waited while it rang, anticipation flooding into my lungs when I heard his gruff voice.

"Hey, Ry," he said, "what's going on? You sick of those two assholes already?"

"We've got a problem." I explained the situation to him, making sure to keep my voice low so Isolde didn't hear me over the running water. "I can't get her back, not tonight. And if I don't, then she'll be here with us until the snow melts."

"Has she talked to her family?" Kodiak said. "Maybe they have a chopper they can use to come get her."

I sighed and pinched the bridge of my nose. "I'll mention it."

"Be careful," Kodiak said. "Watch her. This could be a trap. She could be there to snoop."

I'd thought of that the minute I realized who was in that SUV and what I had to do. "We'll keep our business to ourselves. Luckily, there isn't much she can get into at the Fiver."

"Good," Kodiak said. "And Orion, no one touches her. Understand?"

I almost snorted at the idiotic idea. "Of course, brother. I don't think that will be a problem."

"I'm not worried about you." Kodiak's laugh made me glance up at Lycan and Poe, who were huddled close together by the front door, whispering to each other. Those two had been known to go through women like kids in a candy store. "Make sure they keep their hands to themselves and their dicks in their pants. You're there to work. Got it?"

"Yeah, I got it." I took a deep breath and let it out through my nose.

"Figure out how to get her out of there as soon as you can, and make sure you report into me every day." Kodiak hummed another noise. "If you have to keep her there through the full moon, it's not the end of the world. But it would be better to get her off the property before then."

"Understood." I hung up and rubbed the back of my neck while I took a step closer to my brothers, repeating what Kodiak had told me. "Don't make me have to cut your paws off."

Poe balked but Lycan threw his head back and let out a noise that bordered on a wolfish howl.

"My dick would shrivel up and fall off," Poe said.

"She is hot, though," Lycan added. "And she smells like fucking peaches."

It's strawberries, you dumb fuck.

"No one fucking touches her." This time, I glared at the road captain, daring him to mention it again.

"You're the boss." Lycan held his hands up and cracked a grin, stepping around me to go back to the game of cards the two had been playing before we'd heard the crash.

"You two are moving to the bunks. I'm putting her in the room next to mine." I turned to head upstairs, my shitkickers thumping on the wooden stairs while I walked. Poe followed me so he could grab his stuff from the spare room, and after he'd cleared the space, I grabbed extra linens from the closet and made the bed with fresh sheets. When I came back downstairs, Isolde stood in the center of the space with a towel wrapped under her arms, her long ginger-blond hair wet and dripping down the front of her body.

The shower had made her scent more potent, practically pouring off her in intoxicating waves. Lycan and Poe stared at her, each with a hint of mischief and revulsion mixing in their expressions. And fuck, I could understand what was going on in their minds, even if we weren't connected through the pack.

For as much as I'd said they needed to keep their dicks to themselves, the sight of a beautiful, wet, naked woman wearing nothing but a towel stirred a heat in my most depraved, feral parts.

I shoved that away and raised my eyebrows, a silent ask about what she wanted.

"I don't suppose you have any spare clothes." She cleared her throat and held her head higher. "Mine need to be washed."

"Sure," I said, nodding toward the stairs. "I've made the bed for you. I'll check the lost and found."

"I've got some spare shirts I can lend her," Lycan said, pushing to his feet so he could follow us.

"I've got it, Lycan," I said, ignoring the part of me that didn't want her wrapped in another male's scent.

He pursed his lips and sat while Isolde trailed after me up the stairs. I went into my room and grabbed a few of my white shirts and a spare black hoodie before going to the lost and found in the hallway. I found a pair of sweatpants and boots that I thought would fit her and returned to the room to lay them on the dresser.

"I'm in there," I said, gesturing to the door next to us. "Lycan and Poe are in the one down the hall."

She nodded and gripped her towel tighter, and I focused on the floor, the ceiling, anything except the droplets of water sliding down her perfect skin.

"Thank you," she said, glancing at me before darting her focus away.

"We keep spare jackets and shoes in the closet in the hallway," I explained. "I think these should fit you."

"Is there a washer and dryer?" Isolde fiddled with her wet hair and pursed her lips. "I'd like to try to get the blood out of my clothes, if I can."

"Yeah, I'll show you once you're dressed." I headed toward the door and stopped short when I saw Lycan standing out in the hallway with a shit-eating grin on his face. Pretending not to care, I turned back to Isolde and grabbed the door handle. "Poe will take care of your head wound when you come downstairs."

She nodded as I shut her in, glaring at Lycan while he pinched his lips into a tight line, clearly trying to repress his amusement.

"What?" I barked, shoving him toward the steps so we could go downstairs.

"You all right, veep?" he said through broken giggles. "You look like you've just seen a naked girl for the first time."

"Shut up," I said, sending my frustration through the supernatural tether to both of them.

"Didn't want anyone else's scent on her?" Lycan teased again.

I growled and nodded to Poe on the couch. "Play your card game and go to bed."

Lycan laughed harder while Poe asked him what was so funny, but I pushed all of that deep down inside where I could never examine it again. Sure, Isolde Vanderbilt was gorgeous; Lycan had been right about that, and the mysterious notes of her scent called to my primal nature like a siren song. No one had ever been as alluring to me. But she was also the spawn of the devil, a privileged princess who had never known a day of hard work in her life. There was a reason the three of us came up here, and it wasn't to sit on our asses while the world spun around us.

It was a hard life at the Fiver. We were up at sunrise and we didn't stop until after sunset, and with the way the snow was coming down, we'd have to clear a path to the stables before we could even do anything substantial.

She was just another mouth to feed. A liability. And I'd have to be the one to remind her of that come morning.

When Isolde emerged from upstairs wearing one of my shirts and a pair of spare sweatpants, I nearly groaned in contentment. Seeing her in my clothes turned my insides warm for reasons I didn't want to study. I reminded myself that she was the enemy, even if the way her hair shimmered in the soft firelight made me want to wrap my hands around it and yank.

"I don't think you need stitches," Poe said, sitting on the coffee table while he examined her from her spot on the couch next to Lycan. "It's gonna leave a nasty scar, though."

"That's okay," she said with a wince while Poe used tweezers to pull the cut closed with butterfly bandages. "Thank you for helping me."

"Uh-huh," Lycan said. "Wanna tell us what you were doing out driving around in a fucking snow-ocalypse?"

Isolde wet her lips and frowned, shaking her head after Poe secured the last bandage in place. "It's a long story."

"Well, you're stuck here with us until the snow melts," Lycan said, nodding toward the window. "There's only one way down the mountain, and we've got nowhere to go."

Isolde dropped her jaw, glancing up to me for a moment before righting herself and tilting her chin up. "What about the highway crews? Won't they come plow you out?"

"On county highways, yes," I explained. "But not this far up, and definitely not on roads owned by the Bastards."

She gulped and returned her attention to her lap, as if she'd just remembered she'd been picked up by three fuckers from the local MC. There had been rumors about us, of course. The townies made up stories about why we were so secretive and why we didn't take kindly to trespassers on our land. That part of the lore, unfortunately, had always been true. Humans were spiteful, terrified creatures. If they knew a pack of werewolves hunted in their backyard, they'd come with their pitchforks and torches, shouting, "Kill the beasts!"

"What about your family?" I asked, crossing my arms. "Aren't they gonna be looking for you?"

She laughed a sad sound and sighed, looking despondent. "Yeah, probably."

"You need to tell them you're safe," I said. "The last thing any of us needs is for them to put out an APB and get us arrested." Especially not this close to the moon. No one wanted to shift in a jail cell. There'd be nothing left if we did.

Isolde nodded and folded her hands in her lap.

"Do you think they'd have a way to come get you?" I shifted my weight to my other foot, attempting to get comfortable despite the tension growing between us at the mention of her relatives. "A chopper or—"

"I said I'd call them," she snapped, shooting a glower in my direction before realizing she'd lost her cool and widening her eyes in astonishment. "I'm sorry. It's just—" Isolde cleared her throat. "I'm not on the best terms with them right now."

Poe looked at me, reminding me that he'd thought we should have left her ass to freeze to death. I wanted to ask her what that was supposed to mean, but Lycan pushed to his feet.

"I think that's enough for one night," he said, gesturing to the clock on the wall currently reading one thirty in the morning. "We have to get up early and it's already going to be a hard day without being exhausted on top of it."

Isolde softened her features and stood, forcing a small smile before turning toward the stairs. I watched her shut the door after she entered her room, and I turned to my brothers, raising my eyebrows.

"She's running from something," Lycan said. "I can smell it, and we're stuck in the middle."

"We'll deal with it tomorrow morning, brother." I patted him on the shoulder and moved to the steps, even though I agreed with him. She'd reacted strongly for someone who came from such a supposedly wealthy and happy family. Why weren't they on good terms? And what could chase her out of her life of luxury on such a shitty night?

Try as I might, sleep didn't come easily that night. The sight of her warm, tempting skin had my wolf's attention, and the way water had dripped down her neck made my canines tingle and my tongue ache to lap it up. I wanted to sink my teeth into her flesh. I wanted to rake my claws down her skin and leave deep bloody marks only to watch them heal before doing it again.

Stop that. She's a girl who lost her way. Nothing more.

Besides, she was the daughter of my family's enemy, the most villainous person I'd ever known. Uther Vanderbilt may have inherited a kingdom, but he'd turned it into an empire in the worst sense of the word. When Kodiak and I had been branded into the pack and officially made Royal Bastards, the land dispute between the Vander-bilts and the Bastards had already been going on for a decade.

Uther had publicly blamed us for the death of his wife even though we had nothing to do with it. We were easy scapegoats for his undeniable greed. He had wanted all of the territory on the Missouri River basin, but the Bastards had already laid claim to it. He'd tried to bribe us with money, and when that didn't work, black-mail. Finally, he resorted to more deadly means, hiring assassins from the Scorpions to take out half of the pack in one night and calling it justice.

The change into our animal alter egos wasn't quick or pleasant, and it hurt even more to shift back into human. It took five to ten minutes, depending on the shifter, and in the aftermath of the magic, the person was left reeling and shivering until the adrenaline wore off. The Scorpions had snuck onto our property after a full moon, when we were at our most vulnerable, and slit the throats of those on guard before bleeding out our brothers as they lay unable to fend for themselves. Kodiak recovered first and discovered them in the act, tearing the attackers into pieces until I could join him.

We'd never be able to prove it was Uther, but the assassins pointed to him as the one bankrolling their massacre. We didn't have reason not to believe them. I'd lost both of my parents that night, as did Kodiak.

The alpha at the time lost his mate and went rabid, a condition in which the human-self hurt so badly that the wolf took over as protection. When a shifter lost their humanity to the beast, there was almost no getting it back. Eventually, Kodiak had to put him down to save the rest of us from him. It had been one of the most vicious acts the Scorpions had ever committed, and there wasn't enough vampire blood in the world to make up for it.

In the chaos afterward, Uther had been able to buy out the prop-erty from under us before it could be transferred to Kodiak. We'd been trying to get it back ever since.

The Vanderbilt patriarch ultimately died of cancer, but that wasn't for lack of us trying to take him out beforehand. He had an entire army of people loyal to him, that protected him, no matter what. Not to mention the billions behind his name. He could literally buy this entire state if he wanted. But now he was dead, his army disbanded, and my bloodlust had gone unanswered by the man responsible for it. Sure, I could kill as many Scorpions as I wanted. I could even walk into the next room, wrap my hands around Isolde's pretty little throat, and choke the life out of her in retribution.

That seemed like too small a price to pay. I wanted to take over his entire kingdom. I wanted to get our land back and watch the Vanderbilt empire crumble to ash and dust. I wanted to hand deliver the Vanderbilt ranch to Kodiak and my brothers on a silver platter. Then, and only then, would I consider the debt repaid.

Thoughts like that kept me tossing and turning, and when the sun finally rose, I hauled my tired ass up and headed downstairs to make coffee before the rest of them woke.

The snow still rained down in buckets, and after brewing enough for a mug, I sipped my caffeine and walked out onto the porch. I sat in one of the rocking chairs and propped my boot up on the railing, sighing at the work ahead of us. I'd have to get the tractor from the garage and plow us a path to the barn so we could check on the animals. Once they were fed and watered, I'd get Poe to clean the pens and try to take Lycan down to the lake so we could check that the fence had held up through the storm.

"There you are," Poe said, stretching as he walked outside with a blanket wrapped around his shoulders and a mug of coffee in his hands. "Shit, it's still coming down, huh?"

I nodded. "After breakfast, I'll get us a route to the barn."

He walked around me to sit on the wooden bench swing, his rumpled hair blowing in the wind while he squinted awake.

"Is the Vanderbilt still asleep?" he asked.

"I guess." I shrugged. "I haven't seen her yet."

His hesitation echoed through me like a stab to the gut, like he had a million things he wanted to say but didn't know how to voice them.

"Speak your mind," I told him.

"No one gets away with relaxing at the Fiver," Poe said. "You know that."

"Uh-huh." I took another sip of coffee, sensing what he wasn't saying.

"You think she knows how to muck out a stall?" He laughed.

"I'm sure shoveling shit is an easy trade to learn, no matter where she grew up." I sighed. "I'm still hoping her family will come get her and be done with it."

"They can't fly a chopper in this weather," Poe said. "But maybe tomorrow or the next day."

I nodded. "Yeah, maybe."

"Look, I'm not trying to start shit," Poe said. "But her father killed your parents. He's responsible for more Bastard blood than anyone else in Montana, and those are the ones we know about. What about the other people he took out to build his monopoly?"

I cleared my throat and shifted uncomfortably in my seat, glancing at the tall brother at my side.

"I know," I said, rubbing a hand over my forehead. "But if we sink to his level, we're no better than him." That wasn't the only reason I didn't want any harm to come to her, but I disregarded those protective instincts, telling myself it was just because of the moon, because it had been so long since I'd gotten laid, and because I'd been the one to save her. Damned if I didn't have a savior complex.

Poe laughed and took another long drink of coffee, letting it out on a deep sigh when Lycan appeared, stepping out onto the porch already dressed with his cowboy hat on.

"Princess is in her room," he said, stretching so his hands braced the top of the frame. "Someone want to go wake her up?"

"I'll go get her," I said. "She was fucked-up when I found her; she's probably hungover. So be nice, yeah?"

Lycan balked and looked at Poe with a sneer. "I don't get any special treatment when I'm hungover."

"Yeah," Poe added. "Those aren't the rules at the Fiver. It's all hands on deck, no matter what. If you don't work, you don't eat."

"I said I'd get her," I grumbled, pushing to my feet so I could refill my coffee before heading upstairs to her room. I paused at the door to listen, bracing myself for the onslaught of her scent once I opened the entry. Then, I gave two hesitant knocks before twisting the handle, but the barrier barely moved. I shoved again, this time harder, and it gave, but only at the expense of a chair that she'd evidently shoved under the knob on the other side.

I narrowed my eyes at it before glancing up at the bed, where Isolde sat against the headboard with big, wide eyes, the blanket pulled up to her chin. There could be no other explanation for the chair under the doorknob. She'd been wanting to keep us out, to have ample time to protect herself should we try to break in.

"You know," I said, "if we wanted to hurt you, we woulda done it last night."

She met my gaze with a hesitant one of her own. "Can't blame a Vanderbilt for protecting herself...especially from the Bastards."

I couldn't tell if she'd meant to insult me or if she'd hoped it would come off as a joke. Either way, it rubbed my wolf like a backward pet. Suddenly, I didn't care if she was hungover. I didn't care if she had whiplash or sore muscles from her wreck. Kodiak had told me to watch her, that this could be a trap set by her idiot brother.

"Get up," I snarled, trying and failing to keep my voice level. "Get dressed. We have work to do."

She seemed surprised at that, her delicate mouth falling open into a pout. "Oh."

"Oh?" I raised my eyebrows.

"I just thought...Well, I suppose I thought I could try to get ahold of my family and maybe clean my clothes."

"Hmm," I said, straightening. "No one gets a free ride at the Fiver, and now that you're here, you're another set of hands." I grabbed my plaid long-sleeved shirt and jacket from where she'd dropped them on the same chair she'd used as an intruder deterrent and tossed them on the mattress next to her. "Breakfast is in fifteen minutes."

She scoffed but threw the covers back, wincing as she swung her feet out of the bed, clad only in one of my white T-shirts. Fuck, the sight sent something wicked and depraved coursing through my blood, so I turned and slammed the door behind me as I stalked back downstairs to my brothers.

E very muscle in my body cried as I slid Orion's oversize jeans up my body and tightened his belt around my waist. I slipped the long-sleeved shirt over the white T-shirt I'd slept in last night and inhaled Orion's masculine scent—fresh and sharp and powerful. A girlish shiver raced down the center of my torso, and I leaned my head to the side, breathing more of it in, relishing in how much I liked it.

Wait...what?

I shook my head and berated myself for such a silly thought. I'd only met the guy yesterday, and he was my family's enemy. I couldn't be so reckless as to develop some silly crush on a Royal Bastard, especially when he'd made it clear that he didn't think very much of me in return. My joints ached, my head splintered, and my stomach churned, all the result of dehydration and whiplash. I checked my cell phone, only to see that it had died sometime overnight because I'd forgotten to plug it in.

"Ugh," I groaned. Thankfully, I'd had a spare charger in the SUV and Orion had grabbed it along with my other belongings. Reaching over the nightstand next to the bed, I attached the business end to the wall. While I waited for my phone to turn on, I glanced outside the window and winced at the entire three feet of snow that had fallen. It all came rushing back to me.

The crash. The angel. Orion. The Bastards.

Orion had been the one I made eye contact with at my father's funeral, the one that time slowed down for, the one that nearly stopped my heart and forced the air out of my lungs. What the hell could that mean?

Nothing, you ridiculous girl. It had been from the stress and grief of losing my father; that was all. But even as I thought about him barging into my room and commanding me to get dressed, a tremble ghosted up my spine and the throbbing in my head grew more prominent, almost like the answer was right there, like fate was trying to tell me something and I'd was only *just* too far away to hear it.

"I'm so screwed." I debated my options. I could go downstairs, meet up with the Bastards, and demand they take me back to my car. But one glance outside told me that wouldn't happen any time soon. It had snowed a tremendous amount, and the weather showed no signs of stopping. They'd said as much yesterday, that I'd be stuck here with them until the roads cleared on their own.

Perhaps I should be worried for my safety. I thanked the version of myself from last night for bringing my pepper spray and pushing the chair up against the door. Although, Orion had made a valid point. If they wanted to kill me, they had enough opportunity to do it while I was drunk. Hell, Orion could have left me there to be buried alive in my own vehicle like Poe had suggested when he thought I couldn't hear. The Bastards had that reputation—kill first, ask questions later. But they'd been decent to me. I had no reason to think they wouldn't continue to be.

I ran my hands over my face and imagined what Percy would do when he realized I hadn't come home, that I wouldn't be home for the next few days, if not longer. So much for his silly plans with the Scorpions. So much for getting married right after the blizzard. The president had wanted to get it over with as soon as possible, and now his would-be bride had run away. Would they think the worst?

Would they assume something terrible had happened to me? Or would they think I had gone back on my word?

I wasn't sure which I preferred, but I also knew I couldn't do nothing. If I didn't get in touch, if I didn't let them know where I was, they'd assume I'd been abducted and throw the entirety of Montana's resources into finding me.

Still, I had a few days until that happened. Perhaps I could enjoy this little respite. Perhaps I could use it to figure out what to do next, to get in touch with Guin and come up with a plan to evade my dastardly brother. One thing was for sure, I would do whatever I could to get out of this mess. I just needed time to come up with something.

Digging around in my purse, I took inventory of what things from my old life I'd managed to bring with me: a travel manicure set, a few bottles of polish, perfume, my wallet, an e-reader (fully charged, thank God), and sunglasses.

My phone blinked to life, and I glanced at the missed calls: two from Maeve, one from Avalon, and a text from Guin. I opened that first.

Guin: I'll be home in a few days. Hang in there.

I sighed a deep breath of relief. She hadn't outright said she could help, but I took her *hang in there* as a sign that she understood and would do her best. She'd never had a problem standing up to Percy and kicking him back into place.

I called Maeve back, but she didn't answer, so I tried Avalon. She groaned into the phone after the second ring.

"Hey?" she said. "Where are you?"

"I got into an accident," I explained. "I'm fine. Don't worry about me."

"Percy is freaking out," she said. "Whatever you did to him, you must explain it to me. I need to know how to put him on edge, just for funsies."

"Ava," I started, taking a deep breath. "Will you cover for me for a few days?"

She paused, and I could imagine the confused, rumpled look on her face. "What do you mean? Where are you?"

"I'm taking a break," I explained. "I'll be back before they notice I'm gone." *I hope.* "If anyone asks, just say I'm at the lake house for a quick relax before my upcoming nuptials." I rubbed my fingers over my tired eyes, praying they had coffee downstairs.

"The lake house?" Ava's tone became more concerned. "Sol, where are you, really? Are you okay?"

"I'm okay," I said. "I'll be back once the storm is cleared."

"Okay," she said. "Call me if anything dramatic happens."

I let out a sad sigh. "Okay. Same here."

Yes, Orion and Lycan had wanted me to ask my family to come get me, and we did have a chopper capable of making that trip once the weather got better. But I wasn't sure I wanted to go home, not yet anyway.

Yes, this could work. This could give me the time I need to come up with a plan.

Deciding I would tell my family the truth once they could do something about it, I went downstairs to the living room, ignoring three pairs of eyes as I gingerly limped to the bathroom at the back of the tiny log cabin.

Catching sight of myself in the mirror, I winced when I looked like I'd been put through a meat grinder. The cut on my head had bruised, leaving the area around my temple in angry purple splotches that cascaded down to my cheek. The bags under my eyes hinted at the hours of sleep I needed to catch up on. After I did my business and cleaned up as best as I could, I went to the kitchen, where Orion sat at the head of the table alone. From the sounds of the heavy machinery already running outside, Lycan and Poe must have grown tired of waiting for me. Orion's raised eyebrow and frustrated glare confirmed that suspicion.

"Took you long enough," he said with a twinge of irritation.

"I called my sisters," I said, glancing at the place setting next to him. A cup of coffee sat next to eggs, toast, and bacon. I grimaced, my stomach still too full of whiskey to contemplate eating any of what was offered. Still, I pulled the chair out and sat, swallowing down the rising bile as I took a sip of tepid caffeine.

"It was warm when I asked you to come down." He must have read my expression.

"No worries," I said. "I enjoy my coffee cold with a side of grumpy Bastard attitude."

He narrowed his dark gaze. "You think this is an attitude?"

"I'm sure it can get much worse." I bit into my toast, ignoring how that, too, had gotten hard and chilled.

"If you want your food hot, you'll get down here when you're called." He tilted his head to the side.

"Yes, sir!" I lifted my hand to my forehead and brought it down in a mock salute.

"This isn't a game." His voice came out gravelly, almost a growl, forcing my attention to him. "We don't regularly take in strays, much less ones that have your particular history."

"I'm not a stray," I said, choking back my offense. "If anything, I'm a pedigreed thoroughbred."

"I don't give a fuck what your last name is," he said. "Here at the Fiver, it's all hands on deck. The work is hard and the days are long, even in the winter. You're another mouth to feed."

"Yes, I heard you and your *brothers* whispering about me." I snorted out an indignant scoff while I nibbled on another bite of bread. "I promise, I won't be any trouble."

"Oh, I know that," he said. "You'll follow me around and do whatever I tell you."

Wow. The audacity of this guy astounded me. Growing up with an overbearing father, I'd gotten used to big men ordering me about, but I *had* only just met him.

"You should have left me in the snow," I mumbled under my breath.

"Yeah, I probably should have," he said, "but here you are."

Silence fell on us while I forced another bite, deciding I could perhaps get the eggs down, too. I scooped up a forkful and swallowed, glancing around at the tiny place. Details stuck out more to me this morning than they had last night. Cobwebs lined the corners of the walls and the floors were littered with filth and decades-old patina of who knew what. When was the last time this place had been properly cleaned? I supposed it wasn't like they had a staff that would keep the place up for them.

"Did you sleep okay?" His gruff voice cut off my line of thinking, and I glanced back to him, studying him, perhaps really seeing him for the first time.

I'd thought he was gorgeous last night, an angel sent to rescue me from certain death. In the broad daylight, that was an understatement. His square jaw gave way to high cheekbones and intense eyes that penetrated even my tough exterior. When he looked at me, I felt like I'd been stripped naked in front of him, like I couldn't hide no matter what I did. My cheeks burned at the images floating around in my brain, and I went back to my breakfast, ignoring the way he analyzed every move I made. I could practically hear the wheels churning in his brain, trying to suss out whether I was a spy or just a silly girl that had run too far away from her problems.

"Fine," I snapped, realizing too late how ungrateful I must have sounded. I should have thanked him, but I couldn't let him win. If I gave him an inch, he'd take a mile. That was how the Bastards were.

"Hmm," he said with a scowl.

I balked at his lack of decorum and proper manners but didn't comment, just returned to my breakfast. "Why do they call you Orion?"

"Because my soul is as dark as the night sky."

I snorted. "Orion is a constellation."

"I'm the best hunter in the MC."

I knew the myth about Orion. He'd been a companion of Artemis until her brother, Apollo, grew envious and tricked her into killing him. In her grief, Artemis put him in the sky so she could see him whenever she wanted.

"But Orion isn't your real name?" I drank the rest of my coffee and finished the eggs.

"No," came his one-word response. I waited to see if he would give me more, but he didn't. *Well, I guess I won't be practicing my conversational skills with Mr. Tall, Dark, and Broody.*

My stomach churned and I stood, deciding I'd had enough breakfast for my hungover state. I grabbed my plate and dumped what little remained of my meal into the garbage before rinsing it off in the sink and loading it in the dishwasher. After I cleaned up, I turned to him and raised my eyebrows, silently telling him I was ready for whatever he had in mind.

My joints throbbed and my head ached like I'd had an anvil dropped on it, but when he pushed to his feet and stalked out of the house, I followed dutifully behind him. On the porch, he handed me a shovel and nodded down to the others. Lycan sat behind the wheel of a big industrial plow as Poe steadily carved out a path to the barn.

"Really?" I glanced up at him. "Shoveling?"

"What? Is that too far beneath you, Trust Fund?" He grabbed his own and stomped down the stairs, leaving little room for argument.

In my defense, I'd never shoveled before, and based on how tired and wrecked I felt, I wouldn't do much good today, either. But short of blatantly refusing and stomping my way back inside the house, I didn't see how I had another choice. Even if I did, he'd probably just haul me over his shoulder like a caveman and force me outside anyway. He wouldn't leave me unsupervised, not that I blamed him. Our families had been enemies since before I was born. It would probably be easier to do what he wanted with little fuss, and if it made him tolerate me enough to let me stay here, surely it couldn't be that bad. I clutched the pepper spray in my pocket, reassuring myself that I could use it at any time before stalking down the porch in my ill-fitting boots.

Sure, my siblings and I had played in blizzards as children and even had the occasional snowball fight. But I'd never done anything laborious. After a few minutes, I found a certain calm in putting myself to work, even if my hands trembled and my brain throbbed with every movement. I managed to keep up, though that was probably hubris on my part. Poe cleared more snow in twenty minutes than I did in an hour, but I blamed that on being injured.

Once the path to the barn was cleared, Orion showed me around and introduced me to the animals. I gave Judge and Pete a pat on the head and watched as Poe fed them so that I could do the same if they needed me to. I helped Lycan spread hay around for the mule and the horses, and I even offered to brush them down. Orion told me to stay away from the mare at the far end. She was big and sturdy, named Nemesis for how ornery she was around strangers.

"I can't imagine why," I murmured to myself as I took a step closer to her. Life with the Bastards was sure to turn even the gentlest of beasts into a monster.

"Yeah, I wonder how much worse she'd be if she'd been raised by the Vanderbilts," Orion said low enough that he thought I couldn't hear. But I did, and both Lycan and Poe stiffened before glancing at each other.

"What was that?" I said, turning toward him. I'd done everything he'd asked me to do this morning. I'd gotten out of bed and hauled my exhausted self out here. I'd sweat through my clothes and developed blisters on my hands, despite the gloves. I didn't have the energy for this, even if I might have been the one that started it.

"Nothing," he barked, moving away from me.

"Go on. Say it louder. We might as well clear the air." Fire raged in my gut, probably due to the work and onslaught of hunger, but I'd come too far to back down now.

He shifted his broad shoulders and pulled his lips into a sneer. "Forget it."

"Just like a Bastard," I said. "Coward."

That set him off. He growled and turned to me, towering over me with eyes the color of coal. "Coward? That's real nice coming from you, Trust Fund. Your father killed dozens of my family, my parents included, and never owned up to it. How far does the apple fall, I wonder?"

"Orion—" Lycan tried to cut in, moving toward his fellow Bastard, but Orion held up a hand to stop him.

I jutted my chin up and squared my jaw, refusing to back down. Either we hashed this out or he killed me. It wouldn't be the first time the Bastards had torn apart a Vanderbilt woman.

"Me?" I balked and let out a sardonic laugh. "Your stupid motorcycle gang killed my mother. The least you could have done would have been to leave a body. Give us something to bury. But no, I had to mourn an empty casket. Where's the bravery in that?"

Orion took another step forward, baring his teeth in a menacing display of aggression. I nearly retreated but forced myself to stand my ground instead. My temples hurt, my muscles cramped, and I'd had enough of this elephant in the room.

"You have no idea what you're talking about," he said, towering over me, making me feel small and insignificant in his fury.

"Don't I?" I refused to break eye contact, holding firm. "I lost my mother, you lost yours. An eye for an eye."

He yanked the shovel out of my hands so hard it scraped my fingers. "Stop talking, little girl. The Bastards didn't kill your mother. You sound ridiculous."

I swallowed and finally looked away because I didn't want to give him the satisfaction of seeing tears in my eyes. I didn't have very many memories of her. She'd died when I was only five, but that hurt the worst. His wretched biker outlaws had stolen that life from me, the one where she came to graduations and helped me get ready for my wedding and protected me from my idiotic brothers.

"Princess," Lycan said, nodding toward the front of the barn, "why don't you help me make lunch?"

I stalked past Orion and Poe to follow Lycan inside.

"He doesn't mean it," Lycan said, squirting mayonnaise onto a piece of bread. "You being here...it's bringing up bad memories for all of us."

"He's not the only one who lost people in this insidious war between our families." I put slices of turkey down behind him, making sure to ration three slices per person according to Lycan. "Does he think I *wanted* my father to do those horrible things?"

"No," Lycan said, giving me a friendly smile. Like the other two Bastards, Lycan was gorgeous. He could have been a supermodel in another life, even with the wild, roguish look in his eyes and the scruff on his jaw. "Not that I'm giving him excuses, but his default setting is grumpy and hard to be around."

I scoffed. "Mine is stubborn and angry."

Lycan laughed and put cheese on top of the turkey, following it up with a leaf of lettuce and a slice of tomato. "I'm surprised you stood up to him the way you did. Most people tuck tail and run the other way when he starts growling."

"He can take his growling and shove it up his—"

Poe and Orion stomped inside the house, interrupting my curse, and I glared at the lumbering savage, purposely showing my frustration through my expression. Orion took off his hat and placed it on the peg by the back door, clearing his throat as he eyed the lunch. He walked behind me to sit in the seat to my left, reaching in the middle of the table for the pitcher of water before pouring some into each glass.

"Have you heard from your family?" Poe asked as he took the spot opposite me. "Do you know when they plan on picking you up?"

"Poe," Orion snapped. "Eat." He grabbed a sandwich from the middle and plopped it down on my plate before taking one for himself. I didn't acknowledge the action, choosing instead to sip at the water while Lycan and Poe exchanged another secret glance.

"I talked to my sister this morning," I said, which wasn't technically a lie. "But like you said, there's hardly anything they can do during the storm. They know I'm safe; that's all that matters." I glanced to Orion, wondering if I should continue to needle him. But screw it, right? I was already stomping on thin ice. Might as well break through. "I *am* safe, right?"

No one spoke for a moment, and Orion glanced at me before clearing his throat and nodding.

"You mean to tell me the Vanderbilt family hasn't figured out how to control the weather yet?" Lycan blew out a disbelieving laugh, but it was obvious by the inflection in his voice that he'd meant it as a joke.

"It's on the list for world domination. Just wait a few years." A laugh bubbled out of my throat while I grabbed the sandwich and took a hesitant bite. It was good, but my headache had only increased during the day and, after the argument with Orion, it interfered with my appetite. Forgoing the sandwich, I focused on the soup. That went down much easier.

They talked about what they had left to do and how they planned to keep the animals warm during the coldest parts of the night.

"Poe, you take the first shift. I'll take the second," Orion said. "Lycan, get your ass up early enough to check on them before breakfast."

"Ten-four, boss," Lycan said, giving Orion a mock salute with his middle finger.

Orion rolled his eyes, and I continued to pick at my lunch, my manners battling with my upbringing. I'd never had to shovel out a stall in my life, nor had I slept in a barn to make sure the animals stayed safe. But, it couldn't be that hard, right?

Yeah, they seemed like weathered, grizzled men that had seen their share of hard work, but if they could do it...

"Is there anything I can help with?" I hesitantly asked, taking another slow sip of soup, savoring in the warmth it brought to my belly. "If I'm not *trustworthy* in the house by myself, you might as well put me to work."

Poe pursed his lips, and Lycan rubbed a hand over his mouth, glancing at Orion. The older Bastard stared at me, placing his elbows on the table before intertwining his fingers over his plate.

"Perhaps I was overzealous." Orion raised an eyebrow. "Do you enjoy doing dishes and scrubbing toilets?"

I recoiled and twisted my nose into a scrunch. "Not particularly."

"Well, what do you suppose you'll be doing inside while we're in the barn? Sitting around, painting your nails?" He glanced down at my chipped polish, and I quickly hid them under the table.

"We're planning on mucking out the sheep pen this afternoon." Poe asked, his eyes lighting up with hope. "Pick your poison."

"Princesses don't shovel shit," Lycan cut in, rubbing his hand over the younger man's brown hair. "Only snot nose emo boys from Baltimore."

Poe laughed and shoved Lycan's hand away. "Shut up, fucker."

"Make me, bitch," Lycan snapped back. They stared at each other for a few tense moments before Poe pushed his chair back from the table. Lycan launched himself upright, and the two of them took off through the front of the house, Lycan throwing open the front door while Poe followed him out into the chill of the afternoon snow.

"Shut the door behind—" The slamming of the entry cut off Orion's shout. "Apologies. They weren't raised right but I'm working on it."

I didn't respond, still seething from our argument an hour ago and his continued broody disposition. As I sipped more of the soup, silence fell between us. I normally didn't feel safe around strangers, especially ones that hated me and my family. And Orion certainly looked intimidating. He had strong, angular features and hard, menacing eyes that likely saw far more than they should. When he set that penetrating stare on me, it seemed like he could look right through me, all the way down to the terrified girl inside. Did he know about my brother's deal with the Scorpions? Did he know I hadn't told my family where I was or when I'd be back?

"I'm not opposed to shoveling shit," I suddenly said, trying to draw his attention away from whatever he'd seen when he looked inside my soul.

He sighed, pinched the bridge of his nose, and shook his head. "Poe's just being a prick."

"I understand why," I said. "I'm a liability. A burden." I threw his own words from this morning back at him. "But I can pull my own weight."

"Can you lift a bale of hay?" Orion raised his eyebrows at my silence. "Do you even know how to feed sheep in the winter?"

"I'm a quick learner," I said. "Vanderbilt currency is money, but if the Royal Bastards require more from me—"

"You have no idea what you've stepped in, do you?" Orion rubbed his hands over his face. "You shouldn't have come here."

"I know," I said. "But there's nowhere else for me to go, at least not for a few days. I'll do whatever you need me to do. Would it make you feel better to see me cleaning toilets? Fine. As long as you don't leave me to freeze to death outside."

Orion took a deep breath and pulled his lips into a thin line before placing the rest of his soup in front of me. "I'm sorry for what I said out there."

"Don't patronize me."

"I'm not," he said, softening his tone. "You were a child when that shit went down. Neither of us had anything to do with it. But Isolde, I promise you...the Bastards didn't kill your mother. We had nothing to do with her disappearance." Orion met my gaze with something like kindness echoing out of his. For someone who seemed so stern and furious most of the time, this rare act dialed my rage to a simmer. I wanted to believe him. Everything in my gut told me he was telling the truth. But if that was the case, what *had* happened to my mother? And why would my father lie about it for years?

"Perhaps I was too hard on you," he continued, "Perhaps... perhaps you could spend the afternoon tidying the place up, if you want."

Seeing as my stomach still churned and my brain didn't feel like it fit inside my skull, the thought of being out of the storm for the rest of the day came as a huge relief.

"I can do that," I said.

"Perhaps we can call a truce." He raised his eyebrows.

I nodded and held out a hand between us. "A truce."

He grabbed my palm, squeezed it tight, and gave it a shake. The tentative fervor of safety settled in my gut.

Giving me one last nod, he flipped his hat over his head and headed out the same way Lycan and Poe had. Then, I choked back the rest of my soup before devouring what Orion had left, trying to ignore the fact that he hadn't argued with me when I'd called my presence a burden.

As the second youngest child in a house with seven siblings, I'd gotten used to being seen and not heard. It wasn't until most of them had gone to school that Father paid any attention to me, and even then, I wouldn't call it cozy or familial. We were close, but he was still emotionless and distant most of the time.

I didn't expect the Bastards to accept me with wide open arms, especially not after the way our families had treated each other. Based on the less than twenty-four hours I'd spent with them, I already had a better opinion of the Bastards than I did the Scorpions. No one had assaulted me or compared me to a brood mare. No one had made me feel so out of place and time.

When I finished, I washed the dishes and put them away. It was a strange feeling, cleaning up after everyone, one that I'd never had to experience before. But standing at the kitchen sink, watching the guys work outside, a unique sense of pride blossomed in my torso. Almost like I *enjoyed* it. But that was silly, wasn't it? Who enjoyed doing manual labor, especially when they didn't have to?

After that, I went upstairs and found my soiled clothes from the night before. But then, I stood in front of the washing machine, unsure which knobs to turn or buttons to push. It wasn't like I was completely useless; I'd just never had to do this before. For as hard as my father had been on us, we'd always had staff to handle these things, even when I was at boarding school. Most of my clothes were dry clean only.

I stared down at my designer blouse and tailored trousers and wondered if it was even worth the effort. Besides, how long would I really be here? A few days? A week, max? Resigned, I put my underwear and pants in the opening, added some soap, and turned it to delicate, hoping for the best.

By late afternoon, I wandered around the tiny space with a duster I found in a closet, wiping at the counters and spinning it through the cobwebs in the corners. I paused to stoke the fire before adding a few more logs, and I glanced at the photos on the mantel, recognizing my three hosts among the crowd of other leather-wearing, muscle-wielding Bastards. They looked happy. I had understood the Bastards to be terrible, horrible men, vicious and unruly. But these three had been relatively decent, even if Orion was snarly and grumpy.

I figured the others didn't want me here, either. Poe had argued that Orion should have left me to the elements. Maybe he was right. I made their situation more complicated. Like Orion had said, I was just another mouth to feed. I swiped over the dust and grime on the mantel and countertops, greeting a spider that had made its home in one of the corners of the room.

"I shall call you Spencer," I said, giving the little thing a smile and deciding to let him live. "Spencer the spider."

Instead of making friends with all the insects I found in the proverbial man-cave, I continued my dusting on the lower level before heading upstairs. I did my room first and quickly made my way through Lycan and Poe's, grimacing at the used condoms and empty beer bottles in the trash.

Not my business.

Judging by the suitcases full of clothes, they didn't live here full time, which made sense as I knew they had a bigger ranch in the middle of their property.

The smell of the two men mixed heavily in the air, making my head pound harder despite the food and the caffeine. Some kind of warning instinct in my gut had me turning around and leaving as soon as I was done.

A door at the end of the hallway opened to a rickety set of stairs, which led to an unfinished attic stacked with boxes and plastic containers. I figured I could spend weeks up there and still not go through it all. So I went back to the second level and wandered to the bedroom next to mine, twisting the handle to open the door.

A rush of Orion's clean, woodsy scent bombarded me, so tantalizing and *male*, and I inhaled it deeply, as if it could ease the aches in my body with aromatherapy. It entranced me, luring me in. Sure, he probably wouldn't like me invading his private space, but I couldn't resist. The temptation of him...of being close to him...hit me behind the knees, propelling me into the room.

I didn't understand the compulsion, especially since he'd made it perfectly clear that he didn't like me or want me around. None of that reason or logic stopped the sensation from settling in my veins like aged whiskey.

Where Lycan and Poe had left their blankets thrown about, matching their clothes on the floor, Orion had made his bed this morning. His clothes were hung in his closet or put in the dresser, folded and organized. His spare boots were lined up in their proper spot under his mattress, and another picture of the Bastards sat on an end table next to his bed.

I picked it up and brought it closer so I could see. This one had more people than the one downstairs, women included, and Orion looked like a teenager as he stood on the far end. But my gaze caught on a tall, dark-haired woman in the background. She looked to be in her late twenties or midthirties, like a female version of the grumpy Bastard I loathed, her a radiant smile stretching from ear to ear.

"What are you doing?" The gruff voice made me jump, and I nearly lost my hold on the frame. Orion stood in the doorway, leaning against the jamb with his arms crossed.

Busted.

"Cleaning, like you told me," I said, running the duster over the table before holding the picture up to him. "Who's this woman in the back?"

It had to have been his mother.

He pushed himself upright and walked closer, the sway of his hips reminding me of how a predator stalks its prey. When he got close enough, he stared down at me, the heat radiating off him in suffocating waves that nearly brought me to my knees. He smelled like sweat and deodorant and ice-covered outside, and that, too, entranced me. I wanted more of it. I wanted to bury myself in it.

Orion didn't answer. He just grabbed the picture from my hands and put it back on the nightstand.

"It's time for dinner," he said, stalking to the door but stopping to make sure I followed him. I paused to glance at the photo one last time before moving, turning to my side when I passed him in order to squeeze through the tiny opening he'd left for me.

The tips of my breasts brushed against his lower chest, and I sucked in a breath, ignoring the zap of energy and heat that ricocheted through my muscles.

Nope. Danger. Danger. Do not read into that.

The next few days passed much the same as the first. I woke up to Orion pounding on my door, quickly dressed, and went downstairs to help with breakfast. After we ate, I followed them outside to shovel snow or shit or whatever Orion asked me to do. We mostly ignored each other, save for the few times I glanced up and found his gaze lingering on me. I figured I didn't know the proper way to muck out a stall, but Lycan assured me there wasn't much to it other than to get the shit in a wheelbarrow.

I fed the horses and snuggled the dogs, and at lunchtime, I went inside first to prepare the food Lycan or Poe had set aside that morning. My head continued to throb and my body still ached, but that must have been because I hadn't fully recovered from my car wreck before being forced to work a ranch like I'd been doing it my whole life.

Secretly, I didn't mind it so much. Yeah, I smelled like a barn animal at the end of the day, and I felt it in muscles I didn't even know I had, but I'd never slept as well as I did those first few nights. I didn't even need to read before bed, something I had done since I was a child. I loved books, and if I'd had my way in college, I would have studied writing instead of business. But I'd always thought I'd work for Vanderbilt Holdings one day, so for me and my siblings, there was no other choice. I didn't know Father would die before I could.

The guys had started to warm up to me, or at least, Poe and Lycan had. One morning, I came downstairs to find Poe standing at the stove, stirring something in a pan that smelled delicious. I paused at the sight of Lycan behind him, arms wrapped around the younger man's waist, scraping his teeth against Poe's ear, exchanging hushed whispers and desperate giggles.

Oh...

I cleared my throat and walked forward, grinning when both men glanced up at me.

"Is there anything I can help with?" I asked, quickly adding, "For breakfast?"

Poe raised a skeptical eyebrow as Lycan stepped back and laughed.

"Do you know how to make bacon without burning the place down?" Poe asked.

"I can learn," I said, hooking my hands together behind my back. Poe explained the basics and told me to keep an eye on the eggs while Lycan pulled him toward the bathroom and kicked the door shut behind them. I set the table and made myself as useful as I could until heavy footsteps came down the stairs and approached. When I looked over my shoulder, I found Orion in jeans, a T-shirt, and his flannel, leaning against the beam separating this part of the house from the living room and watching me.

I'd swear I saw his eyes flash blue before he blinked and they turned dark brown again.

I must be concussed. That was the only explanation. I obviously needed more rest.

"Are they like...together?" I nodded toward the bathroom, indicating Lycan and Poe by the sounds of laughter and moans echoing over the running water.

Orion pushed upright and shrugged, walking forward to the eggs. "No idea. It's none of my business."

"Oh, okay." Certainly, it wasn't any of mine, either.

"Why? Are you into one of them or something?" At the hint of a snarl in his tone, I straightened and turned to face him, bracing myself with my hands on the back of the chair in front of me.

"No, of course not," I said, fighting a blush that echoed up my neck and into my cheeks. "I'm a Vanderbilt, remember?"

"Hmm," Orion said, shifting around so he could lean against the counter and stare at me again. "How's your head? Any better?"

"Not really," I said. "It's pounding, but I'll be okay."

A crease formed between his brows as he came closer, and I held my breath while the space between us closed to inches. Without asking, he grabbed my chin and forced my face up to his, his gaze zeroing in on the wound near my hairline. "You've got a nasty bruise. I shouldn't have you working outside. You need rest."

"It's fine. If you're going out, I'm going out." I jerked out of his hold. For some stupid reason, I enjoyed being in the fresh air with them, I enjoyed doing my part to earn the few days I planned to be here.

He made another masculine sound low in his chest, and a tremble shot down my spine, pooling in parts that had no right forming an opinion. I clenched my thighs together, curling my fingers into fists to keep from pushing them through his thick hair.

"But maybe I should make it an early night," I added, more as a reminder to myself.

He nodded and grunted a noise of agreement, taking a step away from me just as the bathroom door opened and Lycan appeared with a towel wrapped around his waist.

"Sorry to interrupt," he said with a smile, glancing between the two of us as he padded upstairs. Poe followed closely behind him, and by the time we were alone again, whatever had happened between Orion and I had been quickly brushed under a rug.

Eventually, Lycan and Poe came back down, fully dressed, and we ate breakfast together before heading outside to work. Other than that one interaction, Orion remained grumpy and aloof, and when dinnertime came on day four of captivity, I figured there would be no breaking through to him. Which was fine with me. For as beautiful as he was, I needed to stay away from him. He made me feel things…inexplicable and undeniable things…that were better left unmentioned.

"All right," Orion said at four thirty. "Let's call it and head inside."

"I'm famished," I said, tossing the last little bit of feed out for the sheep. "But I think I'm getting better at this."

Poe smirked while Lycan barked out a laugh and threw an arm over my shoulder. "We'll make a ranch hand out of you yet."

Orion glared at Lycan but said nothing, just nodded back toward the cabin. "Go gather more firewood from the pile out back, enough to keep us warm through the night."

Lycan grumbled to himself but ultimately stuffed his hands into his gloves and walked around the house. Poe fell behind us, tending to a few things before closing the barn, and I nudged my shoulder into Orion's arm, hoping for a playful grin on my frozen cheeks and wind-chapped nose.

"Not bad for a trust fund baby, huh?" I said, delight squeezing my heart when he set those predator eyes on me. They flashed a bright icy blue, there for a moment and gone in the next, just as they had that morning in the kitchen. I nearly stumbled over a snow pile from watching him instead of where I was walking.

"Yes, being covered in shit suits you." His voice came out in a deep, sarcastic growl, nearly enough to raise the hairs on the back of my neck. "Wait until I have you shearing sheep and wrestling cattle."

Certain I'd imagined the whole changing eye color thing, I clapped in excitement and jumped, thrilled I'd pleased him. I didn't know why. It didn't make any sense. I'd just met him four days ago, but everything in me wanted him to think I'd earned my place, that

I'd done a good job. When did I become so desperate for his approval? And why did I care so much?

I don't. I swear I don't.

The guys walked ahead, but I realized I'd left my gloves in the barn, so I turned back to get them. I slid the door to the side and walked back to Nemesis's stall, smiling as the mare came closer to the gate. She whinnied and nudged my shoulder in greeting, perking her ears toward me.

"Hi, girl," I said, giving her a few quick scratches on her nose before I walked back toward the entrance, shutting the door and locking it like Poe showed me.

I took a step toward the house just as a crack in the woods came from my right. I froze and glanced in that direction. A chill skated down my spine that had nothing to do with the cold air as I thought I saw white fluff scurry by, moving against the snow.

"Hey!" I shouted toward the house, but the guys had already gone inside. I glanced back toward the woods, narrowing my gaze on the moving blob, almost certain now that it was a sheep.

Damn. Had I left the pen open?

No, I'd locked it up. This one must have gotten away while we were cleaning it earlier. I trudged toward the tree line, stomping in the thigh-high snow. Once I got into the forest, the snow drift lowered to my knees, but it was still a pain to chase an animal through the stuff.

"Hey, sheep," I called, feeling like even more of an idiot when the beast kept bucking and kicking its way through the storm. I had half a mind to let it go, to let it get eaten by wolves or bears or whatever scavengers might be out in this mess.

But no. I'd just started getting the respect of the guys, Orion especially, so I kept going. I *had* to keep going. I could catch the damn thing and put it back in its pen and no one would be the wiser about my mistake in counting earlier.

I counted fifty-two, didn't I? What the hell?

I didn't know how it escaped, but I didn't care. The only thing that mattered was getting it back.

As if sensing a game of chase, it sped up, hopping through this shit faster than I could walk. What seemed like centuries later, I finally gained on it, only to have it throw itself over a fallen log with a lingering, "Bahhh."

The sun had started to set and the angry storm clouds made the natural shadows of the forest seem even more ominous, so when I hopped over that same log and lost my footing, I immediately buckled at the knees and rolled down a hill.

The world spun around me, making my apparently permanent headache more intense. I crashed into a thick oak tree with a resounding *thump,* aggravating every nerve in my body that was already sensitive from the wreck four days ago. Warm, sticky blood coated the side of my face from my head wound that had reopened on impact.

"Damn it," I shouted, wincing as stars blinked in my eyes and a sharp stab went through the center of my skull.

All the air rushed out of my lungs, and I lay there for a moment, praying for the strength and the willpower to get back up.

"Bahhh," said the sheep, practically mocking me from a few feet away. I hauled myself to my feet, my shame for having made a mistake turning into full-out rage. Now, I *had* to get the damned thing.

"I'm going to turn you into a tasty lamb chop," I taunted, staring it down as it teased me. "And I'm going to take your wool and make it into a blanket for some rotten kid to snot all over. Would you like that?"

It only bayed at me again before turning and continuing its pursuit into the woods.

"No, you little asshole!" I chased after it, this time getting close enough to wrap my arms around its neck, halting its Houdini act. "Ha! I got you."

It made another "Bahhh" at having been caught, but this time, a deep, rumbling growl punctuated the sound, carrying on the wind. I froze, glancing around at the icy forest ground and thick brown trees blocking my path. Rancid instinctual fear raced through my veins, telling me I wasn't alone out here...and I was severely unarmed.

I straightened and wiped blood out of my eyes, blinking against my stinging vision as I kept one hand on the sheep so it didn't run off again. Looking around, I grew desperate to find the source of the noise. Another threatening snarl echoed off the trees, interrupting the soft tinkling of snow falling around me. My heart pounded and the sickening curl of anxiety rolled in my gut as I struggled to stay calm and debated my options.

I could run. I could throw the sheep to whatever predator lurked in the woods and take off, but after falling down the hill, I had no idea which way to go. I was disoriented and the pounding between my temples had only intensified from the fall. All thoughts stopped when another gnarl accompanied two more, this time closer, seeming to come from all around me.

Oh no. I was surrounded, and this wasn't just *one* predator. No... this was a pack.

Bright glowing eyes appeared a few feet in front of me, giving way to a long brown muzzle with lips pulled back on big, slimy teeth. It snapped at me, and every survival impulse I had told me to *run!* But I knew better. To run would initiate a chase, and their prey drive would take over. They wouldn't stop until they had my throat in their jaws and their claws in my soft bits.

The ground was covered, so even if I thought I could fight them off with a large branch, I'd have to dig to find one that would work. No, I was absolutely screwed. There would be no getting out of this.

Deep in the part of my brain that operated on primal urges, I laughed. I'd been betrothed to a degenerate, forced to live with three Bastards, and this was the way I died? God had a funny way of showing irony.

"Well then," I said, raising my voice as I stared down the biggest and the most hungry looking wolf. "Go on. Come and get me!" I let out a loud roar, seeming to come from the very pit of my soul. If I went down, at least I could say I went down fighting.

"There's something going on with her," Lycan said as soon as we got inside for dinner, raising a suspicious eyebrow in my direction. "I can smell it."

"You better keep your fucking muzzle to yourself," I said. "Alpha's orders." Not to mention the thought of either of them touching her sent a possessive fury through my veins that had no right to be there. I'd only known her four days, and despite the fact she was the most gorgeous woman I'd ever seen, there could be nothing between us. Even if I wanted it. Which I didn't.

I definitely didn't.

I kept picturing the way she'd stood up to me in the barn that first day, jutting her chin out, fire raging in her eyes. No one dared talk to me like that, which made it incredibly difficult to resist her. I wanted to needle her again just to see that scalding fury return to her beautiful stare. My wolf whined, remembering the altercation and how badly he'd ached to tackle her to the ground and force her to submit. She'd be a hell of a ride, one I shouldn't...*wouldn't*...entertain.

"No, it's something else." Lycan scratched at the back of his hair.

"I sense it, too," Poe said from the kitchen. "I know I'm the youngest and I've been a wolf the least amount of time, but she's not —*human*."

I cracked my neck and rolled my shoulders, sensing the tension forming in the atmosphere. "She's had a rough couple of days. Let her be."

"Ry," Lycan cut in. "I think she might be latent."

I rubbed my hands over my face and sighed, exhaustion mixing with exasperation. In this world, the shifter gene was dominant. Even if one of the parents didn't turn furry on the full moon, any offspring from such a union would result in shifter children, regardless.

We went through normal puberty as a human and a second wave as a young adult, usually in our early to mid-twenties, though it could happen earlier for more dominant wolves. We called it the transition. It activated the preternatural gene to force the first change. It was the most horrific experience someone like us could have, and another shifter needed to be there to help them through it, usually someone of the opposite dominance that was already mature.

One of the older Bastards' sisters had helped me when I was fifteen, feeding me her blood and providing the necessary primal requirements to see me through it. I barely remember the few nights in question, but she'd said I'd done well.

However, like all genetics, occasionally the DNA mutated. Sometimes, we produced a child that should have had the magic but never transitioned. A latent shifter.

"The Vanderbilts aren't like us," I said. "We'd know if they were."

"My wolf is picking up heavy pheromones," Lycan said. "He's never wrong."

I took another long inhale and tasted her delicious scent in the air, feminine and fertile and...My beast howled with agitation. He wanted to track her down, bend her over, and sink deep inside her. He wanted to lick up everything that seeped out of her, pheromones and come and—and the fucking thought irritated me. Everything about her irritated me. She was a Vanderbilt: infuriating and spoiled and fucking beautiful and—

"I'm gonna check in with Kodiak," I said, cutting off that line of thought as I headed toward the stairs. "Call me when dinner's ready."

"You're the boss," Lycan said to my retreating form, perhaps sensing my agitation through our pack bond and deciding to let me be.

But I couldn't get Lycan's suggestion out of my head, not even when I called Kodiak to update him on our status. Yes, she'd been snooping, but no, she hadn't found anything except for the picture of the pack before the Scorpion attack.

I thought about telling him Lycan suspected she might be latent, but decided to hold off until I knew more. My baser half yipped in excitement, howling its anticipation of getting closer to her, but I had to calm him down. I updated Kodiak on a few more details about the Fiver, and he assured me the run to meet the WA chapter had gone well before hanging up.

When I came back downstairs, I found only Lycan and Poe in the kitchen, still working on the chicken roast for the night.

"Where's Isolde?" I asked, glancing between them.

Lycan shrugged. "I thought she went upstairs. Is she not up there?"

"No." I glanced at the windows, noticing the sun had already gone down below the horizon. If she went back to the barn, she should have already made it into the house. Alarm blared through my torso, radiating from my heart down to my gut as my wolf growled in warning.

Something's not right.

I rushed outside and stomped through the snow to the barn, grimacing when I found the doors locked from the outside. Footsteps lined a path into the woods, and then my terror wrenched up to eleven. We weren't the only predators this far north, and the darker it got, the more likely she was to run into something she shouldn't.

I closed my eyes and let my animal senses take over, inhaling deep to find her tantalizing scent. It rushed toward me, lodging deep inside my nose, urging me forward.

"Isolde!" I shouted as I took off, racing through the storm, letting my wolf take the lead on finding her. He lunged against my mental restraints, barking in a frenzy, his sense of smell pointing like a beacon into the night. She was up ahead, and *fuck,* she was bleeding. Even though fresh flakes had started to cover her trail, her indescribable pull couldn't be mistaken, and my shifter side had become so attuned to her specifically, I could probably pick her out of a room full of a million people.

I ran faster, harder, shoving my legs through the snow despite the calls from my brothers behind me to slow down. I couldn't, I wouldn't. She needed my help. I didn't know how I knew, only that her fear sliced through me like a hunting knife, like a jagged blade had been lodged in my chest. I had to get to her. I *had* to.

I jumped over a fallen log, regaining my balance before racing down a slope.

"Stay away, you mangy beasts!" came a panicked scream over the wind, and I turned my head to the right at the sound of deep, rumbling growls.

There, my wolf yelled. *There. There. There!*

I nearly stumbled at the sight of four wolves circling her, baring their teeth, snapping and lunging at her in the middle. She'd been cornered against a tree, a lone sheep screeching behind her, wiggling and bucking against her legs. Clearly terrified and unsure what to do, she clapped and shouted, trying to make herself bigger and angrier to hopefully scare them off.

Thank fuck she hadn't run.

I jumped into the middle of the fray, letting my eyes go wolf and my claws grow from the ends of my fingertips, my canines extending in my mouth.

"Back off!" I roared, my voice deep and guttural, the beast in me commanding the animal in them. "Go home! Now!"

They obviously didn't understand my words, but they knew dominance. For decades, my pack had lived in harmony with the local wildlife. We respected them, they respected us. They saw Kodiak as another alpha, and they wouldn't dare disobey. But the hunger had taken over inside them; it echoed out of the leader's eyes. He licked his lips and pulled his ears back, lowering his head as if to suggest he might actually fight me for her.

"Go ahead," I said, puffing my chest out, making myself larger than him, even in human form. I couldn't fully shift until the full moon, but I still had sharp claws and big, pointy canines, not to mention sharper reflexes and increased strength. I sensed when Lycan and Poe had finally caught up, circling around the others as they made their own intimidating growls.

The alpha lunged at me, snapping its teeth millimeters from my face, but I shoved it away. One of its buddies jumped at Lycan, the other attacking Poe, while the fourth joined the bigger one in coming after me. I swiped at it with my claws, sending it whimpering into the tree line. The alpha snarled and lunged at me again, scratching a deep gash down my chest that had me wincing from the twinge of agony that shot through my midsection.

"Fuck!" I reared back and punched the fucker as hard as I could, making it whimper before I picked it up and slammed it down on the snow. It bit my forearm, sinking its vicious teeth into my skin, but I lurched out of the way, grabbing its neck with one set of claws, curling my other around its stomach. "Enough!"

The three others had run off, and now the alpha finally admitted defeat, dropping eye contact and relaxing under my touch, perhaps seeking forgiveness or absolution. I freely gave it, running my hand over his chest, down his furry stomach, and back up again, latching my claws around its neck. This showed that I *could* tear out its throat if I wanted, but I wouldn't. I just didn't want it eating my girl for dinner...err...*our* girl, our guest, the Vanderbilt girl.

I let the alpha wolf go and stood as it got to its feet and scampered off into the woods in the same direction its buddies had gone. Then, I turned to Isolde.

"What the fuck are you doing?" I stormed toward her, not caring that my monster was still in my eyes and the rancid tang of panic in her scent had brought out the most protective parts of me.

She took a deep breath and straightened, her tiny form shivering as she held tight to the sheep behind her. "I was trying to c-c-catch him. He got a-a-away."

"I don't give a shit about that," I said, close enough now to stare down my nose at her, my terror now replaced with fury that she'd be so reckless. "Why didn't you come get us before running off into the woods alone?"

Her jaw trembled as she glared up at me, her eyes filling with tears. "Stop yelling at me!" She squared her chin and balled her hands at her sides. "I just wanted to get the sheep and take him back to the barn. I don't know how he got out. I'm sorry...I swear I didn't..."

Lycan walked up behind her and grabbed the sheep, lifting it up over his shoulders as he nodded back toward the house. Poe quickly followed behind him, but I needed to deal with her. Isolde sucked in air like she couldn't get enough of it, her breaths coming in short, shallow pants. Her face turned pale and her knees gave out. She sagged onto the forest floor, plopping down onto the snow with wild, unfocused eyes.

"I was dead," she whispered, running her fingers back through her hair. "I was going to die. I was dying."

Fuck, she's having a panic attack.

Calm her down, my wolf told me. *Calm her down.*

"Hey," I said, my tone much gentler as I squatted in front of her, "it's okay. You're okay."

"I didn't mean to..." She gasped, struggling to get oxygen, her cold dainty fingers reaching out to twist in my jacket as if pleading for me to make it feel better. "I'm sorry, I didn't mean—"

"It's okay. Shh." I unzipped my jacket and scooted next to her so I could wrap her in my coat and pull her close. I tucked her under my chin and circled my arms around her, holding her as tight as I could. "Take a deep breath with me. Inhale..." I pulled air in through my nose, softening when she did it with me. "Exhale..." We let it go together.

There we sat, huddled together under a bare oak tree while she shook in my embrace. I cooed whatever I could think of to calm her down, things like, "You're okay," and "I'm sorry I yelled." Maybe I had let my own fear of something happening to her overcome what little reasoning I had, and in the aftermath of my rage and the fight with the wolf, I'd directed that energy toward her.

The scratches on my chest ached and the bite mark on my forearm twinged with each movement, but that was secondary to consoling her and making her feel safe.

"Come on," I said, pushing to my feet before bending down to scoop her into my arms, my elbow under her knees, my injured arm around her shoulders. Then, I trudged through the snow to carry her back to the Fiver.

"Fucking hell, you're covered in blood," Lycan said when I stomped into the cabin, ignoring the way Poe winced at the claw marks on his right forearm. This close to the full moon, we'd probably be healed by morning, but there was no way he'd be able to patch himself up like that, much less deal with the deep gashes on my chest that pulled with every step I took.

"I'm fine," I growled, hoisting Isolde higher before stalking through the house to the bathroom in the back.

"You don't look fine," Lycan barked, forgoing his work on Poe in favor of trailing behind me. "Let me at least—"

"I said I'm fine!" After the mile hike back and the way Isolde trembled, I didn't have the patience for him to ignore me like I wasn't the fucking second in this pack, the veep of the Royal Bastards. "Deal with Poe. Leave me to clean her up."

With that, I kicked the bathroom door shut behind me and sat her down on the toilet, kneeling on the floor in front of her. She shivered and curled in on herself, tears streaming down her cheeks as she wrapped her arms around her body. In the wake of her panic attack and adrenaline rush, her hormones had dropped and she'd gotten the shakes.

"Hey," I said, cupping her cheeks with my bloody hands. "You're okay. We're home now."

"I'm sorry, Orion," she muttered, clenching her eyes shut. "I didn't mean to get in danger. I didn't mean for you to get hurt. It was so st-st-stupid."

"I'm okay," I said, brushing her hair away from her face. The scrape on her head from her car wreck had burst open again, the right side of her face now covered in crimson, snow, and mud. "We need to get you in the shower. Do you think you can do that?"

She nodded and ripped her jacket down her arms, gingerly coaxing her shirt over her head. I leaned away to give her privacy, but she didn't seem to mind my presence. When she stood in her bra and jeans, her beautiful skin on brilliant display, she swept her gaze over me for the first time since she'd calmed down and gasped.

"Oh my God," she said, dropping to her knees, her torso nearly flush to mine. "You're hurt really bad."

"I'm okay, Princess," I said. "It's nothing."

"It's not nothing." She grabbed my jacket to push it off me, tugging my shirt out of my pants so she could lift it up my chest, revealing the deep claw marks across my pecs. "Orion, these need stitches."

"I heal fast," I told her. "They'll scab over by the morning."

Refusing to listen to me, she stood and rushed to the shower, turning the faucet on before checking the heat. "We need to get you cleaned up so Poe can—"

"Your head is gushing," I said, rising to my feet so I could get her attention. Sure, my wounds were bad, but I was the shifter here. She was a human. She'd probably scar either way, but if she kept letting it leak like that, she'd pass out from blood loss before she could do anything to help me. "Will you let me take care of you?"

She stared up at me with big emerald eyes, her pouty lips falling open as if she couldn't believe I'd offered such a thing. Which was fair. Less than four days ago, I'd accused her of killing my parents and chewed her out for having the fucking audacity to be born into a family she didn't choose. But I knew her better now. She was kind and smart and funny, and sure, she'd been spoiled most of her life, but maybe I wanted to be the one to spoil her from here on out.

Fuck! Stop that, Orion.

"Okay" came her breathy response.

"Okay," I said, "now sit down and let me get the blood off your face so I can bandage your wound. Are you hurt anywhere else?"

She shook her head. "No, just muscle pains."

"Okay." I grimaced as I reached up to open the cabinet, grabbing some gauze and more butterfly sutures. Then, I found a clean towel and ran it under the water so I could wipe away the excess blood.

"My body hasn't really stopped hurting since my accident," she said as I turned back to her, holding her chin with one hand so I could run the towel over her cheek with the other. She stared up at me while I worked. "I think I'm going to need a vacation when I get back."

I smirked at the idea. "Where would you want to go?"

"The Caribbean, maybe," she said with a silly grin. "Somewhere warm and sunny."

"Yeah, I bet you'll be tired of snow after this." Once her face was clean, I placed the bandages with tweezers, doing my best not to pull her skin harder than I needed to. But the wound needed to be closed or it wouldn't heal right for weeks. After I was done, I nodded to the shower. "Okay, get yourself clean."

"No," she said, pushing to her feet so she could gesture to the toilet. "Your turn."

I raised my eyebrows at the no-nonsense tone in her voice. No one talked to me like that, not even Kodiak. I didn't take kindly to orders, especially not from spoiled little brats like her, but the serious glint in her eyes told me she wasn't kidding. If I put up a fight, she'd likely stand here with her arms crossed, tapping her toe until I complied. Something inside me wilted, and I yanked my shirt off my body with a groan, tossing it on top of hers.

"There's a good boy," she said in a playful tone, but the praise plucked a chord inside me that had never been strummed before. Sure, women had muttered all kinds of shit to me during sex, and it definitely wasn't the first time one had called me good. But to hear it fall from her pretty mouth while she stepped between my knees so she could wipe blood off my chest, well…it sent a spark of fire right through my blood. My balls ached and my cock gave a half-hearted jerk, but I licked my lips and ignored all that.

Not the time. Not the place. Definitely not the girl.

"So," she said, raising an eyebrow while she ran a clean washcloth over the wounds on my chest. I hissed against the burn but kept my hands in my lap to let her do it. They *did* need to be cleaned. "Where do you want to go once this is all over? Once you're free of the Fiver?"

I sighed. "I like it here."

She furrowed her brows and met my eyes again. "Really?"

"I'm not a big fan of—" A moan tumbled out of my mouth when she hit a particularly sensitive area that made me stiffen. "—people."

"No, you don't say?" Her playful smile had me curling my mouth into one, too. "Here I thought you won all the ladies over with that surly attitude and grumpy disposition."

"You're the one to talk." I stared up at her, savoring the gorgeous hue of her sparkling forest-colored eyes—like sea moss or clover in full bloom.

"I'm a pleasure," she said, grabbing my forearm so she could wash the dirt away from the bite mark, too. "Ask anyone."

"Hmm," I groaned, swallowing down the first thousand replies I had to that. Gritting my teeth against the filthy images in my mind, I finally decided on, "Yeah, I bet."

The innuendo hung between us and she froze her ministrations on my arm as she took a deep breath, the tops of her breasts rising over her bra, her pouty lips falling open again. I wanted to slot my fingers right in between them and force her to suck her own blood off them. I wanted to—

"Thank you," she said, "for saving me."

"You're welcome, Princess," I murmured.

"Not just tonight, but after the car accident, too." She swallowed, her face so close to mine that I smelled the snow lingering on her cheeks, the shampoo in her hair, the crisp freshness of her sweat and scent and—*Fuck,* she was damn near irresistible. All it would take would be one tilt of my head, one surge upright, and I could connect our lips together. I could take her to the ground and rip those jeans off and bury myself inside her. I'd bet she'd be so soft and warm and—

Fuck yeah, my wolf howled. *Take. Take. Take.*

"I know you think you should have left me to freeze to death—"

"I didn't say that." The harshness of those words smacked me back to reality, one where she was a fucking Vanderbilt and I was a Bastard and we absolutely could *not* do any of those deliciously disgusting things haunting my subconscious. "I'm sorry I insinuated it. That was wrong. Of course I should have saved you. I'm happy I did."

Her beautiful smile lit up my entire chest, bubbling like champagne in my veins. Reaching up, I brushed her hair back behind her ear, checking that her head wound had stopped bleeding.

"I'm happy you did, too." She whispered it against my forehead, ghosting her tender mouth over my temple, barely making contact but enough to send sparks of the almost connection down my spine and through the backs of my legs.

Fuck it.

I sat up straighter and leaned closer, my heart pounding when she took a step in and bent down to meet me. Our lips collided with an explosion in my torso, an erupting warmth that burned my nerves and set my lungs ablaze. Her mouth was soft and decadent, and I lifted my good arm to grab the back of her neck and hold her tighter, twisting my fingers in her hair.

She moaned appreciatively and wrapped her arms around my neck, the heat of her bare skin melting against me. I darted my tongue out to lick across her lips, begging for entrance, and she opened to let me have it. And fuck, she tasted like woman and snow and blood, and I wanted more.

More, my wolf agreed. *More, more, more.*

My cock pulsed to life as a thick, heady lust bolted from the knot at the base through my stomach and up to my throat in a low, simmering growl. Just as I thought about yanking her to the ground and clawing her pants off, three quick pounds on the bathroom door had her jumping and taking a step away from me.

I set my predator's gaze on the entry like I could burn whoever was on the other side with my mind.

"What?" I growled, standing so I could turn the handle and tug the damn thing open.

"Are you two almost done in here?" Lycan asked, glancing between me and Isolde. "We all need a shower and Poe is about to pass out, yeah?"

I cleared my throat and nodded, suddenly thankful for the inter-ruption. "Yeah. Isolde's up first. Once she's out, you two can have it. I'll go last."

The weight of what we'd done settled around me. She was a Vanderbilt. I was a Bastard. Kodiak had warned me not to touch her, and there I was, pawing all over her like a fucking Neanderthal without a thought in his head.

I turned back to Isolde, who stood in front of the mirror exam-ining the gash on her face. "Don't use up all the hot water. The tank is small."

"Yeah, you got it, boss."

I pretended like the nickname coming from her didn't do anything to reheat the fire in my gut and closed the door behind me as I left her alone. If I'd had another two minutes, I would have enacted those terrible impulses, and then I'd have to explain to Kodiak why I couldn't follow one simple order.

Don't touch her again, Orion. Paws fucking off.

I didn't sleep easy after the attack with the wolves. Yeah, Orion had patched me up, and yeah, adrenaline sizzled through my veins like battery acid, but I couldn't get that amazing kiss out of my mind. Maybe I was concussed, but it had been the best kiss of my life. Fireworks had erupted under my skin, making me clench in all the right places, and when Lycan had interrupted, Orion scowled like he was going to murder his brother. And the way he looked at me? Like I hung the moon in the sky—like I was the most beautiful woman in the world? Surely, he'd seen more gorgeous girls than me, being a Royal Bastard and all. But it made me feel precious and lovable. No significant other had ever looked at me like that before.

I wanted more of it.

I'd had to take a tepid shower to cool off afterward, to remind myself we were sworn enemies, that I couldn't have him and he couldn't have me and letting myself get carried away was a mistake.

During the wolf attack, I could have sworn I saw his eyes turn sky blue instead of the depths of pitch I'd known them to be. I thought I remembered long claws extending from his fingertips, almost as large and threatening as the wolves themselves. But that didn't make any sense. It had been dark and I'd hit my head pretty hard when I fell down the hill, so hard it had burst open my wound and made my vision go starry. I had to have imagined it. I *had* to.

Sometime around dawn, I gave up on sleep and got out of bed, determined to make coffee and be the first one in the barn today. I pulled a fresh pair of Orion's oversize jeans over my legs and stuffed my tender torso into another one of his shirts, taking a long, deep inhale of his dark, woodsy scent. I didn't know why it calmed me or made me feel at home, but it did. How could a smell be so pacifying? On my way out, I stopped to check my head in the mirror, wincing at the violet bruises and bloody scab. My long ginger hair frizzled around my face like a halo and thick bags hung under my eyes as if I hadn't slept in months. I glanced down at my fingernails, which had gotten even more chipped after the days I'd spent with a shovel in my hands.

What I wouldn't give for a facial and a manicure right about now.

After braiding my hair into a plait down the side of my body, I checked my phone to see that I had a missed call from Percy and another from Liam.

"Isolde," said Percy in the voicemail. "There is no time for you to relax at the lake house. Marx is already asking for final arrangements. Get home. Now. Don't make me hunt you down."

I deleted it without listening to the rest and hovered my finger over the power button. Certainly, they could track me if it was on, and for one impulsive moment, I decided I didn't *want* to be tracked, not by him. Not by *them.* So I turned it off and placed it back on the nightstand, resolving to wait until the storm cleared before explaining what had really happened to me. Dismayed that I hadn't heard from Guin, I let myself ruminate on how to fix this before relegating that to Future Sol. Present Sol had work to do.

Shaking away the thought of confronting my stupid brother, I rubbed my tender shoulder muscles to try to work out the kinks, ignoring the chill in my bones and the sour twist in my stomach. The crash and the half a week of work had taken its toll on me, not to mention the wolves. I felt worse today than I had since I'd gotten here, but I blamed it on all of the above and wondered where the guys kept their ibuprofen.

When I opened the door, Orion stood on the other side, reaching into the hallway closet for something on the top shelf. He hadn't yet put on his shirt, wearing only a pair of unzipped jeans that hung low on his hips, and he glanced over his shoulder at my interruption.

I couldn't help my wandering gaze. It traveled from his angular features and dark beard to his broad shoulders and chiseled pecs. His ab muscles had been cut from marble, strong and defined, beautiful despite the wounds marring them diagonally. The dark trail of hair disappearing under the waistband of his boxers made me want to drag my tongue along that part of his skin to see what it tasted like.

At my perusal, he straightened and curled one side of his mouth into a smirk. "Good morning, Princess."

"Morning," I said with a smile. Heat flooded between my legs as the kiss between us in that tiny bathroom came roaring back to life, a thick tether of desire that tangled around my heart, nearly forcing me to beg for him. His mouth had been so soft and inviting. I wanted it on other parts of me. I wanted—*Jesus, girl! Get your head out of the gutter.*

"Did you sleep okay?"

I cleared my throat and lied. "Sure. How about you?"

He tilted his head to the side and ran his assessing gaze over my face like he could read every emotion in my expression.

"Hmm," he grunted before turning back into his room. "See you at breakfast." He shut the door behind him with a quick snick, and I clenched my eyes shut, frustrated by the pounding between my temples that beat in time with the one between my legs.

Oh, for Christ's sake, girl. You are an intelligent woman. You cannot lust after a grumpy Royal Bastard that doesn't even like you. It was just a kiss. A silly, stupid kiss that meant nothing. Get your wits together.

Yes, he was gorgeous in a dark mysterious sort of way, like a monster in a fairy tale that chose to protect the heroine rather than devour her whole. But that didn't mean I had license to fawn over him.

I rubbed at my aching head and went downstairs, successful in my attempt to beat the rest of them there. I made coffee and started breakfast, and after the others joined me, we ate together before going outside. It was another long day of feeding the animals and taking care of the pregnant sheep. Orion and I didn't get a moment alone, so I couldn't ask him about the kiss we'd shared or how he felt about doing it again...if he even wanted to do it again. Instead, we passed the morning in amicable company, the guys only teasing me a few times about taking off into the woods on my own.

"Next time, come get us, all right?" Lycan said with a toothy grin. "This is Montana, not some snooty rich person boarding school."

I rolled my eyes and grabbed another bundle of hay to move it from storage to the barn. "Yes, yes. I made a mistake. I'm sorry. Thank you for coming for me."

Poe shook his head and Orion ignored us altogether, but Lycan wrapped an arm over my shoulder. "I'm glad you made it out okay."

"And you saved a sheep while you were at it." Poe gestured to our flock. "Good job."

I accepted the compliment, recognizing he didn't hand them out easily. At least they didn't hate me and kick me out. At least, my screw-up hadn't cost me their approval. The conversation shifted to someone they knew in their motorcycle club. Poe and Lycan argued back and forth for a while as Orion and I worked.

"I'm not easy to fool," Lycan said, dropping a pile of hay near the door. "I know a fucking liar when I see one, and that dude has never told the truth once in his life."

Without missing a beat, I plopped another bundle next to his and rolled my eyes, blowing a wisp of hair out of my face. "Oh yeah? Is that why Poe keeps kicking your ass at poker every night?"

Lycan's features froze while he straightened and stared at me, but Poe cracked up laughing, slapping his hand on his knee while I resisted the urge to gloat.

"Listen here, your worshipfulness," Lycan said, narrowing his baby blues. "Poe kicks my ass because I let him."

"Oh, okay," I said, giggling as I grabbed the wheelbarrow so I could load it with feed. "I guess you've never played a real poker player, huh?" I hauled it over to Nemesis's stall, smiling when the horse came closer and whinnied at me.

"Are you saying you're a *real* poker player?" Lycan put his hands on his hips and raised his eyebrows.

"Careful with Nem—" Orion started to say.

But I rubbed my hand along Nemesis's nose and scratched at an itch behind her ear, making the horse chuff in contentment.

"I'll be damned," Poe whispered, glancing at Orion with wide eyes.

"What?" I asked, looking back and forth between the three of them. "What's wrong?"

"Nemesis doesn't like anyone except Ry," Lycan said. "What'd you do to get her on your side?"

"Oh." I shook my head and opened the stall so I could go inside and fill the feeder with hay. "She's just got a wild soul." I smirked and ran a hand down Nemesis's flank. "Don't ya? I can relate."

Lycan looked at Orion. "Looks like someone stole your girl."

Orion smiled and took a step toward us, watching as I refilled her feed bin before giving her another loving pet.

"I thought you didn't have experience with horses?" Orion raised his eyebrows and leaned against the side of the stall.

"I said I didn't have experience working a ranch, not that I didn't with horses." I shrugged and closed the door as I left the stall, walking over to the next one to do the same thing with Lycan's horse. "I had a few growing up, one that even looked like Nemesis. Her name was Heather, and she only liked me."

The thought of my childhood horse made my heart shatter, and I regretted that I only had so much time to spend with her before she passed. At that time in my life, she was my best friend, and in many ways, my only friend aside from my siblings. Growing up a Vanderbilt meant that most people only saw dollar signs, so I had built strong boundaries when I was younger. Animals were simpler in that way. They didn't care about things like last names or titles. They loved pure with their whole hearts.

"What happened to Heather?" Orion asked, taking another step toward me, almost like we were drawn together without realizing it.

"She passed a few years ago," I said. "But Nemesis reminds me of her."

"I'm sorry to hear that," Orion murmured, his eyes shimmering with genuine concern that radiated down to my toes and back up again.

"Thank you," I said.

"Hey," Lycan cut in, stealing my attention back to him and Poe at the front of the barn. "Speaking of good liars, do you know what tonight is?"

He raised his eyebrows suggestively, and even though I had no idea what he was talking about, I had a feeling I'd find out very soon.

CHAPTER 9

Orion

We ate dinner together before Lycan busted out a bottle of whiskey he'd been keeping for special occasions.

"It's Friday night," he said, lining up shot glasses before pouring the liquor to the brim of each and placing them down in front of us. "And since Princess can't drive anywhere, there are no limits on how much we can drink."

Isolde laughed, and I focused on the way her smile lit up the rest of her face, erasing the damage she'd done to herself over this week.

"Just one rule," Poe said, raising an eyebrow at me. "We don't play for money."

"Pfft." Lycan sat back in his seat before lifting the shot glass over the table. "This is the Fiver. Money's no good here."

"Then, what are we betting?" Isolde said, holding hers up as well.

We clinked them together while Lycan said, "Clothes," and I swallowed mine.

Isolde gasped and choked, her cheeks turning bright red as she coughed and tried to clear her throat.

"Think of something else," I growled, shaking my head as I turned my shot glass upside down in the middle of the table. Poe shuffled the cards and Lycan let out a howl at the shock on Isolde's face.

"No, it's fine," she said. "It just surprised me, that's all."

"Lycan wants everyone to be naked all the time." Poe shook his head and rolled his eyes at our would-be prankster.

"It's the natural state of being," Lycan said, winking at Isolde. "Clothes are so confining. Besides, it ups the ante."

Isolde shrugged and smiled wider. "Sure. I'm in."

"I knew I liked you." Lycan slammmed his hand on the table with a loud hoot. "Poe?"

"Fine, fine," Poe said. "I can never resist you."

"That's why we get along so well. Ry?" Lycan glanced at me with those cool blue eyes, and I stared at him, reaching out through the pack bonds. When I found nothing nefarious, just him being playful and unruly, I ran a hand over my face and remembered what Kodiak said about not touching her.

But perhaps the one shot of whiskey had already gone to my head because I just sighed and said, "What the hell."

"Fuck yeah!" Lycan flipped our shot glasses over and poured another round while Poe dealt the first hand. "To crossing enemy lines."

I took a deep breath and shot my liquor back, reminding myself not to get too tipsy. Isolde *was* a Vanderbilt, and I could not repeat that amazing kiss in the bathroom. *Could not. Would not.* Even if her family hadn't been able to get up here to pick her up these last few days, eventually she would go home. Anything she learned here could be used against us, and I'd be damned if I let that happen on my watch.

A few rounds later, I sat in my gray sweatpants and my black T-shirt, waiting for Poe to put in his final bet. I'd lost my socks and my hoodie, but the liquor coursing through my veins, combined with the naturally higher body temperature of being a werewolf, kept me warm.

"Read 'em and weep, suckers!" Isolde laughed while she flipped over two queens, completing a full house based on the cards in the middle of the table.

"Man!" Lycan threw down his hand and stood to take off his jeans.

Poe groaned and shook his head, fiddling with the waistband on his gym shorts so he could do the same.

I smirked and narrowed my gaze at her, raising an eyebrow when I flipped my cards over to reveal a four of a kind, beating her full house.

"Sorry, Princess," I said with a grin. "Guess I'm gonna need those pants off you, too."

"Ohh!" Lycan laughed and grabbed the half-empty whiskey bottle, pouring us another round. I bit my bottom lip and leaned back in the chair while she gaped at how the situation had unfolded.

"Fine," she said, standing so she could pull on the drawstring holding my sweatpants around her hips. My heart raced as she yanked it free and shoved them to the ground, leaving her standing in nothing but my oversize white T-shirt. Her nipples pebbled through the material, and her thick, tangy scent permeated the space between us, drawing my wolf to the surface. He panted and pawed at my self-control, begging me to tug her into my lap so I could bury my nose in her neck and *take*. "But just so you know, I only had one pair of panties when I got here, and I threw them in the wash after working in the barn today, so..."

She let that dangle there while she sat down and grabbed her shot, slinging it back like she had the same tolerance as the three of us. But I could tell by the flush in her cheeks and the heat radiating off her that the alcohol had taken its toll.

"You've been sitting here commando this whole time?" Lycan raised his eyebrows and threw his head back to let out a loud wolfish bellow, reminding me the full moon was only a few days away. "Isn't your ass cold?"

She threw a teasing comment at Lycan that made both him and Poe burst into laughter, but I took a deep breath to calm the raging beast inside. He didn't want the other two looking at her long, beautiful legs. He didn't want her scent filling the small kitchen with such a delectable display of femininity. He wanted to save all of it for himself, just him, and the thought of that was so fucking foreign and outrageous that I had to clear my throat to shake the notion from my head.

"One more round?" she asked, her voice light and hopeful.

"One more," Poe agreed. "I don't have much more to bet, anyway." Both he and Lycan sat in just their boxers, and if I wasn't so damned secure in myself, I'd worry over the way she stared at the two of them. But they'd promised not to touch her, and they knew I'd tear their throats out if they tried.

Unless she makes a move first. Unless she's interested in them.

I ignored those thoughts and the quick anger that followed while Poe dealt another round, and when I beat all three of them again, Poe and Lycan made identical groans of disappointment.

"You cheated!" Lycan shook his head and emptied the bottle into our shot glasses before tipping the glass over his mouth and swallowing down the last of it.

"I would never," I said, pretending to be outraged by the accusation. "How dare you."

"C'mon, Lycan," Poe said, grabbing the blond brother by the back of his neck and pulling him in so their foreheads touched. "You never had a problem losing before."

"That's when I was losing to *you*." Lycan bared his teeth at me before shoving to his feet and dropping his boxers to the ground. He stepped out of them, bent over to grab them, and threw them at me with an indignant guffaw.

I laughed and held my hand up to block them from hitting me in the face, but by the time I'd lowered them, he and Poe had taken off bare-assed through the house and out the front door, chuckling and shouting out into the night.

Isolde sipped her whiskey, watching the two of them with a grin before glancing back at me with those mysterious emerald eyes. I'd never seen such a decadent shimmering color on a person before, and something shifted in my gut when her stare turned sinful.

"Where'd you learn to play poker?" I asked, leaning forward on my elbows, enjoying the pleasant buzz from the whiskey.

"I'm the second youngest of seven," she explained. "If I didn't learn to bluff, they would have eaten me alive."

I grunted low in my chest, imagining a younger Isolde surrounded by her older siblings, dealing cards in that monstrosity of a mansion.

"Do you have any siblings?" she asked, taking another drink.

"No. I'm an only child." I shook my head. "But Kodiak and the MC, they're like brothers to me. P—" I cleared my throat and stopped myself before I said the word *pack*. I'd drank too much to toe that line, and even if Lycan suspected she might be one of us—a *latent* one of us—I wouldn't break our most sacred vow before I knew for certain.

"Kodiak?" She raised her eyebrows and leaned in. "That's the president, right?"

I nodded. "He's in charge. It's his ass on the line if something happens to you."

She snorted and shook her head. "Nothing is going to happen to me. Not as long as I don't take off into the woods again."

Giving her my best wolf stare, I leaned in and whispered, "How can you be so sure?"

"I've met evil men," she said, glancing down at the shot glass in her hands. "None of you are evil."

That's because she doesn't know the real us. She doesn't know the demons she's dancing with.

"Like you said, if you were going to do something to me, you would have already done it." She gave me a sheepish grin.

"Yet, here you sit, wearing nothing but a shirt."

Her scent plumed at my words, growing more pungent and intoxicating, roping me to her, making me want to lean in farther and inhale it in one long pull.

"Well, that's not exactly a bad thing, is it?" Her delicate pink tongue darted out and swiped over her lips, and I zeroed in on the movement, imagining what it might feel like traveling down my body. Her mouth was as soft as a cloud, as warm as heaven, and to caress it again...to have it on other parts of me...I'd bet she'd moan my name when she came. I'd bet I could—

The front door burst open, revealing Lycan and Poe, sweaty and red-skinned and naked, with their arms slung over each other's shoulders. In order to transform into our werewolf counterparts, we had to take our clothes off, so I'd seen it all before a thousand times. But Isolde carefully kept her gaze on her whiskey when they came into the kitchen and slid their boxers back on.

"Oh, c'mon, Princess!" Lycan put his hands on his hips and shook his head. "You're still in your shirt? You didn't even give him a peek at his winnings?"

Her cheeks flushed a deeper shade while she steadily avoided looking at me, but I heard the skip in her heart as her thighs clenched together. Ignoring the mental images that coasted through my brain at Lycan's words, I stood instead and grabbed the empty whiskey bottle to toss it in the trash.

"I gave her a pass," I said, "seeing as she doesn't have a clean set of panties."

Lycan shook his head, but the deep, husky sounds of a popular singer filled the night as Poe attached his phone to one of the speakers.

"Ly, come dance with me," Poe whined, throwing his arms up over his head while he swayed to the beat.

Lycan raised his brows, a hopeful expression in his eyes, as he held out a hand to Isolde. "You coming, Princess?"

She stuck her tongue in her cheek and glanced at me with a question in her eyes, seeming to ask if she should. I nodded, and she shot back the rest of her whiskey before grabbing his palm and allowing Lycan to pull her to her feet. Isolde's squeal of delight rang through me, and even though I should have put my foot down at the sight of those two hanging all over her, I liked seeing her smile. Poe pulled her in between him and Lycan, and mixed with the heat billowing off the fire, the whole scene vibrated with the warmth of pack...of home...of family.

Despite the lust between my fellow Bastards, they kept it relatively PG with her. I sensed that neither of them had anything untoward on their minds, just having a good time. Poe put his hands on her shoulders and pressed his forehead to hers, while Lycan held her hips from behind her, swaying back and forth to the music. When the beat picked up into something faster, they jumped up and down, shouting the lyrics at the top of their lungs. I leaned against the pillar separating the living room from the kitchen, sipping my whiskey and watching while they enjoyed themselves.

The familiarity between them should have startled me. It should have made me pause and question why the hell I felt so comfortable around her so quickly. It had only been a few days, barely a week, and this close to the moon, my wolf should have been on edge with a stranger so near our secrets.

But instead, it all seemed so domesticated...like she belonged with us and we belonged with her. Hell, her interaction with Nemesis was proof enough that she fit in. That horse didn't even like Lycan, and he got along with almost every animal he met.

Something stirred in the back of my mind, my wolf begging me to take notice, but after the long day and the whiskey fever, I couldn't figure out what it was. Isolde laughed and smiled, playing with Poe and Lycan while they hopped around. She was so damned gorgeous, from her ginger mane to the cute freckles across her nose to her womanly curves and her adorable little toes.

At the thought, I cleared my throat and straightened, telling myself it was time for bed. But Isolde turned and caught me, skipping over to close the distance between us.

"C'mon, Ry," she said, grabbing my hands. Her skin radiated such fucking warmth, tantalizing me, and at the connection, a thrum of electricity shot up my arms and into my gut, clenching my muscles tight. "Dance with me."

Lycan burst out laughing. "Ry doesn't dance."

"He's right," I said. "I don't."

"Make an exception?" She pouted, sticking out her lower lip and staring up with big green eyes. "For me?"

Fuck.

"Sure, Trust Fund. Only for you." I let her pull me into the center of the living room, moving my shoulders back and forth while she interlaced her fingers in mine, a huge grin on her face. If I forced myself to forget who and what I was, I could disappear into this night forever. I could wrap my arms around her waist and put her hands on my shoulders and inhale her strawberry scent for the rest of my life.

Eventually, the rock ballad ended and something slower echoed through the living room. Inhibitions lowered and, sucked into this intimate moment with her, I damn near moaned as she slid her palms up my arms to my shoulders. I rested my hands on her hips and stepped closer, staring down at her hypnotizing eyes. Up close like this, I saw flecks of gold and honey mixed into their forest green depths. Lycan and Poe danced together a few feet away, but wrapped up in her, we could have been alone.

"You're so beautiful," she said, reaching up to run the back of her fingers along my cheek down into my beard.

It was the first time in my life anyone had called me that. Rugged, sure. Scary and silent, definitely. But beautiful?

I shook my head and bit back a laugh, staring down at our bare feet and the inches of space between us. Heat flared up my neck and into my cheeks.

"What?" she murmured, touching my chin to tilt my face back to hers. "Why are you laughing at me?"

"I'm not laughing at you," I said. "No one's ever said that about me before."

"Well, everyone you've ever met is an idiot." She bit her bottom lip, curling the ends of her mouth into a smile. My canines tingled and extended, and I had to physically stop myself from leaning down to sample her tender flesh for myself again. Kissing her in the bathroom yesterday had been a huge mistake, but this was pushing the extent of my restraint.

My wolf nudged me forward, begging me to taste her again, to take her, to make her mine in every way that mattered to a shifter. But I shoved him back, reminding him we'd all had a lot to drink and this closeness with her would disappear come morning.

Giggles echoed from Lycan and Poe when the song ended, and they disentangled themselves from each other as Lycan pulled Poe toward the steps, leading the younger brother upstairs. Their arousal thrummed through the pack bond, echoing toward me, sinking inside my veins. I took a deep breath and forced it back toward them, determined not to let it affect me. If I did, I'd make a really bad decision.

Isolde broke away from me and giggled, watching them disappear into their room with a soft click of the door closing behind them.

"Woo, I'm dizzy." She rubbed at the space between her eyebrows and collapsed on the sofa, yanking the oversize T-shirt down to her knees.

"Do you want some water?" I headed to the kitchen to pour a glass anyway, no matter what she said. When I came back, she accepted it with a smile and took a sip, and I focused on her delicate throat muscles as she swallowed it down.

What I wouldn't give to sink my teeth into that skin and claim her, to let everyone know that I had. I suppressed a groan and turned to the fire, adding another log before stoking it with the cast iron poker.

"Why do your eyes do that?" she said, narrowing her gaze on me when I stood and came back to the couch.

"Do what?" I swallowed, trying to play it cool like I didn't know what she meant.

"Sometimes, you look at me, and your eyes—" She shook her head and took another sip of water, and I chided myself for being so reckless with my wolf. He'd been riding the surface extra hard since she'd showed up, not to mention the upcoming moon. "Never mind. I've had too much to drink."

"It's okay," I said. "You're safe here."

She smiled and sat her drink on the coffee table, crossing her legs as she turned to face me. "Thank you."

"Of course, Isolde," I said. "I'd never let anything hurt you." I meant it. I couldn't explain this strange attraction to her, other than to say she'd gotten under my skin faster than any person in my life before her.

"Do you really mean that?" She leaned her head to the side as she waited for my answer.

"Yes, I mean it." It was true, and the blatant reality of that smacked me in the face. If I hadn't had so much whiskey, I would have read more into it. If I hadn't been lulled in by the warmth of her skin and the familiar ache of our closeness, I would have realized what this was at the start. But I didn't, and I sat there like a schoolboy with a crush while she grinned at me.

"What did you want to be when you grew up?" she asked. "Did you always want to belong to a motorcycle club and work a ranch?"

I shrugged. "I was born into this life. I didn't have much of a choice." I told her about my parents, about how they'd been in the Royal Bastards before me, and how I always knew I'd end up here no matter what.

"Did you have a good relationship with them?"

She seemed genuinely curious, so in a rare display of vulnerability, I talked about them. I left out the parts about turning into a wolf and roaming the Montana countryside with my pack and anything to do with their deaths. "My parents were good to me. They loved me, and they loved our family."

Her features fell, and despite not bringing it up, I could tell she'd been thinking about when I'd accused her father of killing them.

"It was the Scorpions, wasn't it? He hired them to—to do it," she said, her voice soft and tender. "You don't have to talk about it if you don't want—"

"It was," I said with a somber nod. "We don't know for sure that Uther had anything to do with it, but the Scorpions we captured afterward said they'd been hired by him as revenge."

"The Scorpions aren't good people," she said, and the foul stench of regret and disappointment filled the space between us.

I almost told her they weren't people at all, but again, I bit that back. I wasn't sure what would happen once the weather cleared and her family came for her, but I knew that either way, she'd have to be mated to a Bastard before she could learn the truth about us. And since she was a Vanderbilt, that day would probably never come.

"I'm starting to think my father wasn't, either."

He wasn't.

"What about you?" I asked, trying to draw her away from that depressing topic. "What did you want to be when you grew up?"

"I always knew I'd end up working for Vanderbilt Holdings," she said, a spark of excitement replacing that fear in her expression. "I went to university to get my business degree, but if I had my way, I'd be a writer." She laughed, but I didn't like the thought of her being too entrapped in her family's politics to do what she loved.

"You can still do that," I said, reaching out to brush a stray piece of hair behind her ear. "You can be more than what your family wanted for you."

She turned into the movement, brushing her cheek along my palm, keeping her gaze locked on mine. The touch sizzled up my arm and down the center of my chest, ending in a jerk right to my cock, the knot at the base pulsing in time with my heart.

"I feel so...different with you," she murmured.

"What do you mean?" It was a stupid question because I understood exactly what she was saying. I was comfortable with her in a way I'd never been with anyone else, except for maybe Kodiak.

"You're supposed to be my enemy," she said, running her nose along the inside of my wrist, inhaling deep like she could smell the possession leaking out of me. "I'm supposed to hate you."

"Do you?" I teased, surprised at the grin that stretched my lips.

"No," she said, and the small word forced her mouth to brush across my skin. "Do you hate me?"

My stomach tightened and a zap of frenetic energy coasted down to my balls, urging me to lean her back against the couch and slot myself between her legs and *take take take*. But I shook it off, reducing it to primal instinct and nothing more.

"No," I said, keeping my voice low. The moans and sounds of the thumping headboard upstairs hid our conversation well, but I still didn't want the others to overhear. This moment was meant for us alone, and both me and my wolf yearned to keep it that way.

"If I said I wanted you to kiss me again, would you?" She chanced a tiny peck to my forearm, holding my stare while she did.

That sensation radiated everywhere all at once. I went still, debating my options. This wasn't some adrenaline come down in a confined space. This was lust, pure and simple. I had wanted her in the bathroom yesterday, and I wanted her again here on the couch.

"I would love to kiss you, Isolde," I said, "but we've both had a lot to drink."

She laughed and nuzzled her face deeper into my hand, reaching up to lace her fingers between mine to hold it in place. "So?"

"So...you'll regret it in the morning."

"I didn't regret it yesterday," she whispered, detaching herself so she could stand. "Besides, I still owe you your winnings."

What?

Before the word could leave my lips, she'd grabbed the edge of her shirt and yanked it over her head, revealing her beautiful naked skin, radiant in the firelight. The thick decadent scent of her arousal permeated the space between us as she moved in between the V of my legs, and I gripped the back of the couch to keep myself from touching her...ravaging her.

Instead, I stared. I traced the lines of her body from the shadows of her collarbones over her breasts and perfect pink nipples that I ached to suck. Her curved stomach gave way to a patch of hair between her thighs that begged to be spread and speared with my tongue. She had legs for days, and I wondered how soft and fleshy they would feel against my ears as she came over and over again in my mouth.

"Fuucckk," I groaned, and she smiled, resting her hands on my shoulders so she could steady herself when she put her knees on either side of my hips and sat in my lap. Goddamn, her natural aroma was intoxicating, roping both me and the wolf into a trance. My canines dropped, throbbing in time with my racing pulse. It took every ounce of restraint I had not to grab her hips and rock her over my painfully hard dick, to grind her down on the most sensitive parts of me. And when she bucked her pelvis, bringing that fiery cunt in contact with the ache in my pants, I sucked in a breath, hissing between my teeth.

"Is this okay?" she asked.

"Yes." The word came out hoarse and clipped, like I'd swallowed an entire beach's worth of sand and forgotten how to speak. She ran her hands up my neck to my cheeks, holding them in place while she rolled against me, dragging that delicious pussy along my ridge, leaving a wet spot that I'd likely never wash out.

"Do you feel me?" She leaned in to brush her lips along my forehead and over my eyebrows.

"Yes," I said again, this time lower and deeper in my chest. My hands trembled as I struggled to keep them in place, to not take control of the situation. I wanted to flip her over and force her to present her ass to me. I wanted to pin her down by the back of the neck and slot myself deep inside her, all the way to my knot, and pump until she smelled like me...*only* me. I wanted to wear her scent around like a perfume so all the other shifters would recognize that she owned every part of my soul and always would. But fuck, those were just drunk thoughts of a sex-deprived werewolf so close to the shift.

She continued her exploration down the side of my face, nipping at my beard and jaw before tucking her head into the space between my head and shoulder. I shuddered when she licked at my pulse point, my entire body tensing at the heat of her soft tongue dragging across my neck. I wondered what it would feel like on my stomach, on my dick, on the rest of my body.

"You're shaking," she murmured, leaning back so she could stare me in the eyes.

"You make me nervous," I said, which was true. Kodiak said not to touch her, and though I'd already kissed her, the alpha's orders ran deep in the magic in my bones. Even if I wanted to do it again, Kodiak would know, and he'd have my fucking ass for it. There was only one instance in which a wolf could disobey their alpha's command, and it was when one's mate was involved. That was an idea I didn't want to consider while I was under the spell of her and whiskey and this sensual night between us.

"I think I like making you nervous," she said, rubbing herself harder against me. My cock responded, springing into action as she trapped it between her cunt and my pelvis. Fuck, how I ached to pull the waistband down and bury myself deep inside her.

"Oh, yeah?" I canted my head to the side as she brought her tongue back to my throat, dragging it up my windpipe and over my chin, pausing at my mouth.

"Yeah," she said. "Big, strong man like you afraid of little old me."

"I didn't say I was afraid," I said with a laugh, which steadily turned into a moan when she rocked harder against me, and I clenched my eyes shut, my control teetering on the edge of something vast and destructive.

"If you're not afraid of me, then what's holding you back?" She brushed her nose against mine in a move that was entirely too adorable for the sexy vixen currently naked and straddling my lap.

"If I do this, Princess, there's no undoing it," I said, and she froze to blink up at me, her lips full and her cheeks flushed. "You're drunk and I'm the enemy, remember?"

"I've done worse things when I'm drunk," she said with a girlish giggle.

"Oh, I'm aware." Like crashing her Range Rover into a tree and going home with a fucking Bastard.

"Fuck me, Ry," she said, rocking harder against me, grinding her pussy into my lap, filling the air with that decadent aroma that made my mouth water. I wanted to devour her from head to toe and back again. I wanted to lap up everything she emitted, including her dripping cunt and the hormones emanating out of her neck and wrists. I had a passing thought that Lycan might have been right about her being latent, but it vanished when she murmured those words again. "Fuck me, Ry. Please. I want you to."

God, forgive me.

I crashed my lips against hers and let the feral side win.

The fact that he was reluctant to take this further because I was drunk only made me want him more. Despite that, he took my mouth like he owned it, and the sensation of his tongue wrestling with mine ricocheted down my center to the throb between my legs. Judging by how hard he was, he wanted this just as badly, if not more.

"Isolde," he said my name like a purr, and I loved to hear it fall from his beautiful lips. Everything about him was so gorgeously made, so ruggedly pretty and enticing. I'd never felt like this about anyone I'd known less than a week, and if I stopped to think about it, I might have gone flailing off his lap and running to my room to hide. But I didn't think, only acted, and everything in my body longed for everything in his.

"Orion," I teased, nipping at his pulse point, dragging my teeth down to his collarbone before sinking them in with a tiny nip.

He bucked against me, groaning as his cock swiped over my clit. The added friction from his sweatpants rattled through me, and I whined, wanting more, needing more. He cupped my jaw with his giant palms and tilted my face up so I had to stare him in the eyes.

"I am not an easy man," he growled, "in any way. When I fuck you, it'll be hard and rough and you'll wear my marks for days afterward. I'll demand a lot from you, more than you'll want to give."

Sweet Lord. I yearned for that more than anything, especially because he'd said *when* and not *if.*

"Shouldn't I be the judge of that?" I tried to lean in to kiss him, to end this dance of wills, but he held me firm.

"And what would your family think, hmm? You fucking a Bastard, moaning his name, and wearing his scent?" He raised his eyebrows, canting his hips at just the right angle to stroke my clit again, making me moan from the sensations ricocheting through my body. I shivered at the feral way he looked at me, digging his fingers into my jaw.

"They're not here," I said. "And I don't care."

His irises shifted blue, and suddenly, it didn't matter why they did, only that they flashed for me and me alone.

"I want you, Orion," I said, dragging my hands over his shoulders and up to his neck, brushing the back of his soft, dark hair. "You want me. What's the problem?"

God, what a loaded question. There were so many reasons to stop this, but none of them were as important as seeing it through. I danced on the edge of a proverbial cliff, staring down into the abyss, knowing I needed to jump to *fully* understand myself. But once I did, there'd be no going back. A fierce primal instinct had taken over, one that could no longer be denied. I didn't know if it had been there my entire life or if it was being around Orion that brought it out, but now that it was there, I had to obey it. I had no other choice.

"You shouldn't want me, Princess," he said. "You should want some rich fuck boy who drives a car worth more than my life."

Or a Bloody Scorpion that made a deal with my brother.

I ignored thoughts like that, shoving them deep down inside where they became a problem for another version of Isolde. I hadn't told them about my so-called arrangement, and I wasn't sure I ever would. I planned to fight it, I planned to find a way out, and once I did, it wouldn't matter anymore.

Perhaps sensing this hesitation, he sighed and let me move closer to him, enough that I could drag my tongue across his bottom lip before pressing my mouth against his for another searing kiss. He tasted like whiskey and man and the combination rattled my soul, making my blood thump harder through my veins.

"Fuck," he growled, but that broke the last bit of his hesitation, and he grabbed my ass, holding me against him while he stood and headed toward the stairs. It turned me on even more that he could carry me like this, and when he got to his room, he kicked the door shut behind him before carefully sitting me down on the bed. I scooted back toward the pillows, marveling at the desire dancing behind his eyes and the smirk on his full, delicious lips. "You're in trouble now."

"Oh?" I raised my eyebrows and tilted my chin up in clear defiance. "Do your worst."

He made a dark chuckling sound and leaned toward me, putting his arms on either side of my hips so I had nowhere else to go. I lay down when he crawled on top of me, trying not to shiver from both anticipation and the contrast of the cool night air with the heat radiating off him.

"My worst?" He tucked his nose along my hairline, dragging it along the side of my face to my neck, where he took a long, slow inhale and hummed. "You'll regret that."

"I won't." I tried to match his tone with a ferocious one of my own, but it paled in comparison. I moaned as he lapped his hot, wet tongue over my throat, once...twice...a third time, and I wrapped my hands around his neck to tunnel them through the back of his thick, silky hair.

"How about I save my worst for a day where we haven't been drinking for the last three hours?" He grabbed my wrist and brought it to his mouth where he breathed me in and licked from the edge of my palm to my elbow. "When I take out my inner beast on you, we'll both be sober and you'll beg me for it."

"Please," I said again, my muscles shaking under him. He went to the other wrist, holding it still while he gave it the same treatment, like he was trying to consume me, gobble me whole.

"Patience, little princess." The words rushed against my skin like a caress and I quivered harder, my thighs soaked with desire for him, my lower stomach clenching with each pass of his velvet tongue.

The nickname started out as a taunt from Lycan, but when Orion said it, I became actual royalty, like he was my king and I was his to do with as he pleased, biddable and submissive. I'd get on my knees and grovel if I had to, anything for him to give me special treatment.

He sat back on his haunches, staring down at me with bright blue eyes gone to the wildness of the night. When he smiled, I could have sworn his canine teeth were longer and more pointed, but I was too enthralled to question it.

"Touch yourself," he said, guiding one of my hands to the sensitive skin between my legs. "Go on. Show me how you like it."

I wasn't a virgin by any stretch of the imagination, but I'd never masturbated in front of a lover before. Most of my encounters had been proper and prudent, missionary only and occasionally from behind if the guy was into it. I could count the number of times I'd climaxed with a partner on one hand, but I suspected Orion would rectify that.

Insecurity twisted my stomach, but hadn't I begged him for this? Hadn't I stripped in front of him and summoned the courage of someone else, someone more in touch with their sexuality? I pushed my fingers between my legs and rubbed at my clit, throwing my head back when a moan barreled out of my throat. Sparks of euphoria rushed through my veins, settling my nerves, and Orion pushed my legs farther apart, resting his big callused palms on my knees so he could rub circles over my thighs with his thumbs.

"That's it," he murmured, "that's my good girl."

Chills rocketed down my spine at those two words, tearing through my last bit of hesitation. I loved when he said that. I loved pleasing him and putting on this show. It amped up my arousal, making me wetter, and I grabbed my nipple with my other hand, squeezing until it pinched. But I liked that, too.

"I can smell you," he said, running his hands up my legs, just to the juncture of my pelvis before back down again. "Mouthwatering like woman and need and desire. It's intoxicating."

I let out a demented laugh and rubbed myself harder, dipping lower so I could enter myself and hit that special spot inside that sent me reeling.

"Fuck, you're so wet," he said, moving so he lay next to me, his nose tucked against my neck. "Can you hear it?"

"I can," I said, pumping myself harder, circling myself faster. Being here with him, so exposed and vulnerable, it should have disgusted me. He was the enemy and if my family ever found out, they'd disown me or worse. I was supposed to be engaged to the president of the Scorpions, but with Orion's body heat so close and the feel of his tongue rubbing against the most sensitive parts of my neck, I couldn't be bothered with that. He pressed closer to me, and his cock jerked against the outside of my thigh as he thrust his hips in time with my fingers, almost like he could fuck me through my hand.

The whole experience was so erotic and intimate that I didn't think I'd last much longer, so I turned my face toward him, desperate to kiss him, willing him to connect with me somehow. He leaned his head away, staring into me with those sky eyes, the pupils now so dilated that they were almost entirely black.

"Are you close, Princess?" he growled, rutting into the mattress harder while he ghosted his fingertips over my face and down to my lips.

I nodded and opened them, sucking one finger inside when it got close enough. He groaned and thrust harder, and I furiously swiped over my clit, so gone to the haze of lust and whiskey that I couldn't tell right from wrong. My senses had been left somewhere downstairs, and now the only thing I knew was him and the only thing I wanted was more.

He pushed his finger inside my mouth faster, pressing down on my tongue like he was imagining putting other parts of his anatomy between my lips. At the visual of me on my knees for him, sucking him to oblivion, I lost control. My climax took me with a passion, so hard and quick that I couldn't fuck myself fast enough. I arched off the bed, moaning and crying. And he held me through it, running his hands over my chest and down my stomach, murmuring words that I couldn't comprehend—things like, "Fucking beautiful" and "Mine, only mine," and "Just wait. You're such a good girl."

He whimpered and pushed one last time into the mattress, tucking his face against my windpipe and lapping at my skin with his tongue. In the aftermath, he looked up at me with his hair all ruffled and his eyes glazed over with the aftereffects of our connection. So adorable, nothing like the grumpy man who'd yelled at me in the barn a few days ago.

I smiled and ran my hand down the side of his face, belatedly realizing it was the same one I'd had stuffed inside my pussy. But he turned his head toward the touch and sucked my fingers into his mouth, rubbing his tongue over them like he was trying to get my taste off them.

"You're so beautiful," I said, shaking my head as I wondered how I'd gotten lucky enough to be found by him. It could have been anyone out on those roads. It could have been another Bastard or a Scorpion or hell, no one at all. But Orion had been a gift to me, and I appreciated whatever fates had put me in his path.

"You're really drunk," he said.

"No," I replied, though I was. "I mean it."

The release of hormones had mixed with the liquor in my nervous system, finally catching up to the hard work we'd done out in the barn. My eyelids weighed a ton and his mattress was so warm and comfortable. It smelled like him—pine and cologne and soap and *him*. So decadently him.

I was asleep before I could stop myself.

The next morning, I blinked against the bright sunshine streaming in through a break in the curtains. Voices echoed from downstairs, and I winced as a sharp pang radiated through my head.

"Ugh." I groaned and rolled onto my back, taking a second to remember where I was and what I'd done. Alone in his bed, Orion's thick, heady scent permeated the atmosphere, all the more entrancing for what we'd done last night. Despite having a raging headache and a hangover, I grinned to myself at the memories.

Sure, it had been relatively PG-13 considering how willing I was to take things further, but the sight of him between my legs and the grin on his lips when I came sent a flush into my cheeks.

I stretched and shifted to his side of the bed, taking a long, slow inhale of him, letting it settle my nerves.

He'd let me sleep here. He'd let me stay the whole night.

But then the consequences of what we'd done set in. What would my family think? What would they do when they found out? Percy didn't own me, much to his chagrin, and he couldn't make me marry Marx if I didn't want to. But if I didn't figure out a plan soon... if I didn't contact Guin and work out a different way...the family might suffer. Without ranchers to finish the winter work, the business would take a hit, which would have downstream impacts that I didn't fully understand.

Don't I deserve to be happy? Don't I deserve freedom?

What would Orion do when he found out? *If* he found out? We were enemies. After the snow melted, I would go back to being Isolde Vanderbilt, and he'd go back to being the vice president of the Royal Bastards Motorcycle Club. Nothing had changed...right?

That nascent, primal part of me that I'd discovered last night blinked awake, coating my insides with boiling frustration. I'd only been here six days, but I'd trade the rest of my family fortune if it meant I got to stay forever. Every day, I grew more comfortable with

Orion, Lycan, and Poe than I'd ever felt with my toxic family. I'd gladly shovel shit until I croaked, if it meant I'd never have to go back home.

Does that make me selfish? Is it okay to put myself before my family?

Deciding that was too much for one hungover morning, I pushed myself out of bed and found one of Orion's oversize shirts. After pulling it over my head and slipping my arms into it, I paused to take in his deep woodsy scent, delighting in the delicious warmth that it brought to my heart. I loved it, perhaps too much. I put on a pair of his sweatpants and opened the door, combing my hair into place with my fingers as I made my way downstairs.

"There she is," Lycan said, giving me a big smile from the kitchen table. "How'd you sleep?"

"Great," I said with a yawn, my chest tightening when I didn't see Orion.

Poe stood at the stove, shoveling eggs and bacon around in a pan while he winked. "There's coffee in the carafe."

"Thank you." I walked to the bathroom to freshen up and do my business, and when I came back out, my favorite Bastard still wasn't there. "I apologize for not getting up early enough to help with breakfast. I'll clean up."

"No worries," Poe said, eyeing me with a knowing glint to his brown eyes.

"Besides," Lycan cut in, "sounds like you had a...*hard* night."

Poe snickered, and heat flooded up my neck and into my cheeks.

"Oh, yeah? And how was yours?" I teased, trying to choke back my indignation as I poured myself a cup of juice. "I didn't know the Bastards were so close."

"There's only room for one Poe in my bed and my heart," Lycan said with a dreamy inflection.

"That's bullshit," Poe said, tilting his head to the side. "Lycan would fuck anything with a heartbeat and a warm hole."

The front door opened and boots stomped on the ground. A sharp pang went through my head, echoing down into my heart and lungs, and I blamed it on the whiskey. Panic flooded my bloodstream, squeezing my chest with realization.

What if he rejects me? What if he regrets it? What if he found out my secret?

His footsteps echoed through the house, and I held my breath when he leaned up against the pillar in the kitchen, raking his gaze over the two brothers before landing on me. He shucked off his gloves and nodded.

"Good morning, Princess," he purred. "Glad to see you're in one piece."

"Yeah, most women can't walk after a night in Orion's bed," Lycan teased, ducking quickly out of the way when Orion threw his gloves at his head.

"Are you feeling okay?" Ry nodded to the stove. "Did you get some breakfast to soak up the liquor?"

"I was just headed there," I said, grabbing a plate so I could hold it out to Poe. He scooped eggs and a piece of bacon on it before handing me two slices of toast.

"Make sure you eat," Orion said, straightening. "We don't work as hard on Saturdays, but you still need your strength."

"I will," I said, sitting in the same spot I'd taken the last few days and ignoring the way I lived to please him. I liked when he gave me orders, like it freed me up from the responsibility of having to take care of myself, and there were too many implications of that for me to digest before I'd had my caffeine.

"Have you heard from your family?" Orion asked.

I bit into a piece of bacon, but it tasted sour when accompanied by his question.

"Trying to get rid of me so soon?" I forced myself to swallow down my bitterness, glancing up to where he hovered by the stove. Poe grabbed his own plate and headed toward the front door, followed shortly by Lycan. They must have sensed this would be an awkward conversation, but there truly was no reason for that. I'd figured out where this was heading this morning, and it couldn't be anywhere good.

I was a big girl. I could handle it if Orion had decided what happened last night was a mistake. We'd had a lot to drink. It didn't need to happen again.

"I don't want them to send the cops up here looking for you," he said, finally meeting my gaze with a soft one of his own.

"They won't." I returned my attention to my plate. "Don't worry."

He cleared his throat and moved to the spot Poe normally sat in, pulling out the chair before lowering his body into it.

"Look, about last night," he started, but I figured I'd cut him off to save my pride.

"Don't worry about that, either," I said, taking another bite of the rancid bacon, my stomach twisting, my head throbbing, every joint in agony. "It was only because we were drunk." I tried the eggs, but they too tasted like dirt. The only thing that looked remotely appetizing was the toast, so I picked that up and took a nibble before continuing. "Besides, it's not like we did anything serious, right? We were just having fun."

"Right. Fun." He nodded and swallowed deeply, straightening as he dropped his attention to the ground between us. "It's not because I don't think you're gorgeous or...that I didn't enjoy myself, but—"

"We're enemies," I said, letting the weight of my shame settle in my gut. I'd never be good enough for someone like Orion, no matter what I did or how hard I worked. To him, I'd always be a Vanderbilt. Just like I'd always been the *fourth* daughter to my father and the easiest to sell to my brother. Nothing I did ever mattered. "In the real world. Once the snow melts."

"You'll go back to being you," he explained, "and I'll go back to being me."

"Right." I pursed my lips and gave him a firm nod, blinking back the burning in my eyes and gulping down the fire in my throat.

I'm not good enough for him. I'll never be good enough for anyone. This is for the best.

"Right," he said again, returning his gaze to me. "Call your folks. The weather should be nice enough today for them to land the chopper out by the lake. I'll walk you down there myself."

"And if they can't?" I raised an eyebrow. "It's not like my family is just sitting around, waiting to rescue me."

"You're welcome here as long as you need," he said, pushing to his feet. "But come Wednesday, the guys and I have to take a field trip down to another cabin. No one will be here to keep you company."

I narrowed my eyes. "Can I go with you?"

"No," he said, leaving no room for argument. "It's probably best if you're gone by then."

As if that was final, he stood and headed toward the front door, where Lycan and Poe were likely ignoring their breakfasts on the porch in favor of eavesdropping.

"Eat your eggs," he said, putting his hat back on his head. "We'll head down to the barn to get things ready. Meet us down there whenever you're up for it."

Telling myself it would be childish to cry, I forced the rest of the toast down my aching throat, wondering what the hell Poe had done to it this morning. Was he so hungover that he'd forgotten how to cook? All of it tasted like garbage, even the coffee.

Deciding I wasn't that hungry, I dumped it in the trash, cleaned the dishes Poe had used to make the breakfast, and headed back upstairs to my room, where I shucked Orion's clothes to the ground so I could wear whatever I found in the lost and found. Every time I breathed him in, it reminded me of the way his tongue licked across my neck and that it would never happen again. I couldn't be around it. I needed something neutral.

Clad in oversize apparel that smelled like mothballs, I went to my phone to turn it on and try my eldest sister again. I had a bunch of missed calls from Percy and a few from Liam and Maeve. But the only person I wanted to talk to was the one that could save me from my brother.

She still didn't answer, and when I left another voicemail, I realized it was time to stop fussing around. I'd have to leave soon, and if I went home with no plan, Percy would use that against me. I needed to be prepared to come out swinging, with or without Guin's help. Ignoring it for the last few days had not done me any favors, so now I would start plotting the way my father would have.

While I ruminated, I needed to do something to blow off steam, to get rid of the churning in my gut. Despite the headache and the body chills, the house had been wrecked by our drinking last night. There was a decade's worth of grime in the cupboards, and my skin crawled when I remembered the state of the bathroom.

I couldn't go out and face Orion, not after this morning. He didn't want me, and the sting of not being good enough for him...of never being able to be good enough for him...ached deep in my bones.

No, I wanted to stay inside and give the Fiver a good scrubbing, and as I stood to walk downstairs to let the guys know, I realized I should have been more freaked out by that compulsion. Since when had a Vanderbilt wanted to clean anything?

What the hell is happening to me?

"That was brutal," Lycan said when I emerged on the porch and pulled the front door closed behind me.

"It needed to happen," I said, ignoring the howl of my wolf inside my head. He'd been riding my ass hard since last night, since I kept my hands *mostly* to myself and nutted in my pants like a fucking teenager. He wanted to take her, to claim her, to mark her in a million different ways so no other male, shifter or not, could have her without knowing I'd already staked my claim.

Not only was she a Vanderbilt, but I also hadn't forgotten the fact she might be keeping something from us, perhaps running from something. Why had she been out drunk in a snowstorm in the first place? There was a reason I preferred the Fiver over everyone else. Most people weren't trustworthy, and even if they were, what was the point of letting them get close? Death could snatch someone away in a blink of an eye, and I had no desire to turn into a rabid monster that had survived the loss of its mate.

Not that Isolde was my mate...not at all. Just the thought, in general, made me keep everyone at arm's length.

"You should have shut her down last night," Poe said, taking a long sip of coffee. He rocked back and forth on the swing, eyeing me with an incredulous gaze that said he saw far more than he let on. "Didn't Kodiak say not to touch her?"

"I didn't," I said, adding a mumbled, "Not much anyway."

"Not much?" Lycan blew out a disbelieving breath and glanced at Poe. "What the fuck does that mean?"

"Did you disobey alpha's orders?" Poe raised both eyebrows.

"No," I growled, cracking my neck as rage swirled up my gut into my chest, twisting around my heart. My beast raked his claws down the inside of my brain, whining and pacing, yearning to chase her down and apologize for it all.

"So you didn't touch her?" Lycan's narrowed gaze put me even more on edge.

"No," I said through gritted teeth. "And it's none of your fucking business, anyway."

"Hey," Lycan said, holding up his hands and focusing on the ground so he avoided direct eye contact with me. This close to the full moon and the way my wolf rode inches from the surface, he knew better than to push his luck. "I'm not judging you. If she's your mate, she's—"

"She's not my mate," I snarled, but even as I said it, the words tasted like ash. Shivers raced down my spine, and I clenched my hands into fists to keep from pounding them into the blond brother's face. I needed to release some of the tension that had built up over the last two days...hell, since she'd gotten here. Her damned scent wouldn't leave my nose, and watching her sleep last night had soothed both of my sides in ways I didn't want to examine closer.

That had been the whiskey, and I swore off the stuff for the rest of the time she was here. I couldn't trust that I wouldn't take it further next time, that I wouldn't force myself to keep my hands off. Despite the draw to her, despite how much I ached to sink my teeth into that soft skin by her pulse point, she had to leave. The sooner, the better.

"Okay, brother," Poe said, taking a hesitant step closer to put a hand on my shoulder. The contact calmed me, reminding me we were pack. Brothers. Family. "Okay."

"Let's just get to work, all right?" It didn't fucking help that I was hungover, and the ache had nearly split my head in two. I wanted to crawl back into bed with her, yank her close, and breathe her in deep. And the fact I couldn't, *I wouldn't*, let myself devour her made me want it more.

The three of us walked down to the barn to start the process of feeding the animals and checking in on the barn dogs. Nothing had happened overnight with no one on guard, thank God, but that didn't soothe my agitation. When Isolde eventually appeared, twisting her fingers into knots in front of her and forcing a fake smile, I ignored the pit in my gut telling me to hold her, to tuck her in close and kiss that unsure wrinkle between her brows.

"My family won't be able to come get me for several more days," she said, shooting a nasty glare in my direction. "I'm sorry if that's disappointing."

Lycan raised his eyebrows from where he shoveled hay into his horse's pen and turned to glance at me.

"Did they give you a date?" I asked, clearing my throat when my voice cracked.

"No," she said with a slight clip to her tone. "But don't worry. I'll keep pulling my weight."

"That's not the problem." I ran a hand over my forehead, wiping away the sweat before it dripped into my eyes.

"I'll keep my paws out of the whiskey stash." That too stung more than I'd expected. She'd been the one to tell me not to worry about it, that last night was just *fun*. Was she full of shit?

I smelled the salt on her cheeks from the tears she must have shed before she came out here, and it made me feel like a downright prick that I'd probably been the cause of them. More than that, the beast paced inside my mind like a trapped monster, beating against my heart until I did something to cheer her up.

"Right, well." Isolde took a deep breath and let it out slowly, glancing between the three of us. "The house is a mess. If y'all don't need me out here, I'll just—" She pointed to the Fiver and turned to head in that direction.

Poe faced me and pursed his lips, putting his hands on his hips in a silent display of accusation. Lycan glared, staring holes through my head until it became too unbearable and I cracked.

"What?" I growled, staring back at him.

"If she's gonna be stuck here during the full moon, you're gonna have to fix this with her," Lycan said, shaking his head while he picked up more hay.

"There's nothing to fix," I said. "Even if we could, that doesn't mean we should."

"You want her going back to being the snippy Vanderbilt you found on the side of the road?" Poe let out a harsh whistle at my indignant stare. "You're something else, brother."

Lycan scratched his nose and took a step closer. "I'm telling you. I smell something on her."

I cracked my neck as my own wolf piped up in agreement, letting out a howl that demanded I pay attention.

"It's getting stronger the closer to the moon we get." He put his forearms on the stall, expecting a response, but I ignored him and continued brushing down Nemesis. "You know, I remember someone that thought they were human their whole lives."

"Stop," I said, sensing where he was going with this.

"And then, one day, she met a Bastard alpha. He'd been born into it." Lycan raised an eyebrow. "The more time she spent around the Bastards, the more she started to change. She grew feral during full moons. She started nesting in places she shouldn't have been nesting."

Lycan was talking about the previous alpha's mate. She'd been born and raised human her whole life until she met Kerrick. After spending a few months with the pack, she realized she was latent and went through her transition, leaving her former life behind in favor of running with the wolves.

Latent shifters could be like that. If she hadn't met our alpha, she would have gone on living her normal human life like nothing was ever different about her. But she *did* meet him, and she *did* mate with him, and then a few days before the first moon after they acknowledged their bond, she went through her transition. If Kerrick hadn't been by her side through it, she would have died. But latency did happen, and that wasn't even the first time I'd heard a story like that.

Finding one's mate could change everything about the way a werewolf lived. All of their priorities altered to focus on the survival of their counterpart first, even before the alpha, even before the rest of the pack. It was a law of nature, guaranteeing the survival of the species.

"I'm not saying that's what's happening here," Lycan said, finally close enough to force me to meet his gaze. "But brother, if she's your mate, it's okay. The pack will protect you. The pack will protect *her*."

"Lycan," I said when he'd finally shut his fucking mouth. "Get back to work."

He snorted out a sad laugh and patted me on the shoulder. "Sure thing, boss."

We had no reason to think any of the Vanderbilts could be shifters, least of all Isolde. They'd never presented as anything other than human, and in all our time hating one another, we would have picked up on it by now.

As the day dragged on, I got more antsy at the thought of her going to sleep all alone in her room while I dreamed of her taste in mine. By the time we finished our chores and went in for lunch, Isolde had cleaned and straightened the entire living room. She'd dug old trinkets out of forgotten hiding places, either proudly displaying them on the various countertops or piling them into the garbage can by the door. Now in the kitchen, she'd already prepared lunch for us, which sat on the table while she stood on a stool and leaned in to wipe a rag through the top shelf of a cupboard. All of the plates, bowls, and cups that used to reside in that cabinet now soaked in the sink.

"When was the last time anyone did a deep clean of this place?" she asked, popping her head up when we got close enough. "I'm pulling out things that would make even Lycan vomit." She'd wrapped her hair into a messy bun on top of her head, revealing her long, elegant neck and the curves of her delicate clavicle.

"What are you doing, Princess?" Lycan asked, looking around at the mess she'd made.

"I told you," she said, hopping off the stool and wiping the wisps of hair out of her face. "This place is disgusting."

Poe snorted out a laugh. "Have you ever cleaned anything in your life?"

"Well...no." She pursed her lips and pulled her brows into a furrow. "This is weird, isn't it?"

"I'm not complaining," Lycan said with a playful grin as he gave me a side-eye. An itchy knowing started to prickle up my spine and over my scalp, like spiders that had burrowed under my skin.

"I feel like I'm losing my mind," Isolde said, running her hands back through her hair. "But I can't stay here a minute longer with this place so filthy. It's like...I can't *not* clean it."

Lycan raised his eyebrows as if to suggest he'd been right, and Poe pinched the bridge of his nose before letting out a deep sigh.

"Why don't you come sit down and eat with us?" I asked, taking a hesitant step forward. But I already knew the answer before I'd asked it.

"I'm not hungry," she said, rubbing at her temples in a shy little move that she probably hoped I didn't see. But I did. Which meant her head was still hurting her and had been since the wreck, despite the whiskey and wolf attack.

"Did you eat breakfast?" I continued, biting into the sandwich.

"Just let me get this done, Orion. Then you can pester me." It came out more like a growl. She waved me off and walked into the living room with a bag full of garbage, heading to the front door.

Lycan stared at me until I met his gaze and shook my head. "Don't start."

The transition rarely took a shifter by surprise. There were usually signs in the days leading up to it, and if Lycan was right (which he probably wasn't), this would be one of them. The body aches came first, then the night sweats and a lack of appetite. For more dominant shifters, aggression and irritability presented after that. I'd wanted to put my fist into everyone and everything that crossed my path before mine. For more submissive and domicile shifters, they wanted to nest and clean, something about creating a more comfortable environment for the magic to take hold.

"What if she is?" Poe murmured. "You should tell Kodiak."

"Don't say a fucking word," I said, running a hand over my forehead and into my hair. "I'll talk to him."

"You fucking better," Lycan said. "We're only four days out from the moon. If she transitions with the three of us in the house, you know what will happen."

A snarl rumbled in my chest before I could stop it, and I cleared my throat to shake away his insinuation. For shifters that could get pregnant, their transition was like their first heat—their first fertile period. They expelled hormones that made every shifter with a knot in the immediate area want to fuck their brains out. I'd seen wolves tear each other apart to get to a submissive in such a vulnerable state. I'd seen three or four wolves share a shifter in heat until they were wrung out and exhausted.

I won't share, my primal self roared. *It'll be me or I'll kill them.*

Lycan evidently picked up on that through the pack bonds because he narrowed his eyes and pulled his lips back over his teeth. "If she goes into transition and you don't help her, I will."

"Hey!" Poe cut in, clapping to get our attention off each other and back on him. "We don't know any of that is going to happen. Knock it off."

Suddenly, I didn't want any more of the sandwich she'd made. The room had grown stifling with dominant wolf scent and territorial bullshit, not to mention the lingering smell of *her*—strawberries and woman and something else that had always been there but had grown stronger in the last day or two. Definitely since last night.

I stood and grabbed my jacket to stalk toward the living room. The door opened just as I got there, and Isolde looked up at me with those big, green eyes.

"Hey, what's wrong?" She stuck out her lip in a pout, her cheeks adorably flushed with the cold and her natural glow. Her scent hit me harder, right between the eyes, and a burst of fire-blooded lust shot down to my groin.

Take her. Fuck her. Mark her. Now. Now. Now. Do it before the others can. Do it before the moon.

I groaned and reared back, wincing as I sidestepped her and rushed out into the cool winter air.

Fuck. No. No. No.

CHAPTER 12

Orion

Isolde was already in bed by the time I crawled my sorry ass back to the house, and neither Lycan nor Poe would meet my eyes. That was fine by me because I didn't have much to say to them, either. I reheated some dinner and headed to my room, pausing for only a moment outside her door to consider apologizing for running out earlier.

The next day passed in companionable routine. Isolde busied herself around the house, and when she finished there, she came out to the barn to help with the animals. The closer we got to the full moon, the stronger her scent permeated through everything else. I smelled it when I woke up in the morning. I smelled it when I showered. I smelled it when she wasn't anywhere near me.

Lycan had picked up on that fact and wouldn't let the fucking thing drop.

"You need to do something about this," he said three days before the moon while we were tagging the pregnant sheep. "Her family's not coming before the shift."

"I know that," I said, sliding my red marker over an ear before releasing the critter back to the herd.

"Did you talk to Kodiak?"

133

I grunted but ignored his question because I *had*; I just didn't mention the fact that Lycan suspected she might be latent.

"He knows she's gonna be here for the moon," I explained. "We'll be out in the woods. Nothing's gonna hurt her."

"That's not what I meant," Lycan said, glancing at Poe before standing up to grab another ewe. He dragged it over to me and read off her measurements so I could write it down.

"She's not latent," I said. "If she was, we would have known by now. *She* would know by now." We were so close to the moon, she would have already gone into transition.

"And yet, there she is, rearranging the fucking house."

"It's been lived in by Bastards for decades." The stab of anxiety that went down my chest and into my gut had nothing to do with how right he might be. Nope. Not at all. "It needed a good cleaning."

"She's a Vanderbilt princess," Poe added. "She's never cleaned a day in her life."

"I'm sure she never shoveled hay, either." I rubbed at the back of my head. "Look, I don't know what you two want from me. If she's latent, we'll know soon enough. If she's not, then we'll be glad we kept our distance."

"And what if she's your—"

"Don't fucking say it again," I snapped. "I already told you she wasn't."

Lycan narrowed his eyes and leaned in closer to me, taking a deep inhale before letting out a deep belly laugh and turning to grab another sheep. "Whatever, your holiness, the great pharaoh of the Fiver."

I raised an arm to sniff under my pits, but I didn't smell anything weird. Yeah, maybe I was a little sweaty from the day, but that was it. When I glanced at Poe, he shrugged and went back to work. "What the fuck does that mean?"

"King of Denial," Lycan said with a deep guffaw.

I didn't understand what happened with Lycan until later that evening. Isolde had made chicken and vegetables for dinner, and although she wore a pair of baggy jeans and a huge shirt, I couldn't stop staring at her neck. She'd pulled her hair up on top of her head and joked with my brothers, but my canines throbbed and my wolf paced inside my blood. I was leering, and it was fucking creepy as hell, but Goddamn it, all I wanted was *her*. I couldn't stop.

I wanted to draw blood. I wanted to lap at the skin until she melted in my embrace. I wanted—

"Right, Ry?" she asked, raising her eyebrows in my direction.

I cleared my throat and shook the indecent images from my head. "Yeah, sure." I didn't even know what I'd agreed to.

"See?" She stuck her tongue out at Lycan in a playful retort, but my brother reacted by grabbing the perfect pink muscle between his index finger and thumb.

And I didn't like that shit one fucking bit. A growl erupted out of my chest before I could stop it, and I pushed to my feet, the chair sliding out from under me so hard it smashed into the cabinets behind me.

Isolde jumped and turned toward me. Poe dropped his fork and straightened. But Lycan only smiled and cocked his head to the side, raising an eyebrow in my direction.

"You got a death wish, Mitchell?" The words flew over my lips so quickly that I didn't realize I'd used his real last name in my rage until I'd already said it.

"Whew," Lycan said, holding his hands up in a display of feigned innocence. "You smell that, Princess? It's Orion's bullshit coming in hot and heavy."

"Kodiak said don't touch her." I put my hands on the table, preparing myself to go flying over the damned thing if he made one more wrong move.

"And I guess those rules don't apply to you, do they?" Lycan crossed his arms with a shit-eating grin on his smug face.

"Hey," Isolde cut in. "What's this about? Orion and I agreed that—"

"*Orion* doesn't know what the fuck he's talking about." Lycan sneered, licking his teeth with an indignant swipe of his tongue.

"What?" Isolde glanced at me before looking at Poe for help. I understood what was happening better than Lycan ever could. The full moon was weighing on us, and if she wasn't here, we might have been snippy with each other, but it never would have gotten territorial. But she was here, and she was a viable submissive, healthy and strong and beautiful. Our feral sides were already emerging, and her presence made us itchy.

I was more dominant than Lycan, higher in the pecking order. But that did not stop his wolf from trying to test the boundaries of my patience. If I had to, I'd take him out back and remind him why I was the veep, the second in command, the strongest only after our alpha.

"Back off, Lycan," I said.

"Make me, Morrison." The glint in Lycan's eyes indicated he knew what would happen by using my real last name. It only pissed me off more.

"Hey, enough," Isolde cut in. "My head is throbbing, my muscles ache from cleaning all day, and I'm pretty sure I'm having an identity crisis. The last thing I need is you two tearing each other apart."

At that, the impudent brother snorted and shook his head, dropping eye contact as he evidently decided he didn't want to tempt me further. "I think I'll sleep in the barn tonight." He stood and headed to the front door.

"Lycan," Poe cut in, standing up to go after him. "C'mon."

After the two of them were gone, Isolde stared at me with an open jaw and wide, confused eyes. "What the hell was that about?"

"He's been riding my ass all week," I said. "He shouldn't have touched you like that."

"He was joking around," she said, sitting in the spot next to me with a nearly empty plate. "He didn't mean anything by it."

Wrong. He wanted to provoke me into a reaction to prove that he'd been right about her, that she was more important to me than I let on. But I didn't want to believe that. Even if I'd never touched her, she would still be off-limits by Kodiak's orders. Grabbing her tongue...doing anything to her tongue...would be grounds for an ass-kicking.

I should get my ass kicked.

"You need to eat more than that." I glanced down at her small scoop of mashed potatoes and tiny helping of carrots.

"I'm not hungry," she said. "I haven't felt like eating in days."

"What did you mean that you feel like you're having an identity crisis?" I cleared my throat and tried not to be too obvious.

"I don't know." She rubbed her palms over her eyes and propped her face in her hands. "Vanderbilts don't clean. We don't shovel shit. We don't enjoy manual labor. I should be freaking out, but I feel like...it feels like I'm home, ya know? Like I'm meant to be here. I know that sounds ridiculous, but it's true."

It's the moon, I wanted to say. *You're latent. You'll probably transition come tomorrow night.*

But that couldn't be true. Lycan was projecting his own desires onto a poor woman who had gotten stuck here by bad circumstance. That was all.

"Try to make up with Lycan, okay?" She smiled, her perfect pink lips matching the flush on her cheeks. "He's just being playful."

"Hmm," I grunted, but I didn't agree. When we shifted together, our wolves would take it up among themselves. In the end, we were pack. We'd come out of the shift with lowered hormones and a new mindset on this whole thing. A few days after that, she'd be gone and we wouldn't have to worry about it any longer.

I sat there and watched her move food around on her plate while she talked about tackling the boxes in the attic tomorrow. She still hadn't confirmed with her family about when they might be able to come get her, but she insisted she didn't mind it here.

"It's peaceful," she said, smirking. "I like the quiet."

"Yeah, me too." I sighed and rubbed a hand over my face. "I volunteer to come here more than anyone else, despite the isolation."

"I understand that." She reached across the table and grabbed my hand, tucking her dandy fingers into my palm with a squeeze. But all I focused on was how hot her skin felt in comparison to mine, and I was a fucking pure-blooded wolf. I naturally ran hotter than humans, so if she felt warm, she probably had a fever.

Fuck.

"Thank you again, Orion," she cut in, drawing my attention back to her. "I know I've said it before, but I really do appreciate all you've done for me."

The anxious tone in her voice set alarm bells off in the back of my mind, like there was so much more she wanted to say but held back.

"Anything for you, Isolde." I smiled. "Why don't you go get some rest, huh? You feel warm. You might be getting sick."

She frowned.

"If you still feel bad in the morning," I continued, "sleep in and we'll work the ranch. You can finish cleaning up in here...only if you feel up to it."

"Yeah, okay." Rubbing at her temples, she pushed to her feet and headed upstairs, her food only half eaten. I pretended like I didn't know what that meant, like I hadn't seen the same thing in other shifters teetering on the edge of their transition. I simply would not believe it. The Vanderbilts had a long, complex history with this land, but if they had shifter blood in them, we would have known. I was a stubborn shit. Once I had my mind set on something, it was damn near impossible for me to be swayed...even if all the evidence pointed elsewhere.

Eventually, I went upstairs to pass out. A few hours later, a strange noise brought me back to consciousness, forcing my eyes open in the darkness of my room. A figure stood at the end of my bed panting, but the thick, heady feminine scent made me pause.

"Isolde?" I murmured, sitting up so I could see better.

She didn't answer, just hugged her arms tighter around herself and breathed heavier, her eyes hazed over. Was she sleepwalking?

"Ry," she said, and panic seized my chest, pulsing scalding blood through my veins. "Ry, I need you."

"I'm here," I said, pushing to my feet so I could walk toward her and touch her shoulder, her burning skin nearly shocking me back a step. "Isolde?" I tried again, this time giving her a shake. She didn't wake, just stood there and gasped for air like she was trying to catch her breath after a marathon. "Isolde, come back to me."

"Ry?" she murmured, and relief sank into my gut only for the moment. "What's going on? Where are we?"

"We're okay, Princess. You're in my room." I turned her to face me so I could put both hands on her shoulders. Her normal scent now emanated with something darker and richer, reeling me in, making me want to yank her down on my mattress and bury my face in her neck for the rest of the night.

"What happened?" she asked, rubbing at her eyes.

"You were sleepwalking." I brushed the hair out of her face and ran my knuckles down her cheek, forcing her to glance up at me the same way she had in the dream.

"What?" She winced and took a step back. "I'm sorry...I've never done that before." Her voice cracked, sending a painful jolt right through my chest. "What's going on with me?"

"You're okay." With the way the moonlight trickled in through the window, I saw that she wore a thin shirt and nothing else. Sweat had soaked through the fabric, making her skin shimmer and shine. "You've got the flu, Princess."

Instead of answering, she stared up at me, the confusion behind her green gaze melting away to something else, some mischievous and heated. "Why do they do that?"

"Do what?" I had no idea what she was talking about.

"Your eyes." She brought her hand up and traced it over my cheek, down to my lips. "Most of the time, they're brown. But sometimes, they turn blue. It's...impossible. And beautiful."

Ahh, shit.

I clenched my eyes shut as my wolf protested in the back of my mind. It didn't see the point in lying to her, and there were a thousand fucked-up things about it that I didn't want to analyze.

"It's just the moonlight," I said, glancing down at the ground while I tried to force that fucker back in its cage. The moon was so close now, it was nearly hopeless.

"No, it's not," she said. "I saw it the other night, too. With the wolves and again between us."

"It's late, Isolde," I said, nodding toward the door. "You should go back to bed. You need rest."

"I can't sleep in there," she said. "It's too cold."

Cold? We'd been burning the fire for days now. The second floor had been heated like a sauna, even with the six feet of snow outside.

"Can I stay with you?" she whispered, and the sound rattled right through me, down to my lower stomach and the back of my legs.

I took a deep breath and ran my hands over my face, back into my hair. "You shouldn't."

A tiny whine poured out of her chest, and it broke my heart even more, making my wolf pace and howl with stubbornness.

Pay attention, it growled. *Look at her. Look harder.*

I put my palms on her shoulders again, smoothing them up her neck to her cheeks, her soft skin so fiery under my touch. "Christ, you're burning up."

Instead of answering, she whimpered like an animal in pain and stepped closer, burying her face in my chest, rubbing her tear-stained cheeks against my pecs. Being skin to skin with her felt like heaven, and when I wrapped my arms around her shoulders and guided her toward my bed, I told myself it was just for tonight. Just until she felt better.

She settled against me, her back to my chest, my arm over her waist, tucking her in close. She wrapped her freezing toes in between my legs, and despite the surge of ache at the temperature difference, it pleased both me and my beast that I could care for her like this.

I slept better than I had since the last time she was here with me, and I decided not to read too much into that.

I woke up before her the next morning, making my way downstairs with a headache like I'd been hit by a train the night before. I didn't understand why. It wasn't like I'd been drinking, but Isolde's sleepwalking and how I kept being drawn to her despite the boundaries I'd tried to erect had me on high alert. Her skin was on fire, and she'd hardly eaten anything for days.

It's the flu. Only the flu. She's human, and she's been through a lot this last week.

I put the coffee on and dropped bread into the toaster when something twisted in my gut.

Magic, the wolf growled. *Magic and heat. Take. Take. Take.*

I clenched my eyes shut and shook my head, trying to push it away. I poured myself a hot, steamy mug of caffeine just as the front door opened and Poe stomped his feet on the ground to shake off the snow.

"Morning," he said, narrowing his gaze as he came closer. "How'd you sleep?"

"Fine," I lied. "How was the barn?"

Poe laughed and shook his head. "We didn't do much sleeping."

"Is he still pissed?" I raised my eyebrows as I took a sip, ignoring the strange sensation of creepy-crawlies on my skin, like spiders enveloping me, like a million tiny shocks of electricity rattling over my body.

"I think you should talk." Poe crossed his arms. "You're both stubborn, pigheaded motherfuckers, and one girl shouldn't tear you apart like this."

"We're two days out from the moon," I said. "A warm breeze could tear two dominant shifters apart."

Glancing to the ground, Poe snorted and sighed. "I agree with him, you know."

I raised my eyebrows, refusing to acknowledge his opinion, even when my heart thumped, shouting at me to listen.

"She's different." Poe met my gaze with a submissive one of his own, trying to tread lightly despite what he knew he had to say. "She's not a wolf, perhaps, but something else. Definitely latent, if not completely a shifter."

I sighed and put my hat on my head, deciding to head out to the barn to get started on today's work before anyone else suggested something ridiculous. I found Lycan on the porch dressed in the same clothes he had on last night, sitting on one of the swings with his booted foot on the railing.

"Do you feel that?" He raised his eyebrows as Poe came out with two cups of coffee and handed one to him.

"Feel what?" My voice came out in a growl, and I cleared my throat to keep my wolf from snarling as punctuation.

"That hum in the air." Lycan blew out a breath and wrapped an arm over Poe's shoulders when he sat next to him. "The magic just below the surface."

I wanted to attribute it to the moon being so close, but it had never felt like this before. As much as it pissed me off, I had to admit, this morning hit different. It rattled in my veins, vibrating in my molecules, preparing me for something epic, something that would take every bit of adrenaline I had. I shifted my hips and cracked my neck as a tickle twisted its way down my spine.

"Yeah, you feel it." Lycan gave me a knowing look before curling his lips into a grin. "If I went upstairs, I'd bet I'd find your pretty little princess in a sweaty heap under the blankets."

"Why are you goading him?" Poe cut in. "This is hard enough—"

He never got the rest of his sentence out. An invisible blast poured out of the house in a shockwave of hormones and shifter magic, nearly knocking me back with the force. Her scent billowed toward us next, strawberries and feral animal and wild, untamed female. My monster reared up in my mind, yipping with excitement, urging me forward, yearning to race up the stairs and take what was his.

"Orion, please," came the whimpered call before another blast of the same transition energy blew my hair around my face and whipped my hat clear off my head. "Please, please."

"Fucking hell, I love it when I'm right." Lycan shoved to his feet and went for the door, but I beat him to it, bursting it open so hard I nearly knocked it off its hinges. The three of us ran to the stairs, taking them two at a time until we were on the second floor landing. The pheromones radiated stronger up here, pouring off Isolde in thick, heavy waves that assaulted my senses.

My feral side took hold, awakening every animal impulse I had. My cock throbbed behind my jeans, instantly hard and ready to serve her, and my veins thrummed with the anticipation of being torn open to pour my magic into her waiting mouth. She writhed on top of my sheets, her shirt bunched up around her hips, her skin shiny with sweat and tears. She'd balled the duvet in her tight fists, her knuckles white, and clenched her eyes shut in obvious pain.

"Orion, help," she cried again, and I took a deep breath, savoring the way her delicious taste coated my tongue and dripped down my throat.

"This can't be happening," I groaned, rubbing a hand over my face, disbelief rattling through my molecules. "The Vanderbilts—"

"It *is* happening," Poe said, shoving me forward. "Go to her."

"She's going through her transition," Lycan said. "She needs you."

I froze. I didn't want this for her. She was sweet and tender. She didn't need to know this side of life, this side of me. She would have been better off anywhere else than here with us, especially now that Lycan turned out to be right. "She deserves better than me."

"You don't want her then?" Lycan tried to shove his way past me, but I shot an arm out to the opposite wall and blocked his path.

"Back off." The sound that came out of my mouth wasn't me; it wasn't my voice. The wolf had taken control because the man wouldn't move. Such was the survival instinct of a shifter. We existed in codependence with our animal side—when one couldn't handle something, the other side took over until it could. My vision sharpened and my canines elongated, the first signs of a territorial beast making its claim.

I walked into the room and took a deep breath, letting the magic enthrall me, before turning to face my brothers.

"No one comes in here," the beast said, and I slammed the door, twisting the lock into place just for good measure. They'd listen to me. Fuck, they knew better than to disobey me. I'd rip their throats out without a second thought.

And when I turned to my little submissive, my little princess, my heart sank into my gut. She looked so lonely, so tortured, suffering on the covers by herself.

She needs us, the wolf whispered. *Get in there.*

My hands shaking and my knees turning to mush, I yanked my shirt off and threw it to the side just as another surge of aching hormones blew off her. I grimaced against the tremble in my bones, rattling my teeth so hard, I thought they might break. My cock jerked again, the *want* tightening in my balls. When I was naked, I crawled on my knees toward her, letting the wolf take complete control.

He knew what was best. He knew how to do this. The only time I'd been involved in a transition had been my own, and I barely remembered it. The pain and the agony of the magic taking root in my soul had been too overwhelming for me to stay conscious through it all.

"O—ri—on," Isolde called, thrashing against the duvet, arching her back as another wave took her. It plumed off her body, lifting me into the air where I hovered, suspended with the fury of it. The magic blew through my skin, reaching deep down inside until it wrapped around my soul, yanking me toward its inevitable oblivion.

I'd been such an idiot. Of course this was happening. Of course there could be no other outcome. I'd been a slave to my own blissful ignorance, denying the truth in hopes that I could will it into being.

"I'm here, baby girl," I cooed, hardly recognizing the tenderness in my voice. I'd never spoken to anyone like this, not even Nemesis. "Here, sit up for me." I tucked one hand under her body to help her upright, ignoring the twist in my heart when she whined like I was hurting her. But I had to get her shirt off, and when she failed to lift her arms high enough for me to tug it over her head, I grew impatient and ripped the damn thing down the center. She moaned when it was finally gone, and when I did the same thing to her tiny panties, she bucked her hips up toward me, practically begging me to touch her.

But I wouldn't. Not yet. She needed something else from me first, something only a dominant shifter could give to her. Pushing my canines out farther, I held my wrist up to my mouth and bit into my skin until I tasted copper, my wolf's blood pooling on my tongue. Then, I held it over her lips, letting it drip until she opened wider, seeking it out.

"Yes," I murmured. "There you go. Good girl." When she licked out for more, I watched her latch on to the wound while she sucked and lapped at it, pulling my shifter magic deep.

Fuck, I sensed it inside her, like I existed both in my own skin and hers. My cock pulsed against her hip, causing her to roll her pelvis against me harder. The fragrance of her wet cunt made me dizzy, overwhelming my senses and all of my restraint.

Get inside her, my wolf bellowed, desperation in his call. *Take her. Claim her. Mark her.*

Orion, the man, knew I shouldn't. But Orion, the monster, had long since forgotten the reasons why. It was always meant to be this way between me and her. The shifter knew that the first time he set eyes on her, and now that we were here, my teeth throbbed with the possibility of sinking into her neck and leaving a bonding mark. Would she even want that? What would she think if she were in her right mind?

It didn't fucking matter because I was too gone to the primal side to care. She drank from my wrist until she purred with satisfaction, licking over the wound like a preening cat. Then the wolf and I took what we'd been dreaming about for eight days. I slid down her body, kissing and nuzzling her sweat, damn near rolling in the scent. I wanted it permanently in my skin. I wanted mine in hers, and when I smelled something darker and territorial wafting off me, I realized that would be exactly what happened. We'd leave this room reeking like each other, and the thought shouldn't have turned me on as much as it did.

She didn't even know she was a shifter, and when she came back to herself, she'd have a hell of a reality check. But thoughts like those were so far away from the present moment. I needed to do what the magic required, and right now, that involved my tongue on her pussy.

I situated myself between her thighs and wrapped her legs over my shoulders, staring up at her face like I was waiting for this to stop—for her to tell me she was just fucking around and this wasn't what I thought it was.

Get on with it, the wolf snarled, but even with his insistence, I trembled with nerves. For all that I'd been cocky swagger with every other woman I'd had in my bed, I worried that she'd want someone else, that if she had a choice, she might want Lycan here instead.

"Orion," she moaned, pressing her hips up toward my face. "Orion, please. It hurts."

"Shh," I said, running my fingers up the sides of her thighs, digging my claws into her skin to hold her in place. "I'll make it better."

I'd never known a greater pleasure than sliding my tongue through her silky, delicate skin. She tasted like heaven, better than she smelled. I gathered what I could and swallowed it down, feeling the magic shift inside my own body. The bond between us snapped taut like an invisible guitar string, connecting me so deeply to her emotions that they vibrated deep in my body.

Her cunt shimmered with her slick and my saliva, and I lapped it up like a man starved, like I'd never known what it meant to desire a woman before. Fuck, it was the best thing I'd tasted in my life. I sucked on her clit and stuffed my face as close to her as I could get, pleased when her moans ramped up and her panting grew more intense. She rolled against me harder, spreading her legs wider, the rush of her own pleasure echoing out of her and into me.

Unable to stand it any longer, I thrust my hips against the mattress, finally giving my aching cock some friction, but it wasn't enough. I needed to be inside her.

Not yet, I reminded myself. *She needs more.*

The instructions came from a feral instinct inside my cells, the logical side of me having taken a back seat. The animal was in charge now, and he wanted her to drink more wolf's blood, to swallow down more magical essence, before I filled her pussy with the same.

I reached up to press my wrist against her mouth again, and she greedily accepted, allowing me to shower her with the most intimate of exchanges. And while I went back to feasting on the decadent skin between her legs, she swallowed down the fury in my blood, her euphoria radiating outward.

Just when she reached the pinnacle, another shockwave of hormones surged out of her, blinding and intoxicating. The force of it pushed me off her body a few inches, lifting me over her with a translucent shield of her power before crashing me back onto the bed.

"Fuck," I groaned, my cock now painfully erect and ready to serve.

"Please," she said, finally opening her eyes to focus on me with that hazy, blissed-out stare. "More."

"Okay, baby girl," I said, climbing up her body so I could position my dick at her entrance. At the feel of it, she pushed her hips up and arched her back, wrapping her arms around my neck to pull me down on her. I obliged and dropped to my elbows as I shoved inside her, all the way to the hilt, connecting us skin to skin from the torso to our pelvises and down our legs. "Fuuuucckkk me."

She fit like a glove, like we were made to be one, and I nearly lost my balance on my shaking arms. Her cunt was so warm and tight and wet that I almost came before I even got started. I'd embarrassed myself the other night by busting in my pants, but I knew even if it happened now, I'd be hard again in a few moments. The supernatural magnet of her transition had roped me in, and now that I was under its spell, there would be no escaping it, not until it ran its course.

I pumped my hips against her, sliding in and out with ecstatic ease due to the slick dripping off her, drenching both me and the sheets. Her mouthwatering aroma entranced me, making my head spin, and my wolf rolled around in it.

"Yes," she moaned, leaning up to kiss me. "Please."

I licked against her mouth, tasting both her and metal, and the combination made my canines pulse with need. I wanted to sink them into her throat.

No, my rational brain managed to break through. *If* I ever marked her, it would be with her full acknowledgment and willing participation. My wolf wanted her, but to claim her while she was in transition seemed like a shitty thing to do. So I kissed my way down to her neck and fucked deeper inside her while I licked the salt from her skin.

She scratched my spine, sinking her nails deep into my flesh hard enough to leave traces of her own. But I *liked* it, so I moaned my appreciation and she did it again.

"You're such a good girl," I mumbled. "Taking me so good. You're going to make it, Princess. You're going to make it through this. I promise." I spewed countless affirmations, words that promised a future I wasn't sure we could have.

But that didn't matter, not then, not in the throes of this overwhelming experience. Her climax rose and she tightened her muscles around me, pulling me down on top of her with her arms around my neck and her legs clamped around my hips, but I kept going, recognizing the same anticipation in myself.

Her orgasm rushed out of her and into me, the metaphysical tie between us enabling shared sensations, so when her precious cunt clamped down, the base of my cock expanded, locking me into place deep inside her. My knot throbbed furiously, and I emptied myself with a roar, my teeth begging to sink into her shoulder.

By the grace of fucking God, I managed to restrain those impulses, allowing her to bite me instead. Her new pointy canines dug into my neck, my collarbone, my chest, anywhere they could clamp, and I felt, more than saw, red welts that I'd wear with fucking honor.

Now sated, her hormones ebbed, and she relaxed against the mattress. I held myself up on top of her, my limbs quaking with the force of our union as she ran her fingers down my spine in a lazy caress that soothed the anxious beast in my head.

Care for her, he howled. *Mark her. Take her. Claim her. She's ours. Ours alone. No one else sees her like this. No one else can have her. Not now. Not ever again.*

Still, I ignored that because after this was over, she might walk away from me. She should. Nothing had changed. We were still enemies, and we always would be.

"Orion?" Her voice came out soft and pliant, like she expected me to reject her now that the hormones had momentarily subsided.

"I'm here, baby girl," I said, drawing my tongue up the column of her throat in a primordial display of devouring the essence from her skin.

"What's happening?" She sounded more lucid than she had since last night, but I knew we were far from finished. Transitions usually lasted at least a day, if not longer. This close to the full moon, we might be in this room until it was time for the shift.

"You're in transition," I murmured, meeting her gaze. But it was not Isolde that stared out at me. Her green irises had turned to a brilliant shade of amber, hinting at the feral thing hiding under her skin.

"Transition?" She creased her eyebrows together and clenched her eyes shut, a shock of anxiety and terror shooting out of her and into me. "What does that mean?"

"I'll explain it to you, I promise." Nuzzling my nose farther into her shoulder, I inhaled her exhilarating smell and let it soothe the beast inside my mind. "Just relax for now. I'll take care of you."

"Am I dying?" She sounded so scared, so confused. I wanted to do anything to put her at ease.

"No," I cooed. "You've never been more alive."

"Thank you." She let out a half-hearted sob and nodded. "I'm happy you're here."

"Yes, baby girl. I'm here. I won't leave you." I littered her face with kisses, hoping to reiterate the fact that I wasn't going anywhere, that I would stay until it was over. I'd give her everything I had to ensure she made it safely through. The bulge at the base of my dick started to soften, and I eased out of her, trying to be gentle because I knew how rough I'd been.

But that didn't matter. She was still soaked between the legs, now reeking of both her and me, and that made my monster so fucking happy, he howled at me to do it again.

I barely had time to think that through before another surge of pheromones rolled off her, hitting me right in the center of the chest, and my cock responded with a hard jerk, forcing me on top of her again.

It went on for hours...days...centuries. I lost track of how long I'd spent between her legs and how much blood she'd taken from my wrists. When the wound got to be too sensitive, I encouraged her to sink her teeth into my neck.

Fuck, the sensation of her tiny canines biting through the skin on my pulse point and sucking down my magic had me roaring through a heavy explosion between her legs. My knot chafed and my cock burned, but I couldn't stop it. Her transition had me in a chokehold and wouldn't let me go until it was satisfied.

The sun set and rose again, and still, we stayed in that bed. Eventually, the bouts between her surges lasted longer, and we slept in those lulls. But even unconsciousness was no match for the pull of her magic. It drained me dry, completely and irrevocably, to the point where I couldn't even lift my head. My arms lay heavy by my side, my leg muscles cramped any time I moved, and my jaw burned from how long I'd spent licking her from head to toe. The skin on my dick protested any touch that wasn't her cunt, but that did not stop it from expanding whenever her supernatural side called to mine.

Finally, on that last morning, the day of the full moon, the magic loosened its hold on us. I woke up to a weak burst of hormones and a tiny moan from the woman next to me. I creaked my groggy eyes open, and I tried to will my body into action, but the haze in my brain wouldn't cooperate.

Take her, the wolf howled. *Help her. One last time.*

I curled up, desperate to get my torso off the mattress, but I didn't have the strength and flopped back on the pillows, only to try again with pitiful results. My nerves were fried and my brain had shriveled to the size of a peanut. It didn't matter because Isolde crawled on top of me and spread her legs to either side of my hips, easily positioning me at her entrance before sheathing me all the way down. I groaned and arched into her, coasting my hands up her thighs to her hips while she leaned down to lick at the wound on my neck before sinking her teeth into it again.

"You taste so good," she murmured while she rode me and took what she needed. "Why is this happening? Why does it feel so right?"

The mental fog wouldn't clear, no matter what I did, but I let her take what she needed, hardly able to form coherent sentences. All I managed to get out was a mumbled, "Yours."

"Mine," she repeated, rocking herself against my body, taking me deeper, lapping at the wound to close it again. With my blood dripping from her mouth and her cunt wrapped around my cock, she reached a final climax, launching me into my own. It sputtered out of me, yanked from me despite my exhaustion. My knot expanded inside her, locking us together like that, and I sighed as the transition finally broke its hold on both of us.

She collapsed on top of me, her chest on my stomach, her head tucked under my chin, but I couldn't move. I lay there and panted, my canines tingling, my muscles trembling, my entire body so fucking sore and blissed-out that I had no idea how I would change in twelve hours.

But I'd seen other shifters do it, so I had to rely on the moon to see me through, the same way every pack member had before me. She would be thrumming with my essence for weeks to come, and when she shifted with us tonight, she'd have the time of her life running through the woods, just as I had.

We both fell asleep joined together like that, and when I woke a few hours later, I had regained enough of my strength to climb out of bed. I froze and stared at myself in the mirror above my dresser. I might have lost fifty pounds in two days. My cheeks were sunken in, my ribs showed on either side of my body, and my stomach curved the wrong way, like I could almost see my organs through my translucent skin. Deep bite wounds gaped bright red on either side of my neck in various degrees of healing, matched only by the ones on my wrists and legs. She'd made a mess of me, and I didn't give a fuck.

In fact, pride beamed through my chest and into my gut, and I wondered if the submissive that had seen me through mine had felt the same the day after.

Or was this different? Did I wear these wounds with such joy because there was something *more* at play?

After my transition, I didn't remember feeling so intrinsically linked to the pack mate who had fed me and fucked me through it. Once the pheromones subsided, she had left and eventually mated someone else in the pack. I thought about her no more or less than I had before. It had been a transaction for both of us, something she'd done out of necessity and respect for our family.

But when I put my boxers on and glanced back at the sleeping female in my bed, I sensed her buried in my soul. The connection we'd formed during our time together had not eased when the magic had. Her satisfaction burned in my blood, the warm, gooey sensation of euphoric happiness that I'd been there for her, that she slept in my bed, that she had my scent marking her body. In fact, when I leaned down to smell my own skin, it had changed to accommodate her flowery notes.

Fuck. I opened the door to head downstairs. She'd wake up soon and we both needed food. It had been far too long without sustenance.

Both Poe and Lycan looked up at me from the kitchen table when I appeared. Poe widened his eyes and dropped his jaw, but Lycan only shook his head and laughed.

"Good to see you," Lycan said. "I'm surprised you can walk."

I grumbled something that sounded like fuck off before going to the refrigerator and gathering some of the leftovers. The chicken from a few nights ago still smelled good, as did the vegetables she'd cooked for us. I put those on the counter before going for the lunch-meat and sliced cheese.

"How did it go?" Poe asked, purposely keeping his tone light and innocent, as if to suggest he didn't mean any harm by asking. Through the bond, I understood that he wanted to make sure she was all right, that the worst *hadn't* happened. Even with help, sometimes shifters didn't make it. The magic could be detrimental to the body, and the human could reject it. That hadn't happened to Isolde.

I took a deep breath and turned to face him, running a hand over the back of my neck. "It was—" I didn't have words. How could I describe the sheer magnificence that had flowed between us to someone who had never experienced the giving end of it? How could I put into words the depth of the emotions we now shared? "It was mind-blowing. Life altering."

"You look like hell," Lycan added. "How are you going to shift tonight?"

I swallowed against a dry throat, grabbing two glasses out of the cabinet before filling them from the tap and gulping one down. "The moon doesn't give a shit about how I feel."

"Fair enough," Poe added. "How is our Princess?"

I bristled at him calling her *our,* but if I opened myself up enough, I sensed her there, hovering as an extension of me. She wasn't fully in the pack yet, and she wouldn't be until she shifted, met the rest of our family, and received an invitation from the alpha. But it was enough that likely Poe and Lycan sensed her, too.

As would Kodiak.

I probably should have called him to tell him what had happened, but with the moon coming tonight and everything else going on, neither of us would have time to deal with it. I decided to save that news until after her first shift.

One problem at a time.

"She's great," I said, returning to the plate of food I'd been preparing for us. "She'll be ready for tonight."

"Yeah, I bet she will," Lycan said with a laugh, making me glare at him. "With all that VP blood flowing in her veins, I bet she could run to Pluto and back."

Poe barked out a chuckle, and I shook my head, combing through the chicken for the best bits to put on her plate, opting to eat the other bits myself. When I had a sufficient amount, I grabbed a few bananas and oranges from the bowl before grabbing a knife to peel and slice them into pieces for her.

Lycan and Poe teased each other about how much they'd fucked over the last forty-eight hours, a result of her hormones spreading through the Fiver like a shockwave, but I tuned them out in favor of getting the food ready. I sensed her starting to wake with a soft stirring in my chest and hurried my movements. I wanted to be there when she came to, so she'd know she wasn't alone, that I had kept her safe and would continue to do so.

"So are you two mated now?" Lycan asked, bringing my attention back to them.

"It sure smells like it." Poe leaned in and took a long, slow inhale. "I'm picking up a bonding scent and everything."

Again, I mumbled something unintelligible before grabbing the plate with one hand and her water with the other, walking back up the stairs to my room, quietly shutting the door behind me.

Bonding scent?

Sure, I smelled myself and her and...something else...something darker and more territorial and distinctly primeval. But the bonding scent would only take hold if *both* parties had accepted it, and she'd been out of it for the last two days. There was no way she'd know what the hell had happened to her, much less agree to having mated a Bastard.

Reality started to close in fast, and the private heaven we'd created here in this room began to slip away.

The smell of warm food woke me from sleep, and when I opened my eyes, I found Orion sitting on the mattress by my legs, picking at a plate of chicken. He looked absolutely wrecked, like he'd gone on a juice cleanse and hadn't slept in months.

"Ry?" I croaked, pushing myself into a sitting position.

He glanced at me, his eyes shifting from dark brown to the clearest sky blue, and his scent wafted toward me, a barrage of pine and sandalwood and *him*. He could reel me in with that alone, and I wanted to spend forever pressed against him, inhaling him deeply.

"Hey." He curled his lips into a gentle smile and handed me a glass of water. "How are you feeling?"

"Okay." I clenched my eyes shut and sipped, delighting in the delicious coolness as it slid down my burning throat. The sense of anxiety that had been rotting in my stomach for the last few days was gone, and the thundering between my temples had dissipated. In its place was a newfound curiosity and an overwhelming need to run, to be free. "What happened? You look like hell."

He ignored my inquiry and grabbed a piece of chicken, holding it up to my mouth. "You need to eat."

My stomach chose that moment to rumble, completely wiping away any resistance I may have put up. I opened my lips and let him slide the food inside. The flavors burst against my tongue, salty and flagrant and downright delicious. I'd never experienced anything like it before, and when he held up a piece of orange next, I wrapped my lips around that, too. It was like experiencing food for the first time, like I hadn't eaten in weeks and now dined on the finest fare.

"What happened to me?" I tried to remember yesterday or the day before, but all my mind could conjure was him. Memories of him inside me, of sucking on his wrist and his neck, and...*are those bite marks?* I gasped at the wounds on his throat, violet and jagged. "Oh my God. Who did that to you?"

He sighed and shook his head. "Princess, we need to talk."

I didn't like the drop in his features or the weariness in his tone. "Okay. What's going on?"

"Have you ever heard of shifters?" He held up another piece of meat, and I took it without thinking, chewing on it while I considered his question.

"Like—werewolves?" I furrowed my brows. "I mean, I've read stories about them. But—"

"They're real," he said. "Almost all the legends are real."

I laughed and swallowed, reaching for the glass so I could take another sip. When Orion didn't laugh with me, I paused and blinked, trying to rationalize his reaction. "Wait...what?"

"My eyes," he said. "You asked me why they change colors, that it should be impossible." I vaguely remembered that but after the last however long, it seemed like a fever dream. Like it had happened to someone else. "My eyes are brown. My wolf's eyes are blue. Whenever he's close to the surface, whenever he takes over, they shift."

I couldn't believe it. I didn't want to believe it, especially as he continued talking. He told me his story, how he'd been raised in the Bastards as a child, how almost everyone in the MC was a shifter or a shifter's mate. "Most of us are wolves," he said, "but there's a few coyotes and wild cats. When we reach a certain age, we go through a transition. The magic takes hold of us, mutating our genes so we can handle the shift." He grabbed another piece of meat and held it up to me, but I refused it in favor of trying to comprehend this new information and why he was telling it to me. "If the shifter's personality is more submissive, they'll need a dominant. If they are more dominant, they will need a submissive. Usually, it's someone of the opposite gender expression, but not always. It depends on the person's preference."

I shook my head and swallowed my food, sensing in my chest and my gut that this was significant for more than one reason. "Are you saying you're a werewolf, Orion?"

"I am," he said. "And you are, too. Though, not a wolf, I suspect. But something similar."

I froze, raising my eyebrows as I stared at him.

What. The. Fuck.

"There's a reason you were so tired a few days ago, a reason why you felt the urge to clean the entire house from top to bottom. The headaches, the body chills, they're gone now, aren't they?"

I nodded, taking a deep breath before I swallowed so I didn't choke on both the food and the new information.

"If you were to focus, I bet you could hear Lycan and Poe talking about us downstairs. You could smell the coffee in the pot and the ingredients Poe used to make breakfast this morning. Hell, you could probably tell all the different animals in the barn."

I hung my mouth open like an idiot because he was right. I heard Lycan and Poe flirting and laughing almost as if they were in the same room with us. I smelled melted butter and toast and the specific type of bacon that they'd cooked. I could even make out precisely how much sugar Poe had used in his coffee.

"I know it's a lot to take in," he continued. "Especially since you have no reason to believe me."

"What the fuck, Orion?" I pressed my palms into my eyes, my mind struggling to keep up with this new reality. "How did this happen? Did you do this to me?"

"No, Princess," he said. "You're either born a shifter or you're not."

"How?" My chest tightened and my stomach bottomed out, dropping to somewhere near my knees. "This can't be real. You're fucking with me."

"I wish I was," he said, brushing a piece of hair out of my face. The sensation of him touching my face rattled down my spine and into my toes. I felt him everywhere. I sensed him deep inside me in a way I'd never imagined I could.

Even as I bucked against this, I couldn't deny that I felt different...that I *was* different.

"I have no reason to lie to you." He sighed and tried to feed me another piece of orange. "Please. Eat."

I clenched my hands into fists as I tried to understand, but when I let him place the fruit on my tongue, a new voice took root in my brain. It was me, but distinctly *not* me.

He's right, it said. *You know he's right. You can feel it.*

What the hell is that? I argued with myself, unsure what to do with this identity.

It's me, it said. *It's you. It's us.*

"It's unbelievable and incredible I know," Orion continued, "and there's a thousand reasons why we've kept ourselves hidden. Humans are destructive, and if they knew about us, they'd lock us up in zoos or keep us as science projects."

The betrayal that had been brewing inside my chest subsided, replaced with a hesitant understanding. "That's why you didn't tell me...before."

He nodded and ran his hands back through his hair. "There's a lot more to explain, but for now, I need you to understand that you went through a change, that you're different from who you were."

I opened my hands and stared down at my palms, seeing the same skin that had always been there. But it tingled with excitement and unfulfilled potential, like I had infinite strength, like I could run a marathon if I wanted to. More memories from the last few hours bombarded me, and I remembered biting into Orion's wrists and tearing at the skin on his neck with teeth that had grown sharper than they'd ever been. I ran my tongue over them, widening my eyes when my canines grew. They throbbed in beat with my pulse, and the more I thought about the time I'd spent in bed with him, the more they tingled.

"That's your animal side," he said, reaching out to run the back of his finger down my cheek. "Your teeth will elongate now whenever you get excited or angry or fearful. You might grow claws or... other things."

"Other things?" It came out clipped and rushed, my heart now thundering between my ears. Trying to ignore my rising panic, I raised my eyebrows and took a long, deep breath. He pressed his lips together, his cheeks glowing a faint shade of pink. "Well, go on. You might as well tell me."

"For shifters with a penis, particularly wolves, we have an extra muscle at the base that locks us inside a partner. It's called a knot."

As he talked, the last two days became clearer. He'd rutted inside me, emptying himself and unable to move for quite some time. It had been hazy, of course, but toward the end, I'd been more levelheaded.

"And for shifters with a uterus?"

He cleared his throat and ran a hand over the back of his neck. "You have slick."

"Slick?" I swallowed against a dry throat and reached for the glass of water, suspending disbelief long enough to remember how wet and sloppy our union had been...and it didn't have to do with the blood. "That sounds awful."

Orion barked out a laugh and shook his head. "It's not. At least, not to other shifters."

"What is it?"

He glanced at the space between my legs and cleared his throat. "It's like when you get wet...but more."

My mouth fell open and I fought the burn in my cheeks. "Oh."

"It helps with the knotting." He gave me another grin before picking up the last pieces of meat on the plate and placing them in my mouth.

"Oh my God," I said through chews, suddenly remembering that we hadn't used a condom. "I'm on birth control. Does that still work on shifters?"

"Don't worry," he said. "No one gets pregnant during the transition. The magic is too traumatizing for your body. You have to go into heat to have pups."

"Like a dog?" I didn't like the thought of that.

"Like a shifter," he corrected. "There are other things you should know, too. Skin privileges and feeding times and burrowing, but we have to get ready for the full moon."

"That part's true?" Still convinced that this must be a dream, I swung my legs off the mattress, moving to sit beside him so we connected from shoulder to hip to thigh. Scalding electricity bloomed through me, almost like it had been when I first got here, but *more*—painfully, erotically more.

"Unfortunately," he said. "Shifters can't turn whenever they want, nor would we want to turn all the time. The shift is...well, I suppose you'll see." He glanced away, focusing on the ground, but I put a hand on his cheek and turned his face back to mine, taking in the sheer beauty of his features.

Yes, he looked gaunt and exhausted, but the hard edge to his eyes had disappeared and the vicious set of his jaw had eased. He looked relaxed for the first time since he found me in my SUV.

"Tell me," I said. "I want to hear it from you."

"The shift is painful," he explained. "It takes a few minutes to complete. But it's also..." He trailed off, seeming to look for the right word. "Ecstatic, like you never knew what it was like to be alive until that moment."

I nodded and licked my lips, trying to understand, but Orion's gaze dropped to the movement and he gulped, quickly looking away.

"Thank you for helping me," I said. "You're too good to me."

"Never," he said, leaning down so he rested his forehead against mine. "You deserve so much better."

"How can you say that about yourself?" I murmured, grabbing both sides of his face to hold him up so I could stare him in the eyes—those beautiful clear eyes the color of the ocean. "I think you're amazing."

"I think you're amazing, too, Isolde." He leaned forward to brush his lips against mine, and I moaned into the contact, relaxing against him as the sensation of our kiss echoed down my spine and into the space between my legs. I'd wanted him before this transition, but now I ached for him with a desperation that echoed deep in my molecules. I wanted to crawl in his lap and take him inside me and test all the things this new reality had in store for me.

But when I ran my hands down his jaw to his neck, he winced and pulled back, clutching at one of the wounds.

"I'm sorry," I said with a grimace. "I take it that's my handiwork?"

He sighed and traced his knuckles down my cheek, giving me a soft smile. "It's not your fault. I wanted you to do it. They'll go away after the moon tonight."

I pursed my lips as a small flame boiled in my gut. I didn't want them to go away. I wanted them to stay so everyone knew *I'd* put them there, so that no one else would dare touch him. And if he even so much as thought about helping another shifter through their transition—

Wait...what?

He laughed and grabbed my bottom lip between his thumb and forefinger, giving it a little pinch that brought my attention back up to him.

"Don't pout, baby girl," he said. "All that territorial aggression is part of the shift. That'll go away after the moon tonight, too."

I almost asked him what I was supposed to do if I *didn't* want it to go away, but he stood and I ran my gaze down his body as if I hadn't just had it all to myself for the last forty-eight hours. I still sensed him inside me, like his soul and mine were now entwined on a level I didn't understand and perhaps never would. I glanced down at my palms, opening and closing my fingers. I almost saw his blood flowing through my veins. Could he feel it as well?

"Are you sure you're okay?" he asked again, putting a finger under my chin to lift my face up.

"I can feel you," I murmured, "in my blood."

He nodded and smiled. "I had to give you my magic for you to survive. I only know of a few people who've done it without help. It's not easy."

"Will that go away after the shift, too?"

"In a week or two." He turned to grab a T-shirt off the ground and handed it to me, and a strange purring noise came out of my chest when I pressed it to my nose. It smelled like him and me and *us,* and this new side of me recognized the delicious notes that made up our connection. *Ambrosia.*

"C'mon," he said with a quiet chuckle. "Get dressed. I've got to clean the sheets and you need a shower. You look like you survived a horror movie."

There was so much more to talk about, and I almost told him about my situation with Marx. What would the leader of the rival motorcycle club do when he realized I was a shifter and harbored conflicting feelings toward the veep of the Royal Bastards? I should have said something to Orion, but with all the thoughts rumbling around in my brain, I barely had time to catch up to the new changes in my body, much less confess why I'd been out in those woods, driving through dangerous territory. There would be time to explain. I had to get through my first shift.

I pulled the shirt over my head and got to my feet, meeting my reflection in the mirror for the first time since this started. The woman staring back at me wasn't the same that had come to this cabin just over a week ago.

That woman had pale skin and green eyes and long, wavy ginger hair. This woman had a glowing, radiant complexion and a mane that hung in wild curls around her head. But most startling were the amber eyes that stared out at me, golden and vibrant and magnetic.

"Holy—" I got closer, pulling at my lids to get a better view. "Is that...is that my other side?"

"Yes, Princess," he said, wrapping his arms around my midsection from behind so he could rest his head on my shoulder. "Say hello."

"Hi there," I said, giving my new reflection a grin.

Hi, came the soft internal reply.

"There she is," Lycan said when I emerged from the shower in a different set of Orion's clothes. He held his arms out for me and I wrapped mine around him in a hug before doing the same to Poe. They were the same people...er, shifters...as before my change, but everything about them was different. They smelled more like themselves, deeper and richer and familial, almost like I could sense a piece of myself within them.

Pack, came the voice inside, my beast, my other half.

"I still can't believe it," I said, ignoring that voice for now. "No one else in my family is a shifter. I don't understand how it's possible."

"Sometimes, the magic lies dormant," Lycan said, gesturing to the spot across the table from him. I sat while Orion busied himself with making more coffee. "Until you're stuck in the wolf's den." He flashed me a toothy grin and a wink before nodding toward Orion. "He insisted it was nothing, that I was reading the situation wrong. But my wolf is never wrong, not about this."

"I suppose I owe you an apology," Orion grumbled.

"Don't worry," Lycan said. "You'll find a way to make it up to me."

"Ry said the shift is really taxing on your body," I said. "Aren't you worried about going through it so close to..." I remembered how we'd spent the last forty-eight hours and my cheeks burned. "...what just happened?"

Orion sighed while Lycan scoffed. "He's the second for a reason."

"Second?" I furrowed my brows, trying to understand.

"Our alpha is Kodiak," Poe explained. "He's the president of the MC and the one who keeps us all together."

"In the pecking order, he's the biggest, baddest motherfucker there is." Lycan took a sip of coffee. "The only one who could take him in a fight, the only one who could come close, would be your man, Orion."

My man. I pretended the heat lighting in my stomach had nothing to do with the thought of him belonging to me.

"Am I a wolf, too?" I asked, but even as the words came out of my mouth, I knew it was wrong.

Lycan shook his head and leaned in closer, giving me a deep sniff. "You're canine adjacent, but not a wolf."

"Fox," said Orion, rolling his head around and cracking his neck.

Both Poe and Lycan paused, and I glanced up at the man currently breaking eggs over a pan on the stove. So much about my life had changed so quickly that the earth could suddenly smash into the sun and that would be more believable.

"How do you know?" I worried my bottom lip with my top teeth, trying to grasp all of this. I'd gone to sleep in one reality and woken up in another.

"I can smell it," Orion grumbled, adding a few slices of bacon that made my mouth water.

"I guess we'll know for sure at the full moon," Poe said with a laugh.

"Orion said all the legends are true," I continued. "What about vampires? Or witches?"

"Yes," Lycan said. "You've heard of the Bloody Scorpions?"

I froze, stiffening as a chill raced down my spine. I tried to play it off and act like the mention of the rival MC had no effect on me. But the words brought back everything that had been going on in my life before the blizzard.

"I have." I cleared my throat to maintain my composure.

"They're the local bloodsuckers," Lycan said, rolling his eyes with a pretend shiver. "Bunch of fucking leeches, all of them."

I remembered the sense of foreboding I'd gotten when I'd met Marx and the rest of his gang. He had looked evil, and based on what Lycan shared, I'd been correct in assuming they weren't good men. The words were on the tip of my tongue, and I almost admitted the reason I'd come here in the first place. I trusted them now, and I was sure they'd help me if they could. But my life had literally been turned upside down and everything I thought I knew had changed so quickly. I decided to wait until I could talk to Orion privately. He'd know the best way to break it to the others, and it would be easier to explain to him alone. We could still sense each other. He'd understand...*right?*

"Shifters are born of nature," Poe continued. "You're either born a shifter or you aren't. People like you have the magic, even if it's latent until activated. Vampires, on the other hand—"

"They've been perverted," Lycan cut in as Orion sat down next to me, scooting his chair closer so his arm brushed against mine. His stomach grumbled as he dug into his food, and I watched him eat while Lycan continued. "Their magic isn't from the earth; it's from a curse."

"That's why they need blood to stay alive." Poe shook his head. "It's disgusting, the fucking parasites."

"Do they feed from humans?" I was ravenous for more information. I wanted to know everything as soon as possible, even as I realized it might take me a lifetime to figure out this new mythology and my place in it.

"Humans, shifters, other vampires." Poe pretended to wretch. "I've seen the leftovers from a vampire attack. It's traumatizing."

"They killed most of our parents," Lycan said, glancing at Orion quickly before looking back at me. "They attacked our pack and took out the alpha's mate, not to mention countless others."

Orion paused for only a moment, his fork halfway to his face, before clearing his throat and shifting his shoulders, obviously uncomfortable with something Lycan said.

"They're enemies," Lycan continued with a stern stare. "Now that you're a shifter, you should stay away from them."

"Our blood is an aphrodisiac," Orion explained. "They take great pleasure in draining us dry for months at a time."

I nodded and glanced down to the table in front of me, knowing now that I had no other choice. I *had* to get out of the predicament waiting for me at home. There could be no going back, especially not after tonight.

"But what about the transition?" I asked. "I drank Orion's blood. A lot of it. Isn't that the same?"

"That happens only once, and unless you're into that sort of thing, you don't have to do it again." Lycan laughed but Orion snapped his eyes to him with a sharp glare. "And throw away all of your silver jewelry. It's not deadly for shifters, but we tend to be allergic to it. Notice all our utensils are stainless steel."

"What about the vampires?" I asked, glancing between them. "What's their weakness?"

"The stuff about iron and a stake to the heart is true," Poe said. "Though I prefer ripping their heads off their shoulders."

"And witches?" I said. "Fairies? Other mythical creatures?"

"Witches are real," Poe continued. "They're just as complex as anyone else, some good and some bad."

"I've never met a fairy," Lycan said. "But one of my pack mates swears he met a leprechaun once, and they're fairy-ish."

"I wouldn't trust anything Nix says without seeing it myself," Orion added, biting off a piece of bacon. It made me happy to see color returning to his face while he ate, even if I still worried about the upcoming shift. Perhaps it was his magic inside me or some animalistic drive that wanted to keep him forever, but the thought of him in pain made me want to claw off my own skin. I needed him healthy and safe.

Almost like I'd said it out loud, Orion looked at me and smiled, and the intimacy in our locked gazes reminded me that there were very few barriers between us now. He'd taken me and I'd drank of his magic, and together, we'd created this bright burning affection between us.

I want more, came the voice, unbidden and reckless. But he had the opportunity upstairs to tell me he wanted to do it again, for real this time, and he hadn't. What if this connection was only one sided? What if he'd seen me through the worst of it and believed there was nothing more between us? I hadn't been good enough for him before now. Had anything really changed? I was still a Vanderbilt. He was still a Bastard.

"So what now?" I asked, drawing my own attention away from that complicated situation. "When do we leave for the full moon?"

"I suppose we don't need to leave anymore," Lycan said. "But roaming the woods is always much better than being shut inside. We'll stay close by."

"The snow melted in the last two days," Poe said. "I think it'll be fine to run in the forest."

"Really?" I hadn't even thought to check outside, but when I got up and walked to the door, dread lined my stomach. Poe was regrettably right. What had once piled up to the fifth step on the porch now sank down to the third. In just a short time, it would be nearly gone, which meant the roads would be clear enough for me to go to my SUV...for me to return home.

"You should probably check in with your family," Orion said, and I swallowed against a parched throat as I walked back into the kitchen. "I'm sure they're worried about you, especially since it's been two days."

I forced a grin. "I'll go give them a call right now."

"I'm sure we don't have to tell you to keep this to yourself," Lycan said, narrowing his gaze.

"I told her that," Orion cut in.

"It bears repeating." Lycan crossed his arms and shook his head. "Not even your family. No one can find out. It's the first rule of being a shifter...of being pack."

"Is that what I am now? Pack? Or am I still a Vanderbilt?" I looked between the three of them. "Where's the line?"

Lycan and Poe shifted their attention to Orion.

"Go call your folks," he said instead of answering. "Then we should start to prepare. We'll need to make food and bring extra clothes, even if we plan to stay on Fiver property."

"You got it, boss," Lycan said as I rounded the corner to the stairs and made my way to the second floor. I heard Orion apologize to Lycan again for not believing him about my shifter status, but I shut the door on that because I needed a moment to myself, a moment to wrap my mind around everything that had happened.

My room smelled stale and distinctly human. This new me had a wildness that could have only come from Orion, but standing in what remained of my former self, I couldn't help but think how that person was gone. It had only been ten days, but I was completely different from the girl who had wrecked her SUV. I would run away before I'd marry Marx. I would do whatever I could to rebel against it while still saving my family.

What would the guys do when they found out about Marx and my brother's deal with the Scorpions? I had to figure out how to get out of it. I would tell Orion after the moon and then I would find a new way to help Vanderbilt ranch.

I couldn't deny that I had spent the last two days under some kind of spell, and something had definitely happened to me in the days since I arrived, but a shifter? A fox? Did I really believe in such things?

And hell, Orion had said the transformation would be painful. How painful? My heart started to pound again and I couldn't get enough air into my lungs.

Relax, came that wild voice inside. *Don't freak out. It'll be okay.*

I turned on my phone and winced at the missed calls from my brothers, but I narrowed my eyes on a new text message from Guin.

Guin: I know what happened to you. Call me before the moon rises.

My heart thundered harder as I pressed her contact, bringing the phone to my ear to wait for her to answer. Did she know I was a shifter? Did she know some deeply held family secret?

Admittedly, I'd spent most of my childhood at boarding school or away at summer camp. How well did I know my family, truly? Were my siblings shifters? Lycan said that one was born this way or not. If I had the gene, then my siblings could as well.

Based on that text, she must have suspected something if not outright knew.

"Sol," she said when she answered. "Where are you? Are you okay?"

"I'm fine," I said. "Where are you? I've been trying to get in touch with you for days. Percy has lost his mind, and I got into a car wreck on Bastard territory. I've been staying here, but Guin..." I choked back a sob, all of my emotions from this past week finally catching up to me. I tried not to freak out, but I wasn't doing a very good job. "Things are so messed up."

"I know," she cut in. "You went through your transition, didn't you?"

"What?" I took a deep breath and paused, remembering what Lycan had told me. "How do you know about that?"

"I can feel it," she cut in, "through our family ties. I can't talk long. I'm in Dallas, meeting with the shifters in the Royal Bastards here. I've been trying to research as much as I can about our kind."

"You're a shifter, too," I said, shock rattling through my veins. "How is this possible? How did we not know about this?"

"It's a long story," she said. "Look, I'm working on a plan for Percy, but as soon as the snow melts, you need to go home, or he'll send the cops after you."

I sighed and collapsed on the mattress. "Mae and Ava are covering for me."

"They won't be able to hold him off for very long." She chuckled in a sardonic manner that reminded me of when we were younger and she'd beat up our idiot brother in defense of me and our sisters. "He's such a greedy fuck. We'll figure it out after the moon. Just protect yourself and make it through your shift in one piece. I'll explain everything when I get home."

"How is this possible?" I took a slow, deep breath, attempting to keep my metaphorical wits from going haywire. "How long have you known? Is this real?"

"It's real, Sol," she said.

"You knew. All this time, you knew." I couldn't believe this. The walls of what I knew about my world had started to close in too quickly.

"You're okay," she said. "You're strong. Like me. You'll survive the shift. Just hang in there."

"Okay," I said, blinking back tears as relief sank in my chest. "Thank you. I may not have always said it, but I'm so thankful to have you as my sister."

"Yeah, you too, kiddo." Then she hung up.

When the sun dropped low, we headed into the woods. The snow had melted to only knee deep, and I feared that, by the time we returned in the morning, the roads would be clear enough to travel.

Despite the lore that Orion and Lycan had spent most of the day explaining, I still expected to wander out to the forest, only for nothing to happen. But that couldn't be true. My so-called *shifter side* brewed in my molecules, racing through my veins with a primitive drive that I'd never experienced before. My body temperature ran hotter, and I didn't need as many clothes to stay warm in the cold winter air.

Orion walked next to me as Lycan led us to a clearing about a mile away from the cabin.

"Will I still be me?" I asked, gulping against a sudden panic. My stomach churned with anticipation, the way it felt before getting on a roller coaster or jumping off a high dive. There existed the possibility that this could end badly, but that dread mixed with the almost certainty that it would be okay, pulsing adrenaline under my skin.

"You'll still know you're you, but it'll be harder to ignore the wild side of things." Orion touched my lower back, guiding me ahead of him, and the simple connection relieved some of the tightness in my chest. With Orion here, I could do anything...be anything.

"In case this doesn't work out," I said, "it's been wonderful spending this time with you."

"Don't talk like that, Princess," Orion said, turning toward me. He cupped my face and leaned down to kiss my forehead, conveying so much comfort and kindness in that one move. The tenderness his touch echoed down my torso and the back of my legs, curling my toes. The part of his magic that still swirled in my veins danced, wanting to wrap itself in his arms and never let go again.

"This should be good," Lycan said, glancing around at the snow-covered trees and darkening sky. "We're still close enough to the Fiver to protect the animals if anything happens, but far enough away not to scare them."

He tilted his head to the side and cracked his neck, closing his blue eyes to presumably allow his wolf to take over. He started to yank his clothes off and Poe toed the back of his boots to do the same.

I turned to Orion, taking my cues from him. He nodded and pulled his shirt overhead, so I did the same. I stripped out of my jeans and T-shirt, folding them into a nice little pile and placing them next to the pack of food and water that Orion had brought.

"Come back to this spot when the sun rises," Orion said. "And for the love of God, leave the natural wolves alone."

"Honestly, I don't plan to leave your side," I said with a smile, wrapping my arms around myself to protect my modesty, but it didn't seem like Lycan and Poe had any concerns about that. I figured that I should get over it if I ever hoped to turn with the pack.

"You'll be okay, baby girl," Orion murmured, wrapping an arm around my neck to pull me in. I hugged him and moaned when his scalding skin touched mine, that same electrifying tether sizzling over my body.

I wanted to tell him how grateful I was for him, how much I

needed him now that I'd discovered who I truly was, but I caught sight of the moon low on the horizon and all words stopped. It hung so beautiful there...so radiant and full...so mesmerizing.

I stepped away from Orion when a yank in my stomach punched down my spine, knocking my knees out from under me. I dropped to all fours as fire erupted through my veins, boiling me from the inside out. Groaning, I looked up for Orion, but he, too, was in the grips of his shift. He'd also sunk to the ground, the massive expanse of his ribs rising and falling as he groaned. I tried to remember what they'd told me, that focusing on my breath would get me through it, but the pain overwhelmed my senses. Arching my back into the mind-numbing agony, I zeroed in on that ethereal presence in the sky, that ever present moon that would now dictate my life in ways I'd never imagined.

I'd never been so entranced, so out of control of my own actions, and it terrified me.

Calm down, that animalistic voice said. *Give over to me. Let me take it.*

No, I couldn't. I needed to stay in command of myself. I didn't want to be someone else. I didn't want to lose my mind to a strange, alien creature.

It's okay, it said. *Trust me.*

Unable to withstand it any longer, I wilted into its blinding fury. Flames burned up the back of my esophagus and I heaved on the forest floor, wishing that the contents of my stomach would move so that I'd feel better. But when I glanced down at the ground, I blinked in horror at the sight of my skin sliding from my arms. My face screamed, and I spat out what I thought was vomit, but nearly wretched again when I recognized it as my teeth. My tongue went next, and I pushed it out onto the bloody pile forming on the snowy ground.

Pressure built behind my eyes and I clenched them shut to alleviate it, but the agony grew too intense. When I opened them again, my vision flickered as they popped out of my head onto the pile, replaced by my new animal eyes. *Fox eyes.* I gasped, desperate to fill my lungs with crisp air as my flesh melted from my bones, twisting and reforming. My skull stretched, unhinging my jaw as a soft furry muzzle pushed its way out of my throat, replacing what had once been my face.

I rolled onto my back as my body convulsed, splintering and breaking apart to rebuild around new tissue that hadn't been there moments ago. Claws erupted from my fingertips, chipping my nails and cracking my flesh into long stringy threads that fell away as russet paws took their place.

Give over to me, the fox said. *Give over.*

Relenting, I tried to hold back my panic as my legs cracked, my knees bending backward to form my new hindquarters, accommodating the rear end of the beast. All I knew was the agony, the pain and torture of the Call. The moon had me, the fox had me, and I could no longer deny the fact that this was *real.* I was a shifter, for better or worse, and the damage was irreversible. I couldn't resist anymore, maybe I never could.

Perhaps I would die like this; perhaps it was better for me to disappear into the woods and never return to my former life. Death had finally come knocking at my door, and all I had to do was answer.

Let it take me. Let it end here.

Just when I'd surrendered to the possibility that my life was over, the suffering shifted into something...*more.* Something blissful and euphoric. My lungs cleared, allowing me to suck in sweet, delicious winter oxygen, and my fox's gaze caught on the moon again. The beautiful, powerful moon. Ever changing. Ever calling. Ever calming.

It's okay, the fox side of me said. *We're okay.*

A warm muzzle nudged at my cheek, giving a little yip before touching me again. I rolled over onto all fours and tried to stand, my shaking legs giving out on me so I fell flat on my face. I glanced at the big obsidian wolf staring at me with clear blue eyes, and he prodded me again, pulling his lips back into a grin as he lolled his tongue out of the side of his mouth.

So I tried once more, this time feeling more stable as I took a step. When I had my balance, I looked over my shoulder to my long, bushy tail, half the same color as my coat and the other half matching the snow, and gave it a test wag. Even that seemed instinctual, like thinking too much about it would only make it harder for me.

Yes, the fox said. *Yes. Yes!*

I threw my head back and yipped with excitement, pouncing around in the snow before sitting back on my haunches to launch myself at Orion's massive furry form. He was so much bigger than me, but that didn't seem to matter when I leaped onto my back feet and scratched at his face with my front claws. He pointed his muzzle up at the moon and let out a loud, yawning howl that echoed through the forest. Lycan, now in the form of a big white wolf, joined in, followed by Poe, who had a deep chestnut coat nearly the same color as his human hair. I tried to howl like the wolves, but my noises were more high-pitched and screeching.

When it was over, I leaned down on my forearms and stuck my butt in the air, wagging my tail from one side to the other, an open invitation to play. Orion chuffed and turned away, pretending to ignore me. But the bond between us flowed more deeply now that we were in animal form, and I could tell he'd only done it to be sassy.

Fine then. There was so much else to explore, and I used my new fox nose to smell around the forest. Everything was richer and more amazing. I sniffed along the edge of the clearing, savoring the exquisite wonder of all that nature had to offer. Rabbits and squirrels had burrowed themselves deep for the night, and a few coyotes lingered downwind, perhaps having heard the commotion from our shift and deciding to stick around in case they wanted to investigate.

But it was too much excitement for me to stay still. I raced through the snow as fast as my legs could carry me, jumping over fallen logs and pouncing off trees while I waited for the others to catch up. Lycan indulged my more playful side. He kept up with me, bumping my body with his in an attempt to get me to race. I knew he'd win as he had much longer legs, but that wasn't the point.

Together, we took off into the brush, slinging snow and mud behind us as we ran. I yelled and squeaked, and the thrill of it was so addictive that I didn't think I ever wanted to turn back to human. If the transformation wasn't so traumatic, I'd turn into a fox every night.

I lost track of how long we ran through the woods like that, but being so carefree lifted a heavy weight off my heart. I'd finally found my place in the world, and when I backtracked to saddle up next to Orion's heavy form, I realized it was by his side.

"Having fun?" came his deep, rustic voice inside my head.

I widened my eyes and chirped louder. *"We can talk like this?"*

"Not with everyone," he said. *"But you and I have a special connection."*

"Because of the transition?" I rubbed my body against his, purring when his decadent, heady scent plumed around me and inside me. It marked me as his as much as my scent marked him as mine.

"Sure, little fox," he said, but even then, I sensed that he wasn't being completely honest with me...that there was more to our connection that he hadn't yet shared.

"I love it," I said, my heart pounding as he shoved me with a shoulder and gave me a small bite on the rump. I jumped and turned to face him, leaning down again, hoping that he might take the bait and enjoy a little play.

He did, returning the position before setting off ahead of me to instigate a game of chase. I tore after him, my feet pounding into the snow, and I let out huffs of laughter, my joy nearly overflowing in my soul. I wanted more. I wanted everything.

The transformation back to my human form took more out of me. It was like the initial shift but reversed, leaving me exhausted and on the edge of tears. We found our way back to the clearing, where I lay down next to Orion and shook my body until my fur exploded into nothingness. My bones cracked and reformed, stretching into the shape I'd taken for twenty-five years. The pain was excruciating, and I was suddenly thankful it only happened once a month.

When it was over, I blinked against the brightening sky, the rays of sunshine radiating through the tree line like heaven itself had touched our little slice of paradise. The snow had melted even more overnight, and now blades of grass popped out of the top like tiny dials counting down my imminent return to normalcy.

Lycan and Poe stood first, ambling over to the spot where we'd stashed our clothes, but Orion put an arm over my waist and pulled my back to his chest, burying his nose in my hair.

"You smell like flowers in the summertime," he murmured, and I glanced over my shoulder to see him smiling down at me. Turning in his embrace, I nuzzled my head under his chin and breathed him in deep, relishing the strange comfort that came with his scent.

"You smell like trees and sweat and outside."

He laughed and kissed my temple, running his lips over the bridge of my nose before using his to tilt my face up. I kissed him and sighed into the sensations that tingled down my spine, the very essence of him inside me singing with intimacy.

"C'mon, you disgusting lovebirds," Lycan called, tossing my boots closer to my body.

"I guess we ought to go," I murmured.

Orion nodded and rolled onto his knees before helping me into a sitting position. Aside from feeling like I'd put my body through a few marathons, I didn't mind this part of the shift. The worst was over, and now that the call of the moon had ebbed, my fox had retreated further in my mind.

"It gets easier," he said, "once you're used to it."

"I'm glad you were here," I said, smiling.

"Yeah, me too." He nodded toward the others. "Let's get back to the cabin."

We dressed and ate our sandwiches while we eased our way back to the Fiver, all four of us aching and limping. When we got there, I'd never been so happy to see such a tiny house. It smelled like fire and *us* inside, and the comfort of it unfurled heat in my gut. I never wanted to leave, not even after the snow melted.

Orion intertwined his fingers in mine and led me upstairs to his room, refusing to break contact until I'd collapsed in his bed. Even then, he allowed the separation for as long as it took him to undo the laces on my boots, remove them, and kick off his own. Then, he wrapped his massive body around me, pulled me in tight, and relented to his exhaustion. Truthfully, I didn't know how he'd made it through the whole night. He'd looked like a wreck after helping me through my transition, and though he emerged from the shift without his wounds, like he said he would, I couldn't imagine how tired he must have been.

It irritated me that the bite marks were gone, but as I drifted off to sleep, I told myself I'd just have to make them again...as soon as we got some rest. In my dreams, Orion chased me through the woods in wolf form. I ran as fast as I could, my little fox legs working hard to carry me through the undergrowth. When he caught me, he latched his massive jaw around my throat and held me down, forcing me to submit. I did with mirth and joy in my heart, knowing that he wouldn't hurt me, that this was the game. Our game. Our dance.

Pleasure echoed up my body and brought me back to reality some time later, and a massive hand had replaced his teeth on my windpipe. I gasped as a long, warm tongue speared through my pussy, a hot, decadent mouth latching on to my clit with an unrelenting suck.

"Orion," I groaned, arching my back into the touch.

I reached under the blankets to tunnel my hands through his thick hair, and he laughed against my skin.

"Someone's finally awake," he said before giving me another languid lick. "Good morning, baby girl."

"Good morning," I murmured, rolling my pelvis against his face. Tendrils of lust sparked over my skin, and I wondered how long he'd been at it before I woke because I was terribly close to coming already. I pushed the covers down so I could watch him, and the sight of his dark head between my legs nearly shoved me off the edge into oblivion. He glanced up at me with eyes gone to his wolf, his sky blue irises reflecting in the afternoon sun.

It was more than just the physical sensations of my nerves being lit on fire. He was in my veins, my very soul igniting with wanton desire, my blood singing for him. Echoes of his magic inside me bubbled to the surface, and I gasped, sensing both him and me in my molecules. I didn't end at the edge of my skin. No. I existed in him. He existed in me. And the feeling was so familiar and foreign at the same time, it overwhelmed my senses.

My animal nature took over, the side of me that had connected so deeply to him, and my canines elongated in my mouth as my orgasm ripped through me. I held his head where I wanted it the most, and he dove in with a fury, devouring me like his favorite meal. He wrapped his lips around my sensitive skin, sucking me, nibbling gently with his teeth while flicking my clit with his tongue. Nothing had ever felt so good, and no partner had ever been able to anticipate what I wanted better than him.

The rush of hormones had barely subsided before Orion pulled his lips back over his teeth, flashing his long canines and sinking them down on the inside of my thigh. I hissed in a breath at the stab of agony, but it quickly turned to pleasure when he pulled away, and I saw the marks left behind.

"Do you like that, Princess?" he asked as he swiped a long lick over the bite with a low purr in his chest. "There's no more hiding from me, no more running."

"I like it." I bit my bottom lip as I grinned, luxuriating in the thought of us belonging to each other in ways that had never occurred to me before coming here, before learning what I was.

"You better," he said, crawling up my body to put his hands on either side of my ribs. I allowed myself the indulgence of touching his skin, raking my fingers up his spine to the muscles on his chest and abs. He was so beautiful, it nearly brought me to tears.

"Good," I said, using my body weight to flip us so he was under me and my legs were on either side of his stomach. "Because there are some things I've been wanting to do."

He raised his eyebrows, giving me a wicked grin that sent chills down my spine. "Yeah?"

"Yeah." I pressed a kiss to his mouth before moving over his beard to his throat, pausing at his pulse point to lick and taste the skin there. His scent permeated the space between us, thick and heady and mixed with a new darkness that seemed reserved just for me, just for times like this. I sucked on the skin harder, pressing in my canines so that they left an imprint the same as he'd done to my thigh.

"Fuck yes," he said, grabbing the back of my head to hold me there while he arched under me. "Mark me, baby girl."

I did. I made little love bites all the way down his chest, staring up at him while I descended. He never took his eyes off me, crossing one arm under his head while he ran the other through my tangled ginger hair. When I got to his stomach, I peppered the skin under his belly button with licks and soft kisses, purposely ignoring his perfect cock, which stood straight and hard and begging for attention.

I teased the area around it—his thighs, his groin, the indents on his hips making a perfect arrow toward the tortured flesh.

"Princess," he groaned, bucking his hips toward my face, but I grinned and kept going, raking my claws down the insides of his legs, leaving red welts that pleased the fox. Anyone who dared get close to this skin would see them and know I'd been here before... that I'd claimed him.

I grabbed his cock, finally pressing a tender kiss to the tip before daring to give him a firm lick. He groaned and threw his head back, the movement of his Adam's apple as he swallowed urging me on. I swiped my tongue over the whole thing this time, root to tip, and he growled, clamping his fingers harder in my hair.

"Fuck, you've been wanting to do this for days?" He moaned when I nodded and took the whole thing in my mouth, sucking him back nearly to the edge of my throat before rising up to let him go with a loud *pop*.

"Since you rescued me from the wolves." I laughed when he shook his head and made a noise of frustration, but that was the reaction I wanted. I kept going, paying attention to the noises he made, and when I dropped to the swollen knot at the base of his cock, swirling my tongue around the thick, angry flesh, nuzzling my nose against it while I kissed his balls, he panted, and his legs trembled next to my head.

That really turned me on, the slick between my legs so evident that it dripped down either side of my thighs. That, too, would take some getting used to, and even though I'd just climaxed a few moments ago, I wanted more of him. I wanted to do it again.

"Fuck, right there, baby girl. Keep going. Make me come. God, your mouth is amazing. Everything about you is amazing." The words echoed in my head like they had when we were shifted, and I nearly stopped to ask him why we could still hear each other. But I'd never been one to disobey an order like that. So I kept lapping at his knot, alternating between that and swallowing him down deep. Tears came to my eyes as I gagged around him, tightening my throat when I slotted him in as far as he would go.

It pleased me that I could have such control over him, that I could bring a powerful man to the brink of shaking and pleading. And just when he'd been about to release, he yanked my head off him and sat up to kiss me, grabbing me by the back of the legs so he could maneuver me up his body. He lined himself up at my entrance and I sank all the way down, wincing at the soft ache between my legs. It had only been two days since my transition, and the shift hadn't healed me all the way. But that didn't matter. Once he was fully seated inside me, I rocked against him, the friction amplifying our connection.

"Look at me," he said, and I wrapped my arms around his neck while I stared in his eyes. They were so clear, I thought I could see straight through to his soul. He fucked up into me, thrusting his hips while he held me, our bodies fiery against each other. "You're such a good little princess. You take me so well."

"I love it," I whispered, throwing my head back as another climax threatened to yank me under its terrible weight. "More. More."

He growled again, this time lower and deeper, before latching on to my throat and digging his teeth in, not hard enough to break the skin, but enough to leave a mark.

Oh, how I wanted him to do it for real. How I wanted him to draw blood again, to lap at my life force and feel our magic intertwine the way it had when I'd been under the grips of the change. It was still in me, and when another orgasm clenched through my body, seizing my muscles and forcing me to bear down on him, he found his own release.

He came inside me, filling me with his essence once again, his knot swelling thick and heavy, hitting pleasure centers I didn't even know I had. It was so arousing that even after the apex of our shared pleasure ended, I continued to ride him, to rock my hips back and forth, searching for more.

He hissed through his teeth and stared up at me, clamping his fingers around my hips to slow me down.

"Patience, baby girl," he said with a laugh. I marveled at the sight of his long, sharp canines and ran my fingers over their magnificent length. He let me, moaning out a soft hum when I touched the pointed tip.

"Are they sensitive?" I watched with amazement as he opened his jaw wider to let me explore.

He nodded and hummed a soft approval.

"Sorry," I said, dropping my hand to his shoulder. "I didn't mean to hurt—"

"You can touch me anywhere, anytime you want," he said. "My fangs, my claws, my knot, all of it is for you."

"Such things you say." I let out a sad sigh as reality crashed back around me, remembering that we only had a day...maybe two... before I had to go back to my Vanderbilt mansion and deal with my evil older brother.

"I'm serious," he murmured, lying back on the bed and bringing me down with him so my head rested just under his chin.

We'd be stuck like this for a few more moments until his knot loosened to let me go. But truthfully, I didn't want that. I wanted to stay in this bed with him forever. I rolled my hips against him again, squeezing my internal muscles as I grinned up at his response.

"We have to go downstairs sometime," he said. "We have work to do."

"Hmm." I pushed myself up, pressing my hands into his stomach so I could rock my pelvis, shifting him inside me so he hit that soft, sensitive spot that made me gasp and throw my head back again.

"Fuck," he said, running a hand up my stomach, between my breasts, and latching on to my throat. "You're going to wring me dry."

"I hope so."

With a wicked grin, he flipped us over so he could rut into me, swiveling his hips in a teasing prod that turned me insatiable for him.

I knew what was happening, even as I tried to rebel against it. She was the enemy, a Vanderbilt, the spawn of the man that killed my family. I should have hated her. I should have bucked against the instinctual pull inside me.

But every day that went by after she crashed into that tree, I grew more attached. After her transition and the intimacy of our shift together, I could no longer deny that she completed me in ways I'd never imagined. She brought out the playfulness in me, a side I thought died with my parents, and I grounded her in reality, bringing her down from her life of privilege to how the world truly worked.

Mine, roared the wolf inside my head. *Mine. Ours.*

Fuck, that thought should have scared me more than it did, but I couldn't get enough of her. After we both came, our hormones finally settled to a point where I could think clearly. I rolled off her and collapsed against the bed, wrapping an arm under her shoulders to pull her closer. She draped an arm over my stomach and rested her head on my chest, our combined contentment settling deep in my gut.

I reveled in that intoxicating strawberry floral fragrance that set my wolf to pacing. It had mixed with oak and wood and something distinctly *me*. My scent...my *bonding* scent...had etched itself into her molecules, emanating from deep inside her body.

She smiled and nuzzled her head under my chin, rubbing her tight little body firmer against me, which got my cock's attention. It pulsed again, despite the fact that I'd just gotten done having her.

Fuck, will I ever stop wanting her?

It seemed not because she noticed and glanced up at me with that devious grin.

"Ry, what if I wanted you to mark me...for real? How..." She cleared her throat and bit her bottom lip, making me want to dig my own teeth into that delicate flesh. "How would that work?"

"Hmm." My wolf liked the thought of her wearing my teeth imprint permanently. "So eager for a love bite, huh?"

She leaned forward and lapped her tongue over my pulse, and the touch sizzled through my body, electrifying my nerves and clenching in my balls. I'd had her multiple times already, but I could not stop myself from groaning and giving in to my own gluttony.

"Please," she said. "Tell me how it works. Tell me everything."

"It's easy," I explained, wrapping my fingers in her hair and giving it a firm tug so she sat up and faced me. "Once our primal sides agree on the mating, I'll need to nip you hard enough to break the skin right"—I ran a finger over her collarbone to the part where her trapezius muscle met her neck—"there. My saliva will mix with your pheromones and leave a scar. After that, you'll smell like my scent forever, even if we've spent weeks apart."

That sent me into a tailspin that I didn't want to think about. I needed to be near her. Having her in my bed made all the nights without her seem worth it, and when I woke up after the moon with her flowery feminine scent buried deep in my nose, I thanked whatever fates had brought her into my life. Without that crash, we would have never gotten as close as we did, and I would have never known what it was to be so close to someone else.

I wanted to sink my teeth into her skin to make it permanent, to do all the things I told her about, but now that we were so connected, I sensed her trepidation even more than I had before her transition. Something held me back, something I couldn't put my finger on. It had to do with her being a Vanderbilt, with why her family hadn't been more eager to rescue her from this situation. Did she not tell them the truth about her whereabouts? If not, why had she lied? Was it to protect us...or herself? And if it was to protect herself, what had made her so scared?

I remembered thinking she'd been hiding something when she first got here, and I couldn't shake the thought Isolde was still keeping something from me. Until I knew what it was, I couldn't trust her completely. If I marked her, it would be permanent...even more so than whatever we had now. In a few weeks, my magic would be gone from her blood, and until we sealed the mating, we *might* be able to go our separate ways.

My wolf, on the other hand, snarled at that idea. He'd already made up his mind about her, no matter what.

"Would I get to bite you, too?" Her eyes lit up with excitement, and a thrill of anticipation shot through our connection.

I chuckled and shifted my hips under her, brushing my quickly growing cock up against her soft, warm cunt.

"Of course, little fox," I said, my tone dropping deeper as my beast came to the forefront of my mind. He, of course, *loved* the idea of her sinking her cute dainty teeth into my neck and claiming me for life. But I needed to be patient, to make sure I knew exactly what I was getting into.

"Can we do it now?" Her amber eyes shimmered in the afternoon light, and she moved against me, wiggling so close, all of our skin was connected from chest to toes. The delicious tangy scent of her arousal rose up between us, and I took a deep inhale, my mouth watering at the thought she got off on wanting to bite me. "Can we?"

"It's a ritual," I said, grabbing her hips to try to slow her down. "We need Kodiak to bless the union—"

"Bless the union?" She raised her eyebrows. "Why do we need his approval?"

"I'm a member of his pack. I'm the VP of the Royal Bastards." Despite it all, a part of me loved her impatience, like she couldn't wait to get her greedy paws on all that she could have. I wrestled with the same impatience myself. "Waiting for Kodiak is a part of the deal."

"Okay, if you insist," she said, letting out a small, comfortable sigh. "I never want to leave this bed."

"Hmm." I chuckled and kissed the top of her head. "The work at the Fiver doesn't stop just because we're fucking."

"Hmm," she said, mocking my own hum. "You smell good."

"Yeah?" I rubbed my nose against her head until she looked up at me, where I leaned down to kiss her. "So do you."

"We're starting to smell the same," she said. "Is that normal?"

"Uh-huh," I replied, curling my lips into a grin. "It's normal for us."

"Why?" Furrowing her brows, she glanced up at me with curiosity dancing behind her eyes. "Because we're fucking?"

She deserved the truth, didn't she? I wanted to tell her. But could I trust her?

I took a deep breath and decided it was now or never. I needed to voice my concerns and be out with it, no matter the truth, no matter the reason. Whatever it was, I'd have to deal with it. A shifter only mated once, and they mated for life. It was part of the evolutionary drive to find the most suitable partner and breed. The combination of her magic and mine would make powerful cubs, if we decided we wanted that sort of thing.

"Little fox, why hasn't your family come to get you?" I glanced at her and watched as she shifted her gaze to the tiny space between us, pulling her body away. I reached out to touch her chin and force her face toward me. "What are you hiding?"

"How do you know I'm hiding something?" Her voice cracked, and another rush of rotten nerves radiated from her into my chest, hitting me in the gut. I smelled it in the air, tangy and salty with her sweat.

"I can sense it." I shook my head. "Whatever it is, it's better if you tell me rather than keep it a secret any longer."

She took a deep breath and dug her palms into her eyes, her cheeks turning a bright shade of rose as she exhaled on a sob. "I'm supposed to be engaged."

If an asteroid had suddenly dropped out of the sky and slammed me into the earth, it would have surprised me less.

"What?" The word came out as a growl, and she snapped her gaze up to mine, tears beginning to streak down her cheeks.

"I don't want to be," she confessed, "and as soon as I get home, I'm going to figure out how to get out of it. It was arranged by my stupid brother, and I hate it. I hate everything about it." She told me about how her father had died, and their ranch hands refused to work for a man they didn't trust. I didn't blame them. Her brother sounded like a fucking prick, and the longer she spoke, the more solidly that opinion formed in my head. He'd made a deal with the Bloody Scorpions, and in exchange, those fucking leeches had demanded her as a sacrifice.

I knew what they wanted to do with her. They'd change her into one of them, make her a vampire in service to them for the rest of eternity. And if not, they'd turn her into a thrall, a human servant addicted to feeding them her blood.

Not that any of that was possible now. Shifters and vampires notoriously didn't get along, and if they got a hold of this new version of her, they'd spend days getting high on her blood, draining her slowly for their own pleasure.

"He wanted to marry me as soon as the snow melted," she said, wiping the tears off her cheeks.

"Well, that's not fucking happening now," I roared, barely able to keep my canines from extending in my rage. "Why didn't you tell me?"

"I'm sorry," she said, sitting up and twisting the blankets under her arms to cover herself. "I didn't think it would matter before the moon, and now that I know what I am...*who* I am...I was waiting for the right time."

Fury boiled in my blood from both the fact she'd withheld this massive secret and that her brother could do such a horrible thing to his own family. Of course, he didn't know the Scorpions were vampires, just like he didn't know his own sister had turned into a shifter and now she had a pack behind her. How could he? The one thing both vampires and shifters agreed on was keeping the public out of our business.

"Orion," she pleaded. "Say something. Please. Say you understand. Say you forgive me. Anything but silence."

"Stop," I snapped, perhaps too aggressively because she hissed and grimaced and icy-hot fear echoed down our bond. "I should have known this was too good to be true."

I sat up and swung my legs over the side of the bed, taking a deep breath to try to settle the fire in my gut. I wanted to fucking hunt down her brother and strangle him. I wanted to find the leader of the bloodsucking Scorpions and rip his head clear off his shoulders, regardless of how it might escalate the war between our families. I wanted to tear the bond with Isolde out of my chest and shred it to pieces.

"I've felt terrible about holding this in," she continued. "I didn't know how to tell you. I didn't know what to say. I was hoping I could deal with it when I got home, and it wouldn't matter."

I'd had trouble trusting people all my life, and now that I'd found someone who could be my mate, she'd been lying to me since I met her. Perhaps it was the fading essence of the moon or the lingering exhaustion from her transition, but when she tried to grab my arm to get my attention, I ripped it away from her and stood.

"Ry," she whimpered, her eyes red with tears, her cheeks blushed as her shame spread to us both. "Please."

"You know the Bastards and the Scorpions are enemies," I

snarled. "You know this makes everything more complicated. How am I supposed to bring you into the pack now?"

"What—what are you saying?" Her shattering heart punched me in the gut, nearly making my knees shake.

"I'm saying you should have been honest with me from the start." My voice boomed off the walls as I struggled to contain the wrath scalding through my nerves.

She hung her mouth open and blinked, perhaps trying to come to an understanding about the whole thing herself. Then a spiraling inferno replaced that confusion, and she glared up at me.

"You're the one to talk," she said, crawling out of bed to grab a pair of sweats and yank them up her legs. "Just being around you turned my entire world upside down."

"That's not my fault," I said. "If it were up to me, I would have protected you from all this. I would have sent you home as soon as I could or left you in your—"

I cut myself off before I said something I didn't mean. But she caught the gist of it anyway because her features turned to stone, and she grabbed a shirt off the floor, pulling it over her head.

"So, this was all for nothing, wasn't it? The bonding scent and your magic in my blood." She wiped at her eyes and shook her head, and I clenched my hands into fists to keep from going to her and wrapping her in my arms. I *hated* that I hurt her, and I hated this sudden separation even more.

But if she could lie to me about this for so long, what else could she be lying about? And if I let her in, how long would I have her before Marx came for her and put the whole pack in danger as a result?

When Kodiak found out, he could force me to reject her. I'd disobeyed an order from the alpha, and it had ramifications that could destroy our entire life in Helena. He'd be within his rights to command me never to see her again, and I'd have to make a choice: my mate or my pack. Sitting there in that moment, I wasn't sure which one I would choose. My pack was my family, but Isolde...She was just some girl I'd met twelve days ago, some girl that had snuck under my skin and ripped my soul to shreds. I knew I shouldn't have trusted her. I knew I shouldn't have trusted *this*.

There were too many variables, too many things to be pissed about.

"I'll never be good enough for you, will I?" She let out a deep sob and grabbed a hoodie next, slipping it over her arms. "I'll never be good enough for anyone."

She went for the door and yanked it open, stomping into the hall before going into her room. I thought she'd slam the door behind her and cool off alone. But a moment later, she emerged with her purse and soiled clothes, the only things she had on her the night of the crash.

Stop her, the wolf screamed. *Stop her. Stop this.*

But I didn't. Orion, the man, had to protect both beast and human from any further complications. I needed a moment to get my temper under control, to clear my head so I could think clearly about what to do. But things were slipping through my fingers like quicksand, and my rage got the better of me.

No, the wolf howled. *No!*

"Lycan," Isolde called as she stormed down the stairs.

"Well, good morning, your worshipfulness," Lycan said. "What's wrong?"

"Can you take me home?" Her broken voice and sputtered request launched me into action. I grabbed a pair of jeans, stuffed my legs into them, and followed her downstairs, where I found both Poe and Lycan staring at her while she clutched at her midsection.

"What the fuck did you do?" Lycan snarled, shifting his mean gaze to me.

"It's not his fault," Isolde said. "Please...please can you just take me—"

She never got the rest of it out because the front door slammed open to reveal an angry six-foot-seven figure with a deep, raging glare.

"Orion!" Kodiak snarled, and he was pissed.

Orion

"Oh, fuck," Lycan murmured, grimacing as he stepped closer to Poe.

"Silence," Kodiak said, taking a deep breath as he walked toward us. He immediately took up space, commanding the tiny Fiver with his massive body and his intense presence. There was a reason he was alpha. He was the strongest and the most intimidating, and when he set all that on me, I had to force myself not to squirm under his glare. "Imagine my surprise when I go into the shift with fifty-three pack members and come out with fifty-four."

I probably should have felt guilty. I probably should have dropped to my knees and begged for his forgiveness. But aside from being my alpha, Kodiak was my oldest friend in the world. We were born only a few months apart. Our fathers had been friends before us. We had lived together, raised hell together, and God willing, we'd die together. He didn't scare me, and that was the reason I was his second in command, his veep. I was the only one in the pack that could say that.

His penetrating crimson gaze flitted from me to Isolde to Lycan and Poe before coming back to the girl. "Isolde Vanderbilt, I presume."

She cleared her throat and nodded, taking a step forward to hold out her hand. "I'm guessing you're the alpha."

Kodiak stared at it, pulling his lips into a ghost of a smile.

"Yes, it is quite a pleasure to meet a new member of my pack." He shifted his hard eyes to me. "Especially when I haven't even agreed to their admittance."

"Kod—" I tried.

"I said shut the fuck up," Kodiak snarled. I shifted my shoulders, my wolf bucking against the command. I wouldn't challenge him, especially not in front of two other members of the MC. If it came to blows, that would happen alone—when it was just the two of us and we could be friends instead of alpha and second.

"Not that it matters anymore, but it wasn't his fault," Isolde said. "He didn't know I was a shifter. I didn't know I was a shifter. It all happened so fast."

"Poe," Kodiak said, and my pack mate stepped forward, coming to the alpha's side. "Take Ms. Vanderbilt home. Her family has been looking for her."

She hesitated and looked at me, as if waiting for me to argue with him for her. Or hell, maybe just to say goodbye. But after what happened, after what she'd revealed, it seemed too little too late.

She's our mate, my wolf whined, *Go to her.*

But I didn't. The inferno from our argument still burned in my gut, and I wasn't sure how I felt about it or what I would do next. So I stood there with my jaw squared and my eyes burning into her. My wolf bucked against my restraint, clawing my insides, making my conflict even more unimaginable.

When I didn't move, she shook her head and let out a sad, sarcastic laugh.

"Just like a Bastard," she said. "Fucking coward."

Kodiak growled low in his chest as Lycan's jaw dropped and Poe sucked in a gasp. No one in the pack dared talk like that, not in front of the alpha, but she wasn't just anyone. She was the second's mate, emboldened by my magic. Even if I'd had a tiny passing thought about trying to reject it, it took a special shifter to stand by me. If I wasn't about to face down my best friend's wrath in the face of her secrets, I might have been proud of her.

"Ms. Vanderbilt," Kodiak said, turning to her with his arms crossed. "Our families have been at odds for over two decades. I understand you've mated my second and you're potentially a new member of the pack, but listen closely. No one disrespects my kin and lives to see the next moon. You'll do well to pick your next words wisely."

"I'm not his mate. He doesn't want me." She raised her chin and took a step toward him, shooting daggers out of her stare. "But do your worst, alpha. Tear my heart out. Eat it in front of your pack. What more could happen at this point?"

With one last heartbreaking look at me, she hugged herself tighter and walked out the front door. Poe gave me a sympathetic look before following her, but Lycan shot me an angry side-eye. Then he, too, walked outside.

Kodiak raised an eyebrow and nodded toward the porch. Ignoring the tight ache in my chest and the simmering fury echoing down the bonds from both him and Isolde, I gulped against a dry throat and followed him. He stomped down the steps to the muddy ground, the snow having melted to nearly nothing during the day.

The alpha waited until the truck disappeared down the driveway before setting his hard stare on me.

"What the fuck are you thinking?" he roared, the full brunt of his anger sizzling through the connection between us, igniting my own. "Mating a Vanderbilt?"

"Let me explain." I held up a hand.

"You better start talking."

"She went into her transition," I started. "She was latent. Hell, probably all of the Vanderbilts are."

"I told you to keep your fucking hands off her," he growled, his eyes shifting to a bright crimson red, the same color as his wolf. He pulled his lips over his teeth, baring his fangs to me, bigger and longer than even mine.

My wolf recognized the threat at the same time that he recognized the alpha's dominance. He wanted to fight Kodiak to prove how much Isolde meant to him, to me, to us. But at the same time, the pull of the alpha's order speared through my chest, and I had to keep my feet firmly planted so I didn't back up.

If I did, that would admit defeat. If I moved an inch, Kodiak would take a mile.

"She needed my help," I said, holding his stare so he'd know I was serious. "What was I supposed to do? Let her die?"

"You should have told me the truth," he said.

"I didn't mean to disobey you," I said. "I tried to hold off as long as I could."

"Yes, you're a knight in shining armor." He took another step toward me, bringing his face threateningly close to mine. "Do you want a medal for managing to keep your dick in your pants for a whole week?"

Despite how upset I was with her for keeping her business with the Scorpions from me, my wolf's pride wouldn't stand for anyone talking about her like she was just a warm hole. I shoved his shoulders with a menacing snarl. He pushed me back hard enough to send me stumbling a few feet. But that set off my feral side, and I howled, racing toward him so I could shove a shoulder into his gut and take him down to the ground. Agony exploded through my face when he swung on me, hitting me square in the jaw. Ringing echoed through my ears, and I tilted to the side, giving him enough leeway to roll me off him and slam an elbow into my gut. I wilted, but I'd always been quicker to rebound, and I rammed my fist into his cheek, but it barely did anything.

He was the alpha, and he had the strength of the entire pack at his disposal. He could pull on any of them, all of them, even me if he wanted. Alpha could suck the strength right out of my bones. I'd given him that permission when I'd sworn my allegiance to him and sealed the bond between us.

He snapped his gaze back to me, eyes gone red to the wolf, canines fully dropped, claws shooting out of his fingers. He swiped at me, close enough to sting but not hard enough to draw blood, and I blocked, using my legs to wrestle his weight off me. We'd been sparring like this since we were kids, and he knew my weaknesses. That, of course, made me painfully aware of his. I went for the solar plexus, ramming my fist into his side, but he came back harder, nailing me in the cheek once...twice...a third time, hard enough to have me gasping and lying in the snow while I tried to see straight.

"Stay down," he snarled. "It's over. You did wrong. You know it."

I nodded and admitted defeat, pushing myself up into a sitting position as I wiped blood off my chin. I'd bitten my tongue, and he'd split my lips open, but other than that, it wasn't anything he hadn't done to me before. I deserved it, after all.

"Give me some credit," I finally said when he sat down next to me. "I can't withstand the mating call any more than anyone else."

"She's a fucking Vanderbilt, Orion." His words were softer now, as if the fight had taken the edge off even as his features twisted with torment, the years of animosity against that family wearing him thin. "Her father killed yours...killed mine. They're responsible for so much Bastard blood, I can't even begin to put a number on the body count."

"I know." I hated that fact, but I couldn't change it. I had to live with my regret that things weren't different.

"Does she know?" He raised his eyebrows. "Does she know what her father has done?"

I nodded and explained what she'd told me about her engagement to the president of the Scorpions. "She's in pretty fucking deep."

"Great." He wiped at the blood trickling off his eyebrow and lowered his head with a solemn shake. "So not only have you escalated things with the Vanderbilts, but you've renewed a war with the Scorpions."

"I fucked up." I cleared my throat and wiped the blood off my chin. "With her. With the pack. My wolf has accepted her as my mate, but...she's been here almost two weeks, and she didn't say anything about it. What am I supposed to do?"

Kodiak sighed and rubbed his fingers over his eyes. "Put yourself in her shoes. She's alone on enemy territory with three Bastards who hate her because of her last name. You wouldn't have said anything either."

That made sense, but it still chafed. What made it worse was the thought that I'd done nothing but keep her safe. Why did she feel like she couldn't tell *me*? Perhaps that was what I was most upset about, not that she'd kept it a secret, but that in all the things we'd shared with each other, she hadn't trusted me enough with this.

"The Scorpions will retaliate for this," Kodiak said. "The war will begin again."

"The war never went away," I told him. "It was always going to pick back up once Uther Vanderbilt died. That thin truce with him was the only thing keeping us from tearing each other apart."

"Well, now that you've absconded with Marx's fiancée, I can't imagine he'll be happy to keep the stalemate."

I glowered. "She's not his fiancée. She never was, and she's never going to be." Not if I had anything to do with it.

"Yes, now she's your mate, and you've put me in a very tough position." Kodiak crossed his arms, reminding me so much of his father when he and I would get in trouble as pups. "How do I tell the pack that we need to prepare for another war? How do I sacrifice more elders, more cubs, more brothers, for the sake of *you* and your *mate?*" He said the words like they tasted like shit.

"That's what pack does," I said. "I would gladly lay down my life for any of them, to protect any of them, to protect *you*. And I have, time and time again."

He narrowed his gaze and let out a low rumbling sound that

reminded me I walked a very tight rope. "You are not worth the pack. Not one shifter is worth all of us. You know this."

I did. The lone wolf did not survive, but together, the pack thrived. The pack united. The pack lived.

"If I could break the mating bond, I would," I mumbled, the words nearly choking me as I said them.

"Don't lie to me," Kodiak snarled. "If your wolf has accepted her, then you need to make your peace with it. The beast will go rabid without her. The damage is already done."

"Do what you must," I said, knowing the punishment was coming. I'd disobeyed him, and even though it was for my mate, that didn't negate the fact that I didn't tell him about it. I should have mentioned it the minute I suspected it, the minute Lycan thought she might be latent.

"I am not so cruel as to separate a shifter from his mate," Kodiak said. "And I don't think your wolf would listen even if I ordered you to never see her again."

I sighed and felt a weight lift off my chest. I had suspected he might do that, and he would be well within his rights to command it. He could expel us both from the pack and forbid us from ever coming back again. Disobeying the alpha set a precedent, and it opened him up for attacks from other ambitious members, especially when it was his second who'd done the betrayal.

"You will tell the pack what you've done," he said. "You will face their judgment, and afterward, you will find a way to make it right."

"Fair enough." I cleared my throat and nodded. "If I can make my peace with it, will you accept her into the pack? Will you allow us to mate?"

He snorted out a laugh, finally returning to the man I'd known for decades, my best friend rather than my alpha. "You do right by the pack, and I don't think I'll have much of a choice."

"Thanks, Kodiak." I clapped him on the shoulder.

He wiped at his face again and pushed to his feet. "Your right hook is getting rusty." He held out a hand to help me up. "You need to spend more time in the sparring room."

I laughed and took it, letting him yank me to my feet. "You, too. You used to be quicker. You're getting old."

"Yeah, yeah, yeah," he said, nodding toward the Fiver. "C'mon. Let's have a drink and talk about how to break this to the pack. Then, we'll head home."

I could understand Orion's frustration. I could even understand how he would feel angry by my keeping such a secret from him. But his harsh words continued to echo through my mind on repeat.

"How am I supposed to bring you into the pack now?"

I didn't want to be a part of his pack. I didn't want any of this. But fate hadn't given me a choice, and now I needed to learn how to live with the decisions I'd been forced to make in order to protect myself.

Pull yourself together, the logical side said. *You are a smart woman. You can handle this.*

But my fox, that new feral side of me, it just wanted to take off to Bastard territory to find Orion and make him understand. Our shifter sides were so deeply connected that we wouldn't be able to live without each other, no matter how upset he was.

"He'll come around," Lycan said, bringing my attention back to them. "It doesn't matter what you've done. You're his mate, and there's no undoing that."

If that were true, we'd both have some groveling to do. Sure, I'd kept a hell of a secret from him, but he'd practically *rejected* me in front of his alpha and his pack. How could he do that? How could he live with his wolf after that? It had only been an hour and my fox clawed at the insides of my mind, urging me to fix this any way I could.

I would give him some space, give him time to cool down. He wasn't entirely to blame, my temper had also gotten the best of me. This could hardly be the first time mates had argued or, God forbid, broken up. Once we'd had some breathing room, I'd ask to meet in person to talk it out. We were already far too deep in this to stop it now. My fox had accepted him, his wolf had accepted me. Like Lycan said, it was too late.

Besides, I had to fix this situation with Percy and Marx. I couldn't simply *refuse* to marry the Scorpion. I had already tried to do that. I'd made terms with my wretched brother, ones that included him signing over the controlling share of the company to Liam and Guin. But I had as much of a bone to pick with Liam as I did with Percy. He hadn't protected me from our eldest brother, and I had no reason to believe he would protect any of my other siblings.

No. The only people who would or could protect them were me and Guin. Which left me only one choice...

"Thank you both for being so kind to me," I said when they pulled up in front of the Vanderbilt Estate. I stared at the mansion through new eyes and wondered how the hell I'd lived there all these years. Compared to the Fiver, it was a different world—so unnecessarily lavish and overrated.

"Hang in there, Princess," Poe said. "We'll see you soon."

Doing my best to stay tough, I nodded and climbed out, pulling Orion's clothes tighter around my body as I made the long walk up the stairs to the front door. One of our butlers opened the door with a gasp and wide eyes.

"Miss Isolde," he said. "You're home."

"Yes." I nodded. "Where are my brothers?"

"Liam has returned to Bozeman, and Percy is away on business."

"Business," I repeated, my tone begging for more information.

He shrugged and shook his head. "Something to do with securing his standing in Vanderbilt Holdings."

I smirked and thanked him for the clarification.

Oh, Percy, Percy, Percy. You've underestimated me for the last time.

Perhaps fueled by rage or this new beast living inside of me, I'd come out of my experience at the Fiver with a fresh perspective on what would happen next. I had calls to make and pots to stir, and the sooner I started, the better. I made my way to my room and stripped out of Orion's clothes, blinking back tears at the surge of his scent pluming around me.

Don't think about that now. There are other problems to fix.

After I showered and pulled a stoic mask up around my emotions, I started working. I called Guin to secure her buy-in, and once she got over how proud she was of me for coming up with it on my own, she decided to take half of the responsibilities.

"I can call Jan and Randy. I've been working on them since Father passed," she said. Those two shareholders would be the toughest to crack and would require the most convincing. After all, I didn't work for Vanderbilt Holdings, and other than a business degree, a few semesters of internships, and the right last name, I had nothing to prove that I could do what I had planned. But I knew myself better now than I ever had. I was a shifter. I was a Vanderbilt. I was my father's daughter, and if anyone could outmaneuver that little shit, Percy, it was me.

I didn't know why Father hadn't given me a position in the company when I came home from college, and I never would. Perhaps he really thought I wasn't good enough, but I'd suddenly grown so tired of men thinking that about me.

"If we don't do this," I told Guin, "he'll sell our entire family out to whoever makes him the best deal."

"He's always been a slimy little fucker," she said, "but after this, he'll be backed into a corner. He won't have another choice."

"What about Marx?" I asked. "Do you think we can work a deal with the Bastards?"

"That depends on you," she said. "You spent the last few weeks with them. Do you think Kodiak would be open to it?"

I sighed and rubbed my fingers over my eyes. "Let's take it one step at a time. If we get rid of Percy, maybe the old workers will come back."

"You can start by calling them," she continued. "I'll have our payroll send you a list. See what you can do."

"Okay," I told her. "Thank you for hearing me out."

"Thank you for being so smart." She let out another villainous laugh. "I'm headed home now. I'll be there in a few days. By that time, I think we'll have everything in place."

After I hung up with her, I did what she asked. I made the calls I said I would and explained the new situation to any shareholders that would hear me out. It went better than I could have expected, and short a few old-timers that would rather a man be in charge, I started to feel better about my prospects.

A few hours later, a knock at the door broke my concentration. Hesitation coursing through my veins, I stood and walked closer, the delicate scent of my sisters calming my fox.

"Hi there," I said, opening the door and stepping aside so they could come in.

"Holy shit, you're alive," Ava said, wrapping her arms around me. "I thought we'd never see you again."

"I'm glad you're okay." Maeve said, hugging me next. "Where were you?"

"How was the lake house?" Ava asked. "Are you well rested?"

"Yeah, you seem...different." Maeve narrowed her eyes, trying to figure out what it was.

"Thank you for covering for me," I said. "I owe you both."

"Percy was ballistic," Ava said with a grin. "I've never seen him so out of sorts. Not even before his wedding."

"It was hilarious," Mae said, laughing as she walked closer to the mess of paperwork I'd made on my bed. She squinted at some of the articles, reaching down to pick up a piece before bringing it up to her face for inspection. "Wilbert Walkins...isn't that the guy that Percy—"

I grabbed the paper from her hand and put it down on the bed. "It is."

"Why are you researching him?" Ava furrowed her brows, seemingly begging for an explanation.

I pursed my lips, debating whether I should tell them. Undoubtedly, I could trust them. I knew that. They'd covered for me while I was gone, and if there were two people in the world that I would consider my best friends, it was them. Ava had gone to law school, and she likely knew the legal ins and outs of Vanderbilt Holdings better than anyone. But I didn't want any backlash to hit them. If Percy retaliated in the way I thought he might, he could use Mae and Ava against me...against each other.

"Sol," Mae said, grabbing my hands tight in hers. "What are you doing? What's happened?"

"I promise I'll tell you," I said. "I'm trying to protect you, to protect us all."

"Oh, a devious scheme," Ava said with a grin.

"A devilish plot," Mae added. "How can we help?"

I let them in on the game plan, and together, we worked to try to restore what little respect the Vanderbilt name still carried.

But that night, after Mae and Ava had fallen asleep on either side of me in my enormous bed, I thought about Orion. I remembered the way he'd smiled, as if I was the only one that could make him laugh. Notes of his woodsy scent ricocheted through my mind, and I tried to tamper down my fox's whine.

She couldn't understand the separation. To her, the argument had been petty and ridiculous. Why couldn't he see that I'd done my best? That I'd told him when I thought the time was right, when I could trust him with such information? For as much as they thought I was a spy at first, I'd likewise thought they'd kill me and bury me somewhere no one would ever find.

We'd been separated nearly a day, and I missed him more than I ever thought I would.

"How am I supposed to bring you into the pack now?"

I grimaced at the stinging humiliation slicing down my spine and into my heart.

But Kodiak's words gave me hope, though I suspected he hadn't meant that by saying them.

"Imagine my surprise when I enter the shift with fifty-three pack members and come out with fifty-four."

Did that mean I was already part of the pack? Did that mean I was already Orion's mate, no matter what happened? When we'd been in bed together, before I'd revealed the truth, he'd held me with such affection. He'd said he wanted to do right by me, that he wanted to mark me in the mating ritual. Was that all lies?

No, I didn't believe that. This was an argument, and nothing more. The first of many, I would presume, but the only one that would drive this much of a wedge between us. Once I dealt with this Percy mess, I'd crawl back onto Bastard territory and beg him to forgive me. I'd forgive him, too, and then I'd make him take me the way a dominant takes a submissive. And all would be right in the world again.

My eyes burning with unshed tears, I reminded myself to be strong and let unconsciousness take me.

As it turned out, business moved fast when the reputation of the CEO of Vanderbilt Holdings was on the line. With the twins' help, we'd contacted most of the ranchers the following day and negotiated half of them to return. Once I got the courage to reach out to Orion, I suspected we could make a similar deal with the Bastards.

Now, the only thing left to do was to break it to my savage older brothers.

"Isolde," Liam said, entering the parlor with a smile on his face. "You're home. How was the lake house?"

Of the two, Liam had the least amount of bite. He'd been mostly passive while Percy sold me to that perverted old man, but in doing nothing he had told me what I needed to know. Percy wasn't worthy of the top position, but neither was Liam. If it took bringing him down to topple the monarch at the top, so be it.

"Snowy," I said.

He pulled me into a hug before going to the bar cart at the far corner to pour himself a drink.

"Have you heard from Percy?" Liam took a sip of whiskey and turned to face me and my sisters. I leaned against Father's desk, holding all of the paperwork I needed to ruin Percy's life. Mae and Ava stood on either side of me with matching grins.

"Oh sure," I said, glancing at the clock on the mantel. "He should be here any second."

A few moments later, the sound of loafers on the marble floor preceded the sight of Percy walking into the parlor. He wore an expensive suit with his hair slicked back, his hands in his pockets as his dark eyes flicked between me, Liam, and our sisters before ultimately landing back on me.

"Dearest sister," Percy said, tilting his chin up so he stared down his nose at me. "It's good to see you home...in one piece."

"Hmm," I said, crossing my arms and narrowing my gaze on him. "Yes, it's been quite a revelatory two weeks."

"Well," he said, taking another step closer. "A lot has happened here as well. Our allies have grown impatient."

"I needed time to think," I said. "To consider this *alliance* more fully."

"Is that why you drove onto Bastard territory and wrecked the SUV?" He raised his eyebrows and walked to the bar cart next to Liam, uncorking the crystal before pouring himself a glass of whiskey.

Of course he already knew where I was. He'd probably tracked my phone that first night. He'd probably known all this time and had refused to do anything about it. No, he'd want me to come home with my proverbial tail tucked between my legs, perhaps begging for his mercy. He'd get no such submission from me. My time away had done nothing but emboldened me.

"Oh dear brother." I shook my head. "I've decided I won't be marrying the president of the Bloody Scorpions."

He snorted a disbelieving sound and glanced at Liam, who shook his head and gave our brother an "*I told you so*" look.

"Oh, really?" Percy raised an eyebrow. "And just what do you propose we do instead?"

"I've made my own arrangements." I lifted my chin higher, certain I could smooth things over with the Bastards. Even if I couldn't, the ranchers had decided that working for Guin would be more reasonable than Percy. I'd made promises and compromises that he never would have considered.

Maeve and Avalon snickered, covering their mouths when I glanced at them. Liam shook his head and crossed his arms, leaning against the bookcase.

Percy, for once, seemed speechless. He opened his mouth and blinked, practically aghast with the suggestion.

"And just what, pray tell, are these arrangements?" Liam said. "Certainly not a deal with the Bastards. They hate us. We hate them."

"The past is the past," I said. "From what I understand, our father was not very kind to them. They were forced to do what they had to, and I don't think they killed our mother."

Percy laughed like he couldn't believe my audacity. "Two weeks away and you're already a buckle bunny. Very nice."

"So easy for you to say," I retorted. "Especially when you tried to turn me into a whore for the fucking Scorpions."

"Better a whore for the Scorpions than nothing to the Bastards," Percy said, running his tongue over his teeth and scowling. "You think they'll accept you? A Vanderbilt? You're the daughter of the man who—" He looked at our sisters and stopped himself, clearing his throat before taking another long sip of whiskey. "It's not just about territory. It's about blood."

I opened my mouth to talk, but the sound of the front door opening stopped me. Guin curled her lips into a wicked grin when she saw us all gathered together. She had on a tailored suit and matching Louboutin heels that made her seem even more powerful and sinister.

"Well, well, well," she said as she sauntered in. "A family meeting without little ole me."

"Great," Percy murmured, pinching the bridge of his nose. "I thought you were in the Sierra Nevada, scaring the hell out of old men with mommy issues."

Her dark emerald eyes twinkled. "Oh, baby brother. You know me so well." Guin glanced at the twins before raking her penetrating gaze over me, eyeing me up from head to toe like she was trying to find my fatal flaw. "Welcome back, sister."

I kept my chin up. "You too."

"Have you already broken the news?" Raising her eyebrows, she widened her grin.

"Oh, no," I said. "I've been waiting for you."

Taking another step forward, she glanced back at our brother and shook her head. "Oh, baby bro. You've fucked up big time."

Percy gulped down the rest of his whiskey before setting the glass down on Father's desk. "What are you talking about?"

"Do you know why the ranchers deserted us after Father died?" I asked, glancing around at my gathered siblings. The only one missing was Galahad, and he'd already gone back to school. "Anyone?"

"They didn't trust Percy in charge," Liam said. "Everyone knows that. They told us before they left."

"Hmm." I nodded, pulling my smile even higher. "That's right. Never worked on the ranch a day in your life, so why would they stick by you now?"

"But I know something you don't know," Guin sang. She'd always been bolder and meaner than anyone else in our family, and if there were one person who took after our father in attitude and spirit, it would be her. It wasn't a surprise the workers had decided to return as long as they worked for her instead.

"Do you know who else I managed to convince not to trust Percival Vanderbilt?" She shook her head and stalked closer to our brother, raising an eyebrow as he squared his jaw and stared her down.

"No," he murmured with a grimace.

"Oh yes," she said. "The board of trustees has grave concerns about some new allegations against you, little brother." She grabbed the folder I'd been holding and slammed it down on the desk before clapping his shoulder.

"And luckily for everyone involved," I added, "Guin has recently appointed a new head of Vanderbilt Energy, which means she's freed up her time to run the ranch in Father's place."

"You fucking bitch," Percy said, ripping open the folder to peer through the pages, flipping them urgently as Liam came to stand next to him. "What did you do?"

"The Board has appointed me CEO and head of the trustees," she said. "After much convincing by Isolde and the disturbing reports by your own sisters, who would want you in charge?"

"And there will be no deal with the Scorpions," I continued. "While some marriages in this family have been arranged, times have changed. Father is gone, and the only member of this family with a price on their head now is you."

"And the ranchers?" Liam asked, glancing up at Guin.

"They know me and Guin," I said. "They trust us. I have half of them back. And the other half?" I shrugged. "Perhaps the Bastards would be agreeable to a deal...without the coercive marriage bit."

"Hell," Liam said as he read over Percy's shoulder. "You two did all of this in two weeks?"

"No, we did this in two days," I said.

Guin turned to look at me, her eyes gone a momentary amber before quickly shifting back to green, but I saw it. I knew what it meant. I flashed my own amber back at her with a grin. It had practically taken a miracle, but we'd made it work. Whatever God was on our side had been looking out for us...looking out for *me.*

"Fuck you," Percy cut in. "How could you do this to me? How could you betray your own brother—"

"You better watch what you say next." Guin raised an eyebrow and clenched her jaw. "How could I do this to you? How could you do this to our sister? Selling her to the Scorpions like that?"

"She agreed to it!" Percy's face had turned a beet red and the veins in his throat bulged.

"In exchange for you giving up your controlling share," I said. "But unfortunately, the scales were still too uneven for my tastes. Turns out, I didn't need to agree to anything to get what I wanted in the end."

"We needed to save the ranch," he whined. "This was the only way."

"Apparently, it wasn't," I said.

Percy gave a sardonic laugh and shook his head. "You have no idea what you've done. Sure, get rid of me. Push me to the peripheral, but make no mistake, the Scorpions won't let this slide. They were promised—"

"You think I'm afraid of some silly motorcycle gang?" Guin scoffed and rolled her eyes. "Father kept them at bay for forty years. I intend to do the same."

"That's what I was doing." Percy clenched his hands into fists. "You're the one that's fucked-up, big sister. You don't even know how badly. Your arrogance is going to destroy this family, just wait."

"Better it be my arrogance than your greed." Guin tilted her chin up. "Now, run away, little brother. Go lick your wounds in peace and leave the grownups to take care of business."

Percy shook his head and narrowed his eyes at both of us before storming out of the parlor and turning toward the front door, slamming it shut behind him.

"That was dramatic," Liam said, raising an eyebrow. "Are you certain you can get the workers back?"

Guin raised an eyebrow but didn't deign to answer Liam's question, only turned to me and my sisters before saying, "What's for dinner?"

Later that night, I found Guin in her old room, sitting on her bed with a book spread open on her lap. She'd decided to stay for a few days just in case Percy came back with any stupid ideas, but I figured he'd gone to pout in private.

"Hey," I said, taking a few steps toward her as she glanced up at me. The soft glow from the lamp on her nightstand cast her in a delicate light that reminded me of our mother. She'd hate that comparison, so I didn't bring it up. "Can we talk?"

She nodded and set her book to the side so she could cross her legs and make room for me. I crawled on the mattress next to her the way I'd used to do when we were kids.

"I'm surprised the shareholders were so easily swayed," I said. "I can't believe it went so well."

She shrugged. "They didn't know there was another option. Now they do."

"Just like that, huh?" I said.

"Well," she continued. "I had to scratch a few backs and call in a few favors. But we got it done, so all's well that ends well."

"How did you know I'd turned?" I asked.

"I could feel it." She rubbed a finger over her brow, brushing back her ginger hair that matched mine. "I've known I was a shifter since I was a teenager."

I balked, widening my eyes at her confession. "What? How?"

"It's a long story," she said. "Suffice to say we used to have some day workers that were shifters, and the more time I spent around them, the more it brought it out of me."

I thought back to what I knew about her as a teenager, but I'd been young, no more than five or six at the time. I vaguely remembered a guy she'd liked, a guy around her age that one of the ranch hands had taken in as a child.

"Van?" I said, squinting as I remembered.

Guin sighed and rolled her eyes. "He goes by Vermillion now. He's a Bastard...in more ways than one."

"How? Did you go through a transition? Did he help you?" I was desperate for more information, specifically why she'd kept it to herself. If there was a possibility that any of us were also shifters, she could have said something.

"Sol," she drawled, looking out the window as she closed her eyes. "The Bastards aren't good people."

"Neither are the Scorpions." I crossed my arms as an ache splintered down into my gut. I missed Orion, and I'd only been parted from him for two days. He hadn't reached out since Kodiak sent me home, but admittedly, neither had I.

"You shouldn't have gotten involved with either." Guin pulled one side of her mouth into a smirk. "I'm sorry Percy backed you into a corner."

"I tried to fight him," I said. "I tried to do what you would have done. I just didn't have enough sway at Vanderbilt Holdings without you. I'm glad we worked it out together."

She cast me a sympathetic glance before brushing a stray piece of hair behind my ear in a startlingly endearing move. "Tell me about your time with the Bastards."

I did. I explained how I'd learned to take care of the sheep and feed the horses, how I'd gone through nesting and my transition.

"Orion helped me, more than I could ever repay him for. And then…" I clutched myself tighter, forcing myself to say it. "And then I think we mated each other, but he found out about this stupid betrothal and we got into an argument and now I don't know what we are."

She narrowed her eyes at my neck before glancing over the rest of me and returning to my face. "I don't see a bite."

"We didn't get that far yet," I said. "He wanted to wait for the ritual, for Kodiak to welcome me into the pack…but then I fucked it all up."

"Mates are for life, Sol," she said. "If you truly are mated, he won't be able to stay away from you for long. Nor you him."

I had so many questions. "Are you in the pack? When did you transition?"

"I didn't know anything about this when it happened to me. I was barely eighteen. Vermillion got me through it." She kept her features blank, almost purposely so, like she'd built a wall between this current version of her and the one that had been that girl all those years ago. "And for my first moon, he took me out to a remote part of the woods where it could just be the two of us."

"Are you a fox, too?" I was desperate to know if she was like me, if our animal side ran in the family.

"Yes," she said. "I don't know how the type of animal is determined, perhaps through family or personality." She shrugged. "I met with a Bastard named Ares in the Dallas MC, but his experience is different from ours. He can change at will whenever he wants. I think there's so many kinds of magic in the world that it depends on circumstance."

I winced, attempting to absorb all of this so quickly, even though it pleased me to know I wasn't alone in our family, that I had another person like me. "Is Vermillion your mate?"

At that, she laughed and shook her head. "No, thank God."

"Why do you say it like that?"

She shrugged. "I'm glad I'm not bound to someone so permanently, and if I have it my way, I never will be. Being mated makes you vulnerable. Your world ends when your mate dies, and I have no desire to go through that type of loss. Ever."

Orion hadn't even died, but I felt the stinging pain of his loss every minute we weren't together. I hated the separation. Even still, her nihilism had caused her to miss out on all the good things about being mated—the shared emotions and deep intimacy and bonded magic. Even this far away from Orion, he still hummed under my skin like a low wave vibration.

"And the Bastards?" I asked, urging her on. "Did they take you in? Are you a part of their pack?"

"No."

"Why not?" I couldn't stop myself from blurting out the first thing that came to mind, even if it seemed to make her frown and blink back tears.

"Because I didn't mate the vice president," she spat, giving me a venomous look that could only come from an older sister chastising her younger one. "And I prefer to run alone."

I wanted to ask more about the relationship between her and Vermillion, but Orion had told me that most shifters don't mate the person that helps them through their transition, so I let it go and shifted the conversation elsewhere. "Where do you go on the moon?"

"I lock myself in my apartment," she said. "Or I use the land out by the Missouri. Once I turn, most of the predators leave me alone."

"That sounds lonely," I said, reaching out to grab her hand. She gave it a soft squeeze and curled her lips into a hesitant smile.

"Don't worry about me, little sister," she said. "Those first few moons are rough enough as it is. Focus on yourself."

I cleared my throat and scooted closer to her. "Thank you again for helping me with Percy. I couldn't have done it without you."

"Yes, well." She rolled her eyes and reached over to turn out the light, bathing us in the darkness of the waning moon trickling in through her curtains. "We need to be careful. The Scorpions will be offended once they learn he's gone back on the deal."

"They're vampires," I said. "Did you know that?"

"Oh yes," she said. "They're even more despicable than the Bastards. That's why I worked so hard to get you out of it. But now you're in their crosshairs. They won't leave you alone until they feel the debt has been paid."

"They haven't enacted their side of the deal," I said. "They said they wouldn't until we were married."

"That doesn't matter," Guin explained. "They'll see it as a threat to their pride, to their reputation. Especially when he learns you've mated the Bastards' second."

"I haven't mated him...not really. It's complicated." I bit my bottom lip and scooted under the covers, fluffing the pillow up around my head. It felt nice to be next to her, and even though she was ten years older than me, the company of another shifter, of family, of pack, soothed the anxiety brewing in my gut.

"I can smell him on you, Sol," she said. "Whether the human wants it or not, your other sides have already accepted it. I bet his wolf is driving him bonkers right now, trying to get to you."

I didn't want to think about that, so I changed the subject. "Are Maeve and Avalon shifters, too? What about Liam or Galahad?"

She shrugged and let out a sleepy hum. "I don't know."

"What about our parents? Do you think it was Father or Mother that had the gene?"

"Mother," she said. "If she'd been around, we likely would have had our transitions earlier. Father either didn't know or did whatever he could so we didn't turn out like her."

"Was she a fox, too?" I couldn't help the questions from coming now, as if Guin had become my own personal shifter history book.

"I don't know, Sol," she said, resigned. "Try to get some sleep. You've had a long couple of days, and it's not going to get any easier from here."

I bit my bottom lip and snuggled farther under the duvet, watching as my sister closed her eyes and relaxed her features.

"The Bastards didn't kill her, Guin," I said. "At first, I didn't believe it. But now, I know. I feel it deep in my gut."

"I know," Guin said. "I know."

It didn't matter why the war between our families had started. Blood. Land. Money. Even though our mother had died nearly twenty years ago, the grudge had continued. Someone had to stop it. Someone had to usher in a new pact. The people who had committed these acts were gone now. Twenty years ago, Orion would have been fifteen, maybe sixteen, and he'd admitted to Kodiak being his best friend, which meant that the current alpha had nothing to do with the war between our families. Could I blame them for the actions of people who came before them? Could they blame me for the things my father had done?

Eventually, Guin's breathing evened out, her inhales as shallow as her exhales, and I realized she'd finally drifted unconscious. I closed my eyes and reached out for the part of me that existed outside of myself, the part of me that was in Orion, my other half.

I sensed him in the center of my chest like the steady beat of a drum, like poison in my veins that ached and soothed at the same time. I yearned to reach out to him, to use what little connection we still had to rectify this whole thing.

I missed him. Terribly. It had only been two days since I left the Fiver, but it seemed like an eternity. Everyone had been right. We were truly mated, deep down inside, and the fury with which I longed to be near him was all the evidence I needed.

I grabbed my phone and scrolled over his contact, the same as I had the night before, but this time, I sent a text.

Me: *I miss you, big grumpy wolf. And I'm sorry. Please forgive me.*

I waited for a reply, but after a few minutes with nothing, I swallowed my pride, closed my eyes, and went to sleep.

Little Fox: *I miss you, big grumpy wolf. And I'm sorry. Please forgive me.*

I stared at the text and sighed, running a hand over my face and back through my hair. Now that my temper had subsided, and I saw things more clearly, I missed her, too. But the fact that she'd kept it from me for so long still bruised my pride, and when I clicked my phone shut without answering her, I told myself it was because I had pack business to handle. I had to get through this meeting without being expelled, or worse. Her words echoed through my head again.

"I'll never be good enough for you, will I? I'll never be good enough for anyone. I'm not his mate. He doesn't want me."

That wasn't true. I wanted her then, and I wanted her now, and I would always want her, no matter what she did. I'd reply as soon as it was over and tell her I forgave her. I'd ask for her forgiveness, too. This wasn't the end, it was just a blip, a lover's spat, one of the many more we'd have as a mated couple.

"Welcome home, brother," Moose said, clapping me on the shoulder. As sergeant at arms and third in the pack, it was his responsibility to make sure all these fuckers stayed in line. Should the pack decide I deserved to be punished, it would be him who carried out the sentence. He'd been given the nickname because he was over six foot six with long floppy brown hair that he kept chin length. Aside from me and Kodiak, there was no one that could outman him or best him in a fight.

"Thank you," I said, glancing at Lycan and Poe standing in the corner, talking to a few of the other pack mates. "How were things while I was gone?"

He shrugged. "The Scorpions are up to something. I can feel it."

Yeah, and I knew what they were planning. They thought they'd have an alliance with the Vanderbilts. They thought they'd finally get a bigger piece of the action. They were sorely mistaken, especially since the little fox wouldn't be marrying that fucking vampire piece of shit after all—I'd kill him first. Of course, I feared retaliation from the Scorpions. They wouldn't take the slight lying down, so the sooner I got this done and brought her into the pack, the better.

I hovered my hand over my phone again, my wolf begging me to reach back out to her, to at least tell her I was sorry, too. My knee jerk reaction had done neither of us any good. Kodiak's words shot through my mind like a bullet, over and over again. *"If your wolf has accepted her, then you need to make your peace with it. Or the beast will go rabid without her. The damage is already done."*

My inner monster was already bucking at his cage, howling and whining at the separation. If we didn't reconcile soon, he'd take over for me. He'd hunt her down and claim her in the worst way. Kodiak, unfortunately, had been right.

"They're always up to something." I took my seat at the council's table and nodded as Serpent and Ruby, the pack's enforcers, sat across from us. Vermillion, our tech guru and head of the cleanup crew, crossed his arms and narrowed his gaze at me while he sat next to Larentia, Lycan's twin sister, before Lycan himself came to sit on the other side. When Talon, our treasurer, took her spot next to Moose, Kodiak banged his knuckles on the table to get everyone else's attention.

"Council, pack members, brothers and sisters," Kodiak said, glancing around as the rest of the pack quieted down to pay attention. "Thank you for joining us for this special session."

We'd come down from the mountain shortly after reinforcements took over for us, and though my animal side wanted to make things right with Isolde and take her back up there, I had to face the pack for what I'd done.

The Vanderbilts were our enemies. They'd killed members of our family, and though Isolde had never done anything to harm us, I'd been told not to touch her. I didn't listen.

"Some of you have perhaps felt the presence of a new pack member," Kodiak explained, and I tried not to shift in my seat. I could handle anything they threw at me, even if it was the gauntlet or time spent in seclusion. "Our beloved VP and my second in command has finally found his mate." Kodiak clapped, causing everyone else to join in with loud cheers and hoops of enjoyment.

"Where are they?" Ruby asked.

"When can we meet them?" Larentia added. "Did you bring them home from Fiver Cabin?"

Kodiak held his hands up, asking for quiet before he continued. "It's Isolde Vanderbilt."

That got everyone's attention, and a hush fell over my fellow pack members. I sensed their apprehension through the bonds, the sickly sweet scent of fear, confusion, and anxiety permeating through the room.

"What?" Moose spat from next to me, raising his eyebrows as he turned in my direction.

"Explain," Larentia continued, her eyes turning a dark shade of navy blue as her wolf prowled closer to the surface.

"I didn't mean for it to happen," I said as I stood, glancing at my fellow officers before sweeping over the room. "She went into transition while we were there."

"What was she doing at Fiver Cabin to begin with?" Ruby asked, crossing her arms. Like her brother, Kodiak, she had bright brown eyes that missed absolutely nothing.

I told them the story, making sure to reiterate that I (mostly) didn't touch her until she went into transition, even after Lycan suspected that she might be latent. I explained everything, including her engagement to Marx and how she planned to end it.

"I smelled it on her nearly as soon as she arrived," Lycan added. "You know I have an intuition about these things."

"And she was engaged to Marx?" Ruby asked.

"Yeah, but I didn't know it at the time," I said. "She didn't tell me until after the moon, and after that..." Shame coated my insides, but I wasn't sure what for: that I'd mated her, that she'd been able to keep a secret from me for so long, that I'd pushed her away when she needed me. Maybe all of it. I adjusted my hips as the discomfort of that reality sat in my stomach like rotten acid.

"That complicates things," Serpent said. "It's not just the Vanderbilts. The Scorpions won't take this lying down. If she backs out of the deal, Marx will come for her."

"I'll tear his fucking hands off if he touches her." The words flew out of my mouth on a growl.

"There's been a stalemate for twenty years," Kodiak said. "This could end that and reignite the war."

"Good," Vermillion said. "I've been waiting to tear into some Scorpion throats."

Some of the others clapped and hollered in agreement, but I coughed and ran a hand through my hair. Like Kodiak said, I didn't want any more Bastard blood spilled.

"The Vanderbilts blame us for the death of Priscilla Vanderbilt," Larentia said. "They believe she came on our territory twenty years ago and our previous alpha, Kerrick, tore her apart."

"Did he?" Ruby asked, shifting her gaze to Kodiak.

"Of course not," he answered. "If Priscilla Vanderbilt was a shifter, it's news to me."

"That's...not entirely true," one of our elders said. He'd gone by the name Polar when he'd been on the road, but now that he was well into his seventies, he only left pack territory when he had to and stayed on the sidelines when it came to fights. "She did come to us once, shortly before her disappearance. She claimed to be a shifter and needed help. I smelled it on her. But Kerrick wanted nothing to do with Vanderbilts, especially Uther's wife. He turned her away, unwilling to escalate a war with him. We didn't know if it was a trap or worse."

Shocked, I widened my eyes, the crowd going as quiet as I felt. The Vanderbilt matriarch had been a shifter? How did we not know about this? How had it been kept quiet this long? Why didn't one of the elders speak out sooner?

"What happened to her?" Kodiak asked, raising his eyebrows in surprise.

Polar shrugged. "I don't know. But it was after the birth of her last child. It's possible she ran off and never came back. Maybe she found another pack."

I narrowed my gaze at the old man and took a deep breath, swearing that I would tell Isolde about this as soon as I could—as soon as I made up with her.

"Regardless of what happened to Priscilla," I continued, "I must ask the pack's forgiveness. Kodiak ordered me not to touch Isolde, and the closer I got to her, the more difficult that proved to be." I cleared my throat and met the eyes of some of the fiercest mother-fuckers I knew, some compassionate, others skeptical.

"He tried," Poe added, giving me a sympathetic glance. "I know he tried."

"And he kept us from doing anything scandalous, as much as I might have wanted to," Lycan added, running his tongue over his canine when a low, threatening grumble erupted out of my chest. "What? She's hot."

"Watch your mouth, Lycan," I snarled, "especially when you talk about my mate."

"All right, enough," Kodiak said. "The only thing that negates an order from the alpha is when a shifter's mate is on the line, so I am inclined to forgive Orion. But that doesn't stop the pack from holding it against him or demanding restitution."

The entire room seemed to hold their breath.

"He might have single-handedly restarted the war with the Scorpions," Ruby said. "If we lose pack because of this, it'll be on his hands."

My chest ached at the thought of that, true as it may be.

"The war was always going to restart," Lycan said. "It was only going to take one spark to reignite the whole damn thing."

"Still," she argued, raising an eyebrow at me. "How forgiving can we be not understanding the fallout?"

I'd known Ruby as long as I'd known Kodiak, and she'd always been civil toward me. She'd gotten her road name because of how red her eyes were in her wolf form, even more crimson and bloodthirsty than Kodiak's, but that moniker also referred to her tough outer shell. Like the jewel, she'd been formed under the pressure of her youth, molded and shaped by the violence of the war between our families. She didn't let much get past her, which was why she held such a high seat on the council and why she'd been made the enforcer as soon as she transitioned.

"And where is this mate?" Larentia added. "Will she become part of the pack?"

I pursed my lips, debating the best way to tell them that I'd gotten pissed at her keeping her engagement from me, something I planned to rectify as soon as I could.

"He threw a temper tantrum and growled at her," Lycan answered for me. "She growled back, but Kodiak sent her home. I'm guessing they haven't kissed and made up yet."

I bared a canine at him in a poor excuse for a retort, but he only shook his head and rolled his eyes.

"If she kept this secret from him," Ruby continued, "what else is she hiding? Can we trust her?"

"Once lover boy seals the mating bond, he'll know if she's hiding anything else," Moose said with a laugh.

"I doubt she is," Lycan continued with a wink directed at me. "She seemed really torn up about it. She's a good person, not like her scumbag father. She helped us at the Fiver. She wanted us to like her."

"Yeah, so you didn't kill her when you found out she was engaged to the bloodsuckers," Ruby argued.

"No," Poe cut in. "I was cautious at first, too. She has a good heart, and she stood up to Orion. Which...let's face it, only Kodiak and those with a death wish can do that."

A few snickers came from all around us; even Ruby had to smile at that one.

"I'm not on the council," Poe said. "But you all were wary about me when I first wandered in off the streets. As a lone wolf from Baltimore, who could trust me? But you gave me a shot. I think we could do the same to Isolde."

Moose sighed and shook his head. "If she managed to get the broodiest motherfucker I know to mate, I might be willing to let her into the pack. Even if she is a Vanderbilt."

"It could be the start of a new era," Serpent said, his hunter green eyes glancing at me. "What if we never had to worry about fighting the Vanderbilts again?"

"Uther is gone," Vermillion said, crossing his arms. "Kerrick and his council are gone. No one is left from that time that even remembers why the feud started."

"They took our land. They killed our family," Kodiak added. "But this could be a way to heal old wounds."

"It won't be easy," Talon said, tapping her fingers on the table in front of her, "but Orion and Isolde could be the pieces that put us back together."

"I move to allow the mating," Moose continued, clapping me on the shoulder. "Perform the ritual. Bring her into the pack. As for Orion's *indiscretion*"—he cleared his throat and curled his lips into a lopsided grin—"I believe Lycan and Poe when they say Orion held out as long as he could. The girl went into transition and he helped her. Her fox belongs to his wolf. No one can resist the mating call. He acted the way a Bastard should, the way *pack* should."

"It's hard to resist a shifter going through transition, especially if you're supposed to be the one that helps them," Vermillion said. "Sometimes, that's more fated than the mating call."

His seemingly nervous stance made me wonder what the hell could make him take that position, especially because the quiet, stoic brother had gotten his road name because of the way his temper went from zero to explosive so quickly. He called it seeing red, but I reckoned his animal side lived really close to the surface.

"We've all been there," Serpent said. "She was lucky to have you."

"Especially since the alternative was this wily son of a bitch," Talon said, nodding to Lycan.

"Hey!" He narrowed his gaze at our treasurer and gave her the finger. "Don't talk about my mother like that."

"Yeah," Poe joined in. "Any shifter would be lucky to have Lycan help them through their transition."

"I second Moose's decision to forgive and forget," Lycan continued even as his cheeks turned a bright shade of blush at Poe's compliment. "I was there the whole time. He fought it as hard as he could."

"Thank you," I said, remembering when it had almost come to blows between us. He'd been so sure in his assessment of who and what she was, and now I understood that I'd dismissed it as a way to protect myself. If I had given in, if I'd chosen to believe him, I would have crossed a line much earlier than I did.

"Any disagree?" Kodiak asked, glancing around at the gathered pack members. I took a deep breath and waited for someone to speak up, but Ruby only pursed her lips and shook her head. Larentia gave me a noncommittal shrug and followed suit. If there were any others that believed I should be punished, they remained silent.

Kodiak nodded and glanced at me. "All forgiven, brother."

"But we won't forget," Ruby said. "If she puts a toe out of line, if I catch even a whiff that she's hiding something else, she's gone."

Which meant I'd have a hell of a time maintaining my position in the pack. I held Ruby's glare with a threatening one of my own. If she came after my mate for any reason, she'd have to come through me first.

"Congratulations," Kodiak continued. "Bring your girl around so the pack can check her out."

I swallowed against my parched throat and nodded, grabbing my phone with trepidation boiling in my gut. Sure, I could do that, but first I had to make things right with her. I had to decide whether I could trust her, whether I believed her when she said she was sorry.

"Good luck with the pack princesses," Moose cut in. "You might have a harder time with them."

I shook my head and grimaced, knowing he had a point. The females were the most vicious part of any pack for a reason. They protected their own.

"It'll be fine," Larentia said, flashing me the same grin as her brother before giving me a big hug. "I'm just surprised someone would put up with your grumpy ass."

"All right, that's all I've got for tonight," Kodiak said, banging his rings on the table to announce the end of the session. "Everyone, go have fun."

It was late, but it wasn't too late for me to have a drink with the rest of them, especially after they'd let me off so easily. But before I could walk out front, Kodiak called my name and nodded for me to stay put.

"I need to have a word," he said. I hung back, and he waited until everyone else had left the space before raising an eyebrow at me and shaking his head. "You got off easy."

"You're not mated yet," I said. "The call is irresistible."

"That's what they say." He rubbed a hand over the back of his neck and grinned, and I worried for whatever shifter caught his eye. He wasn't an easy man, even worse than me, and whoever attempted to mate with him would have their fucking work cut out for them. "Since the pack agreed to let it go, I'll perform the ritual at the next new moon. Assuming you patch things up with her."

"Fuck, I don't think I'll be able to stay away from her." My heart thumped and dropped into my gut, anticipation coiling through me at the thought of mating Isolde for real, in every way that mattered to a shifter. "My wolf is already bucking against me."

"I fucking told you that," he said.

I sighed and rubbed at my tired eyes. It had been rough trying to sleep without her these last few days. "I didn't want to mate her. I didn't want to mate anyone."

Kodiak snorted. "My father used to say you don't get a choice. If we did, no one would do it. You saw what happened to Kerrick. Losing a mate is worse than death. Don't let your pride ruin a good thing, Orion."

"I'm grateful to the pack for understanding, but Kodiak—I'm sorry this happened."

He narrowed his dark gaze at me and leaned in to grab my shoulder. "Don't be, brother. This is a good thing. Having a strong mated pair at the top of the pack will keep the younger ones levelheaded. Kai's got the scent of an alpha, and he's on the verge of his transition."

I nodded and eyed the younger pack member out front where he mingled with some of the pack princesses around his age, Kodiak's daughter Henny included. She laughed and threw an arm over his shoulder, clinking her beer against his as he said something that made the others crack up.

"He'll start showing signs soon," Kodiak said, tilting his head to the side to crack his neck. "I'm happy you're settling down. It'll make the rest of us more stable."

"What about you?" I asked. "Do you think you'll ever find it? Do you think you'll ever be able to love another?"

"Nah, man," he said, seemingly remembering his wife, Kendra. "There's no one else for me."

"Yeah, but you all weren't mated, not really." They'd been married, sure, but his wolf had never accepted her as his true match, not in the way mine had with Isolde. There was a difference, some kind of preternatural connection that could only be formed by the bonds of magic. While he and Kendra had been happy enough, and they truly loved each other, it wasn't nearly as intimate or as powerful as it could have been.

"That doesn't matter," he said, taking a deep breath. "If she had lived, we would have, and my wolf won't accept anyone else."

I winced but didn't argue with him.

Kodiak took a deep breath and patted me on the back. "Go on, Ry. Have a good night. We'll deal with the rest in the morning."

I stood, grabbed my phone from the table, and walked toward the front of the clubhouse, scrolling over her text as Kodiak's advice rumbled around in my head.

"Don't let your pride ruin a good thing."

Was that what I was doing? I had always had trouble letting people get close, and most of the time, I preferred my solitude to others. Sure, the pack was family, but I only needed so much time with them to hit my social battery limit. With Isolde, things were different. I'd gladly spend every waking moment with her if I could.

"Put yourself in her shoes," Kodiak had said. Up against three men she perceived to be enemies, could I really blame her? Why had I reacted so angrily in the first place?

You were scared, my wolf said.

Scared of what, I didn't know. Losing her, perhaps. Loving her too much only to have the pack or the Scorpions rip her from me the same way my parents had been.

Aww, fuck.

Taking a deep breath and letting it out on a frustrated sigh, I responded to her message.

Me: *Little Fox, I'm sorry, too. I miss you. I forgive you. Please forgive me. We have to talk. Call me when you can.*

CHAPTER 21

Sol

I woke up the next morning to the text from Orion, and I would have called him back immediately. But Guin and I had a lot to do in order to get Vanderbilt Holdings turned over to us. We drove into Helena to make an appearance at headquarters in order to officially gain the controlling share of the company. The shareholders had agreed to a 51 percent share split 70/30 between Guin and myself. Guin would have the largest chunk, with the option for the split to be more equal as I gained more experience. It was a step in the right direction, one that settled in my gut with a sense of rightness that I hadn't known since Father had been alive.

Now on the drive home, I stared at Orion's text message again. *"We need to talk."*

I wanted to, desperately. But a small lurch churned in my gut. What if he had bad news? What if he didn't want me anymore?

"Oh, stop pouting and call him already," Guin said. "Your anxiety is spilling over the family bonds and driving me mad."

I sighed and worried my bottom lip. "What if he rejects me permanently?"

"He can't," she said. "You know he can't. You can still feel him, right?"

231

I nodded. "But that's the transition magic. He said his power would be in me for a while. It's only been a week."

Guin rolled her eyes and shook her head. "You're more stubborn than a mule, you know that? It's been days since you last saw him. Your fox is suffering. If you miss him, if you want him back, call him and tell him."

"I thought you said mating was ridiculous, that it only ends badly."

"It does," she said. "But it's too late for you." Guin nodded toward my phone on my lap. "Put us both out of our misery and call him. It might be good news. The pack might want you."

"If I join the pack, will you?" The hope in my tone spread between us like melted chocolate, sweet and sticky. I wanted my sister close. I wanted her to stay and run with me in the woods during the next moon.

"*When* you join the pack, I'll consider it." She let out a sarcastic laugh. "As long as Kodiak keeps all that alpha energy to himself. I'm already dominant enough. I don't need some hulking wolf thinking he can tell me what to do."

I didn't know Kodiak very well; I'd only met him that one time. But it was enough for me to recognize strength and power seeped out of his pores. He demanded obedience; it was the foundation on which the pack rested. Guin bowed to no man, not since our father had died. The thought of Guin and Kodiak in the same room made me want to roast popcorn and pull up a chair to see who would come out on top.

We pulled up to a stoplight outside of town and I started to ask if she thought any of our siblings would ever go through a transition now that the two of us had. But the words died on my lips when a black SUV pulled up behind us and another perpendicular in front of us. My heart pulsed, my fox recognizing the trap for what it was. We couldn't move. We couldn't get out of this.

Tension boiled through me, sending rancid fear careening in my blood as the doors opened and heavy black boots hit the ground.

Dread lined my veins, and now that I was a shifter, I smelled the rotting flesh hanging off their bones even through the cars. This was the Scorpions, and when my gaze connected with Marx through the windshield, he pulled his lips back into a toothy grin that sent shivers down my spine.

"Shit," Guin said, shifting the gear into reverse. But it was too late. The Scorpions had closed in on us on either side, and Marx came to stand in front of the SUV, putting his hands on the hood.

"Isolde," he growled, his eyes a deep shade of violet. "Did you think you could run from me? Such a naughty girl."

My lungs sank into my stomach, my nerves lighting with the first signs of adrenaline. I wouldn't be taken by him, at least not without a fight.

Orion! Help!

We were too far away from each other for telepathic communication, and I wished I had called him back when he first texted. I wished he had sealed the mating bond when we had the chance. Would he even know something was wrong? That Marx had come for me? My canines extended and my fox took over, enhancing my senses. I heard at least four guys behind us, and another three still in the cars. We were extremely outnumbered.

I hovered over Orion's name on my phone and pressed call, hoping he'd answer soon enough for me to get out a plea.

"Come now, darling," Marx said, tilting his head to the side. "Don't make a ruckus. This will go much easier for you if you give in."

"Like hell," I said with a snarl, pushing my claws out.

"Oh, dear." He tsked. "I was afraid of that."

Orion didn't answer, and the deep sultry tones of his voicemail message echoed over speaker as glass exploded on my right, one of Marx's vampire cronies punching the window. When he reached inside to grab me, I scratched at his skin, grappling with the force of a man who was clearly much stronger.

"Get off me!" I shouted, biting and snarling at whatever I could, but it didn't matter. "Orion, help! The Scorpions—" I didn't get the rest out. He grabbed the back of my neck and slammed my head forward into the dash, and despite the fact that being a shifter should have made me more resilient to injuries, my vision blurred from the impact.

"Sol!" Guin's panicked cry faded into the background, and I thought I heard a gunshot, but after that, the world turned fuzzy.

I fought against unconsciousness, knowing I needed to stay awake, but my brain simply wouldn't comply. The world whizzed around me, hazy and confusing, and as a strong pair of arms lifted me into their embrace, I prayed Orion would get my message and find us, that this wouldn't end the way I feared.

Focus, my fox hissed. *Wake up.*

I clenched my eyes and winced against the aching burn cascading between my temples. When I opened them again, I had a long piece of fabric tied around my mouth, attached at the back of my head. My arms were bound behind my back and my ankles were roped together. I sat opposite my sister in the back of an SUV, and when my vision sharpened enough, I took a deep inhale of surprise at the blood caking the side of her face. She had a black eye and a bruised cheek, but the way her amber eyes glared at me told me she was more pissed than anything else. Shifters were stronger than humans and able to heal faster, but this far out from the next full moon, our fox selves were too weak to do much.

I started to panic, yanking at the restraints, kicking my legs to get free. I could only pray that Orion got my message, that he could understand what was happening through the screams.

"Stop that," came a voice from the back seat, a set of violet eyes staring down at me as a Scorpion smiled with long pointy fangs.

I didn't know much about vampires. Orion hadn't explained

more than the fact that they were our natural enemies and our blood was an aphrodisiac for them. Iron could wound them, as could a stake through the heart. But it wasn't like there were giant chunks of wood littering the back of the vehicle.

Guin's wide-eyed gaze told me to stay put, to play this out before doing anything rash, but the fox inside me squirmed with the thought of doing nothing. No, we had to get out, we had to figure out a way to stop this before it escalated into something that couldn't be undone.

Orion, I tried to call. *Please, Orion. Find me.*

When I focused hard enough on the thread tying us together, I sensed his apprehension and the thick cloud of confusion. Had he gotten my message? Could he feel how scared I was? Or had he firmly forgotten me, once and for all?

Impossible, the fox said.

He had to know something terrible had happened. Then that confusion escalated into full-blown fury and panic, the scalding rage of a wolf that had discovered his mate had been abducted, and I sighed in relief.

He'll come for us. He'll come. He'll come.

For the length of the ride, I stared at my sister, memorizing the familiar features of her face and finding comfort in how similar we actually were. We both looked like our father, the same ginger hair, the same green eyes. It shouldn't have surprised me that she'd turned out to be a shifter, too, but my world had gone from normal to unbelievable so quickly that I nearly had whiplash. Add in an abduction by the vampire enemies of my one true mate, and I'd swear I was living in a nightmare.

Wake up. Just wake up.

That never happened, and when the SUV came to a stop what felt like a decade later, I braced myself for the worst. The Scorpions got out of the vehicle and two of them circled around to open the back, wrapping their cold, disgusting fingers around my arm to haul me out. They did the same to my sister before I shifted my focus to the enormous building in front of me. At six stories tall and longer than a football field, it looked like it had once been an asylum or an orphanage.

The brick facade had been painted black and most of the windows had dark drapery behind them, turning it into a Gothic haunted house. I swallowed down the terror bubbling up the back of my throat, struggling against my handler when I saw Marx get out of the other SUV and walk closer.

"Now, now, my love," he said, coming close enough to brush a piece of hair behind my ear. I recoiled at his touch, the scent of decaying flesh and old blood permeating off his breath. "If you cooperate, nothing will happen to you or your sister."

I tried to scream, to mumble something along the lines of *Let me go,* but the appalling rag was still shoved in my mouth and all that came out was a series of muffled grunts and groans.

"Oh, you *are* a fighter." Marx threw his salt-and-pepper hair back to let out a loud, dark laugh, clapping as if that was the best thing he'd ever seen. "That's exactly how I like them. I want to hear you struggle."

"There's something else," said the guy holding my arm. "She smells different...from how she did a few weeks ago."

"Really?" Marx raised his eyebrows as he took a step closer and grabbed a piece of my hair, rubbing it between his fingers before leaning in to draw a long inhale. "Oh, how delicious. Are you a shifter, little thing?"

I took slow, measured breaths as I stared him down, biting down on the rag in my mouth to keep from screaming again. My canines dug into the fabric, elongated and penetrating, and I begged for them to be sharp enough to tear it. But I wasn't a wolf, and my tiny fox teeth barely made a dent.

"Fascinating." Marx turned his attention to Guin, who shot daggers through him with her amber gaze. "What about you, huh? The infamous Guinevere Vanderbilt." He took a few steps toward her and leaned down to run his nose over her forehead. "Whew! You both reek of animal. You should be in a zoo."

Funny for him to say. He smelled like a corpse, like he'd be king of the cemetery. And before this was over, I planned to make sure that was a reality.

"Take them inside," Marx said. "Make sure they see our guest."

Guest? I didn't like the way he said that word, and after my handler forced me up the stairs and into the foyer of the building, I gasped at the sight of my eldest brother standing among the gathered crowd.

Percy had his arms crossed with one elbow bent up toward his face, a finger over his lips as he watched these vampire thugs force us inside. I struggled against the Scorpion's hold, determined to get to my brother and claw his fucking eyes out.

"How could you!" I screamed around the gag, but the words were unintelligible, and Percy only winced and shook his head.

Guin, on the other hand, went stoically still at the sight, her fiery amber eyes drilling holes into him. I seethed with hatred, wondering why he would do this to his own blood. We were family. Vanderbilts. Did that mean nothing to him?

As I passed him, I realized that something was different about him. He didn't smell like a human, he didn't have the same glint to his blue eyes or the same blush in his cheeks. His skin had turned into a pale, translucent gray and his eyes were more black than indigo.

No. No, Percy. What did they do to you? And what about your wife?

Before I could question that further, the Scorpions put a hood over my head and dragged me into another room.

Orion

I was in the shower when she called me back, but the slice of panic that surged across our connection forced me to my phone with soap still dripping down my legs. My heart pounded, a burst of pain echoing through my soul when I saw she'd left me a fifteen-minute voicemail. I pressed play and clenched my eyes shut to listen.

"Get off me!" she screamed. *"Orion, help! The Scorpions—"* The muffled sound of a struggle came next, followed by someone else screaming Sol's name. That must have been Guinevere.

"You fucking bloodsuckers," she shouted. *"You fucking demons. You're gonna be so pissed when—"* Another loud bang, then the sound of closing doors and someone picking up the phone.

"Do you hear that, Bastard?" asked a deep voice, one I had to assume belonged to Marx. "I've got your snatch. Come find me if you can."

Then nothing—just dead silence until my voicemail cut off.

Scalding, blinding rage echoed through my body. Even if Sol and I hadn't officially made up, she was still my mate. I *had* to find her. I would. There could be no other option.

I dressed faster than I'd ever had and called Kodiak while I barreled toward the clubhouse in my pickup.

"Ry? What's going on?"

"They have her," I said. "They fucking took her." I explained as much as I knew, wincing against the agony in my chest. Whatever they were doing to her was painful, and it shimmied right through her into me.

"Where are you?" Kodiak's calm voice only set me off more.

"I'm at the clubhouse," I said, turning into the driveway and slamming the gear into park. When I raced out of the truck, Kodiak was already coming out of the door, Lycan and Poe close behind him.

"Sol said it was the Scorpions?" Lycan asked, his eyes gone ice blue with his wolf. I knew mine was close to the surface, too. I could feel him pacing in my mind, desperate to take over, furious that I'd made him be separated from Sol this long and now we faced the threat of losing her.

"Yeah," I said, replaying the message for them. Poe ran his hands back through his hair when Sol screamed, more pack members filing out of the clubhouse to listen in. Vermillion heard Guin's panicked cry and his gaze turned deadly.

"We have to go get them," I said. "Now."

"I told you this would escalate things," Ruby said, pointing a finger at me.

"Are we sure we're ready for this?" Larentia ran her hands over her jeans and grimaced.

"We've been preparing for a war with these fuckers for years," Serpent added, his eyes turning a darker shade of green.

"All right," Kodiak said. "Everyone take a deep breath. Vermillion, trace Sol's call. Let's find out where they were taken." He continued to bark out orders, some to Ruby and Serpent to get our guns in order, more to Moose and Talon to call in the rest of the pack.

But I couldn't think straight. All I could see were those fuckers tearing her limb from limb. They'd smell the shifter on her. Hell, it hadn't been that long; they might still smell *me* on her. And what then?

Would they kill her just to spite the Bastards?

Fuck, I should have completed the mating bond at Fiver. Now, I may never get the opportunity. And worse, I couldn't talk to her. Another bolt of her unimaginable terror ricocheted down our tiny tether and I cracked my neck, closing my eyes to try to get a hold of myself.

It wouldn't do any good to get emotional and worked up. No, I needed to stay levelheaded in order to find her, despite how difficult that might be.

"Brother, I need you to breathe," Kodiak said, gripping my shoulders. "She's been a part of the pack since the last moon. Between your blood in her veins and my tiny connection to her, we'll find her."

"She's not one of us," Ruby snarled, crossing her arms. "Why the hell should I risk my skin to go get her?"

"You wanna watch Orion go rabid?" Lycan shoved her shoulders, getting in her face as she bared her canines at him. "That's what'll happen if we *don't* do it. Be ready to put down the second because he's mated to her. And frankly, I'm more fond of her than I ever have been of you."

Ruby narrowed her eyes at Lycan and growled. "Say that again, you fuck boy piece of—"

"Enough! We can't let the Scorpions show us up," Moose cut in, and as third in the pack, neither Lycan nor Ruby would argue with him. "By now, they'll know she's a shifter and they'll smell Orion on her. If we don't go get her, word will spread that we can't protect our own. It'll be a matter of time before they do it again."

Ruby snarled, rolled her eyes, and stalked back into the club-house. I didn't focus on her disobedience. I'd let Serpent and Moose handle it later.

It had been just over a week since Isolde's transition so my magic still burned in her body. When I closed my eyes and focused on the thread tying me to her, I sensed it coming from Scorpion territory. We had enough intel to know where they holed up, and though I had no desire to go storming through a vampire nest, I'd do anything to get her back. I'd been named Orion for a reason. Between that and the surge of her fear in our mating bond, I should be able to track her down.

We can do it, my wolf growled. *Let's go.*

I struggled to slow him down, knowing I'd need the entire pack if I were going to be successful. The bloodsuckers wouldn't have taken her to Marx's house. That would be too risky, especially once they found out that she and her sister were shifters. They must have known we'd come for them, that we wouldn't let this stand.

"I can feel her, too," Lycan said, putting a hand on my shoulder. "I can tell she's scared, but she's still alive."

"That makes four of us," Poe said, holding his phone up to his ear. "It's small, but it's there."

"We'll be able to use the pack bonds to find her," Lycan continued. "Ry, it's gonna be okay. She's gonna be okay."

Rage boiled in my gut, overwhelming me, and when I opened my eyes again, the wolf and I had merged into one consciousness. He didn't want me doing this on my own, and I couldn't give control over to him completely. I'd need him to find her; I'd need all the help I could get.

We're going, he barked. *Now.*

Wait, I argued. *Wait for the alpha. Wait for the others.*

"We'll have to invade Scorpion territory," I said, the words deep and stoic despite the scalding wrath in my veins. "We need to go. Now."

"Orion," said my oldest friend in the world. "Don't do anything stupid."

My wolf laughed, but it wasn't out of amusement. No, it was out of the audacity of this man telling me what to do about my own mate.

"I've got Vermillion working on the tech side. Guin still has her phone on her, which is a fucking miracle." Kodiak's voice come out gruffer the more he talked, like his own beast was taking over. "He's tracing the signals. Between that and the bonds, we have enough."

"We're waiting too long," I roared, giving over to the anxiety. More anguish blared to life in my veins, Sol's physical pain bleeding over to me. I wilted at the hips, putting my hands on my knees to bear it. I yanked on the tether holding Isolde to my soul, sending as much power as I could through the thin thread, trying to let her know that she wasn't alone, that I wouldn't lose her to those fucking bloodsuckers.

I'm coming, little fox, I tried to tell her. *I'm coming.*

"Do it now!" I couldn't bear the separation any longer.

Kodiak's answering snarl should have warned me off commanding the alpha like that, but I couldn't care less. He could beat me later if he wanted to, or perhaps drag me into another sparring session to settle the dominance again. In that moment, I needed my friend to help me. I needed the alpha, the president of our MC, to protect one of our own, even if it hadn't officially been sealed yet.

As soon as I had her in my arms again, I'd get down on my knees and grovel for the rest of my life. I'd never let her go again. I'd make the mating bond permanent, just like she'd wanted me to that day in bed.

Eventually, most of the dominant members of the pack had gathered, and Larentia had armed as many of them as she could. We weren't fucking around, and we weren't going to waste time. While Guinevere wasn't a member of the pack, Isolde had shifted with us last moon, and a week from now, she'll have officially mated me. That made her family enough for the wolves to descend.

"Vermillion thinks the Scorpions took them to the asylum," Kodiak said, coming to stand next to me. "I'll smell them when we get close enough."

"Fucking great," Lycan snarled. "They'll all be there. We'll be outnumbered."

"Barely," Vermillion said, sitting his laptop on the hood of my truck while he typed. I came closer, watching as he pulled up footage from the nearby traffic cams. "I've been trying to hack into the Scorpion's security system since you called. It's slow going, but I'm almost there. This is the intersection just off the asylum property. They went through there only an hour ago. Based on this and the cell signal from Guinevere's phone, I'd say that was our best bet."

I cracked my neck and took a deep breath, trying to maintain control. The wolf was too pissed off, too furious to think clearly. He'd have us on a crusade to track them down immediately.

"So, what's the game plan?" Talon asked, crossing her arms while she glanced between the alpha and Moose.

"We're loaded down," Moose replied, nodding toward the vehicles that now contained a hell of an arsenal. "But it would be nice to get a head count."

"I'm thinking at least twenty," Vermillion said, clicking his fingers against the keyboard to bring up different vantage points. "Ugh, fucking finally! I'm in." He flipped the screen around so we could all see it, and Kodiak took a spot up front. There were a few Scorpion bloodsuckers mingling around out front, each with an assault rifle strapped over their shoulders that I knew had silver bullets inside. It wouldn't stop us, but shifters did have a weakness when it came to that specific metal. It would slow us down and hurt like a son of a bitch.

Likewise, we had enough iron bullets and stakes to put these fuckers back into their coffins for good. Being a shifter connected us more deeply to the earth, to the natural cycles of the world. But vampires had to die before they could rise up again, reborn with necromancy. They were abominations, and tonight, we would put as many as we could back into the grave permanently.

"Here we go," Vermillion said, clicking more buttons to bring up the cameras inside the massive space. It had once been an asylum for the criminally insane, the biggest one in the United States. In the seventies, it was shut down due to lack of funding and the inhumane treatment of the inmates. Now, it housed much worse than the scum of the human race. It was a breeding ground for the walking dead, the fucking blight of modern lore. "Holy shit. They brought in the calvary."

He flicked through the footage, going room to room while Moose counted vampires behind me.

"That's over fifty," Lycan said, letting out a defeated sigh. "How the fuck are we going to do this?"

Larentia walked closer, attaching the clip of her assault rifle before handing it to her brother. "We do it like we did after the raid."

We were much younger then and too naive to know the consequences of our actions. When the Scorpions snuck onto our property to wipe us out after a full moon, we had retaliated in the most brutal way possible. We'd waited until they were in a feeding frenzy, a massive party they threw a few times a year where the blood ran freely from human volunteers and drifters they'd managed to pick up. Drinking blood was like doing hard drugs for them. It induced an ecstasy similar to cocaine or MDMA for a human, and when they consumed it in large quantities, they lost track of reality.

Once their old leader had passed out, we snuck onto the property and staked them while they slept, while they fed, while they fucked each other in their blood-soaked euphoria. It had been a massacre, but we avenged our dead. That night still haunted my dreams, the screams of exploding vampires so piercing I'd never be free of the horror I'd created.

"We'll have Morwyn on standby so she can heal anyone when we get back," Larentia continued, reaching into her pants for her phone so she could contact the pack healer.

"They're not feeding," Serpent argued, rubbing a hand over the back of his head as he narrowed his penetrating eyes on Vermillion's laptop. "But I've got a few tricks up my sleeve. I could gas the place with a nerve agent I've been working on."

Talon shifted her weight. "What's it do?"

"It's made from shifter blood. It should simulate the effects of their feeding and knock them out for a while." Serpent shrugged.

"I've never actually tested it on vampires before, just their blood. But from what I've experimented with, it permeates their cells in the same way and disrupts their neural signals."

"For how long?" Larentia added, grabbing another rifle before sliding in a clip and handing it to me.

He shrugged. "Ten minutes? An hour? I don't fucking know. I've never used it before."

Kodiak nodded. "It's all we've got."

"Right," Lycan said, gathering our attention back to Vermillion's laptop, where he'd pulled up a blueprint of the building's design from the forties. The road captain ran down the plan, including how we'd divide up and invade through the various access points. I would go with Kodiak, Lycan, and Poe, and we'd head directly for the basement, where we believed they were keeping our girls. Moose would take Vermillion, Talon, Larentia, and the others through the rest of the place, putting down any Scorpions that stood in their way.

"The gas shouldn't affect us," Serpent said, grabbing a few stakes to slide into his thigh and chest holsters.

"Shouldn't?" Lycan balked and let out a sardonic laugh. "Fucking hell."

"I haven't had time to fully test it, but I've been okay." Serpent shrugged. "Morwyn didn't see anything flawed in my research."

"Yeah, except for the fucking screw loose in your head that makes you want to play with poisons all damned day." Lycan sighed and grabbed a gun from Larentia, loading himself with his own iron-made weapons.

"Focus," Kodiak snapped. "Tell everyone in the med-bay to be on high alert." He turned to me. "Chin up, Ry. We're going to get your girl."

They kept us bound and gagged in a dark, dank part of the basement, attached to the stone wall with thick silver chains. I yanked on them as hard as I could, knowing shifters were stronger than humans, but this far out from the next moon it did no good. My skin burned and the toxicity from the metal seeped into my bloodstream, making me feel drowsy and incoherent. The Scorpions must have prepared for that, or perhaps they made a habit out of keeping shifters locked up down here. Judging by the deep claw marks on the walls, that might be true.

When I gave up, I slumped to the ground and stared at my sister a few feet away from me. They'd hit her several times in the fight, bruising starting to swell around her eyes and temple. It pissed me off even more, and as soon as we got the opportunity, I'd sink my canines into anyone who touched her.

Minutes passed like centuries while we were locked down there, both of us still gagged. I had no idea exactly how long we sat in silence until a door opened and heavy boots thundered outside the door, closely followed by the click-clack of heels.

Ten Scorpions filled in around me, their black eyes glowing in the small fluorescent light hanging overhead. Now that I had a better chance to look at them, I recognized the difference between the Bastards and the Scorpions right away. Where the Bastards were full of life and energy, radiating warmth to anyone that came close, the Scorpions were the exact opposite. Each of them had translucent skin, so paper thin I could see the purple veins underneath. They reeked of rotting bodies, like roadkill no one had bothered to clear away.

Marx, especially, was more of a monster than a man. How long had he been a vampire? And how exactly did one become a vampire? Orion had never explained the process, and the lore varied from region to region. Could I base my reality on what I'd seen in films and TV?

"Well, well, well," Marx said, coming to stand in front of me. "If it isn't my bride to be?"

I stared up at him, daring him to make a move. I didn't have a death wish, far from it, but nor did I want to find out what happened when a vampire bit a shifter. Orion hadn't made it sound like a pleasant way to go. But if it was death or being his blood-thrall, I'd take the early grave.

"Did you think it would be that easy to get out of a deal with me?" Marx said, squatting down so he was eye level. Up close, I could make out every scar on his face, a crisscross pattern of fine silver lines. Had he gotten them while he was still a human? Did they happen while he tried to feed from his victims?

I bit my gag harder, my canines extending on their own as he got closer. I winced and pulled away, trying to get closer to the wall so he didn't touch me. But it was no use. He reached out and wrapped his cold, dead fingers into my hair, yanking my head back so I had to stare up at him.

"A deal with me is permanent," he said, shaking his head and tsking to chide me. "It's *unto death* for a reason."

The vampires behind him laughed, and I saw my brother toward the back of the crowd, his eyes wide and shifty as he took in the scene. I'd never been close to Percy. There was an eight year age difference between us, and he'd been well on his way to college by the time I'd been old enough to form memories. But now, I seethed with hatred for him. I'd see him dead and buried before I left here, so help me whatever deities would listen.

Marx opened his mouth into an evil, maniacal grin that showed off his fangs. They weren't like shifter canines, which were elongated versions of human teeth. No, vampire fangs were pointed across the top and the bottom, each tooth made for sinking into flesh.

"Those fucking Bastards are going to come for you, and when they do"—his disgusting smile sickened me—"I'm going to take great pleasure in killing you in front of them."

Guin yanked at her chains, snarling around the gag as Marx's hold on my hair twisted harder, making me whimper.

"Oh, does big sis have something to say?" Marx let out a demented laugh. "How about you, big bro? Why don't you go shut her up?"

Percy glanced between me and Guin for a moment before stepping through the crowd, making his way to our sister. He reached his hand back, and I thought I saw regret flash behind his expression before he brought his fist down on Guin's face hard enough to break her nose. A loud crack echoed through the basement before the metallic scent of blood filled the air. One of the other cronies came forward and stomped on Guin's leg so hard it snapped with an audible crunch and she let out another howl of pain.

Percy brought his knuckles to his mouth and licked them clean, letting out a deep moan at the response.

"Holy shit, that's good," Percy said.

"That's the shifter blood," Marx explained. "It can be tempting to drain them dry, but you need to be careful. There's a reason we're natural enemies, after all."

"Shifter blood can dilute the senses, even more than human blood," one of Marx's cronies explained. I read the nametag on his cut as Kol—Enforcer. "Drink too much, and you'll be out for days."

"What about their bites?" Percy asked. "Can a shifter bite harm a vampire?"

"Only if it's the full moon and they're in animal form," Kol explained, laughing. "That's why they're so fucking weak. Vampires are lethal every damn day, and a shifter can only do damage one day of the month."

I couldn't help myself. They were so wrong, so ill-informed, I laughed. Maybe a shifter's *bite* couldn't hurt a vampire, but I had claws and canines and a surly attitude, not to mention the pack that was coming for me. This got Marx's attention, and he looked back at me, narrowing his sinister gaze.

"Find that funny, do you?" He shook his head and hauled his arm back to bring it down on my face, the way my brother had done to Guin. Pain ricocheted through my body, erupting in my gut before sizzling back up my spine. He did it again, forcing my head to whip to the side, but I had expected it that time and braced myself to glance back up at him, blood pouring down my face from where he'd split open my cheek. I stared at him while he grabbed my chin so he could lick across my skin, capturing crimson on his tongue.

"Hmm, don't you taste magnificent?" He chuckled. "I should let my vampires have you. I should sink my fangs into your jugular and rip out your windpipe."

Instead, he punched me harder, sending me onto my side in the fetal position, where he kicked my stomach with his boots.

Hit him, the fox said. *Bite him. Claw him. Do something to protect yourself.*

I would. The second they took these manacles off my wrists, the minute I got away from the silver weighing me down, I'd fight tooth and nail. I had to. I sensed Orion's fury and panic growing stronger. He must have felt the agony pouring off me. I ignored it and tried to block out the pain. I didn't want Marx to win. I didn't want him to think he had any leverage over me.

"I should let my nest have you," he said, spitting on me like I was shit on the ground. "I should let Kol and his buddies fuck you until you learn some manners. Would you like that?"

Kol laughed, accompanied by a few of his other Scorpion blood-suckers.

"Yeah, I bet you would," Marx said. "That's how you got in with the Bastards, isn't it? You started fucking one of them like the Vanderbilt whore you are. Did they run through you like a train station? I bet they did. I bet you liked it."

Guin rattled her chains again, almost like she was trying to get Marx's attention, but he didn't budge. No, he squatted down next to me, grabbing my hair to pull me back up again. I winced against the ache in my scalp, trying to focus on him through eyes that burned with blood and dirt and impact trauma.

"I bet a little vampire dick would do you some good, huh?" One side of his mouth curled into that despicable grin. "Tell you what. I'm not interested in sloppy seconds, especially when it's a fucking Bastard that's already laid a claim. But Kol? He doesn't mind as much. And neither does half my nest." Marx let me go and turned on his heel to head back toward the gathered crowd. "Kol, if you want 'em, you can have 'em."

"What about the Bastards?" Percy cut in. "Don't you want to keep them in one piece so you can make a statement?"

Was that Percy's sad attempt at protecting us? I grimaced against the sheer torment rattling through my body, made even worse by the promise of rape and torture and whatever else that ghastly looking Kol might have in store for me and my sister.

Marx tilted his head at Percy and clapped him on the shoulder. "That's the human still inside you. Don't worry, the longer you stay with us, the more that will fade. One day, you'll wake up and hardly remember that you used to feel anything at all." Marx nodded to Kol and disappeared into the crowd, the sounds of his boots echoing down the hall.

"Now, which one of you can take a bigger cock, huh?" Kol rubbed his hands together as he looked between Guin and me. "I bet it's you, little sister."

He came closer as I tried to shrink away, but there was nowhere to go, and he wrapped his stony, ice-cold fingers around my bicep to haul me up. One of the other cronies unlocked the chains connecting me to the wall, but left the ones around my wrists before they both hauled me over to a desk in the far corner of the room.

I struggled against them, kicking my legs and swinging my arms as hard as I could, but it did no good. Vampires were nearly as strong as shifters, and I'd only known about my magical side for a week, hardly long enough to harness it when it wasn't a full moon.

My canines extended over the gag, pulsing with the need to sink into vampire skin, and just as I was about to give up, they sunk through the fabric, slicing it in two. I spat it out and leaned down to bite Kol's hand, rancid, tangy vamp blood filling my mouth in a disgusting rush that nearly made me retch. My claws extracted through the end of my fingertips, cutting into my own palms as I swiped out, tearing flesh and muscle.

"Fuck!" Kol winced and pulled back, but it was enough to give me a moment to react. I kicked out at the other vampire, surprised at my strength when I broke his knee and bent it back the wrong way.

"You fucking bitch!" the vampire screamed, but I'd gotten free enough to scramble toward my sister in a desperate attempt to break her out. Fueled by Orion's magic and the strength he sent down the bond between us, I could get her out. And then we could—

Strong arms wrapped around my waist, picking me up off the ground.

"You're gonna pay for that, you feral little cunt." Kol's voice grated like sandpaper on my skin and his blood stank. My heart pounded and I struggled harder, kicking and snapping my teeth at whatever I could get. But another vampire stepped in to help him, wrapping a piece of fabric around my mouth, thicker and tighter than the one before it.

It took three of them to subdue me, Kol pinning my arms to my sides and two others to hold each leg. I squirmed against them as they carried me out the door, my panic blaring into terror as they separated me from Guin. She yanked at the restraints and tried to reach for me, but the silver weighed her down and my last glimpse was of her scrambling to try to get to me.

I struggled, twisting and turning, trying with everything in me to get away from them as we climbed four flights of stairs. Eventually, they took me into a long, dark hallway and turned into a room on the right, my muscles tensing when I saw all kinds of torture implements on the wall. Pincers and maces with thick, stabby points and needles the size of my arms. But the thing that terrified me the most was a syringe containing some kind of shimmering gray liquid—likely silver.

"I've got a surprise for you, shifter bitch," Kol said, throwing me down in the center of the space. I tried to push to my feet so I could run, but one of the other vampires punched me hard across the cheek, and the torment shooting down my face and into my body made me wince. My vision darkened for a moment, only a heartbeat, but it was long enough for them to attach my cuffs to a chain hanging by the ceiling before yanking it taut. It forced me to my feet, my arms stretched up above me, my toes barely touching the ground.

And when Kol picked up the needle containing something that would most definitely burn, I screamed.

CHAPTER 24

Orion

The smoke bombs worked, at least on the levels where we could get them. Vampires dropped like dead flies, seemingly comatose on the ground...at least until I drilled bullets into their chests. The tiny amount of iron in each shot wouldn't keep them out for long, but after I found my girl, I'd come back with a machete and cut their heads off to put them down permanently.

Lycan, Kodiak, and I stalked through the asylum like soldiers invading a hostile country, our alert on high, our rifles at our chests, our trigger fingers poised to pull. The hazy cloud of Serpent's blood poison dissipated as we walked farther down the hall, but I sensed them before they jumped out at me. Two male vampires flashed their fangs in a loud hiss and attacked from around a corner.

I fired two holes into each chest and one in each head for good measure, just to keep them unconscious for now.

"First floor secured," came Moose's voice through earpieces. "We're heading upstairs."

"Be careful," Talon said, echoing my sentiments.

My human side had merged so completely with my wolf that I'd nearly lost all sense of empathy. We remained focused on one thing:

finding Isolde. It didn't matter what happened, it didn't matter what stood in my way. She was still alive and somewhere close.

"This way," Kodiak said, closing off communication to just me and Lycan so the others could focus on what they needed to do. He stepped in front of me, leading us down a long corridor with doors on either side.

I pointed my gun at each as we passed, satisfied the vampires were too doped up to move, but as we got farther down, the poison stopped working.

A Scorpion launched itself out of a room on our right, taking Lycan down to the ground. He tried to shoot at it, but his rifle didn't go off. The vampire snarled and Lycan barely had his arm up in time to stop it, but I leapt into action. I aimed my gun at the vamp's head and pulled the trigger, feeling nothing when it exploded brain and blood all over my brother.

"Fucking yuck!" Lycan spat and rolled to the side, wiping at his face, which was now covered in disgusting vamp insides. "Why are they so fucking gross?"

"You're all right," I said, holding out my hand to help him to his feet, but I noticed the bite mark as soon as he reached out to grab it. "Make sure you get that looked at when we get back to the clubhouse. Who knows what the hell kind of disease they carry."

He ripped off a piece of his T-shirt and tied it around the wound before giving me a firm nod.

"C'mon," Kodiak said. "I can feel something in the basement."

My heart raced and I took long, slow breaths to calm it down, knowing it wouldn't do any good to get panicked. I already sensed Isolde's anxiety and terror pulling through the bond, and I sent her as much of my strength as I could, tunneling it into the magical connection.

What I wouldn't give to be anywhere else with her right now. Perhaps on a beach or somewhere in the woods. Once we were out of this, I'd pray for her forgiveness. I'd never let her out of my sight again. I'd have her in my bed every night and at my side every day. I'd bring her back to pack territory, her family be damned. She was a member of the Bastards now, a part of the Helena shifter pack, and that could never change.

I took another shot when a female Scorpion jumped out of a corner in the ceiling, snarling and screaming and spitting venom, but my gun didn't go off. I didn't know if it was jammed or out of bullets, but she managed to latch on to me, her fangs going for my neck. My wolf reacted, snarling as I sunk my claws into her carotid and yanked. Her throat tore open, spilling more gore all over me, and fucking hell, I'd look like a monster by the time I got to Isolde.

"Nice," Lycan said.

"C'mon," Kodiak said. "We're almost to the stairs."

I fiddled with my rifle, reloading it as we carried on. It felt like it took an hour to walk down the massive corridor, but eventually, we reached a dead end with two exit doors on either side of us and one directly in front of us. Kodiak walked forward and kicked that entry open, revealing a set of concrete stairs that led both up and down. We headed down, our boots echoing like crashing thunder. As soon as we got to the lowest level, the electricity went out. More gunshots rumbled from the floors above us, but I couldn't focus on that.

Moose and the others could take care of themselves. I needed to find my girl and get her to safety. No distractions. Lycan and Kodiak paused to look around, but I took a moment to let my vision adjust to the darkness, to let the scents of the rooms ahead guide me.

The rancid smell of Isolde's fear nearly sent me into a blind rage, and if it weren't for Lycan and Kodiak next to me, I would have gone screaming into the space without any reservations. Instead, I stayed in formation, holding my rifle higher, gripping the trigger just in case I needed to pull it.

Kodiak opened the door on the basement level, where Isolde's scent was the strongest. I followed closely behind him, where I came face-to-face with Percival Vanderbilt. He held his hands up, his red eyes streaming blood down his cheeks as he wept.

"Please," he said, flashing a mouth full of fangs. "Please help them."

"What the fuck is this?" Lycan whispered. "They turned him?"

"Where are they?" Kodiak asked the eldest Vanderbilt son.

"The last room on the right." Percy took a step to the side, letting out another desperate sob. "Please, I couldn't stop it. I tried, I did. But I couldn't stop—"

I shot him in the forehead, right between the eyes. I didn't give a shit if he felt remorseful. It was one thing to be a Scorpion and do this because Marx commanded it. It was quite another to betray your sisters for the sake of money and power. Perhaps Percy felt like he didn't have a choice, but I didn't give a fuck. The motherfucker was a disloyal piece of shit, and as soon as I had my girl in my arms, I'd take his fucking head for doing this to her.

We stalked down the hallway, three shifters with our canines ready to tear into anything that came for us. I grimaced as the pull to Isolde got weaker, perhaps indicating that she wasn't in here...or that she was dead. I damn near sprinted to the end of the hallway, kicking open the door so hard it burst off the hinges.

The first thing I saw was Guinevere hunched down in the corner of the room, her nose and face bleeding, her eyes bruised from what-ever they'd done to her. Two Scorpions rushed at us, but Lycan and Kodiak took care of them as I scanned the room for Isolde...only to realize it was empty.

She isn't here.

"Where?" I growled, my voice sounding inhuman. I had completely blended with my wolf now, and after this was over, it would take some time to fully separate again...if I ever could.

"They took her," Guin said when Kodiak pulled her gag down. "She's upstairs somewhere."

Yes. Go. Upstairs.

My wolf and I didn't wait around. I turned and sprinted out of the room, down the hallway, and back up the stairs. I didn't sense her on the first or second floors, her terror mixing with my fury to make the draw stronger.

Where are you? Where are you?

I took the stairs two at a time, Lycan close on my heels. I probably should have waited for Kodiak. I probably should have made sure her sister and my alpha got out okay before I took off on my own, but I didn't care. The only thing on my mind was getting to her wherever she was.

When I got to the third floor, my wolf bucked in my mind, the bond vibrating in my chest as her scent got heavier.

Here!

I burst through the stairwell door where five Scorpions jumped me. Lycan fired iron bullets, and I clawed at whatever bodies stood between me and my girl, but they were powerful. One sank their fangs into my left bicep and ripped, sharp slices exploding through that side of my body.

"Fuck," I growled, shoving that bloodsucker away. Another snapped at my face and I ducked out of the way just in time to prevent it tearing into my cheek.

"Orion!" Vermillion tugged that vamp off me, swinging a machete at its neck to separate the head from its body. "I've got it here. Go!"

Lycan and Vermillion took on the fight while I disentangled myself from the chaos and raced toward Sol. I sensed her behind the third door on the right, and when I tried to barrel inside, the barrier wouldn't budge. I banged my good side against it over and over again, but it didn't move.

"Isolde!" I threw myself at the metal, my wolf frantic to get through, and finally, with one more good shove, it gave and I tumbled inside.

To my utter horror, Isolde hung from the ceiling by her wrists, her bloody face leaned up against her arm, her pants down around her ankles and her shirt nearly ripped off her body. A huge vampire stood behind her, fangs extended with what I assumed was her blood dripping from his lips.

Something inside me snapped. No one hurt my mate. *No one.* I let out a growl and emptied my clip into the huge Scorpion, but that didn't do enough damage. Unsheathing my claws and extending my canines, I rushed the motherfucker, taking him down to the ground. He shoved at my shoulders, trying to get me off him, but I was too big...too heavy...too pissed off. I sank my teeth into his throat, curling my fangs around his windpipe, and yanked.

The wretched taste of decaying flesh filled my mouth, coppery and disgusting, and I spat it out before I went back for more. One hand under his chin, the other digging my claws into his chest, I tore at his neck until I got bone...and then I went deeper until finally I hit the ground. When I had his filthy fucking head in my hands, I tossed it to the side and stood, immediately looking for Isolde.

She was barely conscious, so I pushed more of my strength and magic down our bond, grimacing as my vision sparkled from the effort. I was losing blood from the bite on my arm, but I had to make sure she was safe. I had to get her out of here.

When I broke the restraints and freed her wrists, she fell into me like she couldn't hold up her own weight. Her head lulled to my shoulder, her knees buckling under the strain.

More, my wolf urged, and I poured my desperation into her, pulling at Kodiak's magic to reinforce what I was giving. He didn't resist. He let me have it, and finally, she gasped. Her head shot upright, her brilliant amber eyes blinking up at me.

"Little fox," I whispered, bringing my forehead to hers. Her pulse beat strong and steady as I grabbed the back of her neck and held her jaw.

"My wolf," she said, and I melted against her, yanking her in close, wrapping my arms to hold her there, certain I would never let her go again.

"Are you hurt?" I said as I looked her over for serious injuries.

"No," she said, clearly choking back a sob. "Nothing time won't fix."

Relief flooded my veins, calming that churning in my stomach that had been there since I first tasted her helplessness. Now that I had her in my arms again, after suffering the thought of losing her, I knew all the shit I'd been angry about didn't matter anymore. I loved her unconditionally. I loved her more than life itself. My mate. My one true love. Finally, the wolf and the human accepted it, and I would never let her leave again. I'd spend the rest of our lives making it up to her.

"I'm sorry," I said. "I'm so fucking sorry. I love you."

She ran her trembling bloody fingers down my face and smiled. "I love you, grumpy wolf."

I didn't care that I had Scorpion blood on my mouth and dripping down my chin, and seemingly neither did she. Isolde brought her lips to mine, kissing me like she'd been gone for years rather than a few days. I held her close to allow time for our primal natures to be comforted in each other's company.

She's alive, the wolf told me. *She's still alive. Never let her leave our sight again. Never again.*

"I've got you, baby girl," I told her. "I've got you."

"You've got me," she murmured back. "Thank you for coming for me...for us."

I hauled her into my arms, one under her knees and the other around her shoulders, ignoring the screaming pain coming from my bicep. However, when I got back into the hallway, my heart dropped into my gut.

Lycan and Poe each had one of Vermillion's arms over their shoulders, their hands on his waist as they hauled his crimson-soaked body down the hallway. His head hung limp in front of him, suggesting he was unconscious, but his pale skin hinted at something worse.

"We need to move," Lycan said, nodding toward the door. We headed toward the stairs, taking them two at a time until we got to the main level. From there, it would be a quick left turn outside and into our SUV. Except when we got to the main level, the smoke had cleared and most of the vampires that we'd put down had started to wake up. Marx stood at the head of the hallway with Larentia in his arms, a gun at her head and his fangs next to her throat.

"Uh, uh, uh," he said, nodding toward Isolde. "That's not yours. Her brother sold her to me weeks ago, long before you could touch her."

I dropped Isolde and pushed her behind me, growling at the Scorpion leader, my canines throbbing with the need to tear into his throat next.

But Larentia wasn't some meek submissive that would go down without a fight. She glanced from me to Lycan and back to Vermillion before extending her claws and sinking them into the vampire's thigh. Marx let out a loud groan and wilted, taking a step back before he could pull the trigger on the gun. I grabbed his hand and pushed it over her head as it went off. Larentia got free and moved toward her brother as I shoved him away.

He grappled with me, hissing and spitting, while I roared my frustration. I had to kill him now. If I didn't, he would keep coming for Isolde. He wouldn't rest until he'd obtained his perceived restitution, and I wouldn't let him hurt her again.

"You bloodsucking piece of shit," I snarled as I swiped out with the claws on my good hand, determined to tear his eyes out of his head. Just as I made contact, Marx swirled to the side, kicked himself off the wall and took off down the hallway, disappearing into the darkness on the other end.

I wanted to go after him. I wanted to hunt him down until it was his blood on my tongue, but Isolde needed me.

"Orion," she whimpered. "Help me. Please."

I'd almost lost her once, and I wouldn't put either of us in that position a second time. I scooped her up and pushed through the exit door into the crisp winter air, where the rest of my pack waited for us by the SUVs.

Kodiak glanced between us, but his grief-stricken focus landed on Vermillion and he jumped into action, shouting orders at whoever was around while he helped Lycan and Poe get our injured brother into the nearest SUV. Based on the gaping hole in the pack bonds and the amount of agony pulling on my dwindling strength, I figured whatever had happened to Vermillion wasn't the end of our casualties.

I sat next to Isolde in the house on our territory built specifically for our pack healer to take care of us in an emergency. We called it the med-bay, but it was more like a rancher that had been converted to a doctor's office.

In the center of the chaos, Morwyn struggled over Vermillion's lifeless body, pushing as much of her healing magic into him as she could. Her dark curly hair had been tied up on top of her head and her bright blue eyes were clenched shut in concentration as she radiated her hand over his forehead and down to his chest.

"Damn it, Vermillion. Respond," she said, her voice shaking. Vermillion was her older brother, so this was no ordinary patient. For her, this was her literal flesh and blood. I felt the horror ripping through her, the grief and the disbelief that something could have happened to him...that she might not be able to save him.

She gripped Kodiak's other hand tight, yanking on the pack bonds, pulling as much strength from us as we could give her.

After I'd gone into the room to get Isolde, he'd taken on ten vamps by himself. According to Lycan, he almost beat them off. But just as he'd brought down the biggest, another one got him in the neck, sinking their fangs into his jugular and ripping it clean out. He sank like a stone, his life's blood gushing from the wound and his mouth and nose. Lycan knew he wouldn't survive without help.

Poe got there in enough time to put pressure on the blood flow and tried to staunch it himself, but he wasn't the pack healer. He didn't have the medical training and the special connection with Kodiak the way Morwyn did. He couldn't pull on the pack's energy to transfer that into curing ailments. That was Morwyn's gift, and hers alone.

But as I sat there, clutching Isolde's hand and waiting for the silver in her veins to wear off, I realized something horrible.

The absence in the pack's bonds was due to the fact Vermillion had died. He was barely hanging on while we were still at the asylum and now Morwyn was plunging shifter magic into a soul that had already passed on.

"Morwyn," Kodiak said, kneeling down beside her. "Morwyn, stop."

"No, I can save him. I can—" She sobbed and wilted over her brother's corpse, and my heart cracked into pieces as I sat helpless and watched her.

He had sacrificed himself for me to save Isolde. He had given his life for someone he'd never met, and I'd never be able to repay him.

My eyes burned as tears gathered in the corners, my muscles shivering under the weight of the pack's collective pain. Sure, there were others in the med-bay with injuries. We'd nearly lost four other shifters in the fray, and Morwyn had already expelled so much of her magic saving them. My arm had deep bite marks, Lycan needed ten stitches, and Talon nearly had her leg sliced off. We were beat-up and bruised, but most of us would recover without any permanent damage.

Now, I sat with my mate's hand in my mine, watching the pack healer mourn her only remaining family.

"Goddamn it, Vermillion," she shouted, beating on his chest. Her wails sliced through me, cleaving me in two. My soul ached for her, and shame rattled through me. "Goddamn it. Don't do this to me. You promised you wouldn't leave me. You promised."

She slumped to her side, exhausted and bereft, and Kodiak

wrapped his arms around her, holding her shaking body to his while she continued to try to revive him.

"He's gone," Kodiak said. A few pack members gasped and some glanced in my direction, raking their gazes over Isolde like it was her fault Vermillion had died. "He's—"

I sensed it at almost the same time as the alpha—the stirring in the pack dynamic, the sudden surge that replaced the terrifying void.

Vermillion sucked in a gasp and arched his back off the floor, his eyes shooting open in that glorious hue of deep mahogany that I associated with his wolf.

"Fuck," Morwyn said, clambering upright so she could put her hands on his throat, pushing more pack energy into him. I gave it freely. I sensed it yank from my soul into Kodiak's and down into Morwyn. Exhausted from the fight and what I'd already poured into Isolde, I started to get woozy, but I didn't stop. I gave everything I had, knowing what the pack had done to bring my mate back to me.

Vermillion thrashed while Poe and Kodiak held him down so Morwyn could give him something to knock him out.

"Shh, shh, shh," Guinevere said, kneeling next to Vermillion's head, brushing the hair out of his face. "Van, it's me. It's Guin."

He tried to say her name, but all that came out was a garbled whisper. And when I'd given all that I could, all that was left in me, I put my head down on Isolde's bed and let unconsciousness take hold.

I fell asleep in Orion's arms on the way back to Bastard territory. Safety and security surrounded me, warmth trickling from my heart into my gut as I finally relaxed. I inhaled his strong masculine scent with every breath, reminding me the nightmare was over, that I was reconnected with the love of my life and nothing could ever tear us apart again.

Sometime later, I woke up in an unfamiliar bed, the scent of my big grumpy wolf calming my fox. One of his heavy arms was draped across my body, the other tucked protectively under my head. The smell of cleaner and latex assaulted my nose and, when I glanced around, I realized we were in some sort of makeshift hospital.

My head throbbed, and I'd obviously swallowed fire judging by how raw my throat felt. Every muscle in my body ached like I'd run full steam into a freight train carrying a planet's worth of bricks. But when I turned to see Orion, the weight that had been on my chest for the last few days lifted.

He'd come for me. He'd heard my voicemail and felt my panic and come for me.

Memories of being strung up in that vampire's hellhole flashed through my mind, the feel of the silver coursing in my veins making me want to shrivel up into a ball. It was the most agonizing torture I'd ever been through, like acid in my blood, fire in my bones. My entire body felt aflame. Tears formed at the corners of my eyes and I tried to blink them back, but a desperate sob wrenched out of my lungs and I struggled to breathe.

Orion's arms tightened, pulling me closer to him.

"It's okay, little fox. I'm here. I've got you." His murmured words soothed the horrible memories, and I turned to face him, tucking my head under his chin to inhale his woodsy scent.

"I'm sorry I didn't tell you about the Scorpions," I said. "I should have said something sooner. I should have done it all different."

"Shh," he said, kissing my forehead before using his nose to nudge me up, so I had to look at him. "I'm sorry I reacted the way I did. I hated the thought of him putting his hands on you, of losing you. I shouldn't have let you walk away. My temper got the best of me. I won't let it happen again."

"Do you still want me?" I hung on the anticipation of his answer, knowing I couldn't face his rejection again.

"I love you, little fox. Forever. I always will."

His words broke me, and I cried harder, letting the weight of everything I'd been through pour out of me. I hated the fact I couldn't get through this without sobbing. I'd just survived a hell of a trauma, but my fox wanted to be strong for him, to let him know I deserved to be his mate because I could withstand whatever this life threw at me.

You're good enough as you are, my fox reminded me. *You deserve him because he's your mate. That's all.*

I needed the cleanse this release brought me. I needed to process the emotional weight of all I'd been through.

"I love you, too, grumpy wolf," I said. "Please mate me. Please let me stay with you."

"You won't be able to run away from me," he said. "Not again. Never again."

That, too, comforted the side of me that needed him to feel safe and whole. We were mates, irrevocably and infinitely.

Sometime later, the healer came in to check on us, and Orion introduced her as Morwyn. She had bright blue eyes and a kind smile, but she seemed exhausted, her features drawn and her skin pale.

"The silver should be out of your system by now," Morwyn said before glancing at Orion's arm. "And you're all healed up, which isn't surprising."

I narrowed my eyes as I wondered what she meant.

"It's because you're with me," Orion said, obviously sensing my confusion. "You'll heal faster when you're with your mate. It's the magic."

"The magic," I repeated, nodded.

"Whatever it is that makes us shift, whatever it is about me that helped you transition, it's what decided we were the most compatible together." He brushed a piece of hair out of my face. "There's a reason for that and a whole host of benefits."

"One of them is healing each other," Morwyn continued. "When you need it, he gives you energy. When he needs it, you give him the same."

"Morwyn is the pack healer," Orion went on. "She can draw energy from us all in order to save the pack. That's how she healed you. Otherwise, the silver would have taken days to clear out."

"Thank you," I said to Morwyn.

She pursed her lips and nodded. "We're all happy Orion has mated, but you should know, Vermillion is still in critical condition. I don't know if he'll ever be able to talk again. Ruby and some of the others are furious."

Orion snorted a disbelieving noise and shook his head. "I'm not afraid of Ruby."

"I'm not worried about you." Morwyn glanced at me and raised her eyebrow. A chill raced down my spine and I tried my best to hide it. "I'll let you two get ready to leave. Kodiak's called a meeting, and you should go."

"What happened to Vermillion?" I asked after she left.

Orion ran a hand back through his hair and sighed. As we dressed in clean clothes, he explained what it had cost the pack to get me and Guin out of there. He told me about Ruby's reluctance to be involved and how she feared the worst would happen. "It almost did."

Guilt settled in my gut, rotten enough to make me feel like I would vomit. I didn't like the thought someone had almost died so I could live. It shouldn't have had to be that way, and now that Marx had escaped, the war would continue.

"It's okay, little fox," he said, grabbing the back of my neck so he could pull me in for a kiss. "This is what pack does. I would gladly lay down my life if it meant saving any one of them. The lone wolf dies, but the pack gives. The pack thrives."

"Will they ever forgive me?" I asked, determined to do whatever it took to earn my place with Orion's family.

"You're the second's mate, the VP's old lady. You've already won over Lycan and Poe. You'll be okay, I promise."

I nodded and prayed he was right. Of course, I wanted more than to be okay. I wanted them to like me. I wanted to be their family.

"Let's go." He held out his hand for me to take. "The clubhouse is a short walk from here."

While he led me across the Bastard property, he told me about how the pack worked. Their ranch sat on a few thousand acres that everyone in the club helped maintain. Each adult member had their own house, but the younger shifters chose to stay in the dormitories together, preferring to be around others their own age.

"Is that where I should be living?" I asked, pleased when he grabbed my fingers, growled, and kissed my knuckles.

"You better be in my bed every night or I'm going to come looking for you." He said it with a playful grin, but I recognized the serious look behind his eyes. He really would drag me back to his room if he had to, but he never would. There was no place I'd rather be.

He turned onto a snowy gravel driveway leading up to a building that looked like it had been converted from an old barn and turned into a large house. Together, we walked inside, and I braced myself against whatever would await me.

Truthfully, I'd been nervous to meet the rest of the pack. Sure, some of them had come to rescue me and my sister, and maybe I had some allies with them. But I feared what this Ruby would say, especially with Vermillion still so injured.

All eyes shifted to us when we entered the enormous room. The floors were concrete and various Bastards sat around at random tables scattered throughout. A large door on my right led to a room in the back with a desk and a long, rectangular table with the Royal Bastards logo burned into it. Across from us, more shifters sat at a bar with a marble countertop, all swiveling around to face us. Behind that were pool tables, but no one stood around them.

I recognized some of the faces from the night they'd come to save me, particularly the woman who'd clawed Marx so Orion could try to take him down.

Larentia, I think.

"There she is," Lycan said, sauntering up to me with his arms open. "How are we feeling, your worshipfulness? All that silver gone now?"

"Okay," I said, giving him a hug. Sure, my head throbbed and my body ached, but now that Orion and I were with the pack, there was a noticeable difference in intensity. As if being with them made it easier to bear. Poe followed closely behind him, pulling me into a tight embrace before turning to point at Kodiak and Guin in the back room.

I raced to my sister, tears burning my eyes at how rough she looked, so much worse than me. Where I'd healed with the help of my mate, she didn't have one, or if she did, she was too far away from him to be of help. Perhaps she was wrong about Vermillion, after all.

"I'm glad you're okay," she said, hugging me despite the fact I knew her love language definitely was not physical touch.

"Me too," I said. "Have you talked to Maeve or Avalon? How is everyone at home?"

She shrugged. "We'll check in after this, okay?"

I nodded as Kodiak walked closer, his massive arms crossed. Objectively, the Bastard alpha was gorgeous. He had bright, intelligent eyes that saw more than he'd likely admit, and his strong body spoke to the hours he must have spent in the gym. I wondered where his mate was because certainly someone like him couldn't be single.

"Isolde," he said, holding a hand out for me to take. "Welcome to the Royal Bastards clubhouse. I'm glad you've healed up."

I took it and gave it a firm shake, recalling the last time we'd been introduced had ended with him berating Orion for having seen me through the transition and mating me without his knowledge. Now, he seemed much friendlier.

"Thank you," I said.

He nodded to the table behind him and glanced up at the Bastards still mingling around. "C'mon everyone. We've got two new pack members to greet and a deal to make."

Deal? What deal?

Orion hadn't mentioned anything about that, but when I furrowed my brows at Guin and she smiled in response, I figured she had worked her business magic on the alpha before I'd arrived.

Orion pulled me over to a seat next to Kodiak before sitting and tugging me down into his lap. A few of the other shifters eyed me curiously as they filed in, but most smiled and waved in a genuinely friendly greeting.

Growing up, I'd had a few friends at boarding school, but none I would consider close enough to call family. I understood this pack's closeness immediately. Because I had mated Orion, I was already in the family. I still had to earn my place, just as I had to at the Fiver, but they would give me the benefit of the doubt because their second in command, their vice president, had mated me. And if a grumpy Bastard like him could find it in his heart to love me, then surely they could as well.

Lycan and Larentia sat opposite of me, and a few other Bastards wearing cuts filled in the rest of the table. Poe stood off to the side while all the members of the club circled around us.

"Brothers and sisters, family," Kodiak started, standing at the head of the table with his fingertips on the surface. "We have much to discuss. First, we have two new members of the pack: Isolde and Guinevere Vanderbilt." He gestured to us. "Both take the shape of a fox during the moon, and they'll be turning with us from now on."

"So she's the one we almost lost Vermillion for?" one of the members of the pack asked, their eyes shifting between me and Guinevere, who stood next to Kodiak—close enough to touch his shoulder. My mate tightened his arms around me for a moment before he took a deep breath and let it go on a sigh.

"That's my mate you're talking about," Orion snarled, his eyes turning sky blue. "Be careful what you say next."

"I feel the bonds to them," Kodiak said before the naysayer could respond, "Even without performing the ritual, they are present."

"Isolde, I understand," someone else said. "She's mated to our second, to the veep. Her sister?" They shook their head. "Forgive me for saying so, but the Vanderbilts are ruthless."

"And what would you have me do?" Kodiak asked, pursing his lips. "Leave a shifter to suffer the moons alone? Her sister is in the pack. She is connected to us in more ways than one." Kodiak shifted his shoulders uncomfortably, like there was more he wanted to say but couldn't. "Know this—if she was not meant to be in the pack, there wouldn't be a bond."

"I can speak for myself," Guin cut in, glancing at the person who'd suggested she shouldn't be here. "I've known about you all for over ten years. I've been searching the rest of the country for shifters similar to us, and the magic is different depending on where you go.

In all that time, I could have screwed you over a thousandfold. I haven't."

"That we know of," grumbled that same person.

"Tell you what, old man," Guin said, turning so she faced the guy questioning her. "If you find out I've betrayed you in some way, you can challenge me yourself." Whispers echoed around the club, some disbelieving, some impressed. "You all like to do that, don't you? Beat each other down to see who's on top? You look like you hit your stride in the eighties. I bet I could have you on your knees, begging me for a reprieve."

Lycan laughed, echoing a few other chuckles coming from other people, including Larentia. But the other female at the table, the one that looked like she could be Kodiak's sibling, only ran her tongue over a canine and raised her eyebrow at my sister.

Ruby.

"Is that a promise?" she asked.

Guin narrowed her gaze on Ruby and put her hands on the table, leaning closer to the pack member. "You bet. You wanna handle this now?"

"Maybe I do." Ruby crossed her arms. "Brother, I told you what would happen if we trusted the Vanderbilts and we almost lost pack because of it. Now, you leave us no room for concern?" She shook her head. "It doesn't sit right."

"Enough," Kodiak cut in. "As alpha, it's my right to welcome anyone into the pack that I deem worthy. I have enough support from the rest of my council to override vetoes from the others."

More grumbles of approval came from the crowd, and his disapproving sister let out a long sigh.

"We'll perform the pack and mating rituals at the next new moon in a week's time." Kodiak pushed upright and cleared his throat. "There are two other matters to discuss. Guinevere?"

She cleared her throat and crossed her hands together in front of her as I raised my eyebrows, curious about where this was going.

"On behalf of the Vanderbilt family, I want to extend my thank-you to everyone that risked their lives to save me and my sister." She glanced around the room, making sure to linger on Ruby before focusing on Kodiak. "We are in your debt."

He nodded, accepting the acknowledgment. And though I didn't know for certain, I figured owing the pack a debt meant something important, more than it did between humans.

"We got into this predicament because our late brother decided to be a greedy little prick and make a deal with the Scorpions rather than wait for me to find an alternative." Guin cleared her throat and straightened, reminding me so much of our father in that moment, I almost could have cried. "I propose a truce. For too long our families have been enemies, divided when we should have stood together. Our lands border each other. We can help each other."

"What are you proposing?" the man sitting next to us asked. His cut read Moose.

"We need workers to help us through the winter. We're already behind schedule, and the ranch hands I was able to secure won't be nearly enough."

"And in exchange?" Moose asked.

"We make you the same deal—money and land. A future with Vanderbilt Enterprises. A treaty with the most powerful and influential family in Helena...probably even Montana."

Mumbles came from around the crowd, and I swelled with pride at Guin's brilliance. This had been what we'd talked about before the abduction. This had been our plan. As I sat there and watched them mull it over, I realized Guin and I may have done what our father never could. We may have ended this feud with the Royal Bastards, and all it took was one offer of good will.

"Think about it," she said. "But time is wasting, so don't take too long."

"We'll discuss it at our next council meeting, and I welcome any and all thoughts from the pack." Kodiak nodded. "Thank you, Guinevere."

"Thank you, Kodiak," she said, smiling at me before taking a step back behind him again.

"And finally, Moose." Kodiak turned to the shifter next to us. "What's the final count on the Scorpions? How many heads did we take?"

"Near fifteen. We burned their bodies and buried the heads, just like you asked," Moose said, inducing a round of hoops and hollers from the pack. I sensed the warm spark of joy emanating from Orion and the others, the thought of fewer vampires in the world an overwhelming feat. "But we nearly lost Vermillion and four others. Opal and Fenris are still in critical condition."

"And Marx?" Kodiak looked to Serpent, who took a long inhale of his cigarette and let it out with a shrug.

"We're still looking for him," he said. "But I'm sure he'll pop up sooner or later. He won't let something like this stand."

"I agree," Lycan said, a deep growl erupting from his chest. "He wants Sol. He feels he's *owed* her. He'll come for her, and he won't stop until he has her."

"He's welcome to try," Orion said from behind me. "But the next time that bloodsucking motherfucker looks in her direction will be the last time he has eyes. I'll tear his head off myself."

More claps of approval came from around us, and I shifted closer to Orion, feeling safer than I had in my entire life.

"Let me know if anything comes up." Kodiak straightened and turned his attention to me and Orion. "It's seven days until the new moon. Rest up. Prepare yourselves. We'll do the ceremony at moonrise."

Orion tightened his arms around me and kissed my shoulder, and a blush burned my cheeks as another congratulatory round of shouts came from all around us.

Sol

Fitting in with the other pack princesses had proven to be a challenge. Most of them didn't trust me, and those that did kept their distance for fear of the others. However, Kodiak's eldest daughter, Ginny, offered to help prepare me for the mating ritual, and in the week since I'd come to that first meeting, she'd become someone I knew would be in my life for the rest of it.

"Hold still, Sol," she said, tracing the brush over my shoulder and down my arms. She'd spent the better part of the last hour drawing spiraling circular patterns over my skin, going over them until they appeared as black as the night sky. "The ones on your arms are the most important. They'll be the ones everyone sees."

"What do they mean again?" I asked, wincing as I tried to remember everything she'd told me over the last seven days.

"The spirals are for the moon," she said with a gentle smile, "and the triskelion represents the never-ending cycle of birth, life, and death."

"Cheery," Guin said, taking a drink of whiskey before coming closer to inspect Ginny's handiwork. Between the two of them, they'd done my hair and perfected my makeup, though I suspected that wouldn't last much longer than the mating ceremony. Once

Orion got me in private, he'd take pride in smearing anything on my face, especially my lipstick.

"The infinity symbols obviously represent you and Orion," Ginny said, finishing her final swoop on my wrist. "Matings last forever."

I pursed my lips and ruminated on that, wondering about all the mates I'd met in the pack thus far. There were a few elders that had survived the last attack by the Scorpions, some of them having been together for sixty or seventy years. Their companionship thrived on each other, and neither would be alive without the other.

"Has anyone survived losing their mate?" I asked.

Ginny winced as she stood and dropped her brush in a cup of water. "My father believes my mother was his mate, that they would have grown into a mating bond had she lived."

"But you don't think that?" I raised an eyebrow.

She shrugged. "They say you go rabid." She told me about the former alpha and how he'd nearly killed a few pack members before Kodiak put him down.

I pursed my lips as I considered. Would Kodiak want someone nearly as dominant and alpha as him? Or would he be better suited to a submissive shifter? And would it be someone in the pack? How did such a thing work?

"I think you're almost done," Ginny said, pulling her curls into a hairband on top of her head before narrowing her eyes on me.

"Are you mated?" I asked.

"Hell no," she said with a laugh. "I'm only eighteen. I hope I'm not mated for at least another ten years. I still have to go through my transition."

"Is it always two people?" I asked, standing so I could smooth out my black dress and examine my makeup one last time. "Or have there been mates of three or four?"

Ginny considered that for a moment. "I suppose it's possible, but I've never heard of it."

I thought about Poe and Lycan. They were close, so close that if any shifters *could* mate the same person, they might...if they didn't end up mating each other. In the shifter world, silly things like gender and sex assigned at birth didn't matter. The magic would pair two people together by compatibility, not body parts. There were several same gendered couples in the pack, and no one batted an eye despite the relatively conservative mindset of the rest of Montana.

"Enough about that. Today's your day." Guin squeezed my shoulders in reassurance, meeting my gaze in the mirror.

"What would our mother think…if she were here?" I took a moment to remember what little pieces I could of her, hoping wherever she was, she was proud of me…proud of us.

"I think she'd say you were about to be late to your own mating ceremony." Guin laughed when I rolled my eyes. We still didn't know what had happened to her, but I no longer believed the Bastards had anything to do with her disappearance. If it was the Scorpions, I would have expected them to use that information against us, but they hadn't. I'd started to resign myself to the idea that we might never know.

"Ladies," Lycan said from the door. "It's time."

I turned to my sister and gave her a hug. "Thank you for being here. I wish Maeve and Avalon could come."

"We'll do the normie wedding with them in a few weeks," Guin said. "Tonight is about the pack."

I nodded and took a deep breath, hugging Ginny as well.

"Thank you for everything. Thank you for being so kind to me."

Ginny grinned. "I have a gut feeling you and I are going to be really good friends."

"I'd like that." It warmed my heart when she gave my fingers one last squeeze before gesturing to Lycan, who winked at Ginny before holding his arm out to me. I wrapped my hand in his elbow, and he led me through the empty clubhouse, decorated for the party afterward, and out into the crisp winter air. Most of the pack, the ones that approved of this mating, had gathered on either side of the path leading to the woods. My pulse raced as my knees shook, the churning in my gut reminding me all these people would have their eyes on me, waiting for me to take a step out of line.

"It'll be okay," Lycan whispered as we walked. "Just keep breathing and stare into Orion's big blue eyes if you start to pass out."

Ever since he'd rescued me, Orion and his wolf had merged in a way they never had before. His eyes rarely shifted back to brown these days, but I kind of liked that about him.

I chuckled and nudged Lycan with my shoulder. "I'm not gonna pass out."

"All right, Princess," he said in a mock disbelieving tone, but I could tell he was trying to lighten the mood. When we reached the end of the group, the pack filled in behind me, following Lycan and me through the forest, along a path that had been walked hundreds of thousands of times before. The dirt was well worn beneath my boots, and despite the frigid night air, I didn't feel cold. Perhaps it was the mating magic; perhaps it was the new moon. Either way, my shivers were due to the fact Orion waited for me at the end, the man I'd been dreaming into existence since I was a little girl.

We matched each other in so many ways. Never in my life did I believe I'd be so fortunate as to find him, and now that I had, the world could split apart and I wouldn't be separated from him. My fox vision helped guide us along the path, but even if I didn't have enhanced sight, I sensed both Orion and Kodiak a few yards up ahead. The pack bond had been growing stronger the more I stayed with Orion, and after tonight, I'd be able to find the rest of them through the alpha's connection.

The trees opened up into a clearing where Orion and Kodiak stood in the middle next to a cement column. On top sat a dark chalice with swirling decorative designs on it, the same as what Ginny had painted onto my skin. Once my focus landed on Orion, I didn't care about the rest of it. He'd been marked with similar spirals and dots, his bare muscular arms reminding me of the power that lived just beneath the surface of his decadent skin. His eyes and forehead had been painted dark, and his hair stuck out at all angles, making it seem like he'd just stumbled out of bed.

I loved the rumpled look on him, and when our eyes met, he pulled his lips into a huge smile, lighting up his whole face. I stopped on the other side of the column and Guin came to stand next to me while Lycan placed my hands in Orion's. He held on to my fingers, taking a step toward me while everyone filled the space around us.

"You look beautiful," Orion said telepathically, brushing his magic along the bond between us in a soothing caress.

"So do you," I replied.

"Brothers, sisters, family, and friends, thank you for coming to the mating of Orion and Sol." Kodiak smiled and opened a book, flipping to a spot in the middle before continuing to talk. But my attention remained on Orion, as if I could tune the rest of the world out except for him.

"You're shaking." He held my hands tighter. *"Are you nervous?"*

"A little," I replied, *"but not about the mating. Just being the center of attention."*

"Hmm, fuck what they think. You look good enough to eat." He ran his tongue playfully over his canine while I held back a snort of laughter. *"And I intend to do that the minute we get out of here."*

"Sol, tonight, you will also join the pack. You will become a Royal Bastard in name and spirit," Kodiak said, using the name my family had always called me.

Isolde Vanderbilt was a spoiled princess that had no idea what life was, desperate for anyone to like her, terrified to step out of line. Sol Morrison embraced her wild side. She trusted that Orion would love her, knowing she deserved this life and everything in it. I had loved Isolde, but that name and her skin didn't fit me anymore.

Kodiak used a beautifully made knife to make a tiny cut on his hand before holding it out, palm up, for me. Orion placed my left hand in Kodiak's as the alpha handed me the knife so I could do the same. I winced as I made the tiny cut, but the wound was only temporary. Once I sealed the bond with the alpha, the magic would heal both of us, thus tying me to him and him to me for the rest of our lives. It was similar to mate magic, but not quite as intimate. Orion would have a mental link to me at all times, but Kodiak would only be able to contact me if he had to. It would reinforce what was already there and make it exponentially stronger.

I turned my hand over his, mixing our blood together as Kodiak put his other hand over mine.

"I recognize you as one of my family," he murmured, staring me in the eyes as he said the words. "And my wolf recognizes you as one of my pack. You have the strength of the Bastards behind you, should you need it. And should the Bastards need your strength, we will require that you give it. Are you willing?"

"I am," I said, and the moment the words left my mouth, the alpha's magic surged into me, snapping the tiny tether taut, invigorating my molecules with everyone around me. I closed my eyes as it poured into me, and suddenly, I could sense Lycan's jovial strength and Poe's mysterious power. I sensed Ginny's calm reserve and Larentia's brilliant fierceness. If I wanted to, I could reach out on any of the threads and pull, but they could do the same to me, and brightest of all was the link to Kodiak—shimmering and splendid and strong. He emanated with the power of his pack, and never had I been more grateful to be a part of it.

"We do not enter into the bonds of pack and mating lightly," Kodiak said. "Once you become family, the only way out is death."

I shivered harder, but Orion gripped my hand in reassurance, sending another surge of warmth and adoration to me.

"Orion, once you complete the bond, there will be no others. You will use your body, blood, and soul to protect Sol. Do you agree?"

"Yes," Orion said, maintaining eye contact with me.

"Sol, once you complete the bond, there will be no others. You will use your body, blood, and soul to protect Orion. Do you agree?"

"Yes," I said, causing a round of shouting from the pack mates in the crowd.

"It is my very great honor to announce Orion and Sol mated in the tradition of our ancestors," Kodiak said. "May you know great joy. May you never be torn apart."

Applause rang in my ears as I stepped forward to kiss Orion. He cupped my jaw and nibbled on my lips, and I threw my arms around his neck, determined to remember the sheer happiness filling my heart forever.

Just as I stepped away from him, my attention caught on a burnt orange shape sitting in the distance, several feet behind Orion.

A fox.

A real fox. It seemed to smile, thumping its white bushy tail on the woods' undergrowth before tilting its head in a display of curiosity and admiration. I'd been about to point it out, to wonder if it might be the same fox that caused my accident to begin with, but it stood and scampered away. And the moment passed.

The pack celebrated my mating the way we always had, with booze, barbecue, and the loudest fucking party in Montana. By midnight, almost everyone was trashed, but it was far past time for me to take my new bride back to our house.

I hadn't been drinking, and as far as I could tell, Sol had two beers before dinner and drank water the rest of the night. So by the time I met her gaze from across the room and whispered a quick, "Let's get out of here," she'd been more than willing to oblige.

I grabbed her hand, intertwined our fingers, and led her out to the parking lot, where Kai waited with my keys around his fingers.

"No newly mated couple drives themselves home from the ceremony," he said, nodding toward my truck. "Come on. I'll have Nix pick me up at your place."

I was buzzing with too much anticipation to argue, choosing instead to help Sol into the back seat. After Kai circled around to the driver's seat and started my truck, I wrapped an arm over my mate and pulled her in close. She smiled up at me, her warm green eyes switching to amber when I tugged on our bond, now reinforced by the pack magic. But once we got home, once I could sink my canines into her tender flesh, it would be a thousand times more potent.

"You two make a cute couple," Kai said as he drove. "I'm just thankful someone got grumpy-gills to lighten up."

I scoffed and rolled my eyes, but Sol giggled and tucked her head closer to my chest. "I like him grumpy."

"Yeah, I guess a wolf doesn't change his coat and all that." Kai grinned in the rearview and made small talk for the rest of the five-minute drive to my house, but once we were there, he quickly hopped into his buddy's car and left us alone.

"Come here," I said, scooping her into my arms so I could carry her over the threshold to our house. She laughed when I didn't stop in the living room, choosing instead to walk her all the way down to our bedroom. Once there, I put her down and spun her around so I could cup her jaw and kiss her fully.

Finally.

My mate. My love. The one magic had decided was *mine.* No one could ever take her away from me.

"I love you," she murmured in between breaths, circling her arms around my neck so she could hold me closer.

"I love you," I repeated, growling as the sensation of her tongue wrestling with my mine surged down my spine and into my toes. I'd been deprived of her all day, and now my cock ached to get inside her, my canines extending in anticipation of biting her to mark her forever. I traced my fingers down her neck to her shoulders, fingering the delicate straps of her dress. "I want to tear this scrap of fabric off you."

She chuckled and backed away, eyeing me with that tempting mix of desire and mischief. "You rip my pretty dress and I'll edge you for the rest of the night."

Fuck yeah! My wolf howled in excitement, and she must have heard it because she widened her grin and sat on the edge of the mattress, leaning down to unclasp her heels. But I didn't like the thought of her undressing herself on our mating night, so I dropped to my knees in front of her, grabbing her beautiful ankle to lift it on my thigh, meeting her gaze as I undid the clasp and peeled the strappy shoe from her foot. I gave the other foot the same treatment before running my hands up her soft calves and under her skirt, tucking my fingers under the waistband of her tights and underwear.

Her flowery scent hit me in the face, mixing with the tangy, delicious taste of her arousal, amping up my feral side. I peeled the thin fabric down her legs and off her feet before rising and gesturing her to do the same. She did, and I slowly placed her hair to one side, pressing my forehead against her crown as I unzipped her dress and dropped it to the floor.

When she stood naked in front of me, her skin pebbled in the cool night air, I took a deep breath to calm the urge to shove her down on the bed and bury myself inside her with no preamble.

"You're so fucking gorgeous," I murmured, leaning down to kiss her again. "And so fucking mine."

"Hmm," she agreed before twisting her little fingers into the buttons on my shirt, plucking them undone one by one. "My turn."

After she pushed the fabric off my shoulders and down my arms, she went to my pants and undid the buckle, whooshing the leather through the loops in one quick movement. Almost like she couldn't contain herself, she hastily unbuttoned my pants and slid the zipper down, divesting me of my trousers and boxers in one go. I helped her by kicking off my boots and socks, and once we were both naked in the moonlight, I couldn't fucking stand the anticipation any longer.

I wrapped my hands around the back of her thighs and lifted her up so her legs went around my hips. Then, I laid her down on the bed and hovered over her, breathing her in deep, allowing this connection to soothe the beast that had wanted to sink its teeth into her ever since I found her in that beat-up SUV.

Wanting to make it perfect, I started to kiss down her neck, a burst of lust hitting me in the balls when she moaned and arched into it. Her perfect breasts rubbed against my chest, her nipples fucking screaming to be bitten and tugged. But she grabbed my arms to stop me from going farther down, and when I glanced up at her with furrowed brows, she shook her head and pulled my face back to hers.

"Do it," she said. "This entire day was foreplay. I need you. I want you. Please. Please fuck me and bite me."

I let out a noise that sounded like a strangled laugh and half a moan before reaching between us to line my cock up at her entrance. And fucking hell, she'd been right. Her cunt was wet and wonderful and fucking dripping for me, the smell of it only making my mouth water more. I wanted to bury my face in between her legs and hang out there for the rest of the night. I wanted to wear her scent like cologne, knowing anyone who came across me would sense her and keep their fucking distance. I wanted to bury myself so deep inside her that no one would ever dare touch her again because they would face retaliation from me.

Almost losing her had nearly made me rabid, and after tonight, I'd never have to face that again. We wouldn't be parted until death, and we'd both sworn to that only a few hours ago.

I pushed my cock inside her, slowly at first, working her up so I didn't hurt her, but she quickly grabbed the back of my legs and yanked me home—all the way to the hilt, all at once.

"Fucckk," I groaned, nearly toppling forward on shaking arms. She always felt like heaven, but tonight, she gripped me like a fucking vise, like she never wanted to let me go. So warm and tight and *mine.*

"Yes," she moaned, rolling her hips against me, finding the special spot that drove her wild.

My arms shook as I tried to hold my weight off her, and I ignored my racing heart at the prospect of sinking my teeth into her skin and filling her with my scent.

"Goddamn it, you feel so good, little fox," I said, trying to rein in my control as I thrusted my hips against her, rutting inside her.

"I love the way you fuck me," she said, murmuring such sweet, filthy things that I didn't think I'd last long enough to seal the deal. I wanted to bite her just as she was coming. I'd been told that made the orgasm even better, that the bite pushed it into the next fucking dimension, and I wanted this to be good for her. "God, I'm so close… so close."

Her rising pleasure erupted into me along the bond, hot and fiery and sheer perfection, and I groaned against the waves, leaning down so I could kiss along her neck, licking her delicious skin to prepare her. I smelled the right spot, the area where her scent was strongest, where she smelled the most like *her,* and I knew—the bite had to be there. Right above her collarbone. Right where her shoulder met her neck.

My fangs tingled, the magic coalescing around us in a nearly visible cloud of pheromones and ecstasy and tangible magic.

"I'm coming, Ry," she said, tilting her head to the side to make more room for me, meeting me thrust for thrust as I fucked her hard. "Do it."

I didn't need to be told twice. I leaned down and sank my canines into her skin for the first time, piercing through flesh and muscle while she screamed in furious relief. I sensed her euphoria, the tendrils of her climax erupting into me as it surged out of her. My fingers tingled and my legs shook, and the most delectable agony twisted down my spine. Fucking hell, it brought me closer to mine. I wouldn't last much longer, not at all. The bulge at the base of my cock had started expanding, and it got harder and harder to pull back from each rut.

Her blood coated my mouth, and I swallowed down what I could before dragging my tongue over her wound to seal it. She tasted even better than I thought possible, and not that I had much of a blood kink, but the sight of my teeth marks in her skin brought me so much fucking joy, I never thought I'd get over it.

"Get ready, baby girl," I said, steadying myself on my elbows so she could return the bite. "I'm almost there. Almost—"

I shoved into her two more times before my knot expanded and her delicate little teeth sank into my skin, much more carefully and pleasurable than she had during her transition. And it launched me into a whole new universe.

Our souls intertwined, our magic became one, and for a brief moment, I'd swear that the heavens parted and rained down pure undiluted bliss just for us two. My entire body floated and imploded. Her nerve endings were mine, and vice versa. We were one body, one heart, one being, and it was the most mind-blowing experience I'd ever had.

We melted down and reformed around each other like two pieces of metal in a furnace, like a blade being reforged into something stronger and better and more resilient.

"Do you feel that?" she whimpered, running her hands over my chest and up to my shoulders while she swiped her tongue over my bite mark. *"Do you feel me?"*

"I do," I replied, collapsing on top of her while my knot locked us into place, my cock kicking with its release, pouring my seed deep inside her. *"You feel amazing, little fox."*

She hummed her approval and ran her fingers down my spine while I licked at her bite and nuzzled under her chin. "I can't believe we get to have this forever. I can't believe you found me."

"I did," I said, tracing the muscles in her throat with my lips, alternating kisses with little nips that let her know this was real, that we were together and always would be. "And you found me."

We lay in silence, our post-orgasmic glow radiating along the bright, brilliant tether between us. It would be stronger than it ever had, and I'd be able to track her down no matter where she went, no matter how far.

It gave me a sense of peace that I'd never known, not in thirty-five years, and now that I had her, no matter what came for her, no matter if that bloodsucking Scorpion motherfucker showed up again, he'd have to go through me and my entire pack to get her.

We were safe now, and we had each other.

CHAPTER 28

Epilogue

Sol

Two Years Later

I rubbed my hand over the scars of my bite mark and smiled at Nemesis, who had been moved to Vanderbilt ranch after Orion couldn't stand to be parted from her for much longer than a few weeks. Since we'd gotten together, he hadn't been going to Fiver Cabin very much, so he wanted his girl closer so he could keep a better eye on her.

Secretly, I suspected he didn't want to have to drag me up to the sticks that often, but couldn't choose between us. Which was okay because I liked the ole gal, even if she had an attitude and a surly disposition to everyone else. She'd always been nice to me.

"Be careful," Orion said from the entrance of the barn, leaning against the wall with his arms crossed and that mischievous look on his face. "She bites, even if she likes you."

"Well, we have that in common, don't we?" I brushed a hand down her neck as she whinnied and bobbed her head as if to agree with me.

287

Orion smiled and chuckled, walking toward me with that cocky swagger that said he had more on his mind than interrupting my barn duties. I'd sensed him coming, of course, but I didn't think he'd stop to say hi. He had a whole list of things to do since he'd taken on the head role at Vanderbilt ranch, and the alliance between the Bastards and the Vanderbilts had been going so well, we even predicted a profit for both companies this year. We'd come so far in the time since we agreed to the deal that our families were practically one and the same. Long forgotten were the days of a rivalry, and after everything that had happened since then, it was difficult to remember we used to despise each other.

My mate wrapped his arms around my waist and pulled me back against his chest, leaning down to run his nose along the side of my neck, kissing what bits of skin he could find along the way.

"You smell…" He licked along my shoulder before caressing his tongue up my throat to my ear.

"I've been out here all day," I said with a chuckle. "Of course I smell."

"No, your scent is different. It's…softer." He took another long inhale before humming thoughtfully and resting his hands on my hips so he could turn me around to face him. "How long ago was that heat?"

My cheeks burned thinking about it. We'd spent two days trapped in our room together, sweating and fucking and knotting before doing it all over again. My heat reminded me a lot of going through the transition, except I was lucid for all of it and there wasn't a blood exchange. Orion didn't have to pour his magic into me, just fill me with his cock and…*other things.*

Some people chose to have Morwyn put them to sleep for the heat if they didn't want to go through it alone, or some even wore condoms through the whole thing if they didn't want to have pups. But Orion and I hadn't.

I'd gone through my heat last year with a roulette mentality. We'd rolled the dice and decided no matter what happened, we would be happy with it. But this year, we set out with the intention to get pregnant. I'd always had a big family and he desperately wanted one of his own, something to call his.

"A few weeks," I said, circling my arms around his neck so I could push up on my toes to kiss him. "Why?"

He narrowed his eyes. "Have you started to bleed?"

I considered this and shook my head. "Actually...no."

Orion curled his lips into a grin and kissed me again. "I think you've got pups, little fox."

"What?" I balked and stepped away from him so I could clutch my lower stomach. "How do you know?"

"I can smell it," he said, leaning down so he could scoop me into his arms. "The mate always knows first."

As soon as he said it, I knew it to be true. If I closed my eyes and focused hard enough, I felt them there—buzzing with magic and full of life. They were strong and healthy and I swore to all the fucking heavens they'd be born into a family that loved them and protected them no matter what.

Orion

"That's right," I told Kodiak, taking a sip of beer as we celebrated the news. "I knocked her up. Finally."

He laughed, his big smile making me grin harder. "Don't say it like that. She's your mate, not a fucking prom date."

"I can't believe you're having kids," Lycan said, shaking his head. "Let's hope they get Sol's sunny disposition and they're not as grumpy as you."

I bared my teeth at him in a playful growl but smiled when he clapped me on the back.

"I'm happy for you," Poe added. "And Sol. I know you wanted them last year, but it happened when it should."

"Do you know how many yet?" Talon asked, tilting her head as she took another long sip of her drink.

"At least two," I said. "I can smell them."

"Twins," Kodiak said, giving me another clap on the shoulder. "I'm happy for you, brother."

"Cheers!" Moose said, lifting his beer in celebration.

"Don't forget the chicken wings," Sol said, brushing her magic along the bond to remind me of what I'd promised before I left her with her sister and Ginny to come to church. Now that the business had been concluded, I needed to head back to our house. I didn't like to be away from her for too long, especially now that she was holding my children inside her.

"I won't, little fox," I said, checking my phone to ensure the to-go order had been processed.

After I headed into town to pick up her favorite treat, I went home and stalked inside to find my favorite girl perched on the couch, Ginny and Guin having just left.

"How are we doing?" I said, putting the food on the coffee table before sitting down next to her. I lifted her feet into my lap, rubbing at the arch of one.

"We're fine," she said, giving me that adorable look that said I fussed over her too much. "I'm not that far along yet. Aside from cravings for buffalo sauce and blue cheese, I'm the same as I was a few weeks ago."

"Hmm," I said, massaging up her calves to her thighs. Never in my life did I think I'd actually find my mate, much less be a father. My own father had been a bit of a hard ass, and even though he loved my mother, they both had died before I had my driver's license. I swore I wouldn't let that happen. I wouldn't bring these children into the world only to leave them before they came into their own, before they even transitioned.

I crawled over my mate and kissed her, rubbing my half-erect cock up against her cunt, aching to fill her in ways only I could.

"Have I told you how hot you are?" I said. "And how much I always want you?"

"Only every day." She laughed and pulled me closer. "And even if you didn't, I could sense it. We're very firmly mated, my love."

"Thank fucking God for that." I growled and let my wolf take over, let him pull her pants down and yank her shirt off so he could stake his own claim. And while her dinner cooled on the coffee table, I took my mate hard and fast and deep, reaffirming the fact we were together and safe and whole.

Afterward, I reheated her food and hand fed her because it was my fucking privilege to do so, because it meant I took care of her the way no one else ever could. She did the same for me, and it filled my fucking heart to bursting.

The End

Want More?

Thank you for reading! If you enjoyed this book, please consider leaving a review. They help other readers find my work and enable me to keep writing. (Seriously, I am a sucker for validation and have a praise kink. Plz love me.)

Keep reading for a sneak peek at the next book, *Blood and Magic.*

You can stay up to date by joining my newsletter. ANNNDDD you get free smut just for signing up.

https://jenadoyle.com/join/

(No spam, only smut. I promise.)

I'm also @thejenadoyle on all the socials. Be sure to follow me for book recs, pictures of my cute dog, and all the news about upcoming releases.

Blood AND MAGIC
ROYAL BASTARDS MC
HELENA, MT
JENA DOYLE

Blood and Magic

Her heart shouldn't beat for him. His wolf shouldn't hunger for her. But death has a habit of changing everything.

Maeve

Something happened to me a few months ago, something that stopped my heart, smashed it to pieces, and restarted it again. I don't understand it, and I'm not sure I want to.

My sisters are keeping something important from me, and when our family's sworn enemies move in on our territory, I become more suspicious than ever.

I am not supposed to like Van "Vermillion" Alexander. He's quiet, broody, and mean. But he's connected to the stammer in my chest, and I'm going to find out why.

Vermillion

I almost died trying to save one of my pack mates earlier this year. Or perhaps I did die and the shifter magic brought me back to life. I'm different now.

My urges are stronger...stranger...darker.

I don't understand these new compulsions, and when Maeve Vanderbilt starts showing signs that she might be like her sisters, I can't keep my inner wolf from devouring her whole.

Chapter One

MAEVE

NOVEMBER

I'd never given much thought to dying.

My mother passed when I was eleven, and though I understood all things must come to an end, I didn't fully comprehend the precarious tightrope upon which we mortals walked until the Grim Reaper gave mine a good shake.

"Do you think Percy will retaliate?" my twin, Ava, asked from across the dining room. She pushed salad around on her plate, her eyebrows scrunched together in a scowl.

"I don't see how he can," I replied. "Guin and Sol have him backed into a corner. Even if he comes out swinging, there isn't much he can use to his advantage."

Ava nodded and glanced back at her food, but neither of us had an appetite.

Our father, Uther Vanderbilt, had finally succumbed to cancer mere weeks ago, and in a move we all should have seen coming, our despicable elder brother, Percy, had made a play for the family business. We were the Vanderbilts, the wealthiest and most powerful family in Helena, Montana. In order of birth, Ava and I were smack in the middle: Guinevere, Percy, and Liam on one side, Isolde and Galahad on the other. We owned over five thousand acres of land where we raised cattle and trained horses, and that said nothing of the wind turbines and natural gas companies we used to sell energy back to the national grid. Our grandparents had made us wealthy, but my father had turned it into an empire.

"Do you think the Royal Bastards will help us?" I asked, bringing my sister's gaze back up to me.

She shrugged. "Sol seemed pretty sure."

Our family and the Royal Bastards had been enemies for years. A land dispute had started it, but the feud escalated when my mother died on their property and my father blamed them for it. He said the Bastards ripped her to pieces, leaving nothing but a bloody patch in the snow. We never found her body.

After Father died, Percy stepped in to take over, and our ranch hands left us, refusing to work for that spineless coward. I didn't blame them. Percy had always had more ego than brains, and he'd never once worked the ranch. Why would they respect him? This had put our dear brother in the frustrating position of having to make a deal with one of the local motorcycle clubs, the Bloody Scorpions. In exchange for our sister's hand in marriage, the president offered his men to help us.

Isolde, whom we affectionately called Sol, had taken a drunken sojourner into the mountains and returned with a lover named Orion from a rival motorcycle gang, complete with the entire Royal Bastards crew behind him. Ava and I had helped her hatch a devilish scheme to bring our dear brother back down to earth, and when he realized he'd been outmaneuvered, he'd sulked off to greener pastures.

It had been hilarious to watch his precious plans crumble around him. I absolutely loathed what he'd done, so I was thrilled to see him sink so low. That had been a few days ago, and none of us had heard from him since.

"I'm not sure I believe Sol when she says they're not responsible for our mother," Ava said. "There's something wrong with them, something off."

"I agree." I sipped my wine, choking back the Cab Sauv despite how much I loved dry reds. The thought of the Bastards always set me on edge. Rumors circulated through Helena that they were vicious beasts that turned into animals on the full moon. It was small-minded folklore, of course. Shapeshifters didn't exist. "Sol seems different now, too. Doesn't she?"

Ava nodded. "Definitely. I don't know what happened to her at that cabin with the Bastards, but—"

"It's her eyes," I said. "I look into them now and see something else staring out at me."

Sol was only eighteen months younger than Ava and me, by all rights our Irish triplet. We were best friends, the three of us. No one else could be trusted, no one who wasn't family. I'd tried to have friends, of course, and I'd even made a few at boarding school. But money corrupted everything it touched, and I could never be sure if they really liked me or my daddy's wallet.

"It was like when Guin started dating that ranch hand. What was his name?" Ava narrowed her blue eyes in concentration.

"Van," I said, recalling the tall, attractive biker with sandy blond hair and dark brown eyes who used to smile at me from under a cowboy hat. "Beautiful Van."

"Right." Ava laughed, drinking her glass of wine. "Of course, you'd remember his name."

I balked and feigned offense. "What's that supposed to mean?"

"Despite being genetically identical, I fear our taste in partners is quite the opposite." She smirked and let out another loud giggle.

"Precisely," I agreed. "I'm a hot-blooded woman, and you're a frigid prude."

She dropped her jaw, half insulted, half laughing, and threw her napkin across the table at me. "Just because I don't screw anyone with a pulse doesn't mean I'm a prude."

"I'm not shaming you," I said, attempting to ease her ire, but a strange tightness in my chest stopped me. My lungs seized, my stomach lurching as a sudden wave of anguish shot down my torso and up my throat. I couldn't breathe. I couldn't think.

Panicking, I clutched at my sternum and gasped for air.

"Mae?" Ava said, pushing to her feet. She scrambled over to my side of the table just as I lurched to the ground. My vision blackened, the world going blurry, my head both light and the weight of an anvil.

The last coherent thing I saw was my sister's frightened stare, a replica of my own, and then the world went dark.

Dying was a peculiar thing, truly. There was no bright white light or angels calling me home to heaven. I thought I might see my mother or father, or perhaps our grandparents, but there was none of that, either—just the tragic droll of nothingness. Eternity of darkness. End of story. Good night.

I woke up with a gasp, electric currents shooting through my body as my back arched off the ground.

"Mae?" said a deep, dusky voice. Bright light flashed through each one of my eyes, and I winced against the splitting pain in my skull. "She's coming back around."

The EMT barked orders at other people around him, but I focused on the ceiling of my family's dining room. A crowd of people surrounded me: staff, paramedics, my sister.

"What happened?" I croaked.

No one answered as I was lifted onto a stretcher and shuttled out of the house. It was only on the ambulance ride to the hospital that I learned I had collapsed and banged my head on the nineteenth-century table on my way down. My heart had stopped, and if it hadn't been for Ava's quick thinking and immediate CPR, they wouldn't have been able to resuscitate me.

Stopped?

What do they mean stopped?

I never got an answer. The doctors at the emergency department ran as many tests as they could and arrived at no concrete conclusions. I didn't have any heart defects, and other than this one incident, there was no indication of illness, genetic or sudden onset. They referred me to a cardiologist, who was as stunned as the other doctors.

Aside from a cracked rib and the scar on my forehead, I'd managed to walk away from death with barely a hair out of place. I had access to the best doctors money could afford. I'd been shuttled to Johns Hopkins and the Cleveland Clinic. I'd flown halfway around the world and back, only for the world's greatest minds to tell me they had no idea what happened or if it would happen again. In the end, they put me on medication to help maintain the electrical current of my heart and said they'd see me again in six months.

"You're okay now," Ava said, gripping my hand on the last flight home. She'd been by my side through it all, through the tests and the endless poking and prodding. She'd been a guinea pig in her own way. As my genetic twin, they could compare our bodies to each other to search for any mutations. But nothing ever came. "You'll be okay now."

I nodded and gripped her hand, giving her a tight grin I hoped was reassuring. But as I stared out the window of the private jet at the twinkling lights below, I vibrated with a hollowness I'd never felt before. It was more than medical exhaustion, more than any doctor or specialist could tell me. It grew into a nagging emptiness in my soul—rotten, dark, and all-consuming.

I hungered for something...I didn't know what. I only knew I had to find it. This yearning clawed at my insides like razors slicing open my veins, making me restless and jittery. My heart ached for the unknown, and until I submitted, I couldn't guarantee I would be okay ever again.

That emptiness stayed with me through winter and into spring. I went back to work at Vanderbilt Enterprises as director of operations, a job I'd been given by my father shortly after graduating from Harvard.

I hate this, I thought as I sat in a leadership meeting about upcoming strategic priorities.

"If we have any hope of remaining in the top five energy producers in Montana, we'll need to increase our operational efficiency by at least thirty percent," said one of our vice presidents.

I blinked against the monotonous corporate speak. This meeting had gone on for two hours longer than necessary, and I should care about the direction the company planned to take, but I wondered if anyone even gave a shit I was here.

I didn't add much value, aside from schmoozing with people who secretly gossiped about me being a nepo baby behind my back while brownnosing to my face. Vanderbilt Enterprises had once been my safety net, the one thing I always knew I would do. Now I dreaded walking into the building.

I rubbed my temples and tried to focus on the metrics on the television in front of me, but what was the point, truly? In the end, none of this mattered.

Death was a tricky thing. It put a lot into perspective. Like how long I'd spent doing things because my father expected me to. Or how much I'd lived in the giant shadow of my sisters. I wasn't as smart as Ava; she'd graduated from Harvard Law. I wasn't as ruthless as Guin; she'd become the heir apparent. And I wasn't nearly as loved by the Vanderbilt patriarch as Sol; she'd been allowed to do whatever she wanted after college.

With this new lease on life, I was determined to find my purpose, to feel alive in all its splendid glory, no matter what that entailed.

NOW

"I can't believe you're going to be gone for two whole months," Ava said, pouting at Sol. "Are you sure you can't take us with you?"

Our youngest sister laughed and wrapped an arm around Ava's shoulders. "Trust me. You don't want to go on this trip."

"Bali would be wonderful," Ava said. "I don't have to spend time with you and your fiancé, Mr. Grumpy Gills."

"Ugh," Guin cut in, twisting her hair into a pin curl before securing it with a bobby pin. "They're ridiculously disgusting together. It's intolerable being in the same room as them."

Sol narrowed playful eyes at her and stuck out her tongue, reminding me so much of the younger version of herself. I sat in a corner, sketching them in my notepad while we gossiped and de-stressed from the week's wedding planning events. I could have wasted hundreds on a gift, but Orion spoiled Sol with whatever she wanted, and God knew she already had everything she could need. Instead, I'd decided to give her a series of portraits commemorating her big day and the moments leading up to it. It was more personal, and she'd appreciate the intimacy in it.

Tonight was a sisters' bonding sleepover. Tomorrow would be the rehearsal, culminating in the big moment the day after.

"I still can't believe you're getting married to him," Ava said, turning to our eldest sister. "You're okay with this?"

I didn't honestly expect Guin to disagree. In the six months since Sol met Orion, Guin had gotten close with the Royal Bastards, too. She had an "understanding" with their president, Kodiak...whatever that meant. Neither she nor Sol had been particularly forthcoming about how we'd gone from hating the Bastards to welcoming them into the family within a matter of weeks.

All they would say was they didn't believe the Bastards had killed our mother, and we needed them to survive. They had gotten us through the winter, and without their help, our company would have tanked when the ranch hands walked. No one had heard from Percy or the Bloody Scorpions in months. The RBMC had stepped up, but that didn't mean I had to like it. And now Sol was *marrying* one of them?

"Sol is as hardheaded as the rest of us," Guin explained. "There's no telling any Vanderbilt what they can or can't do. If she wants to marry Mr. Tall, Dark, and Grumpy from the wrong side of the Missouri River, who are we to stop her?"

"Hey!" Sol brushed wisps of her ginger hair from her face before rubbing in moisturizer. "He's not as grumpy as he used to be. And in two days, he'll be your brother-in-law."

"Not by choice," Guin said quickly.

"Who would have thought our *baby* sister would be the first to walk down the aisle?" Ava shook her head and laughed.

"I hope you didn't think it would be me," Guin said. "I'd rather chew off my own foot."

"Romantic," Ava added. "No, I just thought...well...maybe me or Mae would have gone first." My twin met my gaze. "Do you still talk to Zachary?"

I winced at the thought of my former friend with benefits and shook my head, softening a dark shadow around my sketch of Sol with my finger. I'd have graphite smudges on my hands for days, but that was par for the course. "No. Very much no."

"Pity," she said. "I thought he liked you."

"Well, he ended up marrying a Kennedy, so I doubt he thinks of me at all anymore."

"Okay, back on task," Sol said, grabbing her phone. "We'll be gone from June into July." She went through all of the ranch activities that would need to be done in those weeks. Since the Vanderbilts had made a tentative truce with the Bastards, they'd agreed to help us maintain what our father had built. Orion had taken on the lead rancher role until things were more stable.

Surprising everyone, she had become his right hand. She managed the horses and drew up plans for the cattle, even while maintaining her corporate position on the board.

"Mae, you're still okay with stepping in, right?"

I nodded, reminding myself I could do hard things. I'd grown up on this ranch, after all. Just because I'd gotten a business degree and spent most of my time in an office didn't mean I couldn't return to my roots. Despite having a special connection to my favorite horse, Molly, I'd never really worked the ranch. Father had always hired help for that. But I could shout out orders well enough, and I'd been cleared from my day job to work remotely for the duration.

"I'll be in Europe for that international trade alliance conference," Ava said. "And then I'm doing a networking tour. I'll be gone until August."

My heart ached at the thought of being separated from my twin for so long. Of course, we'd spent time apart before, and we did our best to distinguish ourselves at boarding school and college. But no one knew me the way Ava did, and the notion of two long months away from her formed a pit in my gut nearly the size of Jupiter.

"I'll be in Bozeman for most of it," Guin added. "If you need help, call me. I'm only an hour away."

"I'll be fine," I said. "The Bastards are sending someone to replace Orion, right?"

Sol nodded. "That's the agreement."

"I'm sure whoever that is will know what they're doing," I said. "Besides, we're not losing our ranch hands this time. They've got a well-oiled machine going out there. I'm here more as a supervisor anyway. A face to put on the family name."

"How are you feeling these days?" Sol asked, her eyes full of genuine concern. Since my near-death experience six months ago, I hadn't had so much as a fainting spell. But something still wasn't right. That hollowness had taken hold deep in my soul, my body yearning for something tangible. I just didn't know what it was.

I'd tried a variety of activities to fill it: skydiving, base jumping, heli-skiing. Aside from a massive adrenaline rush and a few new hobbies, it didn't bring me what I was after. My sisters had called it reckless, but I didn't want to squander my new lease on life.

"Okay," I said, trying to keep a poker face.

Sol glanced at Guin, a quick exchange between them that made me curious.

"No headaches or body chills?" Guin said, securing another pin.

"Why do you ask?" Now that they mentioned it, I'd had a twinge between the eyes for the last few days, but I chalked it up to allergies and the stress of a job that didn't truly satisfy.

"Just trying to make sure you're not about to drop dead on us again," Guin said.

"Well, the last time that happened, I had no warning whatsoever." I accentuated a curl on Sol's shoulders and tilted my head to the side, admiring my work. Her nose wasn't quite right, so I took an eraser to the lines on her face and started over.

Again, Sol looked at Guin, who raised her eyebrows once as if to say, "Who knows?"

I glanced at my twin, sending my own mental message.

What are they hiding?

"What's with the secret glances?" Ava said.

I didn't like being kept in the dark. The only two who were allowed to share telepathic communication were Ava and me, and we had identical DNA. Our neural synapses had been formed together in the same amniotic sac. Ergo, we were entitled.

"What? Can't sisters be worried about their family?" Guin rolled her eyes and returned to the vanity mirror, placing another pin curl in her hair. "God forbid."

After our mother died, Guin had stepped into the role of matriarch. She kept the rest of us in line and protected us from the extent of our wicked family. But she never lied to us, not about something important. To see her go from hating the Bastards to welcoming them with a rapidly decreasing frost made me curious.

Ava glanced back at me. *They're definitely hiding something.*

Agreed, I mentally replied.

"You'll let me know if you start feeling different, right?" Guin said. "Both of you?"

"Different how?" Ava asked, narrowing her gaze.

"Just...*different,*" Sol said, glancing at her phone again. I could have sworn her eyes changed to amber and back to green, but perhaps I'd imagined it. After all, no one's eyes changed colors like that, and she'd inherited the same emerald irises as our mother. Ava and I, along with Galahad and Liam, had gotten our father's dark coloring. "Anyway, the rehearsal is tomorrow. Everyone will be here except for Van."

The mention of my childhood crush got my attention, and I snapped my gaze to my sister.

"Why not?" Guin asked. "He's a groomsman. He can't miss the rehearsal."

"He said he had a conflict," Sol said. "Orion told me to drop the issue, so I didn't argue."

"Well, the show must go on, I suppose," Guin said, looking at me before returning to her hair prep.

"Are you sure you don't want a bachelorette party?" Ava said. "We still have time. We could take the family jet anywhere. Atlantic City. Vegas." She gasped as if an idea had just occurred to her. "Monaco."

Sol laughed and shook her head. "No. There's no reason to aggravate my betrothed any more than I already have by insisting we spend the night before the wedding apart."

"I'm surprised he let you out of his sight," Guin said. "Bastards are notoriously territorial."

"Speaking of Van," I said, clearing my throat. "Are you two still together?"

Guin snorted and shook her head. "Heavens, no. As I said, there's no man with hands big enough to carry my crown, and I like it that way."

Sol giggled.

"What?" Guin balked and stared at our youngest sister.

"Nothing," Sol said. "Nothing at all."

Guin returned her forest-green eyes to me with narrowed inspection. "Why do you ask?"

I pretended like my interest in the Bastard was purely professional. He'd worked the ranch in his early twenties, back when I was just starting to go through puberty. He and Guin had been...friends? Friends with benefits? A hearty teenage fling? With her, it was difficult to tell. She treated boyfriends with the same apathetic disinterest as she did strangers.

In the deepest, darkest recesses of my poor pathetic heart, I'd admit I had a teeny tiny crush on him when he worked here. Most of the day workers ignored us or acted like my father might shoot their eyes out for even glancing in our direction. But Van had been nice... decent...dare I say, flirty?

But then he'd left and joined the Royal Bastards and became our enemy. Except now they weren't enemies, and the lines were so blurred, I didn't know how I was supposed to feel anymore. I hadn't seen Van since I was a little girl, but the thought of his bright brown eyes and big smile sent a shiver down my spine, pooling in my lower stomach.

I was twelve years younger than him, barely more than knees, elbows, and braces at the time. But he *saw* me, and growing up in Guin's massive shadow meant not many people did. He'd been a part of my sexual awakening, and if I happened to have a preference for blonds, well, could anyone honestly blame me?

At such a tender age, he'd made an impression.

"Just curious," I said in answer to my sister's question. Shrugging and ignoring the steady thump of my heart as it pounded against my ribs, I kept my gaze fixed on my drawing. The mere thought of Van set my pulse skyrocketing for no obvious reason. I decided it was the remnants of an early girlhood fascination and let it go.

But my question had gotten Ava's attention, and she raised an eyebrow at me.

I ignored that, too.

Sol went through the rest of the wedding plans, and when it was over, we gathered around our family table for dinner.

For the entire night, I tried to hide my relief at hearing that Guin and Van weren't together, even as it mixed with an excited trepidation of seeing Van again after all these years.

Keep Reading!

Acknowledgments

Dear Reader,

Thank you for giving this steamy little paranormal romance a shot. I took all my favorite parts from all my favorite werewolf tropes and put them in a blender to create the Helena, MT pack. I hope you enjoyed it. If you did, please consider leaving a review wherever you get your books. If you like MC romances, I have another series called The Steel Roses MC you might enjoy. Be sure to check it out.

First, thank you to Crimson Syn. I met her at Smutlovers '23, and she was kind enough to let me into the RBMC world. It's been such a ride, and I am eternally grateful to her for giving me a shot. (Seriously, she's amazing. Go read her books if you need more RBMC.)

To my beta readers, Maggie and Rebecca, I bow to your gracious feedback and support. This book would not have been what it is without your advice. My editors, Misha and Kim, you're rockstars. Thank you for reading all my words and making them better. To my ARC readers, are y'all sick of me yet? Thank you for hyping me up before the release, and I hope this one sates your precious palate.

To my partner, thank you for the love and support. I couldn't do this without you cheering me on every step of the way.

And finally, to you, dear reader. Thank you for giving me a shot. May your coffee always be warm, may your pillow always be cold, and may your love of the written word never diminish.

Cheers!

-Jena

Also by Jena Doyle

<u>MIDSUMMER</u>

We Wild Things (Prequel Novella)

Midsummer

Samhain

Solstice

Beltane

<u>STEEL ROSES MC</u>

They Called Him Saint (Prequel Novella)

Crimson Chaos

Savage Saint

Oleander Oaths

Mischief Mayhem

Ruthless Reign

<u>ROYAL BASTARDS MC: HELENA, MT</u>

Blood and Whiskey

Blood and Magic

Heats and Holidays (Novella)

Blood and Trouble

<u>ROYAL HARLOTS MC: ASHEVILLE, NC</u>

Filthy Little Witch